M J WALKER

OPERATION HYPOGEAN

COPYRIGHT ©

The characters and events portrayed in this book are fictitious.
Any similarity to real persons, living or dead, is coincidental
and not intended by the author.

ISBN-13: 9798397762458
ISBN-10: 1477123456

Cover design by: Eden Butler
Library of Congress Control Number: 2018675309
Printed in the United States of America

OPERATION HYPOGEAN

DEDICATION

This book is dedicated to Jay, who gave me the confidence to never give up, and helped make the writing of this new novel a reality.

And to my nieces, Gabby, Evie, and Betsy, who I am so proud of every day.

OPERATION HYPOGEAN

PROLOGUE

The sky grumbled and churned. Thick masses of shadowy clouds moved swiftly across the vast expanse of land. An icy wind ravaged obscured structures and landmarks barely visible to the naked eye. These were the darkest marks. The time one might have called night, when the sun would slip beneath the horizon. No star, however, twinkled in this ebony sky. There was no peace, and no welcoming solitude that once heralded a period of rest.

A savage crash of thunder echoed through the atmosphere as a heavy gust of wind lifted aged rubble off the ground. It swirled above the plane like a tornado. Then it rotated for long moments within the airstream, before falling back to the ground as effortlessly as it arose. A flash of lightening streaked across the sky. The startling intensity and savage intent wrapped its electric claws over the land. Heat infused the natural elements, and a renewed aroma of ashen flesh and charcoal permeated the air.

Securing a thick cloth tighter around the lower half of her facial apparatus, a lone figure squinted in the darkness. As she surveyed her surroundings, her heavy boots shuffled over the ruined ground. Rubble littered her path, but she continued crunching over brittle, charred skeletal remains, barely hearing the cracking of bone and crunch of ravaged nature.

Another fifty steps and she would reach her goal. Huddling tighter into the heavy barriers that adorned her body, she trudged with determination against the ferocious wind. It howled and growled around her, harsh and penetrating. Cold, so very cold this eve. With each gust, larger objects moved across the ground. Bone fragments skittered past her. Having to angle her body into the storm, she pushed forward with determination, slicing through the ever-raging tempest. She took slow measured breaths, pulling filtered air through her lips. The mask covering her mouth and nose was uncomfortable and tight, laced with condensation. It was a sensation she familiar with. The heavy apparatus secured tight around her head was a necessity for which she was thankful.

Nearly home. The safety hatch, although not visible, was well within reach. Reigning in her last reserves of energy, her weary form groaned and pushed forward ten steps, nine–eight–seven. She took another short breath, six–five–four steps. The descending mantra helped to assure her that she was almost home. Three steps, two and finally one. Relief, vast and palpable, flooded her body and she fell to her knees. She closed her eyes, her brows creased deeply, as a sigh rushed past her lips. Reaching out, she groped blindly for the handle she knew was there. Grasping a thick metal rod, she pulled roughly and, with a stiff grunt, released the latch that kept the horizontal doorway in place. Lifting the circular portal with her remaining strength, she slipped through the opening and dropped down into a narrow metallic chamber. The portal slammed shut behind her and she was plunged into the safety of an antiquated elevator that would take her deep beneath the planet's surface.

CHAPTER 1

A trait in all sentient beings with superior brain function is independent thought and free will. In hand with this comes desire in its many forms, the most destructive of such being selfishness, want and greed. Desire fuels all with ambition and determination. From the very beginning, life flourishes and desire blossoms.

As always, we start at the beginning. Life progresses quite naturally, uniting and creating new life, another product of desire, blossoming into thriving families, colonies, and civilisations. As time passes, these civilisations grow and the dominant within its society assert control. Command structures develop and thus create a hierarchy of leadership. These leaders rise and civilisations unite to form superpowers. The desire to evolve strengthens, clouded by burgeoning delusions of grandeur. The taste for power becomes addictive, undulating like rumbling storm clouds expanding overhead. Civilisations become nations. Industry and politics bloom, leaders of nations clash and the struggle for global dominance begins.

It took place during the worlds' first Tri Nation Environmental Summit, televised to stage full disclosure to the global audience. A gathering of the world's Superpowers had never been aired for televisual viewing. Not like this. Hailed as an event to be remembered throughout history, a platform where nations united to face a threat greater than themselves – environmental devastation. Global temperatures continued to rise, causing a worldwide chain reaction of negative effects. The polar ice masses had all but melted away. Ocean levels had risen so much so that islands had vanished. Highly populated oceanside land masses were disappearing under water and global inhabitants forced to move further inland for safety. They lived together like densely populated insects packed side by side, one on top of the other. Entire breeds of wild beings and plant life were becoming extinct. Pollution hung like storm clouds in the atmosphere and, depending where on the globe you lived, on any given rotation the sky would be lit with violet, russet, or even verdant hues.

And so, the summit began. But unknown to the viewers at home, an air of palpable tension fluctuated between the nations' leaders. For cycles, the three continental powers had been in a race to produce the most successful, clean, and renewable forms of energy. Nations pitted against one another to profit from the production of environmentally agreeable sources of power. Thus began the Energy Race, and each superpower had its own agenda.

Central

The Central Continent took lead, concentrating on one form of inexhaustible fuel. Its greatest minds collaborated to use one of the planets natural elements – water. It was Professor Caldicus who devised the system in which to harness its power; a system capable of efficiently splitting water into its two main elements. These elements in gas form served as powerful sources for his fuel cells, and when used in Caldicus' revolutionary Energy Conversion Chambers they became a breakthrough solution for land and sea transportation. So, the Central Continent produced the C.H.E.S, the Caldicus Hydro Energy Stream; a solution with potential to launch the continent to the pinnacle of the Tri Nation Union's power status. They were, after all, the first to sign the Environmental Treaty, global awareness being at the forefront of their known agenda.

The West

The Western Continent had taken an alternate route with a plan to harness the planet's energy beneath its surface. Deep beneath its surface. However, not wanting to rely on one solution, they began separate and more clandestine tests on a second energy source – Subatomic Particle Fusion. Believed to be a powerful and bankable energy supply, work was under way. There was only one location to begin work creating the Geothermal Energy Harvest and that was offshore.

The plant was vast. Easily identifiable from space. The facility had more than one function. For as well as manufacturing the drilling systems and bi-alloy rods to conduct the planet's internal heat source, it also housed a secondary Testing Station. Here The West began tests harnessing sub-atomic power through particle fusion.

It was the nations' leader, Byrk, who acknowledged the possible fact that they might be too late. Too late to create a new power source. Too late to undo the devastation they had already caused, and too late to secure a beneficial destiny for future generations. Because of this, Byrk commissioned the Galactic Nautical Agency to begin design of an off world living structure on the planet's only moon. Work started in earnest.

They invested in researching these projects, while other projects, just as important and community focussed, began to suffer. Geothermal Energy Harvest plans intensified. The need to sell their solution for the environmental predicament and 'cash in' on their product was the key to solving the social economical funding deficit.

The East

Believing self-preservation their greatest concern, and that they could receive help from the work of other nations, The East invested in an alternate plan. They took point on the race to explore the vastness of space. Their Astro Nautical Galactic Probe Mission had already ventured into deep space.

Wanting to flex their continental power, the nation conducted not-so secret tests on atomic weaponry. With laboratories hidden underground, they produced weapons of unmitigated power. Costs were high, but keeping their citizens living in a communist-like social structure kept community funding low. The bulk of their profits were ploughed straight back into the quest for continental supremacy. Clearly priorities differed between continents.

The scene was powerful. The who's who of the three most powerful global continents seated in a cylindrical theatre of descending seats leading down to a staged setting where each leader sat upon a stone platform.

Harlow, leader of the Central Continent, was a statuesque male with pronounced features. His dark hair and even darker eyes gave a handsome appearance. He sat upon the central platform dressed in a light, tailored suit, his hands clasped upon the table, his jaw set firm with tension. Harlow was, upon first meeting, a charming man. Many a female had initially fallen for his suave looks and character. He was a man with a darker side. Power was addictive to Harlow. He loved to have it and he loved to wield it. It was not the democracy of a public ballot alone that gained him his position; extortion and intimidation were valuable assets.

On the Eastern Continent's platform sat Capita. A woman who would stand unflinching, toe to toe with any opponent. With hair mounted in a gravity defying coiffure and a stance stiff and aloof, Capita stood upon the platform ready to begin. She was a woman of advancing age, her stature short. Capita had lived a life serving, initially for her nation as a soldier. Her military background put her in good stead. As she rose through the ranks of power, and a glowing political career, Capita had taken her seat as ruler of the Eastern Continent. Standing now in her military regalia, the ruler of the Eastern Continent oozed tenacity and confidence.

Finally, on the Western Platform sat Byrk. A stout man with hair rapidly receding to the back of his head and russet cheeks that betrayed too many fortified beverages. Byrk's eyes scanned the other two leaders before him. It was a rare occurrence indeed to get all three leaders in the same room; to have the setting transmitted to the entire viewing global population was a first. Byrk was initially against the transmission, but no amount of reasoning had convinced Capita or Harlow to his opinion. In truth, Byrk considered the situation dangerous and unpredictable.

Around the leaders sat their ministers and political aids. Ranked in descending order with the highest status advisors at the bottom seating, closest to their leader. The amphitheatre-like room was full, and as a focussed set of lights illuminated the stone platforms, the summit began.

It was Byrk who spoke first. He rose and addressed not only the people around him but also the televised audience. "Our planet is our greatest asset. It is our home. It is our legacy, and it is dying." He pulled the edges of his suit jacket down as he continued. "This is not news to us. It is a fact we have been aware of for a considerable time." Byrk walked around his platform and stepped onto a central podium. "We cannot stand aside anymore, hoping the abysmal downfall in our climate and the environment will change by will alone." He clenched his right fist as his voice rose. "We are at crisis point and unless we change our ways, not only as a nation but as a global community, our future is bleak," he shook his head. "Our future is non-existent." At his words, the audience around him murmured in agreement and applauded his words. Byrk nodded and looked around the vast room before turning his attention to the lens of the transmitters. "We, your leaders, set ourselves a task; to inject new life into our planet by making the necessary changes needed to aid global equilibrium. To save our planet and secure our future, not just for ourselves, but for every generation to come."

Applause rose again, followed by cheers of encouragement. Byrk looked to both his co-leaders, noting their tense expressions. He turned back to the lens before him. Beads of sweat gathered around his temple. Byrk had to deliver this right. "During my leadership of the West, we have cut criminal activity, increased employment and are making great strides in social funding. With this success came my next task and the task of my co-leaders, Select Ministers Capita and Harlow, a sustainable and clean energy source for our planet. We were each challenged to research the best and most efficient ways to lead our nations towards a better future for environmental harmony. And so, we are here," Byrk pursed his lips; his eyes scanning broadcasting equipment around him, "to present to you all the efforts we have been making to bring balance back to our world."

Applause ensued. Byrk looked again towards his fellow leaders in a gesture to encourage them onto the central podium. It was Harlow who stepped forward first. The tall, handsome man clasped his hands behind his back as he addressed the nation. His shoulders set firm, his posture composed, he emanated self-confidence. "We, the Central Continent, have made impressive, dare I say remarkable, advances in technology. Along with the lead in our research team, Professor Caldicus, we have created the most sophisticated and multi-purpose Hydro Energy Stream." A baited hush ensued. "This system, that we call the C.H.E.S, Caldicus Hydro Energy Stream, has the capability to power our global transportation needs, as well as the potential to fuel our domestic and industrial requirements." Applause started slowly, but with understanding dawned clarity. The applause increased with zeal. Harlow smiled in self-satisfaction. His voice rose. "Would this also have the added benefit of reducing the planet's ever rising water levels?" With this first positive step, a feeling of hope infused the auditorium. If it were possible, Harlow straightened his back further and nodded with increased confidence as he strode around the podium soaking up the acclamation.

Eager to share the light in his fellow leaders' accolade, Byrk rose both hands, urging the crowd to calm. The vast auditorium hushed. "The West too have made extraordinary advances. We had made monumental strides in the production of Geothermal Power. As you are aware, far offshore we have developed and built the world's first Geothermal Power Plant. With self-contained production and construction of materials, we have pioneered not only the structure but successfully drilled deep into the planet's crust to harness our globe's own natural energy source. We have injected our uniquely designed bi-alloy rods to conduct and channel that energy back to the surface." Applause once again. Byrk's voice rose, "With these impressive advances, never before has the Tri Nations had such hope for our future."

This time applause was followed by a standing ovation. All around the centre stage, in the ascending rows of seating, the council members rose with cheers and shouts of support. Both continent leaders watched each other with haughty degrees of self-satisfaction. They basked in the acclamation around them, certain it extended beyond the vast colosseum-like stage setting and around the viewing world. The applause went on for long moments before the leader of the Eastern Continent, Capita, climbed onto the podium. The other leaders stood aside ready for her to divulge the East's endeavours. Capita's arms folded into a tight bind below her chest. With her head held high she surveyed their audience. The auditorium fell silent once again. She appeared to connect with each set of eyes, one by one, before turning back to her fellow leaders.

"Select Minister Byrk, your advances have been impressive. At what cost has this been to your people or the social funding you speak of? And more importantly, are you imparting all your achievements?"

Byrk's expression remained neutral. "Social funding was restricted in the beginning, but as we reach the end of the first phase, we can plough that funding back where it's needed."

"And your experimental advances?" Capita strode slowly around the edge of the platform. "You talk of Geothermal Power, but what of the second level experiments sequestered away in an undisclosed facility on the offshore plant?"

A momentary spark of guarded surprise flashed through Byrk's eyes before he reigned in his composure. The secondary tests were completely Top Secret and known only by a select team of scientists. "Our secondary testing has yet to prove a viable source of energy on mass levels." His careful expression was not lost on either Capita or Harlow. Capita continued her questioning.

"And these tests are-"

"Not ready for disclosure," Byrk finished.

"But surely subatomic particle fusion should not be conducted in such a sensitive location, no?"

Byrk turned his attention first to the broadcasting lenses and then to Harlow. The cautious expression in the Central leader's eyes was unreadable. Byrk smiled with a forced show of confidence. He smoothed a hand over his slick receding hair line and then readjusted his suit. Why was Capita challenging him like this? And why now before the televised audience? What was she trying to prove?

"Our tests are well under control and monitored to the highest degrees of Tri Nation Union standards."

"And yet you kept these tests a secret. Why?"

Byrk remained cool. "Until we could be positive our tests on such a supreme power source could prove successful. Tell us, Select Minister Capita, why the questioning? We are here with a fully candid agenda."

Harlow stepped forward and motioned for the broadcasting to stop, but his request went unnoticed, the scene too captivating to stop.

"All experiments targeted towards the environmental project were to be disclosed."

"It appears they were," Byrk replied, as his gazed stretched between his two fellow leaders.

Capita, still with arms folded, answered swiftly. "It is prudent for global interests that close observation is upheld on all activity."

Byrk's gaze cooled. "But we are doing nothing wrong in testing such a potential power source. This was after all the agreement was it not? The inherent possibilities of success eclipse everything we as a global union have achieved to date."

"What are the dangers if you fail?"

Byrk turned back to Harlow, his cool demeanour slipping. "You talk of dangers. This from a man who sat with me to discuss our concerns over the East's unwillingness to cease their atomic testing and how we can stop them. You talk of dangers?"

"Stop us?" Capita glared at Harlow. "You wished to stop us?" She noticed his demeanour stiffen. "Was this before or after you purchased one of these dangerous weapons from us?"

Around the world the scene unfolded with an array of emotions. The audience watched in amusement, entertained by seeing the world's most illustrious leaders in such a state of conflict. But others, with a feeling of foreboding, watched on in disquietude.

Byrk's swift turn of incredulity in Harlow's direction went unnoticed by the Central leader as he focussed his attention upon Capita. The leader of the Eastern Continent was as calm and controlled as ever. She released the tight fold of her arms and allowed them to fall loosely by her sides.

Harlow spoke with barely controlled rage. "A deal that was agreed with utmost confidentiality."

"Secrets between you both are a source of amusement to my ministers and myself," Capita said as she smiled. "You talk of transparency and yet you deal in secrets. You talk in favour of your people and yet you conspire to gain from them. But most importantly, you speak of a safe future and yet you barter for weapons of devastation." Capita switched her glare to Byrk. "Or begin construction of off world habitations on our moon."

A hush saturated the air around them.

Byrk closed his eyes as he ran one hand over the opposite side of his face. "All contingencies must be considered and catered for." He began to realise that nothing they did was a secret from one another. He should not have been surprised. They were the global superpowers, were they not? It was foolish to think none had the power to unveil each other's secrets.

Capita's eyes glowed with triumph. "Did you consider that we may be too late to stop the downward spiral of our planet's destruction?"

Harlow glared at Capita with escalating resentment. "What are you doing?" He turned to address the broadcasters. "Turn off the transmission." He motioned with an aggressive step towards the televisual team. "Off. Now."

With a sharp flick of her head, members of the Eastern Continent sprang into action, taking hold of the individuals capable of ending the broadcast. Capita continued. "This quest to heal our world's plight might be too late, but our combined advances in alternate power might hold unconsidered possibilities." The powerful woman addressed the ministers of the Central and Western Continent, as well as the viewing world. "We are not here to discuss how we can save this planet from our own destruction. We are here to say there is an alternative solution to our plight. One with the probability of bringing us a world of clean, breathable air, abundant plant life and, most importantly, no fear of environmental devolution." She turned to address the transmitting lenses. "This is our finest solution for an attainable future for us all."

"WHAT ARE YOU DOING?" Byrk's voice bellowed with rage. He glared at Capita, his cheeks burning with fury. His hands trembling with barely controlled ire. The stout man's shoulders rose and fell with his rapid breath as one finger moved to focus on Capita. "You agreed to join us for this summit. Our chance to bring harmony back to the world."

"Hope for our people." Harlow added.

"Hope?" Capita questioned "If you believe so much in hope and the future of which you speak so fondly then this will mean nothing."

Capita turned to one of her Ministers sitting on the front row. She nodded once. Upon receipt of her cue, the slim bespectacled man lifted a communication device to his mouth and uttered a single command.

Harlow switched his attention to Byrk as the stout Western leader watched the Eastern woman with mounting trepidation. "What was that?" he demanded.

There was little reaction from Capita. "What will you do, Select Minister Byrk, now that your contingency plans are being eradicated?"

The russet glow of ire that infused Byrk's cheeks drained away in an instant. "You…"

Harlow placed a hand upon the Western leader's shoulder in a show of support. "Answer us, Capita."

The Eastern leaders' eyes gleamed with villainous intent. "Right now, a heavily loaded warhead has been deployed, aimed directly for the sub-structure currently being constructed on the moon." Capita turned to address the ministers and global audience.

Byrk wanted to call Capita's bluff. He wanted to call her a liar, but he knew she was not. Silence enveloped the room. Disbelief befell with palpable disquiet. Capita allowed the gravity of her actions to stretch on for long moments before she spoke again. However, Harlow interrupted.

"This is insanity." He clenched his fists and bared his teeth with mounting lividity. "The moon? Our moon?"

Ignoring Harlow, Capita again addressed the population. "The best hope for our future is to leave this dying planet and move to a new more habitable home for us all. And I can lead us there. I ask the continents of the planet to follow me, and I will lead us to deliverance." Capita turned to the minister to whom she had given her earlier gesture and signalled again. This time the slight man rose and walked with purpose towards a large monitor situated off to one side of the cylindrical room. He span the device away from the broadcasters currently watching on in horror and towards the podium. The scene changed from the broadcast of their current summit to that of the planet's one orbiting natural satellite. The room, as well as the viewing population, watched as a streaking light hurtled towards the orbiting rock and smashed into it at full velocity. The impact ricocheted on the planet's surface as a powerful explosion of indigo flames tore through one side of the moon. Fragments erupted as a spray of molten rock.

In the auditorium, ministers' voices rose in horror and Byrk stood transfixed by the harrowing scene as chaos erupted around him. Unseen by the other two leaders, who were at that moment overtaken by their own experience of the unfolding events, Harlow ran to his most loyal aid. The man with light cropped hair and a sallow face stood entranced in disbelief. Harlow grabbed him by his clothing and pulled him to break his trauma. He leaned closer and whispered into his ear. As his words sank into the younger man, he turned to look at his leader in alarm.

"Do it," Harlow ordered.

The loyal aid made a direct call.

Capita continued to address the population, intoxicated by her actions. "My work with the – "

"CAPITA," Harlow yelled. He pulled off his suit jacket leaving him in a shirt darkened by patches of perspiration. He waited for the woman to look in his direction, his view of her momentarily blocked as Byrk ran past to his own gathering of ministerial aids. "You once boasted no ruler was efficient without contingency plans to overcome any eventuality."

Capita's eyes narrowed.

"You cannot hold our world to ransom like this, but the damage has already been done." He shook his head. "How could you? Do you have any idea what you have done to this world?" He paused and straightened. "There is an atomic missile heading straight to your launch station. You will not get away with this."

Capita's head dipped slowly to one side as a sorrowful expression ghosted her features. It was at that point that all global broadcasts ceased to send, and static filled the airwaves.

The Environmental Summit, a meeting heralded as the beginning of the restoration of the planet's environmental and elemental harmony, was, in fact, the foundation of its hellish end. It was at that moment, upon hearing of the impending attack on her own launch site, that Capita signalled for two more launches. The first was towards the Central Continent, specifically aimed for its capital and the C.H.E.S production plant. The second was to the West and their offshore Geothermal Plant. Not expected was the secondary reaction one of those explosions would cause.

A heavily loaded atomic weapon, armed with enough destructive power to eradicate the Geothermal plant's structure, hit its mark with calculated precision. The force of the explosion caused the entire structure to fracture, and the frame buckled into the sea in which it stood. Other portions thrust up into the atmosphere within the flaming inferno of destruction that arose from the detonation. It rose accompanied by roaring clouds of fire. Tides, a product of the blast, generated and massed across the surface of the sea. Building in intensity as they moved, they soared from the surface of the ocean, reaching devastating heights as they roared toward the Eastern Continent's Oceanside villages, swallowing the land in its wake.

But it was the impact itself that caused the most catastrophic and unimaginable reaction. The collision, so absolute in its power, ricocheted down the bi-alloy rods drilled into the planet's mantle and resonated into its tectonic plates. Branching out like the fingers of a web, the force vibrated through the globe's lithosphere, shifting and fracturing as it reverberated outwards. Then, rising to the planet's surface with horrifying speed, the ground cracked, split, and separated. Deep gullies began to form above ground as the webbed fractures continued to branch out below the surface. By the time they started to abate, over half the globe was already affected by the tectonic shattering.

On the surface, seismic activity of unmeasurable proportions continued to destroy its foundations. Buildings fell effortlessly. Enormous valleys ate entire cities. The vast gullies that ran deep down into the planet's mantle churned as glowing lava erupted through the apertures, bubbling up through the ground and out into cities as structures continued to fall. Molten rock engulfed the land through the Central Continent and splintered out to the East and West. Smoke filled the sky, mixing with deadly, burning ash, suffocating in its intensity and blinding in its density. Fires spread wildly, consuming all in its path. Molten rock, a product of the moon's destruction, rained down over the planet's surface.

From above, the sounds of screaming, and cries for help, melded into one cacophony of unmitigated terror. The lands below distorted into a churning mass of molten rock, ashen clouds, and billowing flames. And left, what one could only imagine, was the population of a planet gripped by terror, hopeless victims in a world destroyed by perverted desire.

CHAPTER 2

The cranking and grinding of well-used gears seemed to escalate louder, the further down beneath the planet's surface Scout Jensen travelled. Relieved to finally be away from the harrowing land above, Jensen placed her hands onto the metallic hatch behind her. She leaned the weight of her body against its cold surface. And it was cold. Until Jensen evacuated the chamber, this claustrophobic capsule was, to her, a frigid coffin. Her head lagged to the side as she breathed deeply. She still was not able to remove the mask from her face, and its presence was beginning to irritate the skin around her nose and mouth. She yearned to drag her nails over the aggravated flesh. The apparatus was a robust piece of equipment, similar in design to that of an ancient gas mask, but not so cumbersome in weight, and not covering the eyes. A separate set of goggles adorned the upper part of her face, those too increasing in irritation. Jensen was glad she had almost reached her destination and would be able to remove her outer clothing and aggravating headgear. Knowing she was about to return home filled Jensen with relief and dare she say happiness? It had been a simple assignment, but she was glad to be home.

Feeling the capsule decrease in pace, Jensen re-adjusted her stance. She stood to attention with her fingers clasped behind her back facing forward. A final jolt signified the end of her journey. Jensen felt a last flutter of relief trickle through her system. As she watched the double doors slide open, she sighed and stepped out into another confined compartment. This time she was not alone. Looking to her left, Jensen thankfully spied a familiar face. Feeling at once more relaxed, she pulled the head covering, goggles and mask from her face. Dirty blonde hair fell haphazardly over her shoulders, and she shook her head as if to tame the unkempt locks. Dark eyes rested on the welcome features of her ally and the eve shift's decontamination officer, Nicoletti.

"Scout Jensen," Nicoletti greeted, aware to keep their interactions formal while they were on duty. "You were gone quite a while. I believe certain officers might have begun to worry!"

Jensen quirked her left brow at that remark and her full lips curved into a smile. "But not you?" she questioned.

Nicoletti simply shrugged his broad shoulders. Hazel eyes dancing as he replied. "Some of us possess a little more faith."

"Of course," Jensen shook her head, her smile staying as she began to disrobe. First, she pulled a heavy brown rucksack from her shoulders and handed it to Nicoletti. Holding it within his gloved hands he placed it to one side. Fingering the clasps around her neck Jensen slowly dislodged them one by one. "I don't recall you saying that not so long ago." Jensen pulled the garments from her upper body, starting with an outer jacket, followed by three inner layers, the first of which was covered with ashen grime. The three inner layers provided added warmth. Once removed, she was naked from the waist up. "If my memory serves me correctly you were arguing the pros of sending a second scout onto the barrens to search for me."

Nicoletti shook his head. "We grow, we adapt, and we learn to have more faith." He took Jensen's clothing and deposited them in a large silver container, aware of her playful banter. "Just remove those garments Scout Jensen and get yourself into the neutralization chamber. It's quitting time and I need my slumber."

Placing her hands upon her hips, Jensen halted the removal of her lower items of clothing. "Exactly how do you think your spouse would feel if she heard you speaking to me in such a manner?"

"She would think me foolish to tease a scout."

"She is a wise individual."

Nicoletti smiled. "Of course, she is," he replied with a faux arrogant smile as he held his arms out wide in a gesture that Jensen could only read as over confidence.

Jensen's smile softened as she removed the rest of her clothing. She handed the garments to Nicoletti, leaving her naked and without a hint of modesty. This was a routine she had repeated more times than she could recall. It was a well-practiced ritual that ended every assignment on the planets' surface.

Nicoletti took Jensen's final garments and placed them in the metallic container by his side. He slammed its circular lid shut and lifted the barrel in front of him. Heaving the cumbersome coffer carefully, Nicoletti slid it into a vacant disposal hatch. He slammed the container in place and heard the tell-tale sounds of a swift vacuum sucking the clothing away for a thorough cleansing. The process was automatic, as were Nicoletti's actions.

Jensen looked down at her fair skin, unconsciously brushing her palms over creamy white flesh as if to push away an errant piece of grime. It was flesh that had never seen the sun. Pale to the point of transparency. She took a relaxed breath and held her rigid stance, awaiting the next command.

Nicoletti struck his palm over a red, rectangular button. It activated a doorway to the right which opened with a swoosh.

"My favourite part," Jensen joked.

"Come on, Scout," Nicoletti responded, "You know you love that cold blast of anti-infection rivulets."

Jensen glared in mock annoyance. She sucked a deep pull of air though her nose and rolled her eyes. "Let's get this over with, shall we?" Rubbing her hands together Jensen stepped forward and into the purification chamber. She heard a slight chuckle as the door slid shut behind her. Jensen braced her body for the inevitable. Sanding in the third enclosed space she looked around the ivory walls and waited for the tell-tale signs heralding the beginning of the decontamination cycle. Three long beeps began, one an octave higher than the other, followed by a double flash of magenta. Jensen closed her eyes. Three short blips then signalled the commencement of the invasive cleansing procedure.

Jensen's arms rose above her head, and she reached out, grasping metal rings that hung either side above her body. She spread her legs, moving one limb slightly in front of the other and anxiously held her breath.

Although expected, the bitter blast of gasses always took her breath away. Jensen's jaw dropped and she struggled for breath as the neutralizing gas worked its way from her feet and slowly up her body. Her brow furrowed and she grimaced with discomfort. This was something to which she would never adapt. The chilling gas travelled further up her legs, over her hips, her torso and across her breasts. Jensen felt her nipples tighten painfully. Instinctively she squeezed her eyes tighter, feeling the gas travel up her neck and over her face. Jensen held her breath. A moment more and her ordeal was over. A low monotone 'ding' signalled the end of the procedure. Releasing her breath Jensen opened her eyes. Immediately a second door opened, and a blast of warm air flowed rapidly through. Now for her favourite part. Feeling instantly more relaxed, Jensen stepped out of the chamber and into the comfort of the dressing room.

In this room Jensen was alone and free to dress in private. She moved to a row of metallic lockers, finding the third door along and opening it with an antiquated key kept around her neck. Reaching inside, Jensen pulled out a pair of ebony pants and matching shirt. Laying them on the opposite bench she pulled on the clean clothing.

Once dressed, Jensen turned to a full-length looking glass. She cast a disapproving gaze over her frail form and focused on her limp blonde hair, which she pulled behind her head and fastened within a loose knot. Jensen sighed.

"Well come on then, Scout. Time to meet the captain and impart your findings," she muttered to herself. Jensen exited the dressing room. With her head held high she entered the underground world she called her home.

CHAPTER 3

It was the smell that always welcomed Jenson home. Though unidentifiable as a particular aroma, the pungent mix of odours never failed to fill her with a sense of belonging. Throughout her life, the mix of scents had never changed. Sometimes, during her free time, Jensen would try to name the blend of aromas that floated through the Recycled Air Purifiers, or R.A.P.s as they were more commonly known. At various times, one aroma would stand out stronger than the rest. There was always a hint of soil, something uniquely base in its scent. Often the aroma of whatever was being served in one of the two mess units permeated the air with an enticing allure. There was the definable tang of heated metallic ore, as well as some more unpleasant aromas identifiable from underground living. These occasionally included the lavatories, grease compounds, underlying notes of warm bodies and static electricity. One of these aromas might have made for an overwhelming assault on the olfactory senses. As a combination, they were home.

Having spent her whole life living underground, Jensen considered herself at times more fortunate than most. At least she got to escape the sometimes-claustrophobic confines of their underground habitat, even if not for overly extended time periods. It was the 'out' she was sure many habitants may craved. Scout Taura didn't agree. Long-time ally and fellow Scout, Taura believed if the civilian inhabitants were to glimpse beyond their confines, the truth of what lay beyond their safe little world would cause the reality of their current situations to become too much to bear. Hope served as a great ally in the struggles of subterranean living. To Jensen, seeing the world beyond only served to strengthen her resolve to fight for a future. For a greater purpose.

Venturing into their underground world Jensen glanced around. The integration of metallic beams secured into the stone foundations was an impressive feat of engineering. Even after twenty-nine cycles, Jensen still felt a tiny thrill as she ran her fingers over the cool rock and shining ore. The colony was immense. Originally built over a century ago as an asylum for the mentally ill, long before the annihilation of their planet, it had undergone tremendous, vast transformations. Ever expanding to accommodate the population (although controlled) and their growing needs. The true number of inhabitants within the facility was unknown, even to the government themselves.

There were four main infrastructures. These were named by colonies: Governance, Labour, Domestic, and Primary. Governance was the largest structure. It housed all enforcement and political personnel. All scouts, scientists, medics, and upper-level mechanics and technicians lived and worked in the Governance colony. Next was Labour, housing both single and co-habitation dwellings. Most Labour citizens also worked in Governance, but held lower ranked occupations, Education, Catering, Hygiene and Maintenance. Thirdly, there was the Domestic colony. Here families lived a simple existence shadowed by echoes of the past. They lived rotation by rotation, worked for their own survival, and had little interaction with Governance, socialising only with those from Labour. The last and least acknowledged Colony was Primary. This was the oldest part of the facility and officially abandoned over a semi-century ago, too antiquated for the citizens' needs.

The underground facility was called 'The Haven' by its citizens, and though as artificial and occasionally stifling it could be, it was home.

Jensen was born into Governance by scout parents. Rarer that two Governance citizens would unify and reproduce, but as was the law, their offspring had to follow the parents' occupation. Reproduction followed strict regulations. For a united couple to reproduce, they first had to seek government permission. Once received, their reproductive materials were evaluated for possible abnormalities that could result in any physical or mental deviations. Government was ridged on such processes; the need for an indefectible race was pursued with uncompromising resolve. If the Genetic Reproduction Simulation, or G.R.S, was successful, the reproductive cells were fertilised, and the embryo placed back within the child-bearer. It was a cold and clinical process, lacking the affection of more antiquated methods of reproduction, but it had a high percentage success rate.

Jensen held strong memories of her parents. Her mother Tomei was a nurturing woman with golden hair and eyes as dark as Jensen's. It was Tomei who encouraged a love of literature. Her father, Jaxon, had taught her how to be a good scout. Jensen would never forget his lessons on how to walk the barrens, how to slice through the winds with ease, how to conserve energy, and how to defend oneself. Most of all, Jensen remembered how much her parents loved one another. And how that deep loved had resulted in her losing both parents at fifteen cycles old. Upon that rotation, Jensen entered the family vocation. It was a position she had held for the past indiction. She had risen the ranks from a level three to her current level six status.

Within Governance, the grading structure was as rigid as enforcement rankings. The higher up the chain of command, the privier one was to the government's agenda. Jensen was a level six. This meant that not only did she share the common knowledge that their goal was to leave their world for a new planet, but her work involved scouting for precious metals and ores capable of finishing the construction of an immense craft to fulfil that goal. This was their Ultimate Agenda. This was the colonists' dream for their promised land. This is what everybody worked towards.

Jensen brushed her fingers across the cool rock wall as she made her way further into the Governance colony. She passed the Scout Preparation Rooms. These were six rooms, three on each side, stocked with mission equipment, clothing, rations, basic medical supplies, and weaponry. The type of mission dictated the type of equipment a scout would need for an assignment. Jensen checked each room, noting them all empty, before continuing. She ventured through a wide metallic angled frame and walked into the heart of the facility. The usual aroma hit her as she passed through this area. It was the smell of cooking. She was close to the dining hall. Filling her senses with the daily menu's offering, Jensen peered into the vast room noting the empty tables. Those that were filled were with individuals with whom she did not work on a shift rotation. Allies tended to be made within aligning shift patterns. Ducking back out of the mess hall, Jensen continued to the next room. This was the social chamber. Once again it was sparsely populated, but she ventured inside to scan the faces.

This room, the larger of two social chambers, was again sparsely filled with bodies. Its location by the mess hall was an obvious draw. The room was bright and cool in temperature. Jensen took in her surrounds. There was wide, material covered, seating scattered strategically around with low tables between them. There were also eight circular tables with single chairs. These were higher and made of a different material. They were aged and had been re-enamelled repeatedly over time, but the sturdy construction served well for scores of uses.

The din of voices echoed off the stone walls. Jensen spied colonists seated around a table playing a game of cards. Others were reading. A few more conversed quietly. Jensen checked the wall chronometer, noticing the time. She needed to complete her mission by reporting her findings to Captain Lucia. Accepting her ally and fellow scout, Taura, was not in this room, Jensen left. She hoped to speak with Taura before the rest period. Taura was married to Nicoletti, and as such was probably already in their shared unit awaiting his return. All their shifts ended together and there was usually a brief period of social interaction before rest, but possibly not this rotation she figured. With a quirk of her lips, and nod of acknowledgement to several acquaintances, Jensen left the room.

"Scout Jensen!"

Jensen turned, surprised to see Major Vegas approaching. Vegas was a level eight Major within the Governance colony. He was a large, burly man with dark, ruddy features and a thick head of dark hair flecked with ashen highlights. It matched his closely cropped beard. Dressed neatly in his dark cobalt uniform, he was an imposing figure.

"Major," Jensen greeted respectfully. She stood to her full height and laced her fingers behind the small of her back. Though they were acquaintances, on duty protocol dictated proper conduct. As Vegas approached, Jensen remained focussed upon his eyes; he appeared harried. It was always best to keep one's focus on Vegas' eyes, as the horrendous scar in the form of a deep gouge on the side of his neck served as an ever-present reminder of the dangers one could meet upon the barren lands.

Major Vegas regarded Jensen evenly. He was close to her now and slowed his approach. Though almost a score older, he had often served as a mentor for the younger scout. "You were expected to report as soon as you returned from your mission, Scout."

Jenson nodded. "That was my intention, Major, but I wished to stop by my unit on the way and hoped to catch Taura before then. I am still within mission parameters for completion. I believe I was scheduled to meet with Captain Lucia?"

Holding his arm out, a sign for Jensen to join him, Vegas began to walk. However, it was not towards the briefing room as Jensen had expected. Instead, it was in an unexpected direction. She followed without comment.

"Scout, as you are aware we are rapidly approaching the conclusion of Phase Tria. With the swift advance of Phase Quattuor comes a new set of procedures and agenda for senior scouts."

"Of course."

"With the moment almost upon us, the selection committee has chosen you as one of our most capable senior scouts to sub head the new directive."

Jensen regarded Vegas, as she asked, "Sub head?"
Vegas only smiled. "All will be revealed."

***

Following the Major, Jensen remained one step behind him as they walked down a narrow corridor and past a set of rest rooms, before turning right towards a second corridor. Jensen had believed Vegas was escorting her to the briefing room, but this was not the case. She was heading towards areas she had never visited. The further down the twist of corridors they travelled, the more Jensen became unfamiliar with her surroundings. Vegas stopped by a door. The numerals alone showed to Jensen they were heading towards superior level divisions. He activated the lock with a four-digit code. The barrier opened and he stood aside, allowing Jensen to pass through. Vegas followed and then passed her once again leading the way towards never visited sectors of the colony. Jensen noted the further they travelled the more impressive their surroundings became. Rock walls were replaced with sheets of metallic ore. The uneven stone floor transformed into smooth ornate patterns. Jensen had originally figured there wasn't much that could be altered with a rock infrastructure built deep below the planet's surface. She was wrong.

Jensen looked around her. She thought she probably shouldn't be so surprised that upper-level personnel lived in a slightly more impressive residence, but a twinge of jealousy did rear its head. Such class difference always demanded a finer touch. She was glad she lived alone. It was hard enough to live as an individual in a personal unit, let alone a unit for two who still had to share a space not much larger than her own. Overall, the cramped units were small, housing as many personnel as could be efficiently placed in a specified area. Personal interaction was generally conducted in the social chambers. Although kept to an elevated level of cleanliness, they lacked imagination. Much of the furniture had seen well over one hundred cycles of use. Jensen herself had played every game and read every tome more than once. Reading was her favourite diversion, and one of the only ways to gain insight into their past. She only wished there was a greater choice of tomes at her disposal. All reading material was pre-chosen by the government, designed to deliver the right message; to educate and inform more than entertain. The rare unauthorised novels Jensen had obtained came from bartering with level one inhabitants from the Labour and Domestic Colonies. These she kept in the privacy of her unit.

Vegas stopped by a second door and activated the lock. The barrier slid open with a mechanical 'whoosh.' Jensen looked around. She felt a flutter of anticipation. This was unfamiliar territory. She had no idea where she was.

"Almost there, Scout."

"Right, Sir." Jensen followed Vegas down yet another corridor. This one was wider, and she noted their footsteps echoed less in this area. The walls instantly captured her attention. Gone was the sterile metallic ore. Instead, they were constructed of a fine timber. What was more astonishing was three beautifully framed images adoring these walls. Jensen felt overcome with emotion. The first image was of their little world from above. So perfect. So alive. So vibrant. The second image was of an evening sky. A stretch of darkness broken only by infinite stars shining like specs of silver over an ebony shroud. The third was of an emerald meadow glistening with early morning dew. Jensen's breath caught as she tried to memorise every nuance of the image.

"Magnificent, yes?"

Jensen looked up at Vegas, "Sir, I had no idea. I have seen small images in tomes and on the data streams, but nothing compares to this."

Vegas tapped the frame, not daring to place his finger directly on the image. "That's what we're fighting for, Scout, another chance for a world like this."

Knowing Vegas had scouted the barren lands too, Jensen said, "It takes knowing the world as it exists now to understand just how much we have lost."

"Indeed." Vegas took a step away from the images and turned away. The truth in Jensen's words spoke loudly. It was the reason they worked so hard towards their goal. For another chance, who wouldn't?

"We don't want to be late, Scout."

"Of course not." Jensen quickened her pace, following Vegas down the timber lined corridor. She stopped suddenly when she came upon what she knew could only be a senior ranking social chamber. The luxurious setting was something to behold. Overstuffed and overused hide sofas, placed evenly around the room. Timber tome-cases stood from floor to ceiling; filled with more tomes than Jensen could dare to dream. The flooring was a plush neutral material and, in the centre, hung ornate lighting made from a translucent substance Jensen believed to be glass. It was old, but it was grand. There were only several personnel in the chamber, only one of which Jensen recognised. Judging by the grading insignias on their collars they were high ranking Enforcement Officers. Too high to be mixing with lower-level Governance citizens such as herself. Again, the question of 'just how many people did reside in the Governance colony?' entered her mind. It was something she often pondered and was now increasingly curious. There were so many parts of the colony she had obviously never seen and possibly never would.

Jensen resumed her pace to catch up with Vegas. She was barely five steps behind him when she stopped once again as they reached the dining room. Her instinct to look inside was thwarted as Vegas disappeared around a corner. Jensen quickened her pace to catch up and found the Major standing by a wide set of double doors. A metallic plaque labelled it a conference room. There were no windows on this door and the barrier was sealed closed. Jensen looked around, noting a lavatory to their left and another locked door to her right. This door did have a window and she couldn't help but surreptitiously peek through the translucent polymer portal. She saw stairs. Stairs? Jensen had heard there was a lower level to Governance, but she had never seen evidence of such until right this moment. She was stunned and curious.

Hearing the tell-tail sound of a locking mechanism being deactivated, Jensen turned quickly. With a swift inspection of her appearance, she brushed a hand over her clothing and took a relaxing breath. Pulling her shoulders rigidly into line, Jensen re-adjusted the tie that kept her golden unruly locks off her shoulders and away from her face. Once again, she laced her fingers behind her back. Vegas waited for the door to open and then stepped inside. A slight incline of his head requested Jensen should follow.

Inside the room was an impressive, large oval table. Its dark timber was polished to a high sheen, as were the chairs placed evenly around it. All but three of these chairs were occupied with Enforcement and Government personnel. Most of the faces unfamiliar. Caution twisted her insides as Jensen realised, they had all been awaiting their arrival. The silence of the room was soon broken.

CHAPTER 4

"Please take your seats."

Walking around the oval table, Jenson followed Vegas to the empty seats. The moment afforded her time to scan the room. It was of average size for a meeting room, much like all other briefing rooms she was used to. The only difference was that the plain walls were broken up with images of star charts and their planet pre-devastation. Each frame was of an exact size and of equal distance apart. The images lined three of the four walls. It was the far wall that Jensen found the most curious. Dominating and set within its centre was a large screen with no frame or casing, just frosted etchings down one side, which she presumed were touch activated. She had never seen such a piece of equipment before. Jensen wondered if it were a form of televisual device or used for computing. Either way she hoped to see it in action.

Reaching their destination on the other side of the table, Jensen pulled out a chair, noting how easily it slid upon the hard, buff tile beneath her feet. She saw the contrast between the ornate stone floor and her scuffed worn boots. Jensen took a surreptitious peek beneath the table, noting the highly polished sheen on the footwear of her fellow tablemates. Feeling instantly underdressed for the occasion, Jensen took her seat and pulled herself squarely under the table until the table edge hit her ribs. She placed her hands flat upon its cool surface and waited. The silence stretched out for several moments and Jensen used that time to take a quick look at each person sitting around her. She recognised half the faces. Her inspection quickly ended upon an empty seat, and she wondered if they were waiting for the last person to arrive.

"Major," started Minister Pavo, "I was under the impression you were bringing two scouts with you?"

Jensen regarded Minister Pavo. In size and colouring he was remarkably like Vegas, though his air of self-importance made for a slightly less appealing aura. Jensen found that hard to ignore and difficult to warm to. She had always endeavoured to avoid the man as much as possible. She believed him to be… 'slippery'.

Vegas' slight shift of discomfort was not lost on Jensen. She knew this man too well. She turned to look at him with curiosity.

"Unfortunately, Minister, I have upsetting news to report. We will be one member down on the team.

Jensen felt a familiar clutch of dread claw at her chest. She took a deep breath.

"Scout Taura was discovered near the main hatch. Scavengers."

"Is she alright?" Still seated, Jensen pushed her chair away from the table. "Is she in the medical suite?" Her eyes bore deep into Vegas'.

Vegas placed his hand gently on Jensen before removing it and lacing his fingers back together. "Scout Taura was sent above ground to collect the environmental test data samples. Her mission was two marks at most. When she didn't return, we sent Scout Ryan to investigate. He found her body by a distance marker near the main hatch." Vegas paused for a moment, as he unconsciously fingered the wound on his neck. "Scavengers. Her wounds were too severe, and she died from blood loss before she could make it back to the colony."

Jensen felt his words hit her like a harsh blow to her stomach. The air left her body in a silent exhale of breath. Her eyes moved swiftly over the table before her, seeing nothing as she digested Vegas' words. The intensifying cadence in her chest refused to dissipate, as emotion coiled within her. Jensen closed her eyes. Her head sagged. She summoned the strength not to react in the room full of high-ranking individuals, but it was tough to rein in the sorrow that threatened to immolate and overwhelm her. Why couldn't Vegas have told her before the meeting? At least give her time to process the news. Taura; her closest ally for over ten cycles. Jensen fought desperately to keep her tears at bay. Now was not the time. She pulled in a deep breath, opened her eyes, and lifted her head. She looked straight into the eyes of the woman sitting opposite her. She had never seen this woman before, but the compassion she saw shining back radiated like a welcome beacon. Then, just as quickly, it was gone. The woman blinked and the fragile link was broken with cool indifference. Jensen looked away, surprised to see the conversation had continued around her.

"- informed she put up a good fight. She must have been severely outnumbered."

"This is unfortunate," Captain Lucia replied. Lucia was a tall woman. As tall, if not taller than many of the men in Governance. At least those Jensen knew of. She had short, light cropped hair and a sturdy build, more out of muscular strength. Jensen was unsure if the captain had ever been above ground. She wasn't listed as a scout in the history logs. Lucia continued, "We were planning on the input from two of our seasoned scouts in the field for Phase Quattuor. We don't have time to await a replacement. I feel it best we continue." Captain Lucia looked around the table, awaiting their approval.

"Seconded," agreed Minister Pavo.

A rumbling sigh rose from the head of the table. A distinguished gentleman rubbed his palms together slowly, as he considered their proposal. It was Enforcement Commander Tehera. Tehera was a man as mysterious as he was stoic. Jensen had only been in the Commander's presence a handful of times, but from what she understood, he was a man of few words, only speaking when he had something of importance to impart. The Commander never dallied in idle chatter. Jensen cast a surreptitious eye over her superior, always curious about their mysterious Commander. His hair hung past his eyes, giving the appearance of being surprisingly unkempt for a man of his position. He had a beard that was several shades lighter than his hair and more ashen in colour. Jensen found it curious to see the man in his starchy pressed suit to be in such a paramount position considering his scruffy exterior. She watched him closely. This man was second only to the Select Prime. His word, his decision was final in this tactical meeting.

"Agreed," Commander Tehera responded. "Let us continue for now. A replacement can be arranged if needed."

It was Vegas who spoke next, addressing all nine members of the room. "For the benefit of Scout Jensen, maybe introductions are in order?"

"Agreed," spoke the Commander again. He sat back in his chair, seeming to relax as he said, "Perhaps you can do the honours, Major."

"Of course." Vegas turned in his chair and looked towards Jensen. He noted the expression in her eyes and delivered himself a mental slap. Duty and the mission always came first for Vegas. Always. As such it was easy for him to forget, at times, that not everybody was as single minded as he. Jensen was a remarkable scout. That he freely acknowledged, but sometimes he forgot that she couldn't shut down her feelings as easily as he could. Discovering one of her closest allies had been killed while in the field of duty (during a meeting of high-ranking officials) was not the best time to have received that news. Vegas took a shallow breath. "Well, Scout," he started, a little softer than expected. "Firstly, to your left you have Minister Fawkes, scientist and advisor to our Select Prime."

Jensen nodded politely; acknowledging the influence this individual had on the leader of their civilisation. He was a tall man with no hair. Painfully thin, even by their standards of living, with a sallow complexion and eyes that sat a little too close together. The man returned her nod of greeting.

"Next to Fawkes we have Minister Ilkin. Ilkin is our Social Minister. Decisions concerning the running of the colonies are headed by Minister Ilkin."

Jensen wondered if this was the woman in charge of the tome selection on offer in the social chambers. If so, maybe she could ask her for a few cast offs from the impressive offerings of which she had just been privy in the ministerial chambers. Hide-bound tombs, some twice as thick as the palm of her hand. A tempting offering indeed.

"Next we have Vice Lieutenant Lorenzo; head of tactical resources and scientific advisor."

Jensen, again, nodded politely at Lorenzo, briefly acknowledging the short, balding man, before looking at the woman beside him and directly opposite her.

"Minister Kiernan is one of our head scientists, as well as minister of operations and acquisitions. Some of the orders received by scouts for above ground resources come from Minister Kiernan. She calculates what is needed from the Barrens and works with both Enforcement and Ministerial personnel in combing through ancient cartography, blueprints, and reports of our lost world to learn where we might be able to find much needed resources. As you can imagine, Scout, it's a difficult job calculating measure of destruction, ancient documents, and the location of possible assets. It took many cycles to gather enough data to figure out where we may be able to scout the barrens to safely find much needed materials. Thanks to Kiernan, and her teams work, along with scouts such as yourself, we've found precious metal ores, seeds, technology, and scientific data. All of these are valuable to our Ultimate Agenda and continued survival."

With the impressive introduction, Jensen studied the woman seated before her. She must have been late thirty to forty cycles old. With thick auburn hair and emerald eyes, she was an attractive woman. Obviously highly intelligent too. It then occurred to Jensen that Kiernan was probably the woman who had issued the order sending Taura on the mission that took her life. Her mind moved again to her ally. She loved Taura like a sibling. It was hard to believe she would never see her headstrong, argumentative ally again. Scout Taura was one of the most capable of scouts. With her death, only five female scouts remained. Sadness clouded Jensen's emotions, but realising she was being spoken to, Jensen looked up at Kiernan.

"Scout Jensen," Kiernan repeated. "It's a pleasure to finally meet you."

The unexpected timber of Minister Kiernan's voice surprised Jensen. She offered a nod of acknowledgement.

"And finally," Vegas held a hand across to the final four members of the table, "You are familiar with Minister Pavo, Captain Lucia, Enforcement Commander Tehera and Lieutenant Whylen."

"Yes," Jensen smiled politely. She worked with Whylen, and Lucia was the direct officer over all scouts.

Satisfied all introductions had been made, Commander Tehera leaned forward in his chair once again. He regarded each member of the room and spoke quietly. "Phase Quattuor is here. It has been a long time in the making and has taken considerable effort to reach this highly anticipated juncture. We are more than ready for the next phase in the Ultimate Agenda, and are facing some exciting, but precarious challenges. The majority of Phase Quattuor will take place above ground." The Commander cast his gaze around the room once again. His eyes met everyone. "These missions will come in two categories: Engineering and Scouting. It's the forthcoming scouting mission we are here to discuss." He sat back in his chair. "So, let's set down the agenda for this mission," he turned to his right, "Minister?"

All eyes turned to Kiernan. Jensen watched the woman rise and pick up a small remote control. She walked towards the viewing screen, on the far wall, and then turned to face her audience. Jensen took a moment to further watch the woman. She was tall. As tall as herself. Her auburn hair hung just below her chin. Jensen noticed she kept tucking it behind her ear. A nervous habit, maybe?

"Over time," Kiernan began, "We have scouted above ground for much needed assets. Searching the Barren lands was never going to be an easy task. With so much destroyed in the devastations or infected in the post-desolation storms, even we were not prepared for what lay behind the safety of our haven. But with determination and dedication, our scouts have recovered many assets. During first scouting of the Barren lands, we realised there was much to be gained from the southerly areas. We extended our footing to the southeast and southwest of our position. As you are all more than aware, the north of our colony, although not massively destroyed by fires, was highly affected by ash, pollution, and radiation." Kiernan paused. She pointed the remote over her shoulder and activated the wall mounted screen behind her. "For obvious reasons it was prudent to keep clear of these areas." She took a breath. "However, with the arrival of Phase Quattuor we find ourselves in need of crucial resources." Minister Kiernan took several steps toward the screen and swiped her finger over its corner control panel. A large map of the land above appeared. Each scouted area was colour coded. "As you can see," she pointed a laser to specific areas on the map. "Our efforts have concentrated in these areas. They have proven to be most beneficial for what we have needed thus far. We retrieved vast amounts of metal ore, usable debris, and other items imperative to our continued growth and survival. What we need now, are specific artefacts. Among these items are specific components, which can only be obtained from one known location."

Minister Kiernan stepped away from the map and returned to her seat. She sat down and used the remote to manipulate the map in a northerly direction. Jensen felt a twinge of dread deep in her gut. Instinct, an instinct which had served he well over time, knew she would not like what she was about to hear.

"A dedicated effort has been made in researching records detailing experimental technology at the time of our planet's downfall. Our aim was to find the data and schematics for technology we need now. Technology invaluable for our Ultimate Agenda. After careful studies and a lustrum of searching we have narrowed our searches down to a specific clandestine location. A military Testing Station three hundred and fifty furlongs north of the colony."

Jensen had to ask. "Three hundred and fifty furlongs north?" Her eyes focused in on the Minister. "Our scouting has never ventured more than one hundred furlongs north if that. How do you know this facility remains? It's an exceedingly long distance to travel to receive bad news." Realising her negativity, Jensen was quick to add, "I mean no disrespect, Minister."

It was Vegas who answered her questions. "Scout, like most of our Testing Stations much of this compound was constructed underground. It will be there."

"Right, Sir. And am I to understand you are to send a Scout out to obtain these items?" Jensen felt following through with this mission was tantamount to agreeing to her own suicide.

"It's more complicated than that, Scout," the Commander replied. "We are hoping for materials as well as sensitive documents. We will be sending a ten-man team. Major Vegas will head the mission with yourself and the Minister Kiernan as sub-heads."

That cramping feeling of dread doubled in intensity. Jensen's scrutiny flicked from the Commander to Kiernan, just in time to see a sliver of fear shadow the woman's features before it was gone. Jensen noted this woman was very capable in her ability to shut down her emotions. The Minister's expression returned to a mask of cool indifference.

"Sir, can I please clarify? Minister Kiernan will be joining us on this mission?"

"Yes."

"And yet she has never been above ground before?"

"No."

"And Training?"

"Not yet, but –"

"- then excuse me for being out of line, Commander, but this a dangerous idea! If she has –"

"Do… You… MIND-" Kiernan said loudly, as she rose from her chair, "not speaking about me as though I'm not in the room?" The Minister leaned forward, bracing her weight on both hands as she focussed upon Jensen. Ire coloured her cheeks. "I am aware of the environment above ground. I assure you I am ready for this challenge."

Jensen stared back at Kiernan. She leaned forward in her seat. "A challenge? Minister, this is no challenge to be accepted lightly. Knowledge of the location and what lurks above ground will never prepare you for the actual experience. That," Jensen pointed to the scar on the Majors neck, "and this," she pulled the collar of her shirt to one side revealing a similar scar on her shoulder. "And here," Jensen then rose and twisted slightly to expose another scar on her lower back. "This is what lurks above ground. This was the surprise none of us were prepared for. This is the reason Scout Taura is not here with us. This isn't a challenge, Minister, this is terror. Terror for us all." Jensen took a deep breath and released it slowly. She ran a calming hand over the back of her neck to massage out the tension as she sat down. Again, she realised her outburst had been seen by high-ranking department heads and she lowered her head slightly. "Once again, I mean no disrespect, Minister. I apologise for my outburst. I lost a close ally due to this very reason."

The room fell into an icy silence. All other occupants appeared riveted to the scene before them. Even the Commander watched their interaction with interest.

Kiernan calmly sat back down. She placed her chin in her hand as she said, "Given the chance, Scout, this is not a decision I would freely accept without hefty consideration. My presence was requested by both the Commander and the Select Minister." She waved her free hand as she said, "There is too much at stake not to undertake this assignment."

At the mention of the two governing heads of their colony, Jensen knew her argument was lost.

"I will be sub-heading the mission with you, and you will not address me in such a manner again."

Leaning back in her chair, Jensen said, "Then forgive me, Minister, I will never again show concern for your safety."

Silence returned. The women stared at each other. Awkward shifting sounded around them.

"Now that we have cleared that up." Captain Lucia smiled sardonically. "Maybe we can resume our meeting? I'm sure we all have a lot to say before its conclusion."

"Agreed." Commander Tehera rose. "Shall I continue?" He didn't wait for a response. "We will be sending a ten-man team out to the Testing Station. As informed, Major Vegas will head the operation with two directives; to collaborate with Scout Jenson and obtain the electronic data we need, and work with Minister Kiernan on retrieving the scientific elements and experimental compounds needed for our own work." He elaborated no further on the nature of the items they were to look for, leaving Jensen to speculate.

"Scout Jensen, as one of our most seasoned scouts you will be lead advisor. Your field of experience outweighs any other assigned to this mission. As such your input is vital. You will have one rotation to conduct the mission."

Jensen's thoughts froze. "A rotation? Commander it's three hundred and fifty furlongs."

"Indeed, it is," Commander Tehera stood slowly and walked over to the display screen. He tapped the touch control buttons and activated a set of images. "But you won't be walking, Scout. Not this time." Tehera smiled with pride. "In storage we have two land vehicles. One multi person and one constructed for maximum storage." He enlarged the images upon the screen. Jensen looked on, impressed and admittedly a little in awe by what she saw. She was unaware the colony had any working motor vehicles. Jensen was excited by the prospect of getting to drive in the antiquated transportation.

"They need vast amounts of fuel, which is why we have saved them for emergency utilisation only. Three hundred and fifty furlongs is a great distance to travel on foot. Here we have your solution."

"It's the first time these vehicles have been brought out of storage," Whylen said.

Minister Fawkes added, "The Select Prime wishes for this mission to be conducted as expeditiously as possible. Timing is of the essence."

"It will be in two rotations," Lorenzo finished.

Commander Tehera folded his arms, still standing beside the display screen. He turned and looked again at the maps of their forthcoming mission. "This will be our greatest mission to date. Success is paramount." He looked back at the faces focussed upon him. "We must succeed at any cost."

***

Jensen strode numbly through the stone corridors. After being escorted from the meeting, along with Major Vegas, she declined his offer to discuss Scout Taura and instead made her leave. She needed solitude. She needed to think in her own space. Jensen avoided eye contact with every member of the colony that she passed, as she navigated her way towards the private chambers. It was the one place in her world she felt truly alone and at peace. Reaching the entrance to the colonist personal units, Jensen stopped at a T junction and looked left and then right. To her left were the single occupancy units. The passageway seemed to go on further than she could see in the limited illumination, which was activated only by movement. To her right were the double occupancy units. Taura had shared unit ten with Nicoletti. Jensen's memories drifted to the man she had spoken to, not so long ago. She wondered if he was in their unit. The temptation to see Nicoletti was strong, but the need for solitude was stronger. Turning left, Jensen headed for her unit. Each colourless door was marked only by a number and the occupants' name. Jensen stopped halfway down the passageway, in front of her room. She sighed and closed her eyes, leaning forward and resting her head upon the barrier between her and her place of solitude. The privacy of her own space called out to her; with a mountain of emotions, Jensen unlocked the door and entered.

Not wanting to activate the light, Jensen fell back against the solid barrier and slid down its smooth surface. As she hit the ground, she could no longer hold back the tears that she had fought so hard to keep at bay.

They came fast. Jensen pulled her legs into her body. Her head upon her knees, as sobs shook her slender frame. She was shocked by the intensity of her own emotions but was unable to stop them. Jensen allowed herself to weep. She wept for Nicoletti's loss, for her loss. She thought of Taura and their relationship. Then Jensen thought of her mother and father. All lost. All by the same fate. She focussed her thoughts on her parents, but found she was no longer able to see their faces in her minds' eye and she cursed the passage of time for eradicating them from her memory.

Long moments passed before Jensen felt herself relax. She wiped salty tears on her the sleeve and took a calming breath. Jensen whipped her head backwards, feeling it slam against the door with a painful thud. She heard the resulting echo travel down the corridors outside. Jensen held her breath as though scared she may have unveiled her presence to the outside world. A moment passed before she sighed again, satisfied she was safe. Feeling a little more relaxed, she allowed her feet to slide across the floor until her legs were flat upon the stone ground. She gazed up at the ceiling and her eyes follow the natural patterns in the rock to the wall opposite her. She moved her eyes down the wall and into her room. Her unit was small and held little in the way of furniture. A single bed stood to the right and dominated almost half of the room. At the bottom of the bed, and beside where Jensen sat was a small storage unit. To her left there was a rail of clothing and at the far left was another wider unit for storing clothing and other such apparel. Those three items of furniture held all her meagre possessions. It wasn't much, but what else did one need or could even fit into the allotted spaces they were assigned? The only other notable point of interest in her room were two shelves attached to the wall opposite the door. They held her collection of tomes, with several of her parent's personal effects serving as tome-ends. On the top shelf were her father's old boots and a fossilised child's toy that he'd found upon the Barren lands. She wasn't sure what it was, the colourful polyvinyl was melted into an abstract shape that had always fascinated her father, Jaxon. On the lower shelf, her tomes were held in place by her mother's boots and a carved timber box. It was nothing special or ornate in design. Her father had carved it for her mother, Tomei, as a gift. Inside the box, in a hidden compartment, was a key. Jensen never discovered what the key was for, only finding it upon her parents' death. Still, she continued their tradition and kept the key hidden in its own compartment within the box.

Unexpected voices pulled Jensen from her thoughts. She bit her lip and closed her eyes, turning her head to listen as the voices drew closer and then passed her by. Jensen sighed and rubbed her tear-stained face roughly, before rising to her feet. It only took four steps for her to reach the bed. She sat down and leaned forwards, pulling the laces of her boots from their tight knot, and then kicking them off. She twisted her body around and lay down. The rough sheets were an instant comfort to her. Their smell familiar, with a floral hint designed to enhance sleep. Jensen closed her eyes. It was only then she realised she hadn't reported her mission findings. However, since Captain Lucia was also in the meeting, she was sure the older woman wouldn't mind waiting until the following morn. It was a report worth waiting for.

Jensen rolled onto her side; aware she hadn't removed her clothing. Not to worry. There was nobody she had to impress. She reached around and pulled her flaxen locks from their binding and closed her eyes once again. Her mind drifted to the woman she had met in the meeting. Minister Kiernan. A mild hint of irritation returned, as she recalled the way she had spoken to her. Jensen was adamant she was correct in her beliefs. They were after all ingrained from cycles of training and experience. The older woman had no training, and they were sending her onto the Barrens? Either they were incredibly foolish or... Jensen opened her eyes and frowned. She rolled onto her opposite side... or whatever she was being sent out to find and retrieve was too sensitive, even for her and the Major's eyes. Jensen sighed and rolled onto her back. She stared up at the rock ceiling. The ranting in her mind continued. The woman had spoken to her with such superiority that she had taken an instant disliking. Level nine or not, there was a measure of respect by which all colonists regarded each other.

Jensen rolled onto her side again. She curled one arm under her head and stared down at her free arm, seeing the device strapped around her wrist. Upon conclusion of the meeting, they had each been handed a unique piece of communication equipment. It was like that of a timekeeping device, but instead of the sweeping hands known with such time pieces of antiquity, there was abbreviated digital information. This was to be their means of communication during the mission. She stared at the instrument in disgust; certain it held a location transmitter. A way to keep track of her whereabouts. Another new piece of technology they had, yet never used until this mission. She felt a tiny sliver of growing resentment and resisted the urge to remove it in anger. Apart from the fact it was a futile, and possibly childish, act, it had been calibrated to her body signature. To remove it would cause an alert. Not good when you wished not to be disturbed.

Jensen closed her eyes. She needed to sleep. Her shift had stretched to be much longer than expected and slumber beckoned. Bunching the pillow around her arm, Jensen tried to relax her body. She ignored a growl from her stomach, reminding her she hadn't eaten in a significant amount of time. She was too tired now. Too tired to remove her clothes; and as sleep slowly claimed her, Jensen's last thoughts were of the upcoming mission. Of the woman who sat opposite her and the haunted expression of fear that clouded her eyes. Knowing what lay in waiting upon the Barren lands, that fear was well justified. Jensen's features relaxed, and her lips parted slightly as sleep finally claimed her.

CHAPTER 5

The science laboratory was vast. A room that anybody who was fortunate enough to see the facility found highly impressive for its technological ability and capability. Right now, it was early and as such held the presence of only one individual for the untimely phase of the morn. Most science officers hadn't yet risen, but Minister Kiernan hadn't yet gone to bed. On many such occasions, the woman had been known to fall sleep in her laboratory, slumped over her desk. A position in which she would be found the following morn by the early shift rotation.

Seated at a wide desk, Kiernan was positioned before a computer terminal. Her slim fingers flew rapidly over the metallic keyboard, the insistent tapping echoed through the vast room. Situated at different points around the laboratory were secondary computing terminals, racks holding vials of bio-hazardous test specimens, a range of equipment, and electrical components. Complicated circuit boards lay on temperature-controlled pads, while tools designed for the construction of minute componentry sat in specially designed toolboxes. Each space was individually designed by Kiernan, the scientist in her as fastidious as the minister was thorough. Within the centre of the room stood a tube-like mechanical structure, slightly taller than Kiernan herself, which at that moment sat in idle suspension, a hazy fluorescent light emanating from its centre.

Minister Kiernan paused from her incessant tapping and reached to her right. She lifted a narrow container of rapidly cooling liquid to her lips and took a reluctant swallow. Her lips grimaced, bored of the same manufactured libation, which she had always believed was nothing like the original steeped-leaf beverage of times past. Placing the container back on her desk, Kiernan stifled a yawn. She looked back at the data screen and frowned. She was tired. So much so that the algebraic equations upon the screen appeared to meld together to form abstract animated shapes. She needed sleep. Unfortunately, her mind had been on overdrive since the meeting earlier. She couldn't pull her thoughts away from the impending mission. She could admit, if only to herself, her thoughts hadn't strayed far from the mission since she had discovered their plans and her part in them fourteen rotations ago. Since then, she had dedicated her free time to reading mission statements. She had read over two hundred reports, and with each narrative she read, she was chilled a little more.

It was during her analysis of those reports that she had first discovered those by Scout Jensen. Instantly, the colourful pictures Jensen had pained captured her attention. Not only were they professionally detailed mission accounts, but the scout also tended to deviate from her logs to include up-to-date descriptions of the landscape, environment, and its adversities. The Minister found Jensen's reports both compelling and frightening in equal measure. Kiernan realised she was at times unable to pull herself away from these mission statements, despite the content, impressed by how they could move her with descriptive beauty and yet fill her with unrivalled horror. Scout Jensen intrigued her, like an avid reader might become enamoured with a preferred writer. As a personal rule, Kiernan had little to do with anybody but her direct co-workers and ranking ministers. Like her good ally Major Vegas, she was ascetic and dedicated to their cause. However, for the first time in her forty-two cycles, Kiernan found herself wondering if her life was lacking. It was an unfamiliar notion to the austere scientist who spent every rotation working upon one project or another. Success in her broad field of ability left little room for more recreational pursuits.

Bringing her thoughts back to the present, Kiernan raked her fingers through her unruly hair. She yawned again and blinked tiredly, as she rested her chin upon the palm of her hand. She needed sleep. It had been too long since she had last experienced the relative comfort of her bed. She missed the floral scented sheets and their reassuring embrace.

"No more of this," Kiernan muttered.

Another yawn confirmed her decision, and so Kiernan powered down her computer and rose from her desk. She switched off the data screen and then pulled off her lab coat, draping it over the back of her chair. She headed for the exit; her features momentarily lit by the fluorescent nucleus of the device standing in the centre of the room. Even from where she was standing, she could feel its vibrating hum rattle through her chest.

As Kiernan passed through the door and into the outer mechanics area, she was greeted by Lieutenant Whylen, who was at that moment bent over a desk staring at a circuit board.

"Good morn, Minister," Whylen greeted without looking up. "Finally, off to bed?"

"I most certainly am," Kiernan said with a smile. She walked around Whylen's workstation until she faced him. Whylen was a traditionally handsome man with dark hair and sharp features. The Lieutenant didn't look up as he said, "Interesting briefing."

"Yes."

"Unexpected," he continued. A tiny smile outlined the corners of his lips. It wasn't visible to Kiernan, but she heard it in his voice.

"Indeed," she replied.

Whylen, realising he wasn't gaining the reaction he hoped from Kiernan, placed down his tool, and looked up at his superior. "So, what do you think of Scout Jensen. Quite the fireball, isn't she? I've come to blows with her more than once myself."

"She's quite infuriating," Kiernan agreed.

Lieutenant Whylen chuckled. "To say the least. I must say it's been a long time since I have heard you raise your voice like that. Scout Jensen is headstrong, persistent, and quite able to back her bark with a ferocious bite!"

Kiernan folded her arms. "Then we are very lucky to have her on this mission with us, Lieutenant."

Whylen smiled widely. His eyes twinkled, as he looked back down at his work. "Indeed."

Too tired to interact further, Kiernan turned towards the exit. She needed sleep.

"Sweet dreams, Minister."

"Thank you, Why-" her words halted as the doors burst open and Scout Ryan burst into the room.

"Minister, we need you urgently."

"What is it?"

Scout Ryan held the door open for Kiernan to follow him. "Another body was found close to where Scout Taura was discovered."

"Who is it?" Whylen asked as he followed Kiernan and the younger Scout into the passageway. They exited the room, just in time to see a second Scout pushing a gurney toward them, upon which lay a zipped-up body bag.

"Who is it?" Whylen asked again. "And please tell me you have undergone de-con!"

Ryan joined the scout pushing the gurney and helped in directing it to towards the medical suite. Kiernan followed. "Of course, we have, Sir, but only the outer bag has been processed. The body inside has not."

Kiernan, still silent, unlocked the medical suite door and stood back to allow the Scouts access to wheel the body inside. Her eyes remained focussed on the dark bag atop the metallic trolley before she looked up into Whylen's concerned expression. The gurney was pushed to the centre of the medical suite before they stopped.

Scout Ryan turned to address his superiors, confident now that they were out of hearing distance of any passers-by. The anxious expression in his eyes wasn't lost on either Kiernan or Whylen. "It's not a 'who'. It's a what."

Kiernan frowned. "Explain."

Ryan elaborated. "It was I who discovered the body. It's… it's not a colonist."

Lips slightly parting, eyebrows drawn together in confusion, Kiernan stared intently at Ryan. "Are you saying-?"

"Yes, Ma'am"

"Are sure-"

"I am, Ma'am."

Kiernan's expression hardened. "Are you sure it's dead?" Concern was clear in her features now. She took a step towards the corpse filled bag and paused. "We've never-"

"It's dead," Ryan assured Kiernan, and a stunned into silence Whylen. "A shard of metallic ore is still buried deep in the kill wound."

Kiernan opened her mouth to speak again but closed it rapidly. She looked around the room in paranoia. She had to be sure nobody else was in the medical suite. The room was empty apart from four examination beds, trays of apparatus, supplies and various pieces of examination equipment. She wasn't a medical physician herself, but she had used most of the room's offerings at one time or another. Being a scientist in Kiernan's field gave her access to much of the scientific and medical instruments available.

The four occupants of the room were silent as the gravity of the situation settled upon them. Slowly, a putrid aroma began to invade their senses. It quickly permeated the air around them, eradicating the sterile scent of the medical suite. Each person took two steps backwards in revulsion. The aroma was foul. Kiernan placed the forefinger of her fist upon her top lip to block out the stench.

"So that's…"

"It is," Rylan responded.

"I had no idea it would smell so- "

"Gut disturbingly rotten," Ryan finished. "The first time I smelled this I threw up my breakfast, lunch *and* dinner!"

Kiernan smiled at his comment. She thought quickly, and then shook her head.

"I can't do this now. My mind needs to be clear. I haven't slept in over a rotation. I need rest before I study the body."

Whylen's expression hardened. "Minister, we can't sit on this discovery. If the Commander knows what we have here, he will demand immediate action." He took a step towards her. "You know what this means."

"I'm well aware, Lieutenant," Kiernan said, using her rank to place the man back in line. She took a shallow breath, disgusted by the stench surrounding them, certain it wouldn't wash out of their clothing! "But not now. A few marks rest will do wonders for concentration." Fear ran its sharp fingers down her spine as she looked at the body bag and imagined the possibilities of what lay within. After the reports she had read, Kiernan needed time to prepare. "Who else knows about this," she asked the scouts.

"Just the four of us now, Minister," Ryan replied. She could see the fear plainly in both his and his fellow scout's features. Never had such a thing been brought down from the Barren lands. And dead? It was unheard of.

"Tell nobody of this." Kiernan looked each person in the eye. She ended with Whylen, saying, "That is an order."

"Of course," Whylen conceded.

"I need time to prepare for the examination. If word gets out about what we have, it could ignite mass hysteria. I don't want that and I'm positive neither does Select Prime Abrahams or Enforcement Commander Tehera." Kiernan looked again at the scouts. "Agreed?"

"Yes, Minister," they both replied.

Kiernan covered her face with both hands and took a deep breath. The prospect of what lay before them, putrefying the room with its unimaginable stench, overwhelmed and frightened her. This must have been what killed Scout Taura. Luckily and in an absolute first, it appeared Taura had managed to return the favour.

"Double bag this body. No, triple bag it if it helps eradicate this smell. She looked around. "Put it in cold storage and re-calibrate the lock to accept my signature only. Later, I shall inform the Select Prime and Commander of your discovery and request a dissection of the remains." Kiernan waved her hand in a dismissive manner. "A formality only. It shall be agreed." She watched Whylen step towards the gurney and place both hands upon its sides, as he looked at the dark bag and imagined what lay within. "I must stress again the need for secrecy now. "What we have here is of monumental potential to our survival. Do you understand?"

"Yes, Minister," both scouts replied again.

Looking back at the body bag, Kiernan realised her hopes for a restful sleep had significantly reduced.

CHAPTER 6

What was that noise? A series of three short, sharp beeps sounded in quick succession repeatedly. It was then accompanied by an annoying vibration that irritated the base of her wrist. The incessant shrill intensified.

Still within the clutches of sleep, Jensen batted at the annoyance around her wrist. It persisted, causing her to flip over in her bed. Soft sheets around her lower body further tangled themselves around sprawled legs and restricted her movements. Jensen, with eyes closed tight, tried to find a comfortable position, but the annoyance continued. Tired eyes opened reluctantly. Jensen's blurry vision focussed upon the communicator strapped to her wrist and she hit it hard. It was a lucky strike. The pads of her fingers connected with the correct deactivation button and silence resumed. Dark eyes slipped slowly back behind fragile lids and sleep reclaimed her. Brief moments past before another, not so loud, but just as irritating sound resumed. Jensen released a deep moan that quickly turned into a growl of disapproval as she stumbled out of her bed. She was still fully clothed.

Standing in the centre of the room, Jensen yelled at the device around her wrist, "What do you want?" She threw her arms in the air, "I'm up; I'm up!"

Blinking unfocussed eyes, Jensen allowed her vision to clear and then looked again at the device, remembering Vegas' instruction on how to use its communication feature. With a frown she hit a side button and said, "This is Jenson. Very tired and still asleep, Jensen. What?"

There was a brief pause before she received a reply. Unsurprisingly, it was Vegas, "Meet me in the medical suite in half a mark."

"Major, I-"

"Problem, Scout?"

"No, Sir." Jensen rubbed her tired eyes, as her arm fell to her side. Not bothering to speak again, she began collecting the necessities needed for a quick shower.

In no time, and with clean clothing and a towel under her arm, Jensen opened her door, only to be confronted by Officer Nicoletti, hand poised, ready to knock. Jensen froze as she stared into swollen, desolate eyes.

"Hey, Jen" he said.

With that, Jensen dropped her clothing to the floor and pulled Nicoletti into a hug. "I'm so sorry I didn't come to see you," she whispered.

Nicoletti held Jensen, as his tears threatened to return. "I didn't want to see anybody."

"Me neither," she said, feeling the sting of tears return to her eyes. There was no way she could hold back, and her body shook with silent sobs. "I'm sorry", she whispered again.

Nicoletti didn't respond for several moments, as he fought his own devastation. Eventually he said, "What am I going to do?"

Jensen pulled away enough to look deep into Nicoletti's eyes. They were awash with tears, causing her own to increase in intensity. She sniffed and wiped them away. What was he to do? There was nothing. There was no revenge to be had. No comfort in the knowledge of the easy passing of his spouse. Her death was unimaginable in its terror and to know Taura had died alone? Jensen could form no words of comfort for him. Then one thought did come to mind.

"At least they brought her back to you."

That was a crucial factor. No scout who had presumably lost their lives upon the Barrens had ever been returned.

"I haven't seen her," Nicoletti said. "It's not advised."

Jensen nodded in understanding. She could only imagine.

"I just want to hold her again. To say goodbye." His eyes filled again with tears.

"And you will," Jensen assured him. "I shall make certain of this. I shall speak to Physician Angeles myself."

Nicoletti nodded. "Thank you." He took a step backwards. "You need to go?"

Jensen bent down and retrieved her clothing from the floor. She shook off imaginary specs of dirt. "Major Vegas has summoned me." Jensen pushed her door open further and stepped back. She motioned for Nicoletti to follow. "However, Vegas can wait."

"Jensen-" Nicolette warned, but still stepped into her unit.

Jensen shook her head. "Right now, Nic, this is more important."

With a forced smile, Nicolette strode into the centre of Jensen's unit, and she pushed him backwards until he sat down upon her bed. She then took a step backward and perched herself on the opposite unit. “Can you tell me what you know? What were you told?”

Taking a breath, Nicoletti began.

CHAPTER 7

It was over a mark later that Jensen made her way into Medical Suite three. This was a sub-treatment room situated off the main surgery and used for the purpose of above ground physical preparation. It wasn't a large room, and as such was filled to maximum occupancy. She looked around, seeing who she accurately presumed to be the mission team. Jensen was impressed. They had picked an impressive group for the most part. Jensen's eyes landed upon Kiernan and two enforcement officers from the Labour and Domestic Colonies, easily recognisable by their uniforms. She knew these individuals had no above ground experience. How could they? Their job was to patrol the colonies, aiding the enforcement of law-abiding peace. However, this made for three of the ten-man team who lacked the experience of the environment they were about to enter. Jensen added an extra couple of notches to her internal danger monitor. Quietly she stepped further into the room, making her presence known. A row of faces looked in her direction. Jensen couldn't hide her smirk. It was inoculation time. A pre-requisite for each mission. This was to be a great undertaking and so Jensen knew the injection was going to be a hefty dose. Still, it was needed to aid the body's lack of ability to combat infections and possible radiation poisoning. An injection lasted for up to four rotations, beginning to degrade after three, so it was a high priority for all scouts to keep up to date with their inoculations.

Standing before the row of occupied chairs, Jensen noted Vegas and Kiernan seated at the end of the row. Kiernan looked tired, very tired, and Jensen wondered if the woman had slept at all. The Major on the other hand looked annoyed, and Jensen wasn't surprised.

"Scout, good of you to join us. I see you discovered how to mute the volume on your inter-communicator."

She had muted the communication device, but it wasn't an easy feat. After the third time it had shrilled at her, Nicoletti had discovered how to silence it before Jensen had launched it at the wall.

Jensen smiled unapologetically. "I was with Nicoletti," she said simply. She noted the Major's face tense, as he quietly ground his teeth in annoyance. Jensen knew he would still reprimand her, but at least he would accept her reasoning.

Vegas rose from his seat. “Scout, if I order you to be at a certain place by a certain time, I expect that order to be executed without question.” He held up one finger as Jensen tried to speak. “If there are issues, contact and updates are mandatory.” Vegas’ eyebrows rose as Jensen tried to speak again. “You do not silence a communique from a superior officer.”

“Apologies, Sir.”

Vegas rubbed his dark bearded chin and then checked the chronometer. “Kiernan was behind schedule and Physician Angelus is also running late,” he shook his head. “Great start to the mission.” His eyes were hard, with an unidentifiable shadow of tension that Jensen could only detect because she knew Vegas so well.

It was at that moment that Physician Angelus entered medical suite three.

“Try to contain your excitement,” he said upon instantly seeing the team’s mix of expressions. Some were familiar with the pre-mission medical procedures, several of them were not. His sarcasm was lost on several members of the team, not used to Angelus’ bedside manner.

Jensen peered surreptitiously at Kiernan, seeing her shift uncomfortably. It was then Jensen noticed her state of dress. Kiernan was clothed in standard issue mission fatigues, far removed from the elegant attire she’d seen Kiernan in on the rotation before. The Minister had yet to make eye contact with anybody. In fact, Jensen noted she seemed distracted. Considering their soon to be mission she could understand.

“Scout Jensen,” Angelus called, drawing her attention from the silent woman. “One of my most frequent visitors. You will, of course, still be covered from your last trip.”

Jensen took her seat between Scout Ruben and Major Vegas. “Just following orders, Angie.”

The physician, who at that moment was pulling on a tight pair of latex gloves, stopped and narrowed his eyes at Jensen. He released the skin-tight material with a snap and arched a single brow. “A booster shot for you, Scout.”

Jensen winced. Booster shots were delivered in a different part of the body and as such were more painful. She shook her head. She should have known better than to tease Angelus.

“Ready to drop those pants,” Vegas muttered, just loud enough for Jensen to hear.

“Bite me,” Jensen responded a little louder.

Kiernan turned and peered at them curiously. “You do know that although the rump is the ideal location for a booster shot, the opposite arm to the one originally injected is an acceptable location.”

“WHAT?” both Jensen and Vegas said together. They looked swiftly at Angelus, who was preparing a tray of hypodermic needles. Angelus cast a passing glance at the two before he shrugged his shoulders. “I’m all for ideal locations,” he said as he lifted a needle and inspected it with deep interest.

The pair simultaneously folded their arms and peered down at the floor in discomfort. Kiernan found herself smile for the first time in several rotations.

“Right.” Angelus carried a metallic tray over to the seated team and placed it down upon a narrow trolley. “Nine inoculations and a booster.” He wheeled the trolley to the start of the line. “Scout Raziko, let us start with you, shall we? However, before I do let me add an explanation.” His eyes connected with Officers Jorca and Jax. “The injections, for those not aware, aid your body in adjusting to the environment above ground. Not only is the radiation still present, which, of course, your clothing helps to protect against, but it’s the toxins, air-born and otherwise, that your body needs the most protection from.” He lifted a syringe and peered at the amber liquid within. “Bites and other such hazards must be considered and adequately safeguarded against.” Angelus readied his first syringe. “Scout Raziko, shall we begin?”

Kiernan, who had listened quietly, whispered to Vegas, “I’m not a fan of injections.”

The dark man smiled. “It’s just a little prick, Kir.”

“That’s not comforting.” Kiernan jabbed him in the ribs, unaware Jensen was listening.

Vegas chuckled again. “Kiernan, we’ve known each other for over ten cycles. Have you ever known me to be anything other than sensitive to your needs?”

“How long do I have to consider that question?”

The Major chuckled again. “Look it’s not that bad. Although I’m very much aware how adverse you are to little pricks.”

Jensen pursed her lips, holding a snort that was determined to force its way past them. She was sure Minister Kiernan noticed her reaction, as she uncomfortably cleared her throat. Their conversation was interrupted by Physician Angelus.

"Raziko, Jorca, Ziran and Jilya accepted their injections with little commotion, officer Jax. I assure you it's perfectly safe. If you will just lift your sleeve, we can get this over with."

"Leave me until last," Jensen heard Jax say.

Jensen leaned forward and peered down the line. "Come on, Jax. It's one insignificant little prick," she said with a smile, her words not lost on Kiernan. "Be thankful you don't have twenty of them in a tight circumference pounded into your butt cheek."

"Yes," Angelus took Jax's arm and pushed up his sleeve. "As Scout Jensen so eloquently expresses, be thankful for little pricks!" He administered the injection to Jax's arm as the blonde enforcement officer looked away. "There you go, no trouble whatsoever." Angelus continued down the line. Xoren and Scout Ruben accepting their inoculations with no comment. Next came Jensen and she watched him wheel the trolley to her with a keen expression.

"So ideal location is it, Angie?"

The physician glared at her. He lifted what Jensen believed to be a monstrosity of a needle into the air and inspected it with obvious delight. "If you will, Scout. Usual procedure."

Jensen stood and released the belt to her clothing, allowing her trousers to fall to one side. It was just enough to expose her upper left cheek. She braced one foot upon her chair and leaned forward just a fraction, bracing her arm upon her knee. Jensen then turned to watch Vegas and Kiernan who were both looking politely ahead. Unexpectedly, Kiernan then turned and then made eye contact for the first time since Jensen had entered the room. Feeling mischievous, Jensen winked and smiled, forcing Kiernan to look away with a blush. She felt the sting of the needle enter her flesh.

"So, Angie, why such an obnoxious needle for a booster shot?"

"What this?" Angelus held the monstrosity up with delight and studied his instrument fondly. "This is for making fun of my height, my name and generally being the most uncongenial patient, I have to work with."

"You mean it's not part of the standard booster procedure?" she asked as she readjusted her trousers and sat down between Vegas and Ruben.

Angelus shook his head innocently. "No. Not really."

Holding back a smile, Jensen nodded her head. "Well played!"

"Indeed." Angelus pushed the trolley towards Major Vegas. "Never mess with a man who works with needles."

"Indeed," Jensen echoed. Leaning forward, Jensen looked down the line of team members. Commander Tehera had chosen well. The best of the best. Scouts Jilya, Zira, Ruben and Raziko were skilled scouts with many cycles of experience between them on the Barren lands. Officers Jorca and Jax were a surprise. She had heard of them, and their commendable work as enforcement officers within the colonies, but never expected to see them on the team. She was sure neither had above ground experience. However, they too were highly regarded with stellar reputations in their field.

Then there was Xoren. Xoren had started as an Enforcement Officer, then a Scout, but had worked his way up the internal ladder, taking his place as right hand to Enforcement Commander Tehera as his trusted advisor. A highly irregular jump in promotions. From what Jensen did know of Xoren, he hadn't walked the Barren lands for many cycles. His presence on the team perplexed her. Was he there to document the mission, or ensure the Commander's orders were executed, but wasn't that what Vegas was there for? Jensen pondered deeply as she leaned back in her chair.

"Can we do this in another room?"

The Physician forced out an exaggerated sigh. "Please, Minister, an educated scientist such as yourself should not be afraid of a little injection." Angelus seemed almost bored now.

Kiernan looked down the row of team members, noting not one of them seemed particularly interested in what was going on. Most were conversing between one another, all in fact apart from Vegas and Jensen, the only two who seemed concerned by her current predicament. Kiernan realised now was not the time for modesty or discomfort. She held her breath as she began sliding the sleeve of her right arm up past her elbow. It was Jensen who was shocked by what she saw, as extensive scarring was revealed upon Kiernan's upper arm. She said nothing but turned away respectfully.

"All done," she heard Angelus say. Surprised by the swiftness of the physician's work, Jensen turned back to see tears in Kiernan's eyes. Now she understood why she was so resistant to the injection. Having scar tissue herself, Jensen knew how painful it could be, especially to needle penetration. She'd received many herself during the healing period of her own wounds. It did pose the question; how did Kiernan receive such an unpleasant looking injury? Would this be another mystery to the austere woman?

Jensen looked up at the ceiling, as she pondered the rest of their schedule. It was to be a lengthy process of intensive briefings and mission outlines, but they still had to gain enough rest before departure early morn. Jensen wondered who would be able to sleep. Even she had trouble sleeping before a trip above ground. She wondered how the less experienced team members had been prepared for the mission, especially a certain Minister without combat or environmental experience. Who would be looking after her? She was a sub-mission head. She certainly had no plans to be protecting a tagalong on a dangerous mission. Jensen pushed herself further into her seat, annoyed at her situation and herself for her thoughts. There was so much more to the mission. Nobody had ventured as far north as they intended. There was no telling what they would find. The horrors of the planet's downfall and eventual destruction was something only the Scouts had seen. Visions nobody should see. Ever. Fear of the unknown always held the strongest grip.

The rattle of metal drew Jensen from her musings. She was surprised to see half the team had left, and Angelus was finishing putting away his equipment.

"That's my work done here," he said. "If you will excuse me, I have other matters to attend." Angelus made eye contact with the Major and silent communication passed between them. Jensen watched their interaction with curiosity, and it suddenly dawned upon her what the non-verbal conversation was about. She stood quickly, her gaze darting back and forth between Angelus and Vegas.

"Scout," Vegas warned. "Now isn't the time."

Xoren and Kiernan, the only other occupants of the room, apart from Ziran who was watching the scene closely, stopped their quiet conversation. They too watched closely.

"Major, I-"

"No, Scout-"

"Sir-"

"We don't have time for this."

Jensen took a persistent step forward. "I wish to pay my respects." Emotion clouded her voice, as she gazed imploringly at Major Vegas.

Realisation dawned upon Kiernan. "Vegas-"

"Kiernan," the Major turned to her. "The body is to be incinerated."

Reaching out to take the Major's arm, Kiernan said, "Then allow her this one last time to say goodbye to her ally. If it were you, wouldn't you want the same consideration?" Kiernan gently squeezed his arm. She'd had little dealings with death up until recently. Working in the field of science, Kiernan had been surrounded by the same individuals for most of her adult life. She never had to deal with the loss of her parents. She never knew them. Compassion for the younger woman flowed through her, as she realised just how much death Jensen must have been exposed to. In comparison, Kiernan felt she'd lived quite a sheltered life. "Don't make me out rank you, Major." Kiernan smiled endearingly.

Vegas narrowed his eyes, "I out rank you."

Kiernan continued to smile. She knew him well. "Then I out age you, by almost a full cycle."

Turning away, the Major shook his head. "Fine but make it quick and go with her." He'd never been able to refuse Kiernan.

The Minister continued to smile. She turned her head to see Jenson look upon her with surprise and her smile faltered slightly.

"Thank you," Jensen said earnestly.

Kiernan nodded. "We must be quick."

Jensen then looked towards Angelus. The physician simply nodded his head and then motioned towards a door which led to a back entrance of the surgical bays. "It's the first door on your right." Before Jenson could move, Angelus added. "Scout, don't move the sheet any lower than her chin." His warning followed a serious look that gave little room for doubt as to the severity of his words. Suddenly, the prospect of being alone in the room with Taura's body filled her with unease.

Jensen stepped forward but stopped as Ziran pulled her to one side. He took her hand, while placing the other on the side of her opposite upper arm. A show of support. Silent acknowledgement passed between them, before Jensen followed Kiernan out of the room and towards Surgical Bay Two.

Kiernan took a calming breath, wondering what she had gotten herself into. She had never seen a dead body before. It was one of the reasons she had put off the immediate examination of the body discovered on the Barrens. She needed time to mentally prepare. Kiernan thought she might want to remain outside the surgical bay, but she pushed that feeling aside. She needed to show support to the younger woman. Her sense of grief, although foreign to Kiernan, was nevertheless real to Jensen. If only to herself, Kiernan could admit to feeling a little ashamed by her lack of experience in such areas. One may have considered that a positive, but not now. Not in their reality.

Jensen stepped into the side room through a back doorway, set away from the main entrance. She noticed the silence of the room. It seemed to stretch beyond the doorway and draw them in. If Jensen wasn't mistaken, she would be sure it added a weighty presence. She then noted the single gurney situated in the centre of the small space. Taura's body lay upon its surface. A thick poly-cotton sheet covered her corpse. The sheet was designed in such a way that no matter could soak into its fibres. Jensen looked around the sparse room, seeing the familiar apparatus of a medical suite. Above Taura's body hung a single soft emitting light. It was only then that Jensen noticed a quiet, high-pitched hum coming from that light.

Jensen stopped halfway in her approach towards the trolley, as she heard Kiernan enter behind her. The older woman stopped beside the door. She was silent. Respectful. Biting her lip, Jensen approached Taura's body. With profound sorrow, she reached out to pull the covering from Taura's face, but just before her fingertips touched the sheet's dense fibres, she froze. Her hand hovered over the material. Her mind in turmoil.

"Scout?" Kiernan enquired softly.

Ignoring the Minister, Jensen took the edge of the cover and pulled it off Taura's face. She was careful to keep it laying beneath her chin. The thoughts alone of what may lay beneath were a strong deterrent. A choked sob hit the back of Jensen's throat and she covered her lips with the back of her hand. Tears filled her eyes as she gazed down upon Taura's face; or what was left of it. Ragged breaths assaulted her chest and she struggled to breathe, yet Jensen refused to allow grief to overcome her completely. She closed her eyes, allowing a single tear to roll down her cheek.

"Taura," she whispered, and pushed strands of dark hair away from her battered and swollen face. "What happened out there?"

From her vigil by the door, Kiernan watched with growing sympathy. She tried to grasp onto the sense of horror one should feel, looking at the bruised body of Scout Taura, but all she could recognise was the deep pain Jensen revealed as she stood by her body. Kiernan's eyes travelled over the blanketed form, thankful indeed that it was covered. She had read the reports. She knew what lay beneath. It was horrifying.

Jensen brushed her thumb over Taura's cheek. She leaned forward and whispered. "I promise you. You won't have suffered for nothing," and kissed the only area of unmarred flesh upon the side of her forehead.

So many lives had been lost. With each spark extinguished, so the loss lay heavy in her heart and mind. Jensen wondered how much more she could take. How many more lives would be lost so horrendously to their cause. Taura was the first to ever make it back to the colony. If her death was anything close to the Scouts they'd lost before on the Barren lands, her parents, how much more could anybody take? How much longer until their Ultimate Agenda reached fruition and they could leave this planet?

Knowing they were running out of time, Kiernan spoke softly. "Scout Jensen?"

Jensen turned, but instead of seeing the grief that leaked so overwhelming from her eyes moments before, Kiernan saw emotionless chips of ice.

"Take a good look, Minister," Jensen said. She pulled the gurney around until Taura's battered face was in full view to Kiernan. "Tell me again how you are so prepared for this challenge." Anger clouded her mind.

Shock propelled Kiernan backwards, and she took several steps away from Jensen to regain her equilibrium. Her hand covered her fallen jaw in horror at the sight before her. She wanted to look away, but she couldn't. If Jensen was pushing her, testing her, she would not back down. However, not even reading the report of Taura's death could prepare her for the reality. The young woman's face, swollen, bruised and split open. Teeth missing and fragments of bone exposed. Terror clawed at her spine.

Jensen wanted to shock Kiernan, to launch her mind into panic about their upcoming mission, but seeing her reaction caused remorse to fill Jensen's conscience. She quickly pulled the cover up over Taura's face and lowered her eyes. Her body sagged with dejection as she turned away from Kiernan.

"I'm sorry," she whispered. It was soft, but loud enough for Kiernan still to hear.

Any other words died upon her lips, as a gentle tapping at the rooms main entrance broke the tension. Jensen looked up at Kiernan, an unreadable expression in her eyes. The look caused a nervous tremor in the pit of Kiernan's stomach.

"It will be just a fraction of a mark," Jensen said, causing Kiernan's nervousness to increase. Her frown deepened as Jensen walked towards the main door and opened it. She saw Ziran standing on the other side of the barrier. What did he want? Kiernan continued to watch, as Jensen peered out of the door and look to the right. Then Jensen stepped backwards and opened the door a fraction wider. Officer Nicolette stepped into the room.

"No!" Kiernan rushed forward. "No, you can't. Scout Jensen, what are you thinking? The radiation. The infection!" She looked between the body and Nicolette. "Jenson… her injuries," she said in a lower voice.

Jensen said nothing. Instead, she pulled a pre-loaded syringe from her pocket. A syringe Ziran had covertly handed to her just before she left the medical bay. She looked swiftly at Kiernan as she said, "This is the only way he will be able to see his spouse, Minister. Would you deny him that? Or do you not recall your speech just moments ago in the medical suite?" Studying the syringe, Jensen said, "Leave now if you wish."

Kiernan was silenced. They would be in so much trouble. Their actions broke so many well-placed protocols in the control and containment of radiation and infection. Even with a stolen syringe of the serum, they were still acting without authorisation.

"Please," Nicoletti whispered. "Allow me to see her one last time," he said: eyes swollen, voice weak with emotion.

Closing her eyes, Kiernan looked away. "Potentially you both could lose your status for this." She took a step backwards; once then twice more.

"But we won't," Jensen assured her. "Because this is the right thing to do." Without another word, Jensen pushed the arm of Nicoletti's shirt up past his elbow and sunk the needle into his flesh. The man barely moved. His gaze never straying from the shrouded body of Taura upon the gurney.

Kiernan wasn't devoid of compassion. She had merely never found herself in many situations where she had to exercise such caution in response to her emotions. Her life had always been so precise; so controlled and ordered. Kiernan turned and headed for the door. "Make it quick," she said, delivering one last vacant look at Jensen before she left the room.

CHAPTER 8

Major Vegas studied Scout Jensen and Minister Kiernan with knitted brows. Neither woman had spoken since leaving the surgical bay, to each other or anybody else. They now sat in the briefing room looking pale and subdued. Vegas rubbed his stubble chin in thought as he turned his attention back to Tehera. The Commander was in the middle of the room, talking the troops through their mission requirements. They sat in the centre of a small space, ten chairs in two lines of five. It was Kiernan who entered the room first and had taken a seat on the back-end row. Jensen arrived later, taking a front seat on the opposite side. Their choice of seating was obviously deliberate. Something was amiss. By nature, Kiernan was always a congenial, talkative woman. She was at her best around the company of others. It was one of the reasons Vegas was so secretly enamoured with the woman. He had, on more than one occasion, considered the possibility of taking Kiernan as his spouse, but struggled to see past the deep ally-ship they had cultivated. She was a strong woman, intelligent and not afraid to voice her opinion. As such, he had never seen her so subdued. Had escorting Jensen to see Taura caused this? Vegas' brows furrowed deeper still. Yes, something was amiss.

Slouched in her chair, Jensen stared blankly ahead. She listened as well as she could, but her mind refused to remain in the present. Instead, it wandered back to the surgical suite; to Taura, Nicolette and Kiernan. She felt guilty. Not for her actions, she would never apologise for helping Nicolette spend one more moment with Taura. Luckily, he had heeded Kiernan's words and had not moved the covering from her face. Instead, he took her hand, just the left hand, and had held it close to his cheek as he spoke softly to her. Words of love; words of goodbye. It was then that Jensen had left, knowing Ziran would be sure to remove any evidence of their presence. Ziran was as close to Nicoletti as a big brother and would look out for him and herself. Jensen felt guilty for the way she acted with Kiernan. She could not explain the resentment she felt towards the woman who had been nothing short of professional towards her, and yet she still felt the need to direct her anger towards her. Jensen took pride in her occupation. She was a scout. It was a difficult job, and dangerous without a doubt. Her parents were scouts, and she wanted to follow their example, to make them proud. But Kiernan, she spoke of entering the Barren lands as though it were a challenge, she was ready to face. That provoked Jensen, feeling as though Kiernan was underestimating the dangers upon the Barrens. Little did she know, Jensen thought, but seeing the look of horror in Kiernan's eyes as she swung Taura's body around, showed how it had affected her so. She could still see Kiernan's expression, and she hated being the cause. She had nothing to prove. The Barrens would do that. Jensen turned to look at Kiernan and found the woman looking back at her. Both women looked away, one in shame, the other in discomfort.

"You will leave at 09:00," Tehera said. He pointed to the room's chronometer. "As it's almost lunch, why don't we take a break and meet again at 14:00."

Jensen stared at the chronometer blankly.

"We will reconvene in storage facility one. As you are now aware security clearance is required going forward. You have all been programmed into the system. Your keys will be acknowledged upon entrance. Until then you are dismissed."

The team rose quickly and filed out of the room. Jensen followed, avoiding eye contact, as she disappeared.

Vegas watched her leave with concern. He turned his attention to Kiernan and reached out to take her arm. "Hey."

Turning, Kiernan regarded Vegas evenly, knowing what he was about to say. "It's nothing, Vegas."

"Really?"

Kiernan blew out a forced sigh. "Really. Scout Jensen was upset."

"Understandable." The Major waited.

"Yes."

"Yes, and?"

"And" Kiernan shook her head. "She didn't react too well to seeing Taura. They were close allies."

"I never expected she would. That is why I sent you along in there with her."

Kiernan felt her ire rise. "It wasn't pleasant for me either." She didn't want to think about what happened after. "I've never been in the presence of a body before. I've never seen anything like that. I mean I knew what was up there, but I've just never… I didn't know how best to comfort her." Although speaking the truth, Kiernan hoped Vegas wouldn't push further. She needed to steer the topic towards a different direction. She wasn't ready to deal with her current emotions. Luckily, the room was empty, leaving only Vegas and herself. "I must admit," she sat back down in her chair. "The closer the mission comes the more nervous I become. I do understand the logic in sending somebody in my position and I know the person best suited is myself, but I fear I won't be able to face the challenge."

Vegas grabbed the back of a chair and turned it around to face Kiernan. He sat down. "That certainly isn't what you said yester-rotation."

"Yester-rotation I hadn't seen first-hand what awaits us up there. It's certainly different reading about it," she smiled ruefully, "In the safety of your own unit. To come face to face with that reality." Kiernan sat backwards in her chair and wrapped her arms around her torso. "I'm worried I will hinder the mission."

Vegas shook his head. "We have two land vehicles, as well as the backing of an experienced team. You have nothing to worry about. I assure you." He leant forwards and placed a reassuring hand on Kiernan's knee. "The General himself selected you with the Select Primes backing. That shows faith."

Kiernan nodded silently.

"Do you doubt your abilities?"

"In the laboratory, never" Kiernan said adamantly. "This is different."

"Alright, but then will you do me one favour?"

"What's that?"

"Don't doubt ours?"

With a smile that mirrored the Majors, Kiernan acquiesced. "Yes, Sir!"

***

Staring down at the bowl in front of her, Jensen prodded its contents half-heartedly. She had long since given up trying to figure out the composition of their daily meals. They may have tasted banal, they have had the ascetic appeal as a slice of card, but they did hold all the nutritional requirements for a balanced diet. Having known no different, it wasn't the lack of taste that left Jensen feeling somewhat bereft as she sat in the dining hall staring down at her lunch. The hall was surprisingly empty. Many colonists having already consumed their second meal and left for a moment of personal relaxation before re-commencing their designated posts. Jensen didn't mind sitting in the dining hall, unlike some of her allies, the cacophony of voices and clash and clanking of pots and plates were a welcome distraction from her thoughts. Still, she wished for further distraction. Anything to break her inner voice. She scooped up another spoonful of beige mush.

"I read, cycles ago, food was bursting with colours and flavours and textures."

Jensen looked up to see Kiernan standing in front of her. She really must have been lost in her thoughts not to hear her approach. The older woman placed her tray opposite Jensen and sat down. She tucked her hair behind her ear. "Good thing you can't miss what you never knew, huh?"

Placing her spoon down, Jensen said, "Is that what you remind yourself every time you have to swallow down a mouthful?"

Kiernan laughed. "No. I just count my blessing I was born without a sense of taste."

"Really?"

"Yes. I mean I can still smell things so it's not so bad, but I have no ability to taste which can at times be a great advantage. Unexpected draw back from the preliminary stages of Genetic Reproduction and Gene Cleansing. Before the techniques were perfected and advanced more recently by yours truly." Kiernan winked.

This forced a smile from Jensen. "And you never thought to see if you could reverse the defect?"

"Goodness no," Kiernan laughed. "If you had the chance, would you?"

"Fair point!" Jensen was silent as she watched Kiernan eat. She was thankful Kiernan had taken the step to show she had accepted her apology. Jensen was aware of her short temper. It had at times gotten her into trouble, as had her impulsive nature.

"Are you going to eat that?"

Jensen blinked, realising she had drifted away in thought. Kiernan's spoon was poised over Jensen's bowl. "Oh sorry; I was thinking. No please go ahead." She watched in fascination as Kiernan dove into her bowl with enjoyment. There was advantaged to a lack of taste buds after all. Jensen stared at the older woman, "Minister-"

"Don't, Scout."

"Don't?" Jensen hesitated. "But you-"

Kiernan placed her hand over Jensen's, effectively stopped any further words from passing her lips. "Please. You don't have to say anything. It's difficult, but I do understand and it's alright." Kiernan paused,

"Well, the little stunt you pulled with Nicoletti really wasn't alright. The vigilance we must uphold in making certain no infection or radiation makes it into the colonies is a constant concern for us all. And stealing an inoculation vial?"

"Technically, that wasn't me."

"Not to mention the lack of permission." Kiernan pointed her spoon at Jensen. "All I can say is I'm glad I left the room before I saw any illicit behaviour. I know nothing. Nothing at all." Kiernan arched a single brow before continuing to eat her bowl of thick beige stew. She paused, "Jensen, I'm sorry about Scout Taura. By all accounts she was an excellent Scout."

"Yes, she was," Jensen replied,

With a nod, Kiernan went back to eating Jensen's lunch.

Jensen was silently surprised. She studied the woman before her. How could she have lived twenty-nine cycles in the colony and never have set eyes upon this person before? Maybe she had, she considered, but she was just another face among thousands who lived and worked in the colonies. However, she was sure she hadn't seen her before. She'd quickly gathered Kiernan was a solitary individual outside of her duties, and she did have access to upper-level facilities. With all those tomes. The reading potential!

Seeing that Jensen's thoughts had again wandered, Kiernan continued enjoying the younger woman's lunch. Maybe it was strange to enjoy eating something she couldn't taste, but maybe it filled an emotional void, she thought. She rolled her eyes internally at the thought.

Across the table, Jensen turned her attention to her desert. Straight to the sugary treat. Her sweet tooth thanked her. It was one advantage to living in the Governance colony. They had access to cultivated sugar cane in their meals. Deserts were, without a doubt, her favourite.

"So, Scout, tell me," Kiernan's lips eased into a smile. "What is your defect?"

"My defect?"

"Yes." Kiernan paused. "Oh, come on, Scout. Until approximately eight cycles ago, before I perfected gene cleansing, all births came with some form of minor defect. Most can be quite easy to figure out. A sixth toe was the first defect. One group have the same, dare I say, rather large mole on the upper left side of their back. Maybe not all can be classed as defects. Unless you are referring to mine that is. However, there are the odd exceptions. I can usually tell by the age of a colonist what birth defect they are likely to have." Kiernan tapped her spoon against Jensen's empty lunch bowl. "Judging by your age, at that period of the genetic cleansing, there is one of two options."

Jensen recognised Kiernan's playful smile. "So, what do you think it is?"

"Well, you either have a second navel caused by the twin umbilical defect –"

"Or?"

"Or you have two… of a certain other delicate part of one's anatomy"

"Delicate you say?" Jensen asked.

Kiernan leaned back in her seat. "If you have them, you will know what I mean. If not… you have the second navel."

"How mysterious!"

With a nod, Kiernan smiled. "Very true. So, which two do you have?"

Jensen looked down at her bowl. Lunch was over. "Well would you look at the time! The Commander will be wondering where we are. Break's over, Minister."

"Scout!"

Jensen laughed. "If you really wanted to find out my birth defect then you could check my files. I would presume you have access to them. Why ask?"

Kiernan rose from the table. "Firstly, Scout, I am not in the habit of reading colonists' personal information without prior consent. Unless it pertains to my work."

"And secondly?"

The Minister arched her eyebrow.

"If your intentions were to embarrass me, you failed. You have a lot to learn about me, Minister Kiernan."

Kiernan walked around the table and placed her hand boldly on Jensen's stomach. Her fingers felt around inquisitively. The russet tinge to Jensen's cheeks caused by her bold move made Kiernan smile. "You were saying?" The older woman nodded her head once. She had her answer. Without waiting for a reply Kiernan left the dining hall.

Jenson watched her leave; bemused.

"So, what is it?"

Jumping, Jensen turned to see Scout Ryan seated behind her. "Excuse me?"

"Well, we're about the same age," Ryan said. "I'm curious!"

Shaking her head, Jensen turned to leave, swiping her hand against the back of Ryan's head as she went.

"What?" He asked with a laugh.

CHAPTER 9

It was a remarkable sight. Two genuine, classic land vehicles. Jensen was sure they had to be over one hundred and fifty cycles old. She had seen images of such things in antiquity files. They were basic in design and powered by an internal combustion engine. These were obviously pre Hydro Energy Stream, solar or electrical power. The vehicles were large and cumbersome in design, but Jensen still found them fascinating. To see something she'd only ever before read about in tomes; Jensen ran her hand over the larger of the two. A vehicle designed for mass transportation of bulky items. It looked pristine and had obviously been well kept. The paint was a standard governmental colour used in their uniforms. It shone in the underground lighting. Its body was smooth and cold. Jensen rapped her knuckles on the side panel, it echoed on the inside. Intrigued, Jensen slid open its side door and peered inside. Timber lined its sides and floor. She was impressed, as it would be able to hold a lot of material, but how much were they expected to retrieve, she wondered. Jensen slid closed the side door and pulled open the driver's door.

"Wow," she whispered, peering over the driver's control panels. A large steering wheel was surrounded by many buttons and controls. Much had been fitted after the vehicle's original construction, that was obvious. Jensen hoped it wasn't too complicated as she would have loved to drive the vehicle. Her focus moved to a palm-sized button in the centre of the steering wheel. She couldn't help it. The vehicle wasn't activated. She had to press it.

A loud horn erupted from outside the vehicle, causing Jensen to jump as it echoed around the storage room. She stepped away from the vehicle and pushed its door closed. Luckily, Jensen was the first person to arrive and so nobody else saw her almost lose control of her bladder; she chuckled at her own reaction. Jensen moved to the second vehicle. This one was smaller and classed as a multi-person utility vehicle. Similar in colour, the smaller vehicle had blacked out windows and so Jensen once again opened the door to peer inside. There were eight seats, not overly comfortable in design Jensen noted as she pressed a seat with the palm of her hand. She wondered how fast the vehicle could travel. Neither appeared particularly aerodynamic in design. Jensen closed the vehicle door and stepped back to visually appraise both vehicles. Officer Jax had already been confirmed as driver of the passenger vehicle, she wondered who the second driver would be.

It was at that moment that the storage facility doors opened, and the remaining members of the team began to file in. The line ended with Major Vegas, Minister Kiernan and Enforcement Commander Tehera. Jensen watched the Commander closely.

"Getting acquainted with our vehicles, Scout?" he asked.

"Simply appreciating a piece of history," Jensen replied. She refrained from asking who the other driver would be, though she desperately wanted to know.

"These vehicles have been in storage here since the facility was first constructed, almost two hundred cycles ago. They may not be swift, and they may run on fossil fuel, but they are all we have. We've been saving them for when they will be most vital to the agenda. That time has arrived."

"Out of curiosity, Commander, you say this transportation runs on fossil fuel," Raziko asked, "I thought fossil fuel was depleted."

Tehera nodded thoughtfully, "Indeed it is, Scout, however, we've since converted these to run on fuel cells."

"Fuel cells," Jensen muttered. She looked covertly in Vegas' direction, just in time to see the Major exchange glances with Kiernan. She watched their exchange curiously.

"What fuel cells," Raziko asked.

Tehera looked away. "New technology we've been working on. Each cell lasts no more than a twenty-four-rotation period, it's the preliminary stage of a new fuel source. In fact, Tehera pushed his hand into his pocket and pulled out a small oblong cell half the size of his little finger. It radiated a bright, luminous glow. "One of these will run a single land vehicle for twenty-four rotations."

Jensen took a step closer and examined the tiny cell between Tehera's finger and thumb. How could something so small generate so much power? She looked again at Vegas, to see him talking quietly with Kiernan. Her curiosity increased.

"Each vehicle will receive a backup cell. Merely a cover for any unforeseen circumstances. The technology is still new."

"And what if both cells fail," Zora asked.

"They won't."

"Forgive me, Commander, but you send a backup, in the event a cell would fail… but they won't fail?"

"No, they won't." Tehera placed the cell back into his pocket, effectively ending the conversation. "Now let's get to the reason we are here." Tehera looked at the group who stood in a half circle around the vehicles. "Time for formal introductions of your team and their rolls." Tehera walked to the beginning of the line. Officer Jax was first for introductions. He placed his hands upon Jax's shoulders.

"Officer Jax; driver of the light haulage vehicle."

The fair coloured man nodded his head in acknowledgement.

"Some of you may wonder why an enforcement officer has been drafted into this mission, but I can assure you Officer Jax's bellicose combat skills are supreme. He has put many marks of practice into familiarising himself with this vehicle and perfecting his driving ability. Officer Jax has been briefed on his mission requirement, and when not seated at the helm of the LHV, that is light haulage vehicle for those of you interested," Tehera offered, "he will serve as personal protection aid to Minister Kiernan."

At this Kiernan looked up in obvious surprise, an action that was noted by only one person paying attention. Jensen watched Kiernan, their eyes met, but Kiernan looked away swiftly. *Too late*, Jensen thought, *I saw that*!

Tehera moved along the row. "Next is Officer Jorca. The second of our recruits from the Enforcement Team and our second driver, who along with Jax, has logged many marks herself in the vehicular co-ordination training."

"Better than you," Jorca said as she pushed her co-officer, Jax, playfully.

"Doubtful," the burly man replied.

Their playful ribbing ensued, and Jensen watched as the officers joked amongst themselves. She took them in visually. Both officers were tall and sturdily built. It was well known Enforcement Officers were preferably chosen for being aesthetically intimidating. Jax and Jorca were no exception. Jorca herself was almost as tall as Captain Lucia, but noticeably wider and with clear brute strength. She had closely cropped dark hair, a style most Enforcement Officers adopted.

Tehera moved on. "You all know the next person very well. Major Vegas. I need say nothing more about your team's mission head, except that you have one of our most experienced men with many above ground marks logged on your side. Listen to him. Learn from him. You are all valued members of this team and Vegas is the best lead we can give you."

Vegas wanted to stand proud and tall as he listened to Tehera's words. He wanted to. He should have been gratified by the introduction. Something held him back.

Jensen watched another brief, barely visible and ever-so silent exchange between Vegas and Kiernan. Her curiosity increased further.

"Now for those of you who have not yet been formally introduced, this is Minister Kiernan. Kiernan is one of our lead scientists, also having a political background as Minister of Acquisitions. Her presence on the mission is of paramount importance. The facility you shall be seeking out has much needed data vital to our Ultimate Agenda."

Kiernan smiled softly, as she looked around at her new team. "It's a pleasure to be collaborating with you all."

"And who do we have next, but four of our colony's infamous scouting team, Scout Raziko, Scout Ziran, Scout Jilya and Scout Ruben. We are lucky to have these men on our team who bravely venture up onto the barrens, mapping out the land, conducting repairs to our venting systems, collecting test samples, searching for material wares… all vital to our continuing survival." Tehera moved along the line. "Advisor Xoren."

Jensen studied the older man standing to her right.

"Xoren, as some of you are aware, was a scout cycles ago, but bravery, intuition and a host of other commendable skills has moved him up the internal ladder." He patted Xoren's back, a not so well-hidden sign of favouritism. "Xoren is my chief assistant and advisor."

And you are sending him on this mission? *Why*? Jensen thought. She had decided it was prudent not to voice so many of her internal questions. To keep her inside thoughts, just that.

"And finally, Scout Jensen." Tehera stood beside Jensen. "One of our longest serving scouts with more marks logged on the Barrens than any other. Along with Minister Kiernan, Jensen is your mission sub-head. A highly skilled, and formidable scout."

Several whoops resounded from her fellow scouts, forcing Jensen to look down the line. She delivered a playful glare towards her workmates. They only grinned in response.

Tehera walked around the group and stood before them. He silently surveyed the team. "I present to you the team for Operation Hypogean."

Officer Jorca began to clap, but realising nobody else was following suit, her clapping evolved into a swift wipe of her hands, and pat down of her upper thighs, as she brushed away imaginary dust from her clothing. Officer Jax shook his head. Jorca slapped his arm. Jax flicked her ear.

Ignoring the officers, Tehera held a hand towards Xoren. "If you will, Advisor?"

Jensen took a moment to appraise the older man. He had officially become a scout the same time she. Upon her parents' death two places needed to be filled. Jensen inherited the position, Xoren was recruited into it. However, he only lasted one cycle before his role once again changed, and he was promoted to advisor. Jensen hadn't had many dealings with Xoren since he left the scouting ranks. She knew of only one thing. She didn't like or trust him.

"This mission has been many rotations in the making. Almost half a cycle. During that time, I made it my aim to assure the best of the best were drafted into Operation Hypogean. I have spent many marks working with select team members to assure they were trained for their role."

And she found out about the mission the rotation before? Jensen folded her arms in frustration. She wanted to speak to the Major.

Xoren ran a hand over his shaven head. "The vehicles have been equipped with our best technology, rations and medical supplies have been stored in both…" he paused, "and the strongest weaponry we have to offer."

Jensen turned to Major Vegas, before looking back at Xoren. "Different from our usual weaponry?"

Methods of self-defence had always been a matter of deep concern. Weaponry was in short supply. During early habitation of the colonies, much of the weaponry had been dismantled and reduced to its base alloys. Stock piling weapons wasn't, at that time, considered imperative when the demand for essentials needed to be met. Resources were limited and every useable fragment of metallic ore had been recycled for more vital use. All that remained were tonfas, staffs and mallets. If a scout was lucky, he or she might find a makeshift weapon of choice while out on the Barrens, but it was rare. The weapons were crude, but still effective if used well.

Jensen considered Xoren's words. She tapped her bottom lip as a thought occurred to her. She knew what she had to do. Jensen looked around and saw Vegas watching her closely. The Major noticed her mind had wandered in thought and he delivered a curious glance. Jensen nodded politely and looked away quickly. He was too perceptive. She turned back to Xoren and realised she had missed the end of his address. He began handing out Personal Data Consoles.

"On these, you will find the last known map we have of the area, pre-devastation. It also holds the facility blueprints. Memorise the data well. We cannot afford a margin of error. Time is of the essence."

Tehera stepped forward. "You were all chosen because you are the best in your fields. I don't need to stress to you anymore the importance of this mission or the hazards you will face." The commander ended his speech, as he walked towards the exit. "Get plenty of sleep. Return here at 0600 marks," and just like that, Tehera left the room.

As the team began talking among themselves, Jensen decided she need to run an important errand before she could retire for the eve. Slipping the data console into her trouser leg pocket, Jensen headed toward the exit. Single-minded in her goal, she never saw two sets of eyes watching her.

"Follow her."

Minister Kiernan turned swiftly. "Excuse me?"

"Follow her," Vegas repeated.

Kiernan shook her head sternly. She needed to talk to him about the body she had stored away in refrigeration. "Absolutely not, I –"

Vegas silenced Kiernan, as he put his arm around her shoulders and steered her towards the exit. "If I know Scout Jensen as well as I… look I do know Jensen… and she is up to something. We do not have time to argue."

"I don't think –"

"Something not entirely legal," Vegas pressed. They reached the door. "Follow her and make sure she does not do anything that could jeopardise this mission. We need her."

Kiernan did understand what Vegas was referring to. She had read in Scout Jensen's reports how she had, on three separate occasions, served a two-rotation incarceration as punishment for breaking roaming laws. On each occasion, she had returned from either Labour or Domestic sporting varying degrees of cuts, grazes, or contusions. Although the belief was Jensen occasionally suffered from a simple case of wanderlust, Vegas knew better. There was underground knowledge of a clandestine bartering system existing in the Labour and Domestic colonies. It was ignored, believing the colonists needed that little bit of freedom to feel they were exacting some form of a rebellious nature. Vegas believed Jensen partook in the bartering system, and occasionally those transactions may have gotten out of hand.

Her impulsiveness and quick temper often lead Jensen into trouble. Vegas knew Jensen, and he could read her well.

"Now! Before she disappears."

Dumfounded, Kiernan said, "And what if she catches me?"

"Even better," Vegas opened the door. "Now go, before you lose her!"

With one last exasperated look, and no idea how she was to thwart Jensen's 'wanderlust,' Kiernan left.

CHAPTER 10

Travelling on the outskirts of Governance, Jensen noted the familiar signs foretelling her approach to its lesser-known border. She had taken this route more times than she could remember. The first sign was a thinning out of people. The second was lessening of metal beams supporting the rock structure. She slipped soundlessly down rarely used corridors, through unknown doors, further and further away from the general population. The route was memorised. The location a secret she never shared with another soul.

Finally, Jensen reached a dead end. The narrow passage ended with a dusty rock wall. Jensen approached the wall and stopped a breath away from it. She looked down and swirled her booted foot around the thick dust at her feet. A hollow 'clunk' resounded from the ground as her boots' sole connected with a timber plank. She flicked her foot back and forth to move the dirt and then took a step backwards. Leaned forwards Jensen slid her fingers between lumber slats and lifted the grate from its bed. It opened on aged, rusted hinges. The opening was wide enough for her slight frame to drop through. She did so, letting the grate close behind her. Jensen hit the floor with a light thud. Total darkness surrounded her. She stayed in a crouched position, and on her hands and knees, Jensen crawled for ten paces before reaching another dead end. This time Jensen reached up and lifted a second timber grate. Dim light filtered into the low space and Jensen pulled herself out of the crawl space and into another tunnel. The aroma was that of damp soil and rotten timber. It wasn't entirely unpleasant, but it was strong. Jensen reminded herself it was nothing compared to the scents she was soon to greet.

Staying in a crouched position, Jensen shuffled through the tunnel. She felt the aged boards' creek under her weight. Shafts of dim light filtered through the beams. Jensen could see heavy dust floating within them. The particles ticked her nose and irritated her eyes. When she approached an opening Jensen remained low. The sound of voices filtered through the air. Jensen peered carefully through the gap found at the top of a high wall. It was a venting duct. Voices grew louder, closer. Jensen watched as bodies walked below her and then disappeared. More voices followed. She kept low and waited. Footsteps disappeared and then there was silence. She waited. Nothing followed. With no more approaching bodies, Jensen swiftly swung her body around, and dropped down into the corridor below. She had entered the Domestic colony.

Taking a moment to regain her bearings, Jensen's eyes adjusted to the dimmer light. The ambiance of the Domestic colony was different. The walls were a mix of rock and lumber beams. The environment was no way near as sterile as the Governance colony, but Jensen was comfortable here. The relaxed atmosphere put her at ease. Jensen took a moment. She leaned back against the wall and took a breath. Although she would never wish to live in Domestic, she did enjoy her visits. It was refreshing to see the young children. Once she had visited the school room, in her role as a Scout, to talk to them about her job and what she did for their future. It was the first time she gained insight into what the Domestic colony genuinely thought of those who lived and worked in Governance. To an extent, Jensen found they were revered as saviours of their planet and their continued survival. The children, aged between two to sixteen cycles, looked upon her in awe. It was a unique experience. Jensen recalled talking to the children and telling them about what it was like up on the Barren lands (minus the Scavengers of course). Their young faces looked upon her in wonderment, some scared, others thrilled by her descriptions.

Footsteps brought Jensen's thoughts back to present. She heard shuffling, talking, and rustling around her. She started to move. The passageway was broken by an arched doorway composed of russet blocks. Jensen passed through and into a throng of moving bodies. Like the Labour colony, Domestic lived a simpler existence defined by echoes of their past. Modern technology was almost non-existent and reduced only to what was essential to survival. As Jensen navigated her way through the walkways, she felt comfortable in the family like atmosphere. Here, law and order were still supported, but it was more relaxed to a simple, peaceful way of life. No way near as regimented as Governance. For this reason, Jensen did like to visit both Colonies, even though she had gotten herself into trouble in the past. Visiting without authorisation was frowned upon and often lead to disciplinary action. That was not to say the Colonies were not allowed to mingle, however a permit was needed to cross the borders. It was only valid for one rotation.

In the past, Governance colonists had fallen under the spell of the simple ways of Domestics life and had sought permission to leave. That wasn't for Jensen. She enjoyed her position. She also enjoyed breaking the rules when the mood struck her.

Life was much simpler in the Domestic colony. A single child was born to every family. The government ever strict on that policy. The meticulous control they exacted over the reproduction procedure, managed to high standards. Life ensued with schooling, entertainment, and even amateur dramatics. News was broadcast over an intricately built speaker system, which filtered through from Governance. Just like the other colonies, a communist-like existence had evolved through the simple need to work to live, for the good of the colony. There was no money, no commerce, just the act of doing one's part for the colony and their continued survival. Many saw it as an ideal existence. Others not so much. Frequent patrols by Enforcement Officers always kept order. The Enforcement unit, controlled by Governance, kept the peace in all three colonies, as well as checking their borders. It was these officers who, on three separate occasions, had reported Jensen's unauthorised presence in Labour and Domestic. For this reason, Jensen kept out of sight, moving through lesser used corridors, doorways, and tunnels. She was still a distance from her intended destination.

***

It was when Kiernan found the wide gap at the bottom of the dark shaft she had just crawled though, that she realised Jensen would be in serious trouble if she was discovered. She knelt, peering through a narrow opening to see Jensen take a right turning, and disappear out of sight. Three people then appeared around the opposite corner and Kiernan waited for them to pass, willing them to move swiftly so she could slide out of the narrow opening. As soon as the area was clear, Kiernan turned, rolled onto her stomach, and slipped as gracefully as she could into the Domestic colony. Her feet hit the ground and she stumbled slightly, holding onto the rock wall to remain upright. She needed to move swiftly if she were to gain ground on the distance Jensen was sure to be making between them. Without another thought, she set off.

Kiernan was annoyed. She should never have relented to Vegas' request to follow Scout Jensen. She was a scientist. She was not supposed to be skulking around in dark passageways. Was she too old for this? Kiernan looked down at her dust covered clothing and brushed her hands over the dark fabric, as she wondered once again where Jensen was heading. For a tenth of a mark, she followed the Scout through passageway, after passageway. Although she had spent a fair amount of time in the Domestic colony in relation to her work, she had never seen these areas before. So much so that Kiernan knew she couldn't stop now even if she wanted to. She wasn't sure she would be able to find her way back to Governance. Kiernan cursed inwardly, as she turned another corner and walked for only several paces, quickly realising she'd reached a dead end. She spun around quickly, turning back to the passageway from where she had ventured. There was nothing but timber beams and rock walls. Kiernan turned again. She looked left and right. Anxiety rose and churned within her stomach. Suddenly, a body dropped down from above and landed beside her. Kiernan yelped, hand on her chest, as she stepped away from the surprise figure.

"Why are you following me?"

Releasing a sigh, and feeling her heart rate return to normal, Kiernan wanted to be glad to see Jensen. She thought maybe she should feel guilty at being caught. Instead, she chose annoyance.

"How long have you known I was following you?"

Jensen shrugged her shoulders. "Not long. Now you answer my question, Minister."

Kiernan didn't relent. "I can't believe you're speaking to me in such an accusatory fashion when you are the one breaking laws." She stood defiant, toe to toe with Jensen.

"Regardless of my actions, Minister, you have yet to answer my question."

"I don't think-"

"A simple question will herald the answer to any question you have." Jensen offered.

Kiernan was silent for a moment, before she relented with a sigh. "Vegas asked me to follow you. Let's just say he has a way of talking me into doing things completely out of character."

To Kiernan's surprise, Jensen smiled. "Vegas? Noted."

Kiernan frowned. "You don't seem upset… or concerned."

"I'm not."

"Why?"

"Because Vegas sent you," was Jensen's only reply, as though her answer obvious.

"And you're not worried you will get into trouble?"

"No."

"Why?" Kiernan pushed, felling utterly confused by Jensen's cavalier attitude and lack of clear communication.

"Like I said, Vegas sent you. If it had been anybody else asking you to spy on me"

"I'm not spy-"

"Oh, come on," Jensen pushed. "If it had been anybody else, I would have been worried, but Vegas knows what I know. He also knows he's not able to do what I'm sure he's thinking I am going to do."

Was she speaking in riddles? Kiernan shook her head. The younger woman had obviously spent too much time skulking in dark and dusty corridors. Her brows furrowed together. "Well, I'm lost." Her countenanced conveyed her confusion.

Jensen placed her hand upon Kiernan's lower back. "No, you're not. Come on."

"Where are we going?" Kiernan fell into step beside Jensen.

"Firstly, I'm taking you back."

Kiernan froze. "Oh no you are not." Seeing Jensen was about to argue, Kiernan pulled rank. "Firstly, Scout, you cannot give an order to a superior rank. By rights if I tell you to take me wherever it is you are going, then by goodness you will take me. Secondly, if you don't want me to report back," She smiled, "You will allow this clandestine trek to reach its conclusion with myself in tow."

Jensen's head fell backwards, and she scanned the dimly lit rock ceiling. No reasoning to be found there! "Minister, you have no idea what you are asking of me, and you have no idea where I am going. This is dangerous. There are so many reasons why I can't comply."

"Scout, this isn't a request. You are the one breaking colony laws. Entering Domestic unauthorised, and-"

"I'm using the back passages as those damned Enforcement Officers watch me constantly."

Kiernan's apathetic expression never left her features and Jensen knew she had no choice but to relent to Kiernan's demand. She only hoped she was ready for what she was about to see. "Alright, but just remember I warned you. Be on your guard." Jensen reached out and slipped her hand into Kiernan's trouser leg pocket. The older woman stepped back slightly in confusion as she pulled out her data console.

"What are you doing?" Jensen didn't reply. Instead, Kiernan watched as Jensen accessed the devices memory and wiped it clean. "Why did you do that? We need that information," she said incredulously.

"We can load the information again." Jensen pulled out her own date console and did the same, wiping its memory. She then placed them both into her pocket. "Are you ready?"

Kiernan was confused. She was curious. She felt a rockslide of emotions tumble down upon her, but surprisingly none of them involved fear. "Yes," she heard herself say.

"Then follow me."

CHAPTER 11

Kiernan noted the further they travelled the danker the atmosphere and more pungent the aroma. She would have been lost if not for Jensen leading the way. Kiernan had never travelled so far into the Domestic colony before. She could only trust Jensen in her knowledge of the area they traversed. The air continued to grow stale, reeking strongly of damp timber, soil, and other more repulsive aromas. Kiernan parted her lip, to pull gulps of musty air through her mouth to bypass her olfactory senses. She wished it was her sense of smell she was lacking.

"What is that" she finally complained.

Jensen smirked. "You may not wish to know the answer,"

Kiernan wasn't pleased by the response, but she didn't show it. She continued her pace, a step behind Jensen.

They eventually stopped by a wall, and it was then that Kiernan noticed something quite unexpected. It was a door. A timber door. She looked upon the aged barrier with curiosity. What surprised her most was the brass-coloured insert halfway down the door to the right-hand side.

Jensen knelt and reached into her boot. She pulled out a long metallic object and pushed it into the lock, twisting it twice.

"That's a key!" Kiernan said, in both surprise and confusion.

"You really are the observant scientist," Jensen said, trying to hide her caution with an air of sarcasm. When the door was unlocked Jensen pulled the key out but made no move to open it. "Before we enter, I need to warn you about where we are heading, Minister"

Kiernan tucked her hair behind her ear and waited with a feeling of trepidation.

"As you know, when the underground colonies were built, they were originally formed of four divisions, Governance to the north, Labour to the west, Domestic to the East and the Primary colony to the south. Do you know why the Southern, or Primary, colony was so quickly disregarded?"

"Of course. It was constructed from the basement cells of a mental asylum. The whole structure was considered too antiquated in design," Kiernan offered. "I must admit I completely understand why. It was originally built a lot closer to the surface as it was a hospital for those sick in mind. The structure continued to be added upon in subterranean levels as they constructed a prison for mentally ill prisoners. This all started maybe three hundred cycles ago. However, the subterranean footings heralded the groundwork for the building of the colonies. Over the period of about a hundred cycles, the entire network of the north, east and west colonies were construed from those original footings. Unfortunately, the original and more antiquated construction of the original foundations, the Southern or Primary colony, were considered unsuitable for habitation due to the potential dangers presented."

"Indeed."

"It was a wise move." Kiernan continued, lost in her knowledge of colony history. "Seals were unfinished, the construction was never 'watertight', as they say. Plumbing was unsatisfactory and again antiquated in design. Sewage had no outlet. The air ducts were not fitted safely, and ventilation was poor. Energy was never routed securely through the link-way connections by which we all are connected and-" Kiernan paused, realisation just dawning upon her. "You can't be serious?"

Jensen arched her brow. "I'm really not known for being a joker." She tapped the key on her fingertips. "After over fifty cycles, the inhabitants of the Primary colony have adapted to their environment adequately. Although their efforts may seem crude, it's reasonably safe from radiation and…" she licked her bottom lip with a pronounced pause, aware of the information she was about to impart. "The inhabitants have been living a relatively peaceful existence now for at least forty cycles."

Kiernan blinked. Then again. She looked at the door separating them from the unknown occupants of the Primary colony. It had long since been abandoned and considered an unsafe environment for occupation and growth. Did the government have any idea this was not the case?

"But what about the-"

"Minister, these are the forgotten people who will be left behind."

"How many?"

Jensen shrugged her shoulders. "I'm not sure even they know the answer to that. Minister Kiernan, I need you to understand," Jensen took a step closer. "Life is basic. Very basic." Jensen pushed the door open. "People still migrate here to disappear off the government's radar. All for varied reasons, fear of comeuppance on a misdeed or disagreeing with the Ultimate Agenda. Some just because they are too driven by their baser needs." At that Jensen smiled as she ushered Kiernan through the door.

"Baser needs?"

"Kiernan," Jensen stopped in a dark, narrow passageway. It wasn't big enough for the women to stand side by side. The lighting was dim, and Jensen could barely see Kiernan through the darkness. "Before the government took such a direct approach to controlling how we procreate, how do you think we brought life into this world?"

The Minister was incredulous. "I'm very well aware of that, Jensen."

"Hmm…" Jensen closed and locked the door, enveloping them in total darkness. She pulled out a small torch and turned it on, directing the beam under her face. Her distorted features shone in the darkness. "For those who care to indulge I'm told it's a pleasurable act. For many of these people, it's to ease boredom and tension, as well as an aid to relaxation. Granted, I am more taken by a good tome." Jensen directed the torch beam down the dark passageway. "Downside, there can be a high production of offspring. This needs to remain below radar. One way to do this is defect to Primary. More out of need than an actual desire to do so; as I'm sure you will soon gather." Jensen turned to Kiernan and smiled. "What better place to hide?"

As Jensen stopped talking, Kiernan became aware of voices. Many voices, filtering in through the darkness. Silently, Jensen turned and led the way down the narrow passage. The women took a left, then right and then two more lefts before ascending several flights of metallic stairways. Soon, they were stepping out into what Kiernan could only describe as a small yet strangely organised bazaar. It was a wide-open space with corridors that branched out in every direction. She saw a set of steps that led up and disappeared to the right and out of sight. The walls were a mix of solid dirt and soil, rock, sheets of timber and even corrugated iron. It was, without a doubt, the most unexpected sight she had ever seen. Again, the mix of aromas changed rapidly. The air was infused with a potent fusion of pleasant and some not pleasant scents, but together they offered a unique banquet for the senses.

In the centre of the 'market' stood a fire pit constructed of a terracotta-coloured stone. What surprised Kiernan most was the unidentifiable food stuffs that cooked above the pit on a metallic grate. The scent wafted towards her in a light, smoky essence. It was unlike anything Kiernan had ever experienced in her forty-two cycles. She watched the aromatic smoke dance seductively in the air and rise slowly up, until it disappeared into a chimney. Many colonists filled the space, moving from one stall to another, offering objects in trade for other desired items.

Kiernan's attention moved to the colonists around her, noticing their appearance. Their clothing was tattered, their skin smudged with dirt. It was clear hygiene wasn't an imperative factor in the Primary colony. Children ran around her in various stages of undress. What surprised her was how happy they all appeared, and ignorant to her arrival. Kiernan found that somewhat concerning. Still, she couldn't help but smile at their joyful expressions.

To her right stood a group of people engaged in what Kiernan believed to be some form of recreational activity. They stood a distance from a narrow container and tried to throw stones into it. Each successful hit would result in eruptions of cheers and hollers of triumph.

Jensen watched Kiernan's open expression of wonder and smiled to herself. She was sure the first time she visited Primary she must have looked just as enraptured by the scene. Placing her hand on Kiernan's back she led her towards the centre. Conversations escalated around them. People spoke animatedly on topics Kiernan had little frame of reference for. She watched their interactions with an expression somewhat liken to wonderment. Jensen watched Kiernan surreptitiously, enjoying the vicarious thrill of the older woman's experience. When she first met Kiernan, she found her uptight and entirely utilitarian. However, the more she got to know her, dare she say, 'new ally', the more she found her charmingly endearing and somewhat entertaining.

Pulling herself from her internal musings, Jensen realised Kiernan had wandered away. She noticed with some alarm that Kiernan was heading towards the centre fire pit. By the time Jensen was back by her side, Kiernan was in conversation with the cook. He was a short man, with thinning hair and eyes that were far too close together. He had a permanent squint, which Jensen had always believed to be the smoke affecting his eyes. His hair was rapidly receding, and it was to Kiernan's surprise that she noticed he had very few teeth remaining. The cook handed Kiernan a skewer loaded with five chunks of an unidentifiable form of edible substance. She took it willingly.

"Um… Kiernan," Jensen said cautiously.

Kiernan quickly realised there would be no use of occupational titles in the Primary colony. "Jensen have you smelt this? I've never smelt anything like this before! For the first time I think I mourn my lack of taste buds!"

The vendor, of whom Jensen knew was called Dicken, frowned at her comment.

Kiernan pulled a morsel off the skewer and offered it to Jensen. "Tell me what it tastes like?"

Jensen took a step backwards. "With respect I'll pass." She looked over at Dicken, quick to note his disappointed expression. Jensen knew he prided himself on creating food for the colony. No bartering was needed for his services. It was personal enjoyment.

Seeing his expression fall on her rejection of his food, Jensen took the morsel from Kiernan's fingers and bit lightly into a corner. She chewed it mechanically, not really tasting or savouring the experience, and swallowed quickly. She smiled; her lips thin with lack of enthusiasm that was only noticed by Kiernan. "It's pleasant."

Dicken puffed his chest with pride. Kiernan narrowed her eyes.

"And how does it taste?"

With a smile of thanks, Jensen steered Kiernan away from Dicken's stall and into the crowd of people. "Kiernan," she whispered. "Where do you think food here comes from?"

Kiernan stopped walking. "I… I don't know!"

"Exactly," Jensen said. "And I don't care to know any more than I must. I don't want to know. The banal offerings in Governance are suddenly much more appealing compared to whatever that is."

Kiernan looked down at the skewer, still within her grasp. She swallowed thickly and without a second thought handed it to a passing child. The little child, with dark, messy hair and equally dark eyes, accepted the food excitedly. He began eating with gusto. "I never considered," she said regretfully. She watched the child run off to join his comrades.

"Food consumed in the past has always played heavily on my conscience," Jensen said. "I've heard of the mass of species we consumed back in the time before the devastations and can say with complete certainty that the actions of our ancestors fill me with shame and horror."

Not wanted to delay their journey anymore, but eager to understand Jensen, Kiernan said, "Meat was a staple diet of our ancestors. Would we really have changed so much now if not for a lack of choice? Just because our diet consists of carefully produced nutritional compounds."

"And are we not all fit and healthy on the foods we manufacture and grow through aeroponic production?"

Kiernan looked again at the young child who had finished his skewer. "So, what was that? I have a feeling you know."

"Not exactly." Jensen frowned, "But I know food production here goes side by side with carefully controlled solutions to the insect population."

Kiernan visibly paled in the bazars artificial light; suddenly glad she hadn't consumed the offering. "I… I'm… I'm in no position to question the life choices of others about their survival."

"Spoken like a true politician." Jensen brushed a hand over her face roughly and surveyed the area.

Kiernan bristled at Jensen's comment. She took a breath to calm her ire. "Where are we heading?"

Without another word Jensen once again placed her hand on the small of Kiernan's back and led her through the crowd. They passed another rickety table offering food. Kiernan was positive she spotted hard shelled insects in large clay bowls. She swallowed as her stomach lurched in revulsion.

They increased their pace, Kiernan a step behind Jensen, as she followed her to their intended destination. She continued to look around, noticing they were heading towards a timber framed doorway which had been re-enforced by securing multiple layers of planks over each other. It was visually unsightly and obviously constructed without skill. However, it did its job well. Kiernan then turned her attention to the people around them. She scanned the mix of faces with a closer eye and something clear struck her. All these people, in one way or another, showed signs of radiation exposure. It wasn't debilitating, but it did detract from their aesthetic comeliness. Patchy loss of hair or teeth, skin discoloration, stunted limb growth and even mild, and she hoped benign, tumours, all appeared present in these people. Kiernan was also stuck by one other point of note. A lot of these people appeared to know Jensen, making eye contact, waving, or nodding their head in a way of greeting. She wondered how long Jensen had been visiting the Southern Colony.

Jensen stopped as she reached the timber doorway. It was only then that Kiernan noticed a long, stained sheet stood as its door. Jensen pushed it aside and led her through the opening.

"Where are we?" Kiernan asked, as they entered a large, dimly lit room. She noticed the walls were covered in a worn, tatty padding. "This was part of the asylum!"

"It was," Jensen confirmed. "A prisoners' cell." She stood in the centre of the room and yelled, "Flick!"

Although startled, Kiernan remained still. She took a closer look around the once padded cell. The walls were so dirty she was positive she could print her name in the grime. What was strangely notable were the pictures adorning the material walls. Obscure shapes and images. She stepped closer. The picture was of a land, vibrant with colour, but unrecognisable to her. Even the language was in a text she was unfamiliar with. "So where are we?"

"Our final destination." Jensen stepped towards the only item of furniture in the room. It was a low counter formed of aged, rotted timber. She slammed the side of her fist repeatedly on its surface. "Flick, get out here you have business."

At that moment, a short man almost fell through a second curtained doorway. He wasn't incredibly old, Kiernan suspected no more than twenty cycles, but he had lost most of his hair on the top of his head. Nothing but a small offering of dark strands sat above his ears. Upon closer inspection Kiernan noted a scar that ran down his left cheek. He walked with a slight limp and when he spoke his voice was horse and broken.

"Jen, I wondered when you visit." He offered her a semi-toothless smile as his attention turned to Kiernan. He gave her a slow appraisal, making the older woman feel instantly ill-at-ease. "Have something for you," he said, turning back to Jensen. "Been holding it for a while."

Flick pulled out a small, tattered tome from beneath the counter. He brushed the dust off its faded cover before handing it to Jensen. Kiernan leaned over to look at the tome, curious to see two people locked in an embrace. Her eyes flicked up to read the title, but Jensen pulled it from the young man's grasp and placed it on the counter, face down. Her hand covered the back of the tome.

"Not now, Flick, I'm in need of more specific items."

"Like?" he asked, his eyes once again straying to Kiernan with undisguised interest.

Jensen watched his expression with annoyance, and she reached out, physically pulling his gaze back to hers. "Weapons," she said seriously, in a tone that left no room for argument. "I want weapons. What do you have?"

Kiernan looked at Jensen in alarm.

A slow, sinister smile stretched Flicks lips. "Moment please, customer." He disappeared back behind the curtain.

"What do you think you are doing?" Kiernan whispered harshly. "You can't bring unsanctioned weapons with us." She paused as Jensen's request struck her. "What weapons still exist?" She felt nothing should surprise her anymore.

"I'm doing whatever it takes to ensure our success and survival. Vegas knew this. Why do you think he sent you to follow me? Not stop me, slow me down, or try to convince me otherwise. He knew I'd do what others weren't able to do. I have a feeling you are here to make sure I don't get caught by the wrong people!" Jensen stepped closer. "We're venturing into the unknown. Now I don't know about you, but I'm willing to do whatever it takes to increase the odds in our favour. I won't risk anybody's life." She looked seriously into Kiernan's eyes. "Would you?"

Kiernan felt disarmed, but a response died upon her lips as Flick re-entered the room carrying a large, rusted box. He placed it down upon the countertop and then rubbed his nose repeatedly. Kiernan hoped her internal grimace didn't sculpt her external countenance. She then had to turn away, as Flick wiped the viscous nasal fluid, from his fingers, down his lose fitting shirt.

"Allergies?" Jensen asked.

"Yeah," Flick replied with a sniff. He took a tattered cord that was secured around his neck and pulled it over his head. "I have what you are looking for." He pushed the key into the lock and twisted it back for forth before jiggling it and pushing it in and out of the lock opening again. "Sometimes gets stiff. Nothing can do but wiggle it. Tis over one hundred cycles old." Flick slammed the side of his fist onto the top of the box and the lock gave way. "See?" The lid jarred open. "What you looking for?"

"What do you have?"

Flick reached into the box and pulled out two knives. "These? I like to sharpen them. Might slice a finger off."

"What else?"

"This one," it was another knife, bigger, more intimidating in design. "Nice and sharp."

"Keep going."

"These," Flick then pulled out two antique, automatic firearms. "And this one." He pulled out another, but smaller in size. "Got ammunition too."

Kiernan looked down at the selection weapons. "Do they work?"

"Don't do trade in faulty goods."

Jensen picked up one of the automatic firearms. "Flick knows I'd scalp him if he sold me anything faulty; right?"

The young man grimaced. "Not got a lot to lose, but yeah." He ran a hand over his bald head. "So?"

Jensen looked down into the box and pulled out the clips of ammunition. "I was hoping for more… maybe bigger. This is all you have?" She wanted more, but Flick was the only person she could go to at such short notice, who would have anything close to what she was looking for.

"Tis all I have. Unless I get trades."

"Right," Jensen pushed the empty box back at Flick. "Then I'll take them all."

The young man's eyes widened. "Smashing!" He pulled the ratty curtain aside, exposing the inner room of his dwelling.

Jensen noticed Kiernan's frown, and she shuffled her feet uncomfortably. "Not this time, Flick," she said swiftly. "I've got trade for you." She reached into her trouser leg pocket and pulled out the data consoles. "One of these, in my opinion, it worth all of what we have here. I'm offering you both. Call it credit on anything else I'm in the market for. What do you say?"

Picking up one of the consoles, Flick tapped the screen. His features lit up as the device came to life. "Both?"

"Maybe you'll throw in that tome as well?"

It only took a moment for the young man to reach a decision. "Deal. I'm done looking that picture." He pushed the tome over to Jensen and she took it, placing it in her leg pocket.

"Not my favourite way trade with you, but I get loads for these!" Without so much as a thank you, or goodbye, Flick disappeared into his back room.

"What was all that about?" Kiernan asked Jensen in confusion.

Jensen shrugged defensively. "Who knows?" She undid the fastening of her shirt and pulled it off, leaving her wearing only a sleeveless, dark top. The colour was a stark contrast to her pale skin. "I'm not sure even Flick knows what he's talking about half the time. He's a law unto himself, with a complete lack of decorum." Jensen laid her shirt out on the countertop and started placing the weapons in its centre. "He's harmless. Too many knocks to the head losing him more than just teeth."

Kiernan reached for the tome, sticking out of Jensen's trouser leg pocket, and read the title. "Interesting?" she asked, hiding her amusement.

Jensen snatched it from her grasp. Her blush was hidden in the dimly lit cell. "Don't know. I haven't read it yet."

With a smile, Kiernan watched Jensen push the tome back into her pocket and then become entirely focussed on wrapping the weapons in her shirt. Kiernan's eyes travelled down the young woman's narrow arm. It was pale to the point that she could see the veins under her skin. It was then she noticed another scar gouged into the side of her upper arm. It would have been a deep wound. Kiernan winced; sure, it would have been incredibly painful. The area was still crimson, showing the wound was reasonably fresh.

"Are you ready?" Jensen noted the faraway look in Kiernan's eyes.

"Oh, sorry, yes. Where now?"

"Back home. Unless you feel the need to sample more of the colony's edible delights?"

Kiernan blanched. "I've had my fill but thank you for offering."

Jensen arched her eyebrow. "Anytime you need an education you let me know, Minister. There's plenty more delights to be experienced here!"

Laughing, Kiernan followed Jensen out of Flicks domain, and they walked back into the main bazar. They noticed the mass of people had dwindled and tables were very quickly emptying.

"Where's everybody gone?"

Jensen watched as children were gathered up and ushered away through a maze of corridors. "No. No, no! We need to move. Now!"

"What's-" Kiernan's query was cut short, as Jensen took her hand and pulled her towards their exit.

"We need to go now. Run!"

Jolted by the urgency in Jensen's voice, Kiernan did as she was told, and picked up a swift pace behind Jensen. They ran through the makeshift bazar of the Primary colony and on towards the network of stairs, tunnels, and passageways, which would lead them back to the safety of the Domestic colony.

CHAPTER 12

They ran, and although Kiernan had no idea why, the urgency in Jensen's voice urged her forward. Hand still within Jensen's grasp, Kiernan held tightly so as not to lose the younger woman, who she was sure would be able to run significantly faster than she. Kiernan was grateful Jensen knew exactly where she was going. Without her, she would have been lost, scrambling through a maze of endless corridors and narrow passages. They continued at speed towards the Domestic colony's clandestine entrance. Kiernan felt her lungs burn, trying desperately to take in much-needed breathable air, limited as it was in the subterranean tunnels. She wanted to slow down, but Jensen's firm grip and rapid pace pulled her forwards. Suddenly, she felt her foot slip in moist soil, and she stumbled. If not for Jensen's hold, she was sure to have fallen, but momentum propelled her clumsily forwards and so she did all she could; she ran.

"Almost there," Jensen shouted and directed Kiernan right and up several flights of stairs. She never released Kiernan's hand, even as they rounded the final corner, and their exit came into view. They ran at the doorway, colliding into it at speed. Their bodies caused a heavy thud. Jensen used herself to protect Kiernan from the impact.

"Where's the key?" Kiernan asked, struggling to catch her breath.

Jensen pulled the instrument from her pocket and unlocked the door, pulling Kiernan through and slamming it behind them. She locked it quickly.

Heavy breathing filled the narrow space for long moments. Kiernan leaned forwards and placed her hands upon her knees, as she laboured for breath. She pulled air into her desperate, burning lungs.

"What… what was?" Kiernan took slow, deep breaths. "What… was… that?" She looked up at Jensen, feeling incredibly out of shape at the sight of the younger woman standing beside looking her entirely composed.

Jensen dropped her makeshift carrier holding their weapons, to the ground. "It was the Militia."

Kiernan leaned against the wall. "Who are the Militia?"

"Long time, self-appointed law of the Primary colony. They've been running longer than I've been scouting."

Feeling her body sag against the cool rock, Kiernan looked at Jensen incredulously. "You're kidding me!" She wiped a hand over her forehead and removed a thin sheen of grimy sweat.

Jensen shook her head. "They claim to keep order, but really they're a band of brutal heavies."

Taking a calming breath, Kiernan stood straighter. "So why were we running?"

"They don't like me very much." Jensen grinned, despite herself.

A sardonic smile passed over Kiernan's lips. "However much I'm not surprised by that, care to enlighten me why?"

Jensen leaned down and picked up her package. She tucked it under her arm as she motioned for Kiernan to follow her back towards Governance. "Believe it or not, it has nothing to do with my charming personality. They don't like me because they know I'm from the North."

"North?"

"Northern Colony; it's what they call Governance. I'm not sure how they came about that information, but nevertheless, they were kind enough to enlighten me to that fact when they fractured my cheek bone."

"What?" Kiernan stopped in her tracks, but Jensen kept moving and so Kiernan jogged several paces to keep up with her. "They did what?"

"The leader is a guy called Devlin. Occasionally makes a noble appearance, but more often sends his guys to do the dirty work." Jensen frowned to herself. "He's also the reason Flick's missing most of his teeth. He's one sadistic individual." Jensen winced more to herself at the memory their discussion conjured, and what Devlin's militia had done to her on a previous occasion. "He removed each one personally with a pair of pliers."

Kiernan stopped again. This time she reached out and stopped Jensen. "What?"

With a shrug of her shoulders, an attempt to pass off the emotion those memories caused, Jensen said, "He punished Flick for trading with me. Made quite a mess of his face. It wasn't a pretty sight. He then got his militia to target me. It did scare me away for a while." Jensen paused. She studied the ground beneath her feet. "Only for a while. Truth is, Devlin is hiding something and my link to Governance spooks him. I want to find out what he's up to. I will find out," she added with certainty.

"Even though Flick had half his face bashed in he still trades with you?"

Jensen chucked, as she resumed walking. "Minister, in case you didn't notice Flick isn't a very smart guy."

"Hmm," Kiernan picked up her pace, intent to keep up with Jensen. "And what's your excuse?"

"Incredibly stubborn."

They walked for long moments in silence. Kiernan studied Jensen from behind, her mind carefully processing the information she had learned over the past mark. A thought occurred to her. "How did you know we'd be safe? With a lunatic stalking the Primary colony, I'd have thought you'd want us to steer clear."

Jensen turned to look at Kiernan briefly. "You invited yourself, Minister. I did tell you it wasn't a good idea."

Kiernan couldn't argue with that. "Alright, but what about this Devlin person. What if he made an appearance earlier? What would you have done then?"

It was a valid question. Jensen hadn't thought that far. She had Kiernan with her, so they ran. It was that simple. However, if Kiernan hadn't have been with her. "If you weren't with me, I might have followed him. As I said, I want to find out what he is up to."

With an expression halfway between disbelief and fear, Kiernan said, "The guy's militia beat you up. He pummelled your hairless ally to a bloody, toothless pulp. Now I hear you say you would have further risked your safety on a hunch? Excuse my bluntness, Scout, but I thought you had more intelligence than that." She narrowed her eyes. "What are you not telling me?"

"I'm not 'not' telling you anything, Minister. Devlin has secrets. I want to find out what he's up to and stop him. If anything, the residents of the Primary colony deserve to live with a feeling of safety. They have little else. They've spent cycles afraid of Devlin and his stain on their lives"

"But-"

Jensen held up her finger, swiftly cutting Kiernan short. They froze at the sound of approaching footsteps. Jensen placed the finger over her lips, as the footsteps grew closer. Her eyes bore deep into Kiernan's. She looked around quickly when she realised those steps were heading straight in their direction, and then noticed a narrow crevice to their right. It was just big enough to slide inside. Jensen moved Kiernan first and pushed her into the crevice. She swiftly followed, wedging her body inside just before two Enforcement Officers turned the corner. Jensen and Kiernan stood side by side, their backs to the opposite walls. It was a tight fit. Jensen slid her arm up and placed her finger upon Kiernan's lips, willing her to remain silent. If ever there was a time to assess Kiernan's sincerity it would be now. A higher ranked colonist could easily hand her over to the Enforcement officers if they so wished.

Kiernan couldn't move, trapped as she was in the narrow space. She reached up and pulled Jensen's finger from her lips, hoping Jensen could see her glowering ire in the semi-darkness. However, the younger woman chose to ignore the glare she could feel burning into her side. She peered out into the passageway. Two officers approached and Jensen recognised them both. They were the same two whom had escorted her out of the Domestic colony on two separate occasions. Jensen held her breath. It would be just her luck to be caught a third time with an arm full of unsanctioned weaponry. She forced herself a little further into the crevice, which in turn forced Kiernan to do the same. It got impossibly narrower. She moved her lips to Kiernan's ear.

"Enforcement Officers. Two of them," she whispered. "Give it a couple of moments for them to pass and then we're out of here. We're almost home." She felt Kiernan nod. The patrollers passed. "And try not to slow our return with any more irrelevant questions."

"Why I-" Kiernan felt Jensen's hand cover her mouth.

"Skulk now… talk later."

Kiernan pulled Jensen's hand off her mouth. In a shaft of light, she saw the glimmer of a smirk on Jensen's lips. Kiernan ground her teeth and bit her tongue.

CHAPTER 13

By late evening, Minister Kiernan sat in her personal chamber. Enclosed within the safe confines of her separate bedroom she sat upon a small, but comfortable chair beside her bed. A tall reading light to her right created a perfect silhouette upon the wall to her left. This was her favourite way to spend the end of a working rotation. She reclined lazily in the chair, her feet braced upon her bed. One arm lightly scratching the back of her neck, the other holding a new data console, as she read their upcoming mission details. The first thing Kiernan had done upon returning home with Jensen was to obtain two more data consoles loaded with the relevant data. Her parting words to the younger woman were to keep out of trouble, study the information well, and not trade this device in for any more questionable reading material. Jensen could only blush as Kiernan bid her a good evening. Kiernan had smiled to herself, happy to have flummoxed Jensen for a change.

Kiernan yawned and placed the console on her lap. She rubbed the bridge of her nose wearily and then looked at her large bed. She could almost hear it calling her to rest. She needed sleep, but her overstimulated mind refused to calm. Events of the eve continued to play in her mind, and her thoughts reeled in response.

Was the Government aware of the Primary Colonists? Kiernan found herself in a difficult position. By rights she should inform the ranks of her knowledge. Unfortunately, she didn't know what the outcome would be. Added to that was the fact that Jensen had put her trust in Kiernan. She was loath to break that trust. Kiernan looked again at her bed, but just as she rose a knock sounded from her door.

"No," she whispered, but got up anyway, walked out of her bedroom and into the outer room. Kiernan knew of only one person would knock at such a late time. She pulled the door open. "Vegas."

"Have a moment?"

"I was just about to go to bed!"

"Want company?"

Kiernan arched her brows. "Want your nose relocating on your face?"

Vegas chuckled as he said, "A moment of your time, please?"

Kiernan stepped aside and Vegas walked in. She closed the door behind him.

"So?"

Kiernan knew exactly what he was referring to. However, a secondary thought also occurred to her. "You knew where she was going didn't you."

"To trade," Vegas replied.

Kiernan nodded. "And you know where?"

"Probably the Domestic colony, she's been brought back from there twice before, so it isn't hard to guess." Vegas paused for a moment to study Kiernan's expression, but it stayed neutral. "Weapons?" he asked.

"Indeed."

Placing his hands in his pockets, Vegas turned from Kiernan and walked around her room. "We need all we can get for this mission. I'll take the fall if there's any backlash from her procurement."

"What?" That surprised Kiernan.

"We have too much riding on this, Kiernan." Vegas stopped and looked at a window in Kiernan's room. Inside the frame was a poster view of a rural setting. Her view.

Kiernan stood beside him. "I have to tell you something."

Vegas nodded.

"I'm telling you now, as I know I can trust you."

He turned to look at Kiernan silently.

"I have a body."

That wasn't what he expected. "Excuse me?"

Kiernan closed her eyes with a shake of her head. "Sorry. What I mean is… The Scavenger that killed Taura… she managed to deliver a fatal kill wound to her attacker. Scout Ryan discovered the body," she paused. "The body of a Scavenger. I have it in refrigeration in the medical suite."

Vegas digested her words. Slowly, as understanding dawned upon him, his calm features developed an anxious disbelief. He grasped her shoulder firmly. "Are you sure? Kiernan, this-"

"Of course, I am.

"We have a Scavenger on ice?"

"We do."

"And you chose now to tell me? Why wait so long?" Vegas stopped as understanding dawned upon him. He knew why Kiernan would hide the information. Not only would the ramifications be severe if managed poorly, but she knew she would have to be the one to investigate the corpse. A sliver of fear traversed his own spine. He had experienced Scavengers personally. Her reticence was justified. "This couldn't have come at a worse time!" He folded his arms over his broad chest. "Who else knows?"

"Apart from you and me? Whylen, Ryan and a new scout, whose name, I'm ashamed to say, I can't recall!"

"Probably Harvey then." Vegas thought for a moment. "I'll speak to them first." His expression turned serious as he looked at Kiernan, "but you will be examining the body."

"I know."

"I can stay with you if you wish?"

Kiernan smiled. "I'll be alright but thank you for the offer."

"A scavenger!" Vegas rubbed his chin in thought. "Unbelievable. Did you see it?"

"Body bag."

"Smell it?"

"Most vile stench I've ever had the misfortune to experience."

Vegas laughed lightly in agreement. "Isn't it?" He backed away from Kiernan. "Look, I know you need your rest. I do too. We begin at 0600 marks."

Kiernan tucked her hair behind her ear and nodded with a ragged sigh. She took a deep breath and released it slowly. "Yes."

"You'll do great."

"So will you," Kiernan replied to which Vegas laughed.

"Sleep well, Kiernan." He opened her door and disappeared. Kiernan pushed the barrier closed and leaned back against it. Her thoughts were once again turbulent. Sleep wouldn't be easy after all. Kiernan pushed away from her door in frustration. She walked back through her outer room, with its simple sofa, table, freestanding shelf, and poster view, and back into her bedroom. She closed the door behind her. Back within the closed quarters of her bedroom, Kiernan mechanically shed her clothes and crawled into bed. The cool fabric instilled a feeling of familiar contentment. Rolling onto her side, Kiernan picked up the data console that was still lying beside her pillow. She opened the device, but instead of accessing the mission details, Kiernan instead accessed personnel files. She opened Jensen's file determined to gain some insight into the woman who was causing such waves in her once content little world. Her eyes felt heavy as she scanned through the information. Most of this she already knew. She delved further. Sleep grasped at the edges of her consciousness. The information she was reviewing changed as she read of Jensen's parents. A curious revelation almost roused her to wakefulness, but as Kiernan felt her heavy eyelids close, sleep finally claimed her.

***

Across the other side of Governance Jensen lay on her bed, resting upon her stomach. She too had spent her last waking moments reading their mission data. She'd scanned over it twice, committing the details to memory. It was a task she found easy after repeating the procedure more times than she could recall. The data console slipped out of her grasp and Jensen placed her head upon her pillow. She sighed, spying the bundle of weapons she'd traded for earlier with Flick. Jensen rolled onto her back, placing one hand behind her head and the other resting lightly upon her stomach. She knew taking Kiernan with her to the Primary colony was a risk. A mistake that could have cost them both. As for Kiernan herself, she still didn't know if she could trust her. The woman had upper-level political standing. She didn't follow rules like the rest of the colony. She helped shape them. Without a doubt her original impression of her had been quashed, but did that mean she could be trusted? And why did she feel she could?

Jensen closed her eyes, resolute not to make any closer allies. The pain of loss was too much to bear. Jensen didn't know how many more people she could lose to the harsh, unforgiving lands above them. Her thoughts returned to Taura. Her closest ally. Without warning tears creeped into her eyes. Jensen willed herself not to cry again. She needed to remain focussed. *Think of the mission*, she said to herself and took slow, deep breaths.

There was a knock at her door.

Only a slight hesitation on whether to answer entered Jensen's mind before there was a second knock. This one louder than the last.

"Coming," Jensen called, as she jumped out of bed, pulling on the clothing she had discarded upon the floor to her weary body. She then grabbed the weapons package and pushed it under her bed.

A third knock.

"I'm coming!" Jensen said louder. She pulled the door open. "Major."

"Do you have a moment, Scout?"

"I was asleep," she said unconvincingly, but stood aside all the same to allow the Major entrance into her unit.

Vegas turned to look at her. His posture was relaxed, showing at once his visit was informal. "I think you know why I'm here." He looked around her small room. "Do you have them?"

"You've spoken to Kiernan I see." Immediately Jensen wondered just how much Kiernan had imparted to the Major.

"I have. So?"

"Yes, I have them. They are-"

"No, you don't need to tell me." He crossed his arms over his chest. It was a move that always made him look impossibly wider. His expression was thoughtful. "I just want to inform you that my knowledge of your acquisition means I will take responsibility regarding the obtainment and utilisation of any such unsanctioned weapon on this mission."

Jensen stared at Vegas confounded. "Ugh, why?"

Vegas' gaze softened. "I have my reasons, Jensen, but I will say that I'm impressed by your courage to take such steps. This doesn't not go unnoticed by me, or others for that matter."

"Others?"

"Rest well, Scout," Vegas walked towards her door.

She chose to ignore his avoidance of her question. "Sir, Vegas… I need to tell you something. Since I returned from my last scout of the Barrens, I've not had a chance to impart my findings."

"You didn't log them?"

Jensen shook her head. She'd had little opportunity to do anything other than dedicate her time to mission prepping. "This was something I really wanted to relay in person. I did hope to speak to Captain Lucia, but I know you are within the chain of intelligence transfer."

"Alright?"

Suddenly Jensen didn't know where to begin. She paced thoughtfully around her room. "Sir," she tapped her fingers on her thigh in thought. "I think… no… more than think. I did see it. I just couldn't believe it. It's taken me all this time to really believe what I saw, but now I know. I am confident. I did see it. I know what I saw."

"Saw what?" Vegas was more than a little frustrated by Jensen's anxious rant.

"There was a clement and I saw a break in the cloudbank."

"A break?" He'd never known of a break in the toxic cloudbanks.

Jensen closed her eyes, her minds' eye conjuring the image she recalled from memory. "For the first time in all my cycles as a scout, Sir, I saw the thunderheads part. Just for a moment." Jensen paused again to gauge Vegas' reaction. "Sir, for just a moment I saw the sky. Our sky. I saw stars!"

"Stars."

"Just a small patch. A handful maybe, but bright twinkling little specks of light. Just like they told us about in our schooling. Just like in the pictures. Real stars shining in the eve sky." Vegas seemed to be hanging onto Jensen's every word. She smiled in memory of the vision, still bright in her minds' eye. "It was eve time, the darkest marks. It must have been as there was no colour, but there were lights. Tiny little specks of light in the darkness."

Vegas took a step away from Jensen, as her description sunk into his understanding of their situation and the ramifications this would cause. "We need more proof."

"I know we do," Jensen agreed.

"But if this is true-"

"It means the thunderhead is clearing and the cloudbanks are dissipating."

Vegas didn't want to get too encouraged by the news, but he felt the tiniest glimmer of hope. "For the first time in almost one hundred cycles-"

"We may see the sun again!" Jensen, who was spurred on by the hope she heard in Vegas' voice was then confused by an expression of unease that shaped his features. "What?"

Vegas was silent for long moments. He looked down at his feet and then back at Jensen as his eyes narrowed. "It occurs to me," he said, his gaze seeming to drift. "What will the world look like? When the cloudbank dissipates, and the sun finally breaks though what will our planet look like?"

Jensen hadn't wanted to consider that. The possibilities for positive outcomes had outweighed her thoughts of the negative implications.

"And honestly," Vegas said seriously, "Would we want to see that?"

CHAPTER 14

06:00 marks found the team filing into the storage facility. Major Vegas had arrived a mark before and had prepared the vehicles for departure. He stood to the back of the room; arms folded over his wide chest. The Major appeared relaxed and well rested. His perceptive eyes watched as the team entered the space until he spied the individual he was looking for.

As Minister Kiernan stepped into the room, she spotted Vegas trying to capture her attention. With a nod of acknowledgement, she headed towards him.

Vegas offered a reassuring smile; aware Kiernan would probably be feeling the magnitude of their endeavour. “Ready?” He noticed dark circles around her eyes.

“I am,” she assured him. “But I didn’t sleep as well as I hoped to.” She rubbed her stomach through her heavy clothing. “I also considered requesting maintenance install a revolving door in my bathroom!”

Vegas laughed. “You will be fine. You still have a sense of humour at lease!”

Smiling, Kiernan dropped her backpack to the floor. There wasn’t much contained within the carrier, mainly mission guidelines and her own directives for Operation Hypogean. Directives she was to follow alone. The orders came from the Select Prime himself and were known only by one other individual. That person was just entering the room.

Commander Tehera strode slowly past the team as he entered. All conversation ceased. He walked into the centre and looked around. There was still one person missing. Kiernan noticed too, as she looked around spotting Jensen’s absence. “Vegas,” she whispered.

“She’ll be here,” he assured her.

At precisely that moment Jensen entered the room looking refreshed and ready for whatever the mission would herald. Dressed in her standard issue scouting attire, she carried a backpack upon her back and held her breathing apparatus and protective eyewear in her left hand. Her eyes connected with Vegas as she offered a single nod in greeting.

“Now that we are all here,” Tehera began and looked around at his team. “You are about to embark on the most daring mission ever undertaken by a scout, let alone a scouting team. There are dangers yet unknown, and time is limited." Tehera connected with each team member. "We must succeed. All directives must be completed to exact standards." He turned his attention to Minister Kiernan as he said, "This is our future, and nothing can stand in our way."

Kiernan gave a faint nod and looked away. She scanned her fellow team members, noticing several pairs of eyes upon her, Jensen's included. The younger woman gave her a reassuring smile to which Kiernan nodded back. The nerves in her stomach began triple backflips and impressive summersaults.

Tehera peered down at his console. "Officer Jorca will take control of the storage vehicle accompanied by Advisor Xoren and Scout Ziran. The rest of you will take the multi person carrier with officer Jax." Tehera paused for effect, as he placed the console in his pocket. "I now hand you over to the leadership of Major Vegas," he began to walk away, "and I wish you all a safe return."

Vegas hesitated as he watched Tehera walk away. A hush fell over the room, each team member waiting for him to speak. The Major stepped before his team and Kiernan followed, standing beside Vegas with her hands clasped behind her back.

"Once we get to the Testing Station, we will split into two teams. Scout Jensen, Jilya, Ruben, Raziko and I will take material detail. Minister Kiernan, Xoren, Ziran, Jorca and Jax will take information." He began a slow pace around the team. "There was a time when we thought the toxic atmosphere on the barren lands was fatal, now we know better. The toxin bonded with our genetic makeup on a cellular level and…" he paused, "altered those who remained above ground. This is nothing new to you. However, more than ever we must exercise caution. The latest evidence confirms the scavengers are becoming more self-aware and less motivated by their prey drive. They are reproducing in vaster numbers. They are showing increasing intelligence. They are evolving. Two rotations ago we lost Scout Taura. We will not lose anybody else. Are there any questions?"

The room remained silent.

"Good; then let's get moving."

***

They left the facility through a previously unused lift. Again, Jensen was left wondering just how much more there was to the colony she was yet to see. She still hadn't discovered where the staircase led that she had seen outside the briefing room two rotations ago. Was it only two rotations ago? It felt like much more time had passed. So much had happened since then. Now a mechanical and well-maintained lift was transporting them to the planet's surface. Instead of intrigue, Jensen was instilled with a feeling of caution.

The lift rose slowly. Weighed down by its cargo, it made a steady ascent. The grinding of its gears working in well-timed synchronicity. The ascent was in complete darkness. None of this served to allay Kiernan's apprehension. Sitting beside Jensen in the very back passenger seats, she peered out of her side window and into darkness. Slowly, her vision cleared as a hatch at the top of the lift opened and a marginal shaft of light filtered into the lift. They had reached the planet's surface. The platform ceased moving.

Instantly, and driven by learned knowledge of the world in which they lived, Kiernan looked up at the sky. A toxic, swirling cloudbank churned above them. Amber clouds broken only by darker russet thunderheads that undulated within the upper atmosphere created almost deafening clashes as they collided in the sky. Kiernan flinched as the first clash of thunder ricocheted above them. Faintly, she heard the vehicle engines rev into life and the chatter of Jax and Jorca as they discussed the route ahead. Vegas had ordered that until they reach the Testing Station and break off into their separate groups, that they keep an open frequency between the teams to maintain a constant communication link.

Kiernan continued to look up at the sky. She was mesmerised. It was nothing like the images of history. Instead, it felt she was looking up into a bubbling cauldron of turmoil. Transfixed as she was, Kiernan never felt the vehicle begin to move until Jensen nudged her side. She blinked, bringing herself out of her fascination and back to her current surroundings. Jensen smiled to herself, aware of the sky's hypnotic draw. Sometimes, while scouting, even she would stop to watch. Occasionally she was almost convinced the sky was putting on a show just for her. In truth, the deadly billowing gasses had long since shrouded the planet from the sun. They halted the world's ability to begin healing itself. Jensen was still hopeful that was soon to change. If so, then maybe too would the ultimate agenda.

"It's frighteningly beautiful," Kiernan said.

Suddenly another two thunderheads collided above them. Kiernan jumped and then laughed. It would take her a little time to get used to the cacophony of sounds.

A flash of lightening streaked across the sky. Its forked fingers raking through the atmosphere and for a moment it lit up the land around them. Kiernan saw the skeletal remains of burnt trees and demolished shells of what may have once been residential homes. All gone. This part of the continent was incredibly lucky not to have been swallowed up by mass fractures in the land mass, but it did suffer horrifically from lava flows and the fires.

The vehicle jolted as it increased its speed. Kiernan held onto the seat in front of her. Like most of them, it was her first time in a motor vehicle. The experience was indeed unique. It occurred to Kiernan that, as taken as she was by the sights, sounds and new experiences, she had for a moment forgotten where she was. About the device secured to her head, aiding the inhalation of clean air and the goggles protecting her eyes. She didn't consider the horrific remains and burnt carcasses solidified to the ground. Forty-two cycles of her life, Kiernan had never seen the outside world. She felt a small measure of freedom wash over her, however tainted it was by the stark truth of their reality.

Another crash of thunder. Kiernan jumped again. She looked over at Jensen with an unseen scowl. "Do you ever get used to that?"

Jensen nodded, her expression unseen behind her protective headgear. "After so many cycles, yes. Believe me, if all we had to worry about was thunder and lightning my job would be a whole lot easier!" Jensen looked out of her window. They were moving north at a steady pace. She stared out at the land. They were still in familiar territory. Jensen recognised the landmarks, but she knew it would soon change. They were fast approaching unfamiliar terrain.

The vehicle hit a large stone and rocked to the side, swerving to miss a second, larger boulder. Its inhabitants bounced around like lifeless dolls. Jensen grabbed the seat in front of her. Scout Raziko was in that seat. She could see him studying his data console. The light from the screen reflecting on the vehicle's window.

Jensen had to admit to herself she was enjoying the unique experience of travelling at speed across the land. She looked behind her seeing the lights of the storage vehicle, but unable to see its occupants within. However, judging by the erratic movements of the lights she was certain they too were enjoying the same bumpy ride as they were. She held a little tighter. There was still a long way to go.

Beside Jensen, Kiernan leaned back in her seat. She closed her eyes, willing the rumble of the motor to lull her into a more relaxed state. It was a fruitless attempt. A thought occurred to her, and Kiernan re-opened her eyes. She nudged Jensen and the younger woman turned to her.

"Yes, Minister?" Jensen asked, aware all other members of the team could hear them, and presuming it was a question relating to the mission.

Although she too was aware of the open communication link, Kiernan asked, "I've read possibly all of your mission reports and accounts of the Barren lands." She couldn't see the surprised expression on Jensen's features. "But one thing occurs to me. Never did you offer much detail on the scavengers. Why is that?"

"You can't blame me for that, Minister. Writing these accounts can at times be tantamount to reliving the experience. To give too much mind to the scavengers has been known to cause a disruption to my sleep pattern." Jensen smiled unseen. She heard several of her fellow scouts laugh at her remark. Although she was making light of their situation, the truth was that they had been the cause of some horrifying sleep terrors. It had taken time for Jensen to construct her own way of dealing with the thoughts and dreams of the scavengers, so they didn't overcome her ability to conduct her job. As physician Angelus had advised, it was better for her psychological state to find a way to eradicate the thoughts from her mind. Advice she had followed in the way of meditation, cognitive re-training, and lots of reading. Mental fitness was just as important as physical fitness for all scouts. Jensen liked to believe she now excelled in both.

Kiernan understood, but her thoughts persisted due to a need to prepare herself for what lay ahead. "Could you tell me a little about them now?"

The request surprised Jensen, but she felt the need to assure Kiernan. "It isn't a wise course of action to discuss something that I'm sincerely hoping we will avoid on this mission. Why un-nerve yourself unnecessarily? There are times I can go as much as ten missions without the sight of a single scavenger. Even then, most times I can avoid them."

Kiernan was jostled in her seat, as the vehicle took a sharp left, avoiding an object in its path. It hit a ditch and both women held the seat in front, desperate for an anchor of stability.

"Close one there," Jax said with a nervous laugh. They heard Vegas laugh and murmur in agreement. The Major was seated next to him.

"Please, Scout, I need to know."

"Nothing can prepare you," Jensen advised, needing Kiernan to understand what she was asking.

If Kiernan could have delivered her most pleading expression she would have. However, hidden behind her headgear she could only say, "Please?"

At the front of the passenger vehicle, Vegas listened carefully. He looked up into a mirror, which afforded him a view of the vehicle's rear inhabitants. Although he could barely make out Jensen and Kiernan on the very back seats, he knew Jensen wouldn't be able to refuse Kiernan's request. If he was in Kiernan's position, he too would want to feel as fully prepared for their mission as possible. He also knew there was a reason the scouts never offered full disclosure when logging their information on the scavengers. Nothing could prepare you for an encounter.

Jensen released a sigh, realising Kiernan was adamant in her request and sincere in her desire to understand more about the environment they were entering. However much nobody liked to discuss them, she relented. "Tell me what you do know." Jensen felt her stomach clench and churn. It was a familiar sensation whenever she thought of the scavengers. Long ago she had learned to control the emotional reaction they provoked. However, unease always lingered in the background, just waiting to sneak upon her and unnerve her once more.

Kiernan looked away, her vision instead turning to the passing scenery, such as it was. "I know the scavengers are… I mean they were just like you and me once upon a time. In the beginning. They were survivors of the devastations who never made it to adequate safety or protection from the toxic fallout. How ironic that they survived the worldwide earthquakes, the fires, the missile attacks, but it was the toxicity of the air that did something far worse than a quick death ever could. Now they live a relatively basic existence but are forever changed."

Understatement, Jensen thought.

"What is most surprising is that they are still managing to reproduce!"

Jensen's thoughts drifted for a moment, as she recalled being pursued by an infant scavenger. Even one of such relatively low cycles, it was fully aware of its base instincts, it was strong, fast, and ferocious.

"The scavengers are at the top of the food chain, and we are their choice delicacy," Jensen said. "I don't know how. I don't know why. All I know is that they seem to be evolving in intellect and strength."

"How do they hunt?" Kiernan knew the basics of this, but she wanted to hear it from Jensen. To know a first-hand account by the scout who she admired for her descriptive, mission writing abilities.

"They are always in groups of at least two. Never alone. Almost like a pack mentality with a ferocious prey drive. The larger the group the more confident an attack they will make. There is still so much we don't know about them, even where they dwell. One thing I have noticed however, is that they have clan-like behaviours. I've seen a pack attack another pack, which I believe was from a different genus. For this reason, they will also survive eating one another if they are of a differing clan. We are still their prime choice of delicacy." Jensen thought for a moment. "I think our non-toxic flesh must taste pretty good."

Jensen tried to remain impassive, as images flooded her memory. Fighting for her life, kicking, and punching as a pack of two Scavengers attacked, one taking a bite out of her side. The searing pain, as blunt teeth tore into her flesh, ripping it from her body. Her scars healed, but the memories were still as fresh as when it happened. The pain simmered just below the surface. Jensen looked away, her gaze drifting to her view outside the window. A chill passed through her. "Just never look into their eyes."

"Why?" Kiernan asked with genuine curiosity. She could hear the haunted tone in Jensen's voice.

"Because their lack of emotion hits you right here," she placed two fingers on the side of Kiernan's head. "And here," the then moved them to the centre of her chest and tapped twice. "They're empty. Hollow. Void of any trace of emotion, empathy or anything that would have once made them a sentient being with the capability to love and feel compassion. They are gaining intelligence, but still have no ability to connect with another on any meaningful level. They seem to exist only to feed and fornicate. I can only surmise that all species keep the will to survive and reproduce."

Utterly shocked by Jennens words, and yet not surprised, Kiernan looked away. Her hand held the seat in front tighter. Her breathing quickened, as did the cadence of her heartbeat.

"How do you do it?"

The question was little more than a whisper. Although unsure herself whether it was a question or a statement, Jensen answered. "Because I believe in the Ultimate Agenda. I believe we deserve the chance to live our lives anew in a world away from here. Away from this world of devastation and death."

Kiernan looked down at her lap, and Jensen was confused by her behaviour.

"Don't you, Minister? You work at the heart of our agenda. Your work is one of the reasons we all live in hope." Jensen frowned as Kiernan didn't acknowledge her words. She placed her fingers under her headgear and turned the older woman back to face her. "Minister?"

Kiernan appeared to sag a little in her seat. However, she was extremely aware their conversation was not private. "I do believe; of course, I do. I work every rotation for our Ultimate Agenda." She thought for a moment. "But sometimes I fear it has taken so long that we will not see our plans reach fruition in our lifetime. I know it sounds a little selfish, and I really don't mean that to be the case. I guess like all scientists we wish to see the fulfilment of our work." It was a rebuff and Kiernan hoped Jensen would accept her explanation. She looked down the vehicle, positive she could see Vegas' eyes upon her from the front seat.

Jensen released Kiernan. "I try not to allow my thoughts to stray. 'We will fight with constant determination for our liberation'."

Hearing the Select Primes rehearsed and overused rhetoric, Kiernan nodded solemnly. She looked back out of the window. Another bolt of lightning lit up the sky, but Kiernan didn't flinch. She didn't notice. She pressed her head against the glass and stared out at the Barren lands as they passed. In the distance she could see the wind had picked up, increased in intensity. It lifted ash and debris off the ground, suspending it in the atmosphere. Kiernan watched the airstream rotate in swirling funnels across the land creating mini tornadoes as they caught rustic hues of light. The fascination she should have felt at the spectacle died within her. Jensen's words haunted her, and she was unable to express to the younger woman exactly why. Kiernan bit her lip, and let her head hit the window again with a light thud.

Outside the wind increased in it's ferocity. It pushed hard against the vehicles. Jensen heard Jax curse as he tried to keep their motor under control. Its wheels swerved and hit a large obstacle. The vehicle bounced violently causing the taller members of the team to hit their heads on its roof. It was Vegas' turn to curse, which quickly turned in an order for Jax to keep better control.

Jensen smirked to herself. She did like Major Vegas. Although occasionally gruff and somewhat stern, he had always been open and fair with her. He did have a short temper, but that she could understand as so did she at times. With a sigh, Jensen sunk down in her seat. The pack she brought with her was nestled between her legs on the floor. She took comfort in its presence, knowing everything she needed was contained within that pack. Every team member brought their own utility pack, but Jensen was convinced only hers held unsanctioned weaponry. She wrapped her legs a little tighter around the pack, trapping it between her calves. Kiernan noticed but remained silent.

CHAPTER 15

The team's journey continued with uneventful ease for another half a mark. Their vehicles fought valiantly over the land's harsh terrain, lightening supplying just enough brightness to illuminate the land around. They were halfway into their journey when rainfall began. Vegas looked out of the side window as he heard the tell-tale sounds of heavy droplets hitting the reinforced structure of their vehicle. His caution rose. With precipitation came the onslaught of more concentrated pollution.

"Officers Jax and Jorca, you are most informed on the land vehicles, what is the vulcanisation concentration of the wheels?"

Jensen listened carefully.

"Nothing to worry about, Major. The wheels are reinforced to four times the density. Not only should they last four times as long, but they are resistant to increased acidity and heat. In fact," Jax added, sounding impressed himself, "the whole vehicle's body has been coated with a high-density resilience treatment designed to withstand heavily polluted downpours."

"Impressive," Vegas replied, happy in the knowledge their vehicles would not fall prey to the land's hazardous conditions.

Jensen was impressed. She looked back at Kiernan to ask her a question but found her still staring out of the window. She hadn't spoken since their earlier conversation. Although she hadn't known Kiernan long at all, she knew this was a little out of character for the normally congenial woman. Jensen could just see her eyes staring into the distance, occasionally catching the flash from a bolt of lightning. Jensen tried not to stare, but she was once again confused by the enigma that was Minister Kiernan. She always seemed to leave her with more questions than answers. Jensen found herself compelled to figure her out. What was it that could so easily extinguish the light in her eyes? Always something balanced upon the tip of her tongue, which she never set free. Jensen wanted to speak and break the unwelcome air of tension that had unexpectedly risen in the cab. However, she remained silent.

***

Almost another mark had passed before Jensen felt the vehicle slow down and then stop completely. Pulling her attention from the window, Jensen looked towards the front of the vehicle where Vegas was speaking with Jax.

"What's our current location, Officer?"

"According to data readouts, Major, we're approximately sixteen furlongs away from our destination." Jax rubbed his hand over the windscreen to clear the view of the scene before them. He leaned forwards in his seat to gain a better view.

"Then why have we stopped?" Vegas looked in the rear-view mirror, seeing the storage vehicle flash its lights at them.

"*What's the situation*?" Jorca asked through their inter-communicator.

"Officer?" Vegas pushed.

"Major, there is a high-density rubble field ahead." He moved the vehicle several paces forward to bring their barrier into view and then activated the vehicle's overhead beams. A high field of rubble stretched out in both directions, disappearing into the distance. "Our low range sonar suggests it stretches at least four furlongs in either direction, Major. There's no telling how long this rubble field is, but what I can say with absolute certainty is that-"

"It's too precarious for us to drive over," Vegas finished for Jax with an emphatic sigh. "Damn it." He slammed the side of his fist on the dashboard and then looked back into the vehicle. "Ideas people?"

"We have two vehicles," Jilya said. "We could drive out in opposite directions for as far as we can stay in communication range and see if either of us can find either a beginning, an end or even a break in the barrier."

"It's an option," Vegas said.

Jensen leaned forwards, peering through the seats. "Major, for the purpose of this mission I find it advisable and advantageous that we stay together."

"I concur," Raziko agreed.

"Ideas?"

Kiernan broke her silence. She looked down at her data console. "As Jax states, we are no more than sixteen furlongs away from our destination. I believe we should try to make our way over the barrier on foot. The incline isn't too severe."

"That is far too dangerous," Ruben said in alarm. "There must be a way through. We must at least try."

"Time is a priority, Scout Ruben," the Major looked to the other members present in the vehicle.

"I agree with Kiernan," Jensen said. "Straight over. No messing."

Vegas took a breath. "Officer Jorca and team, any suggestions?"

It was Xoren who responded. "*I'm all for staying together, but climbing over that barrier shouldn't be our first choice. We should at least try to find a through-way. If the sonar is unable to find a break in the debris at four furlongs, maybe we should extend a manual search to eight furlongs together. We keep strength in numbers, and we gain a greater opportunity of finding safe passage.*"

Vegas stared out at the mess before them. Rock, metal, and many other varieties of melted compositions formed the convoluted mass before them.

"Alright. We will travel for eight furlongs left and if unsuccessful we will travel back. We will then repeat the procedure to the right. If we have no luck, we will traverse the debris on foot. That is all the time we can allow." Vegas turned back in his seat and looked at the sonar readout. "Eight furlongs, Officer Jax, and direct the roof beams to the debris. Take a steady route, I'll keep an eye on the readouts. Team, all eyes on the barrier. If there is a break in the rubble, I want it found."

Taking the journey together, both vehicles took a right turning. They began a slow drive along the side of the barrier, their journey hampered by loose rubble littering their path. After a journey of almost nine furlongs, Vegas ordered they head back and try the left. Jensen felt the first stirrings of frustration hit. Just a few moments more and they might have found a route through the debris. They might have. They turned and all the team members continued to watch the barrier as they headed back to their original destination.

"Let's try the left side," Vegas said. This time they pushed their search to an optimistic ten furlongs, with no success. Deflated, Vegas ordered they retreat. "We need to progress forward and not side to side," he said in an exasperated voice. Enough time had been wasted.

Reaching their starting point, both vehicles slowed to a halt and disengaged the engines. There was a moment of silence before Vegas spoke to all members of Operation Hypogean.

"Team… fate it appears, dictates we travel the remainder of our journey on foot. Minister Kiernan, approximately how long do you calculate it will take to reach the compound?"

Kiernan stared down at her console, her fingers flying rapidly over the illuminated screen. "We could make it in a mark, not counting the climb over the debris."

"*Major, we won't be able to retrieve all viable materials*," Xoren protested over their inter-communicator.

"Unforeseen circumstances dictate we change our plans, Advisor Xoren." He looked out of his window to the storage vehicle parked next to them. Vegas could just make out Xoren's silhouette in the passenger seat. "We will collect all we can."

There was no reply.

"Let's move."

The team began collecting their equipment. Jensen turned to Kiernan. She took her arm gently. "Are you ready, Minister?"

"Of course," Kiernan answered with bravado. The slight tremor in her voice was not lost on Jensen.

"Hmm," the younger woman said, as she took the pack from between her calves. "Just think of it as a routine mission. Nothing to be worried about." Jensen paused and thought for a moment. All the tomes she had read. All the multi-syllabic words she had digested to educate herself further, to sound more learned, and she fell short when she needed eloquence the most. There was nothing she could say to reassure Kiernan. In her experience of the Barren lands, Jensen could testify that true horror could come in many forms and was often just around the corner. She wondered again what was so important that Commander Tehera believed only Minister Kiernan was cleared for its retrieval. Demands for answers would be ineffectual, she knew that, and so with a sigh Jensen grasped her pack and waited to exit the vehicle. It wasn't long before its door swung open, and the team disembarked.

Kiernan looked up at the sky in awe. She was relieved the rain had stopped. What transfixed her were the toxic cloudbanks swirling chaotically within the atmosphere. Accompanied by a roaring wind, thunderheads massed and collided, creating shattering clashes above them. Kiernan found herself jumping again, the magnitude of its cacophony all that more terrifying when standing directly under the thunderheads. And the force of the tempest! Kiernan had to stand with her legs a good distance apart to sturdy herself against its merciless force.

She was mesmerised by the colours. The density of the cloudbanks revealed their toxicity. The darker and rustier the hues, the denser the concentration of toxic gasses. Kiernan rubbed her gloved fingers over her goggles, removing ash and dust from her vision. She took a small torch Scout Ruben handed to her and attached it to the right side of her head gear. She didn't activate the beam, knowing it could stretch far beyond their meeting point. Luckily, the torch light could be controlled to a level of distance. A function which was much needed in areas where one didn't want to alert any form of unwanted attention.

The team closed in around Vegas as he began to speak. The use of their inter-communicator, placed in their ears, vital over the howling tempest.

"Stay close. Follow single file up the debris. One of our most experienced climbers will take point. Plan is up and over as expeditiously as possible. Our aim is to reach the facility within a total of two marks." Vegas still found himself shouting to be heard over the storm. He stepped forward, bringing his team into a close huddle. "Stay tight. Keep illumination to a minimum if you are to the rear. Scouts, you know what to look for. High alert. We are in unknown territory."

Jensen nodded in darkness. It truly was a journey into the unknown and with that came many added pitfalls. Being their most experienced in climbing, she knew she was to take point. Finding the safest route over the rubble was her task.

Within the centre of the huddle Kiernan stared down at her console. She was calculating the most direct route to the underground facility. She would then transfer the co-ordinates to Jensen, who would use the information to create an avenue in which to traverse the distance efficiently. She wiped dust away from her goggles again as the console ran programmed calculations. Within moments a direct route was illuminated upon the screen. She sent the data to Jensen and Vegas.

The Major finished strapping a pack to his back. He then attached a baton to his waist before assuring the rest of the team were equipped and ready. Jensen held a tonfa in each hand. She slipped one either side of her waist belt. The weapons she traded with Flick would stay within easy access to one side of her backpack. Their presence on this mission would not be revealed unless needed.

Jensen looked over at Kiernan. She watched as the Major handed her a baton and wondered if the Minister had been trained to use the weapon. Maybe it didn't matter. She intended to make sure Kiernan took one of her stealthily procured firearms. Not that any of them had training in the usage of such things, but how hard could it be to point and shoot? Hope for the best? The odds still had to be better than fighting up close, using only a blunt object as a means of defence; right?

"Scout Jensen's taking point. I will bring up the rear. Keep close everybody."

The tempest continued to increase in ferocity, and Kiernan found she had to angle her body into the gusts to remain upright. Its force was unlike anything she had experienced. The intensity almost overpowering. Almost. Kiernan had never felt anything more than a gentle draft from the R.A.P.s in the colony. The biting wind surged in ferocity.

Jensen made her way to the head of the group. Her dark eyes scanned the high debris barrier, silently calculating areas for safe footing. She had turned her torch to a narrow beam and studied the shaft of artificial light up the rubble as a pathway began to form in her mind.

"Here," she shouted, pointing to a previously molten block of metal. "We start here." Jensen placed her foot on a solid block, "Perfect," she whispered to herself.

A strong blast of wind blew from the west as a clash of thunder resounded above them. Jensen reached out, bracing her hand on a large rock to keep balance. She hoped the rain wouldn't return. Finding her next step, Jensen pulled herself further up the barrier. Their ascent had begun. For small sections of the journey, Jensen found they would be able to walk, other areas they would need their hands and feet. It would be a difficult undertaking.

"Follow my route," she called back to the team and received several voices of acknowledgement through her earpiece.

They started slowly. One by one the team followed the same path behind Jensen. She took her time, carefully judging each step. One miscalculation could result in a painful fall, not just for her, but for those behind as well. The further up the barrier the more devastating that fall would become.

The tempest raged on. Howling against them like a sentient being intent upon their failure. It was a slow process, but Jensen judged each step with a well-practiced eye. She'd spent many a mark climbing in and out, up, and down obstacles. This was easy. Her greatest foe was the persistent gales.

Within half a mark Jensen could see the summit. She felt a trickle of relief flood through her knowing they were at least halfway through the task. Jensen took another step and found purchase of a boulder which enabled her to pull herself to the summit. The wind felt stronger, and Jensen held tight to whatever she could to aid her balance.

"Careful people, the wind is strong up here!" She looked down at the train of climbers behind her. Scout Ruben was next, followed by Kiernan and then officer Jax, Kiernan's appointed personal guard.

As Ruben reached the summit Jensen moved over. The plateau was reasonably level and wide enough for the full ten team members to ascend in safety. He looked around them. "What was this?" he asked in wonder. "What could have created this wall of debris?"

"The facility was built near a large city of commerce," Kiernan said as she reached the summit. Her breathing laboured; she could feel sweat trickle down her forehead. Unable to wipe it away, she tried to ignore its irritating tickle down her skin. Kiernan placed her hands upon her hips as she looked out across the rubble. "I can, of course, only surmise that a directional blast angle caused an entire city to be reduced to such an unexpected formation."

Jorca appeared behind Kiernan. Her face contorted in disgust. "I saw three skulls as I climbed this."

"Only three?" Jensen asked. "Keep looking, Jorca, there's plenty more to be seen." She walked over to the other side of the debris and looked down. "You're wiping more off your goggles as we speak."

Jorca pulled her hands from her face and looked down at the dust covering her fingers. "What the…" she shook her hands aggressively and then wiped them upon her legs.

Jensen turned away from her, deciding now wasn't the ideal time to begin a conversation on respecting the land and the millions of people who had died at the hands of a heartless dictator's deeds. They had all learned about the planet's history in their schooling, about the arrogance of a continent and its leader's single-minded plans.

Jensen peered back over the summit and began her search for a safe route down. She couldn't see the ground below but didn't want to extend her torch beam to locate it. The darkness held too many unwelcome surprises. Caution. Always.

The team finished reaching the debris summit and Jensen sensed somebody behind her. It was Vegas.

"Thoughts?"

"Just the same, but the wind and slope angle will make for a more hazardous descent."

"Was it too much to hope for an easier decline," Vegas' voice boomed over the roar of the wind. "Lead the way, Scout."

"Sir." Jensen twisted her body around, angling herself into the slope. She began her decent. She was only two steps down when she felt her foot slip off a loose block of rubble. Jensen felt herself begin to fall, her body hitting the rocks and metal as she slid down the debris. She reached out, desperate to find something, anything to grasp onto. A sharp pain jarred her thigh, but she blindly grasped onto an unseen anchor and her body stilled. She found safety. Jensen sunk her fingers deeply into the source of stability, as she cautiously regained her footing. She took a breath. Her heartrate returned to normal. Jensen looked up, surprised to see nobody had witnessed her stumble. With a small shake of her head, Jensen pulled her body tighter into the debris and looked to where her hand had found stability. Her fingers were firmly embedded into the eye sockets of a skull encapsulated into the rubble.

"Damn it," she muttered, feeling the need to swiftly remove her digits respectfully from the charred remnants and onto a more nondescript part of concrete and congealed polyvinyl.

Her progress was slow, fighting against both wind and gravity. The tempest ever vengeful from a world intent on revenge. Jensen felt something sharp slice through her thick gloves and into her flesh. The warmth of fresh blood ticked down her fingers.

"Careful," she called, "exposed sharps."

Several voices responded.

"*Got it.*"

"*Understood.*"

Jensen looked up and saw Rubens left foot searching blindly for sturdy footing. She reached up and grasped his boot, directing it to a solid juncture.

"Thanks Jen," she heard him say.

Jensen's nod was unseen as she continued her careful descent. Hampered by the gales, Jensen was at least glad it was what had once been termed 'the light marks'. Although there was no sun to brighten up the land, there was a degree of illumination in the amber hues of the dense cloudbanks.

Feeling the slope even out, Jensen looked down and found she had reached the bottom. Palpable relief flooded through her. She stepped back, allowing Ruben to follow. Reaching even ground filled Jensen with an unexpected sense of accomplishment. She looked around, feeling as though they had entered a new land. Nothing was familiar. No landmark stood out as a clue to her location anymore. Jensen looked to her left; in the distance she could just see what she believed may have once been a forest. Nothing remained but charred stumps. However, she had seen enough remains of trees to form a well-educated guess.

Voices interrupted her observation and Jensen turned to see the remaining team members reach level ground. Kiernan was once again checking the information on her data console. Vegas stood behind her and all eyes turned to the two awaiting their next instruction. She could see Kiernan wordlessly point to the screen and Vegas nod in agreement. He looked up at the team, pointing two fingers in the direction they were to begin. This time Advisor Xoren took point and begin leading the way towards the Testing Station. Torch illumination was kept to a minimum, not allowing the beams to stretch more than six steps ahead. The direction of their location rested solely upon the data calculated by Kiernan alone. Ultimate care was taken on the unfamiliar terrain. Their journey lasted almost a mark before Jensen felt a hand upon her shoulder. She never turned. Recognising the touch, she waited for Kiernan to reach her side.

"Does it ever change?" she asked.

Understanding what Kiernan was asking, Jensen said, "Sometimes. The storms are almost always constant, but on an exceedingly rare occasion I have witnessed a moment of calm. Surreal is it seems at the time, it's beautiful to see. I -" Jensen paused. Did she see movement in the distance?

"What is it?"

Shaking her head, Jensen sped up her pace. "Nothing… maybe. We need to keep moving, Minister."

They continued trudging through the winds. The scouts unsheathed their batons, unsettled by Jensen's words. Jensen too had unsheathed her tonfa, strong hands gripping the lumber tightly. She felt the dried blood from her wounded fingers crack and fresh blood seep from the cuts.

Another fraction of a mark and Jensen stopped behind Xoren. Kiernan looked down at her console.

"Report," Vegas boomed, as he made his way towards the head of the team.

"According to the data we should be here," Kiernan said with relief.

"Good," Vegas released a sigh, as relieved as the rest of the team. "Now we need to locate the entrance."

Daring her next move, Jensen increased the lambency of her torch light. She shone the beam around them, illuminating the team members one by one. Jensen moved in a slow rotation to the left. As Xoren came into view, so did the crumbled, blistered remains of a building behind him.

"There," she said. "I think that could be a-," Jensen froze as her torchlight caught a familiar and terrifying vision in the darkness.

CHAPTER 16

Jensen felt a tight grip around her left arm.

"What was that?" Kiernan said, alarm clear.

Jensen deactivated her touch light, as she ordered the other team members to do the same. She looked at Kiernan, and then to Major Vegas who appeared by her side. There was no doubt in her mind what she had just seen. Vegas' sudden appearance told her he too had seen what they had. He un-sheathed his baton.

"Where's the entrance?" The urgency in his voice spurred Kiernan to look down at her console and retrieve the data rapidly.

"I… I don't know. We're here, but…" Kiernan paused, as she tried to calm her nerves. They were so close, but the land was growing darker. Her fingers trembled as she urgently scrolled through the data. "Come on… come on!"

Jensen's grip tightened around her tonfa. She scanned their surroundings. Frustration coiled within her stomach. They wouldn't just attack. The Scavengers were too smart for that. She spotted only two possible attackers; against ten, the odds were not in their favour, they were outnumbered. Fortunately, Jensen knew to take no chances. In a gut reaction she turned her torch back on.

"What are you doing?" Several of the team shouted in unison, including Kiernan and Vegas.

"Preventing the summoning of re-enforcements," Jensen said, as she examined the visible remnants of the building. She increased the reach of her torch and swept it over the structure. Windswept debris floated past, obscuring her view.

"Come on!" Jorca yelled.

"Feel free to take over," Jensen replied calmly, but ignored her retort. She saw them again. Eyes. Two sets of eyes glowing in her torch light. Deep amber. A vision that haunted her slumber.

The glowing eyes moved out of view and Jensen followed them with her torchlight. One set of eyes re-emerged in the darkness and then just as quickly they disappeared.

"There you are," she whispered. With a tighter grip around her tonfa, Jensen called for Jilya and Ruben to back her up as she sprinted towards those emotionless, amber eyes.

"What is she doing?" Kiernan screamed. Her heart hammering out a rapid beat.

Vegas watched as Scouts Jilya and Ruben sprinted past him and disappeared into the darkness. "She's making sure they don't alert back-up of our presence," Vegas said. He looked back at Kiernan and pointed to the console. "The location of the entrance, Kiernan. Now!"

Kiernan trembled. She looked out into the darkness. The ebony veil surrounded her, obstructing their view almost completely. The sporadic and chaotic dancing of Jensen's torch light was all they could see. The wind howled, the sky churned and crashed. Feeling the urgency, Kiernan looked back at the data before her.

Suddenly, from out of the darkness, there was an ear-piercing scream. It echoed over the storm.

Vegas grabbed Kiernan's shoulder. He held her firmly. "The entrance. NOW!"

***

It was that cry, that soul tormenting, shrieking battle cry that haunted Jensen's dreams. The scavengers didn't speak. Not a word passed their lips, but that screeching howl was their prelude to attack. Even as the sound met her ears, and she saw amber eyes charging towards her, Jensen knew once again that howl of attack would haunt her for rotations to come.

Sensing Jilya and Ruben flank her position, Jensen stood her ground. She gripped her tonfa impossibly tighter. Her knuckles protruding through the material of her gloves. The scavengers approached rapidly. Jensen swung out, hitting one soundly across the face. The fight was on. Her impact did little more than knock the scavenger off balance. It staggered to her left. Jensen sensed Ruben close in beside her, and then kick out, connecting with the second scavenger and pushing it away from Jilya. Jensen swiftly adjusted her head torch to a wide beam. She found the first scavenger. Its amber eyes shone in her torch light, its grim mouth hanging open wide, exposing broken, blunt teeth; its pallid, grey flesh cracked and broken with seeping fissures. Jensen lifted her tonfa again and swung hard, but it dodged her attack. The force of her blow caused Jensen to stagger forward. She recovered quickly and hit out again. Another solid hit, which was followed by a gasp as the scavenger tried to pull her towards teeth that ached to sink into her flesh. Jensen dropped quickly, falling, and taking it with her. She lifted her leg, and using the momentum of the fall, she pushed the scavenger over her head.

Beside her Ruben delivered another solid kick to the second scavenger's face. It fell to the ground. Jensen jumped to her feet in time to see Jilya fall to his knees behind the first scavenger. He took its head in his hands and twisted firmly. If not for the howling wind they would have heard their foe's neck crack soundly. Her relief was short as she turned to see Ruben trading blows with the second scavenger. It knocked each of his punches away with gnarled, bony hands. She watched, waiting for an opportune moment to dive into the fray.

Ruben took two steps backwards and kicked out again. The scavenger was propelled backwards, and Jensen took her chance. She ran forward, using her weight to knock the scavenger to the ground. As she loomed above it, staring into emotionless amber eyes, Jensen was momentarily frozen by the lack of sentience staring back at her. That moment was all it needed to throw Jensen off and roll away. The impact, as her head hit the ground, jolted Jensen's torch and she was plunged into darkness.

"Jen!" she heard Jilya shout though the turbulent darkness.

She saw Ruben silhouetted as he activated and widened the beam of his head torch. He directed his beam to their opponent. Jensen and Jilya ran towards it. It was Jilya who reached it first, dodging grasping, wild hands as he wrapped his arms around its waist and used his forward running force to knock it to the ground. Jilya rapidly twisted his body around and forced his booted foot under the scavenger's chin to push it firmly backwards. It was a well-practiced move that scouts used to take down a scavenger. He wrapped his arms around its frantically scrambling legs. In an instant, Jensen was beside them, and from the corner of his vision, Jilya saw Jensen pull back her tonfa and swing with full force. The solid timber collided with the scavenger's head. Its force was enough to sever the scavenger's spine and deliver a killing blow.

With heavy breath, Jensen stared down at lifeless pools of amber. She watched as the colour drained away and darkness shadowed the once glowing orbs. Its expression no different to when it was alive. Her hand twitched, fighting the instance to hit out repeatedly. It was dead. The force of her blow made with practiced precision.

"What the…" Jilya jumped off the body. He was by Jensen's side in an instant. "That was slick!"

Ruben rushed forwards, blinding them both with his torch light. They shielded their eyes as he adjusted the beam. When Jensen was bathed in a softer glow, he slapped her back roughly.

"Good blow, Jen."

The scouts took little time to recover from the battle as they ran back to the team. The scavengers had been brought down, but there was no way to know if more were in the vicinity. As such it was not safe to stay away too long. They needed to get off the Barrens as expeditiously as possible. The question was, had Kiernan found the entrance?

***

The Minister in question looked up as she sensed more than heard the scouts approach. Vegas was leading them toward the upper entrance to the station. She hadn't had a chance to calculate its exact coordinates before Xoren had located the entrance point. Much to Vegas' relief, the team was removing a pile of bricks and concrete to gain access. Kiernan was relieved to see all three scouts return safely. They'd all heard the fight, even with the clashes of thunder and obfuscating darkness.

"They've found the entrance?" Jilya was relieved.

Kiernan nodded. She felt a little helpless having been placed between two crumbling walls to remain safe and relatively out of sight. Their encounter with the scavengers had shaken her more than she wanted to admit. Kiernan had never wanted any preferential treatment. She wanted to be treated like every other member of the team. However, seeing those soulless amber eyes glow in the darkness had chilled her more than she expected. At least there were only two, she had told herself. Her attention turned back to the clearing of the entrance, willing them to complete the task. If she was positive Vegas wouldn't order her back to safety, she would join them in their endeavour.

"Damned with it," she muttered, and she stalked out to help regardless.

Jensen stood before the entrance, watching her team clear heavy rocks. Vegas stood behind her.

"Good job, Scout. The threats were soundly eliminated?"

"Yes, Sir." Jensen didn't turn to look at Vegas. She concentrated solely upon watching the rest of the team, as she tried to regain her emotions. To her right, Ruben was in a similar state. He stood looking into the distance. His adrenalin simmering, he found he was unable to release the tension from their fight. He stayed in a state of high alert.

"Take a moment and then join the team. Time is against us. We need entrance into the station. We're losing sunlit marks."

Darkness wasn't their ally, that she knew. "Yes, Sir," she responded hollowly. Jensen wondered if Vegas had forgotten the feeling. That empty, harrowing sensation one experienced after an encounter with a scavenger. She closed her eyes, but her mind's eye conjured up the image. Vacant amber eyes, skin stretched taut over bony features, and the stench! Open fissures scattered the ashen skin, oozing pungent puss. Jensen felt bile burn the back of her throat, and she swallowed thickly. She could still smell it. The fetor clung to her like it had penetrated the fibres of her clothing. Jensen swallowed again. Her mouth filled with saliva, as she felt her stomach drop. She willed herself not to react. Breathing apparatus were not ideal when the contents of one's stomach needed release. Jensen took deep even breaths. I am calm. We are safe. Think of the mission.

"Ready to go?" Vegas asked, once again surprising Jensen as he appeared by her side.

Without a word, Jensen nodded. The rubble had been cleared from the station entrance and the team were ready to enter. Upon first seeing the building Jensen was surprised to see it was still in a semi-standing state. She presumed being a military facility that it was constructed to reinforce the structure from possible attack. There was no roof, but walls remained, and a door that must have been constructed of high-strength metallic ore still clung to its hinges. The team had cleared the rocks away and the door was open. From outside, the building appeared to be a simple shop front. Jensen wondered what lay within, and what the establishment had once sold. It couldn't have been the station's only entrance or exit, but it was the only access they had been able to uncover with their limited supply of data.

The team entered and passed through three large rooms. The walls were still partially standing, but barely stable. The sky was visible above them. Xoren led the way, directing the team to an elevator shaft near the middle of the building. It took no time at all for them to remove the sheet plating covering the shaft.

Vegas peered down, seeing what he believed to be the elevator at the bottom of the vertical drop. He nodded to Jensen.

"Sir." Jensen investigated the shaft, seeing metallic rungs attached to one side of the wall. She slipped into the duct and began to traverse her way down the makeshift ladder. She was impressed at how well it had stood the passage of time. Within a fraction of a mark, she had reached the bottom. Jensen turned her torch to full illumination and looked around. She had passed straight into the elevator cabin and stood facing a set of closed double doors.

Ziran appeared beside her. “You have a wedging tool?”

Jensen was already pulling the tool out of her pack. She waved it at Ziran before jamming it between the metallic plated doors.

“I’m going to need extra force with this,” she said, and moved a little for Ziran to help. Together they prised the doors open. A gush of air rushed past them as the barriers parted.

“First time in almost one hundred cycles,” Ziran noted, in his trademark deep voice. Ziran was a mountain of a man, half as wide as he was tall, with hands like shovels and the strength of two scouts. His speciality was engineering. When upon the barrens, it was his job to check and repair the above ground motors and venting systems that helped to keep the colony running. Unfortunately, Ziran’s size made him a little on the clumsy side, and as such hand-to-hand combat was not his forte.

They investigated the dark corridor ahead, almost able to see the stagnant atmosphere fizzle into life. Specs of dust floated in the torchlight. Ziran stretched out between the doors to hold them open. “What can we use?”

“Hmm.” Jensen looked quickly to the floor, finding pieces of broken alloy. She used them as wedges, and jammed them into the bottom of the doors, holding them open. “How is that?”

Ziran moved his arms. The doors remained open. “Perfect.” He stepped out into the dark corridor.

Kiernan appeared next and stood beside Jensen. For the first time in marks, she felt relative calm. Gone were the sounds of howling winds and crashing thunderheads. Her ears adjusted to the silence. “I almost forgot what it was like to hear my own voice,” she said, her volume still too loud in the muted atmosphere.

Jensen smiled but said nothing as she allowed Kiernan to step into the passageway. She followed closely behind as Jorca was next down the shaft. She needed to keep the space clear.

Re-adjusting her goggles to her forehead, Jensen rubbed her eyes with a sigh of relief. “That feels so good.” She looked around the hallway. Although illuminated by torchlight alone, she could see the walls were still reasonably well preserved. At one point they would have been a brilliant polished, colourless brick. Ziran was reading a plaque attached to one wall, and Jensen added her torchlight to the illumination.

"Well, that's handy," Kiernan commented. She ran her finger over the information contained upon the plaque. "Look here, this shows the location of a back-up generator. We might be able to get this started and get some power with an adapted power cell."

"Possible," Ziran said.

"Excellent idea," Xoren agreed, as he entered the hall. "Where is it?" He pulled a power cell from its protective casing. "Dependent on the systems used, this should be able to give us a few marks of energy."

Jensen carefully took the cell from Xoren's grasp and held it up to her torchlight. "Can this really give so much power? Who created this?"

Xoren inclined his head and nodded in Kiernan's direction.

She looked to Kiernan in surprise. "You?"

"Why are you so shocked by that, Scout?"

Not sure if she detected an air of defensiveness in Kiernan's response, Jensen was quick to say, "Not shock, Minister, I'm impressed and in awe if I'm honest. How did you… I mean… how?"

"Long story. I'll tell you about it at some point," Kiernan said. She momentarily recalled her original work creating the energy cells and the first explosion that nearly ended her life. It took her some time to stabilise the power outage and create the power cells. Jensen didn't know their primary usage.

"So, this will work," Vegas asked. He had been listening to their conversation on the inter-communicator.

"Ancient generators worked on fossil fuel," Xoren said. "If this is a fossil fuel generator, we won't be able to adapt the cell. However, if it's one of its more modern counterparts we will be able to bypass the conduits for conversion of the solar or wind and adapt the cell into the generator's conversion matrix."

"My head hurts," Jorca whispered to Jax.

"Does your face hurt too?"

Jorca frowned. "No why?"

"Because it's killing me," Jax jumped to the side as a fist marginally missed his midsection.

Kiernan looked back at the location plaque. She ran her finger over the image. "Looking at this; we're not far from the generator room. Down the corridor, second right, first left and two more rights."

Vegas watched the remaining team members enter the passageway. More torchlight illuminated the narrow space. "Good. Hoping we get power; we will then split into our teams and conduct our directives. Understood?"

His response was a wave of nods.

"Then let's get started."

Multiple beams of illumination lit up their path. The team started its journey towards the generator's location in silence. Having programmed the location into her console Kiernan led the way. Jensen peered over her shoulder studying the screen's information with interest.

"Why is your console bigger than mine?" she asked, as she noticed the screen was twice as big as hers. A fact she had only just realised.

"Jealous, Scout?"

"Curious."

"I like to read; this makes it easier to access not only reports but a vast database of tomes."

Jensen stopped in her tracks, causing Jorca to walk right into her.

"Watch it," Jorca complained, "People walking."

"Excuse me?" Jensen said, ignoring the officer. She jogged back to catch up with Kiernan. "Tomes? Tomes as in fictional tales? As in-"

"Yes," Kiernan laughed. "Tomes, Scout Jensen. Fiction. Non-fiction. Whatever one cares to enjoy."

"Hmm!" Jensen's mind slipped into overdrive.

Raziko adjusted his face mask, as a thought occurred to him. He pulled a small rectangular device from his chest pocket and activated it via a small switch to its side. Three lights flashed and a series of short beeps began. Raziko stopped walking, not noticing Jax brush past him as he stared down at the atmospheric contaminant register. Each light changed to a distinct colour and then flashed. "Major!"

Vegas turned to Raziko.

"Look," he said and held the A.C.R up for Vegas to inspect. I've never seen this before, Major."

Vegas took the information from Raziko and looked down at the results in confusion. "Kiernan," he called. "You're a scientist…"

"Perceptive as always," Kiernan said with a smile. "Are you making a statement or," she was struck dumb as she too stared at the data read out in confusion.

"Can you identify these compounds on the A.C.R readout?"

Jensen was behind Kiernan in an instant. "What the…"

Kiernan took the A.C.R from Raziko and scanned the data. "That can't be." She read a little further and then looked up at Vegas. "Good news is that the air is breathable."

"Yes!" Jorca pulled the apparatus from her face.

"But that data confirms evidence of a decaying poison."

The breathing apparatus that moments before had been removed from Jorca's face flew back so fast she hit her nose in the process. "Ouch, damn it."

"Slick" Jax commented.

Vegas gave the pair a side glance. "Continue please, Kiernan."

"The air **is** breathable," Kiernan stressed, "But there are traces of a deadly neurotoxin still present. It's degraded now. It isn't harmful in the slightest, however its presence is highly unusual."

"Why," Jensen asked, as she too removed her breathing equipment along with the rest of the team, Kiernan included.

"Amphibulartoxin, a hundred cycles ago, was a deadly neurotoxin with no known treatment. What it's doing here is confounding."

Looking up from the task of securing her facemask to her belt, Jensen asked, "Any speculation as to why it would be here?"

They began walking again, Jilya using Kiernan's console to lead the way.

"Speculation is all I could offer, Scout."

"Speculate away, Minister," Xoren said, who had been silently listening to their conversation.

"My only guess could be that… it's a horrendous notion… we would need proof, but…"

"We're here." Jilya announced.

"This is it; the generator room." Kiernan stopped by the door and tapped its keypad enthusiastically.

Vegas laughed. "No power, Kiernan." He received a look that removed the smile from his face. "Prizing tool anybody?"

Raziko offered up the bar they had used earlier. Vegas wedged it into the doors and, along with Raziko, they prized them open. Another rush of air blasted through, as the barrier parted and slid into the walls. Ziran took over and slid down one side of the doorway until he was sitting upon the floor. He used his frame to hold the doors open; his back and booted foot keeping them apart.

"Make it quick before my butt goes numb."

Vegas stepped over him, followed by Kiernan, Xoren, Jensen and Raziko. Raziko looked around the room. He enhanced his torch light to maximum illumination. With the increased light Jensen looked around. The room wasn't large. In the centre was the generator, which dominated most of the space. Around it stood metallic shelving housing a varied array of items from tools to spare parts. Raziko circled the generator and studied it closely. As the engineer of the team, it was his job to test power conversion of the antiquated machinery. Xoren would help.

"Think you can work with this?" Vegas asked hopefully. They needed power to gain full access to the facility.

Raziko knelt to study the machine closer. Strands of dark hair fell into his eyes, and he pushed them away. "Quietly confident, Major." He looked around the room. "I might need some of these old tools." He opened his pack and routed within, "but let's see what I have first."

Jensen looked to a narrow side door. It wasn't easily visible due to being a similar colour to the walls. She moved her hand in a sweeping gesture towards the barrier. Always enthusiastic to discover something new, "Shall we?"

Kiernan rolled her eyes but smiled. She pulled the door open. They both peered into the darkness. Standing behind Kiernan, Jensen directed her torch beam into the cupboard. The Minister was comforted by her presence. They were finally away from the Barrens. Kiernan felt calmer. At least for now. Her only lingering concern was the journey back. It sat in the back of her mind and infiltrated her thoughts when she least expected. She was disconcerted to realise it wasn't fear of what lay in wait for them that instilled those concerns, but the possibility of those eventualities. With some of her closest allies and blossoming new allies, Kiernan recognised the prospect of loss. For the first time, she understood the risks, terror, and heartache a scout must endure. Her respect for Jensen, for all scouts, grew.

Jensen looked around at what was apparently a storage cupboard. She pushed the backpack down her arms and dropped it to the floor. The room was square and no wider than her height. It was lined with shelves against the walls. Jensen was excited. This was the closest she'd ever gotten to rummaging through artefacts from their past. The possibility of what she may find thrilled her. Maybe a tome, maybe a piece of technology? She stepped closer to a shelf holding a sturdy card box and pulled it towards her. She peered inside. Kiernan was beside her, curious to know the contents.

"Would you look at that?" Kiernan reached inside and pulled out a ceramic container. "This was for hot liquids." She studied the picture of a bright animated figure.

Jensen reached inside the box herself and pulled out a stack of glossy papers bound together in such a way that they resembled narrow tome. They were, however, much larger than a tome. Jensen directed her torchlight to the top cover and gulped. She dropped them back into the box.

"What is it?" Kiernan asked.

Jensen shook her head. "Nothing," she lied, feeling a blush creep up her neck and cover her cheeks. Thankful she was still shadowed in enough darkness for her embarrassment not to be noticed. She peered innocently at the next row of boxes, as she pushed the current box back on its shelf.

Kiernan directed her torchlight onto Jensen's face and noted her russet-coloured cheeks. "Scout Jensen, may I remind you that subterfuge doesn't work on me. I may not have known you long at all, but I'd say dilated pupils and flushed cheeks shows you are trying to hide something." She narrowed her eyes. "Out with it."

Jensen glared at Kiernan for a moment before pulling the box back out and retrieving the contents. Kiernan looked down at the glossy stack of papers. Her eyes bloomed in shock.

"Oh… I… I." Feeling the tables had turned, Kiernan felt her own cheeks flush with embarrassment. She knew this existed back before the devastations, but she never thought she would see such a thing. Kiernan heard a snigger from the woman beside her. "You could have warned me."

This time the chuckle crept past Jensen's lips. "What was that about flushed cheeks, Minister?"

Kiernan knocked the torchlight from her face. "I knew items like this existed. I'd read the archives. I never expected to see such a thing. It wasn't exactly included in the history lessons during schooling!" Kiernan pulled the dirty magazine back into view. "Do you think that is real?" She turned several pages over. "Oh," she exclaimed and swiftly returned the magazine to its box and place it back on the shelf.

"No souvenirs?"

The Ministers mock glare was delivered in full force. "Jensen laughed again, her lips turning into a crooked grin. She picked up her pack and lay it upon an empty space on the shelving and then took one of the magazines, rolled it up and placed it into her pack. At Kiernan's astonished countenance, she said, "Bedtime reading!" Jensen's smile faded as her thoughts drifted to the contents of her pack. She looked back into the generator room, seeing Raziko hard at work, adapting a fuel cell into the generator, as the rest of the team watched with varying degrees of interest.

"Come here," she whispered.

Kiernan looked up, "Excuse me?"

"Come here," Jensen said again, not wanting to be heard by the occupants of the main room.

Stepping closer, Kiernan saw the expression in Jensen's eyes change as she reached into her pack. She pulled out one of the automatic firearms.

"I need you to take this and before you protest, I want you to listen to me." She took Kiernan's free hand and placed the weapon upon her palm. "You are the only person here with no combat training. We are working in a highly unpredictable environment. I need for you to be able to defend yourself." Seeing Kiernan was about to argue Jensen pushed further. "Minister," she said, her voice low. "Please take this. As much as I understand the situation that I'm putting you into, I need for you to be safe. I hope you will never have to use this. If you don't, you can return it to me once this mission is over and I'll hand them all to Vegas." Jensen wasn't yet sure if that part was true. "And if you do have to use it, then our actions justify the necessity." Jensen took her hand away, leaving the weapon with Kiernan. "The scavengers fight back. Even if you break a limb, they have no sense of pain. I use several different methods to kill or maim a scavenger. To kill them, you must sever the spine at the back of the neck. It's swift and efficient. You could pierce whatever they may have in place of a heart, and they will still come for you until the last drop of blood drains from their bodies. Just aim and shoot for the throat. Try and hit the spine. Render them immobile. It's the quickest way to take one down.

Kiernan gulped. Her stomach felt cold.

"Unfortunately, it's not always that easy to gain the advantage; there are several effective ways to incapacitate a scavenger. You can use this to shoot at the eyes or incapacitate their ability to walk." She handed Kiernan two clips of ammunition, placing them straight into her pocket. "Can't say I've ever used one of these before, but I've studied it. You slide the ammunition in here, the trigger is here, and the safety button is here. Simply aim and fire." She looked at Kiernan beseechingly. "Please take it."

Staring down at the firearm upon her palm, Kiernan assessed its weight. Her mind conjured many reasons as to why this wasn't a good idea, and why she should hand the weapon back. However, she nodded.

Jensen sighed. She placed her hand back over Kiernan's. "Put it away" she said softly.

"Scout Jensen, Minister Kiernan." The call came from the main room.

Slipping her pack back onto her back, Jensen and Kiernan left the cupboard. No more words were spoken. Kiernan's eyes darted around the generator room as her mind processed what had happened. She placed her hand unconsciously upon the weapon tucked into her right-side pocket. A shiver trickled down her spine.

Scout Raziko was on his knees. He tinkered inside the generator. Jensen noticed Xoren was now searching containers stored upon freestanding shelves. She idly wondered if he would find anything as interesting as they had. To her right, she noticed Jax had entered the room and stood over Raziko's shoulder, watching his progress with interest.

Vegas watched the women. "Scout Raziko has almost finished the conversion matrix transfer. With luck, we should have power soon. Luckily, this generator ran on solar input." He studied Kiernan. "Anything interesting in there?"

With a shrug, Jensen said, "Interesting yes, but nothing usable."

"Not unless you count pornographic paraphernalia as useable." Kiernan added with a simper.

Vegas pushed away from the wall and arched a single brow. Fortunately, it was Jax who asked, "What's that?"

"Boring paperwork," Jensen answered, her eyes upon Vegas with an imperceptible smirk.

"Reading?" Jax waved his hand. "Pfft,"

Kiernan rolled her eyes. Jensen grinned.

Vegas covered his smile with the side of his fist. "How are we getting on, Raziko?"

Insulated wiring hanging out of his mouth and grease smudging his cheeks, Raziko nodded. "Almost there. Just need to connect the energy cell module to the distribution relays." He fiddled within the machine for a fraction more. "Right. Here we go. Who wants to do the honours?"

Vegas stepped forward. "Just start it up."

Rising to his feet, Raziko stood over the generator's control panel. He tapped a sequence of buttons and then pressed a large, square, emerald pad.

Nothing.

Frowning, Raziko tried gain. He pressed the button.

Still nothing.

"Raziko," Vegas peered over the generator. "I'm losing confidence."

"It will work." Raziko pressed the button again.

There was a clank. A groan. A whine. Then there was nothing.

"It's been a long time."

Jorca strode into the room. "Seriously?" She walked around the generator and studied it closely. "Press that button again."

With nothing else to try, Raziko did as told.

Clank… Groan… Whine.

Jorca kicked hard.

The generator growled into life and the team cheered as lighting illuminated the room.

"Good work people." Vegas laughed, relieved. "Right. It's almost time to split into our designated teams. We have a mark to conduct our directives and compete our orders." Vegas stood between Jensen and Kiernan. "We'll disconnect from open communications. Luckily, the air is breathable enough that we won't need to use it now unless we require connection to the other team. Minister Kiernan is Team One and Jensen is Team Two. We will meet back here once our directives are complete. Are there any questions?"

Silence.

"Then let's do this."

Vegas led the way out of the generator room and into the brightly lit passageway. The team looked around, seeing their surroundings for the first time. They didn't have much to observe. At the far end of the narrow space was an electronic door. Earlier knowledge of the facility layout told Kiernan this was the main entrance into the heart of the station.

"Just there. That's the way forward."

Vegas nodded and the team followed him to the doorway. Jensen was directly behind him. She needed to talk with him privately and was searching for a moment in which to take advantage. Vegas reached the door controlled by an electronic keypad. A scarlet light flashed repeatedly.

"Raziko, another one for you."

"Easy." The scout pulled a slim metallic strip out and ran it under the keypad. The scarlet light flashed to emerald, and the door slid open as a whoosh of air was sucked into the corridor beyond them. "Engineering sorcery."

He handed each team member a similar strip.

“How does it work?” Jax asked with interest. She held it up to the light.

“It emits a small electromagnetic pulse that shorts out the control unit.” Raziko was proud of this device. He had designed it himself. “I created it with Captain Lucia. It’s a hobby of mine.”

“Some hobby,” Jensen said with interest. She was both extremely impressed and convinced this was another item she may unfortunately *lose* by the end of the mission.

As the team stepped over the threshold, motion activated lights sprung to maximum illumination. What they saw caused several hearts to freeze in horror.

Lying upon the floor were the bodies of eight individuals. Jensen looked on in shock. She walked further into the corridor. Though almost one hundred cycles had passed, the bodies were still reasonably well preserved. This was due to the station’s shutdown creating an airtight environment which slowed down the decomposition rate. Taught, leathery skin clung to the skeletal remains of military personnel still dressed in full uniform. Jensen knelt beside a body slumped against the wall. She could tell it was a female. The body had long hair and a skirt which stopped just below the knees. The ranking insignia upon her chest was different to what they used now. She was unsure who this person was in terms of position. Jensen’s eyes travelled up the body to her face. The eyes were closed, and her mouth hung open in a silent scream. She spotted a full row of white teeth.

“What did this?” she asked Kiernan, who knelt beside her. Jensen took a small device from the body’s grasp. She had no idea what it was. She pressed several buttons but to no avail. “It must run on an independent power supply,” she muttered.

Kiernan took out her diagnostic scanner. “Let’s find out what happened here.” After a quick inspection, Kiernan pulled a strand of hair from the corpse’s head and placed it into the bottom compartment of her scanner.

“I’m sure we have a pretty good idea what killed these people,” Vegas said from behind Kiernan. He watched closely, waiting for the results to show.

“Indeed.” Kiernan watched as the scanner broke down the separate elements of the sample she had placed within; the results flashed upon its screen. She hadn’t ever worked on deceased individuals. Kiernan tried not to think about the fact this person was once a sentient being. Her actions became mechanical as she conducted her work.

Around them, the team inspected the bodies with curiosity and morbid fascination.

Xoren took still images for their mission report. He knelt beside Kiernan. "How did they die?"

Kiernan read out the results. "As expected, high concentration exposure to Amphibulartoxin." Her brow creased in consternation. "From my research, this was a highly unpleasant way to expire. It starts with paraesthesia, followed by sialorrhea, ataxia, paralysis, seizures, and then respiratory failure ending in cardiovascular collapse." She fought an internal shiver.

Major Vegas approached and knelt beside Jensen. "So, it was Amphibulartoxin."

"A high-level concentration poisoning. This was murder." Snapping her scanner shut, Kiernan rose. "Why did this happen? Judging from the concentration of decaying compounds this was a high-yield spread. Nobody would have survived." She looked over at Jensen. "I'm pretty sure these won't be the only bodies we find." She turned back to Vegas. "So why did this happen?"

With a deep sigh, Vegas rose. "Mass extermination. I can assume that due to the nature of the facility's, work this was a protective fail safe. Somebody or something decided what happened here should never be discovered. Nobody would escape alive."

Jensen looked around. It was clear from the distorted, preserved faces that these individuals had died an agonising death. "What did they do down here that was so important? And is it a danger to us now?" Jensen folded her arms and glared at Vegas. An arched eyebrow reaching perfectly towards her hairline, made it glaringly obvious she expected honest clarification. It had also occurred to her that Kiernan's presence on this mission, as a scientist, might have held more significance than initially presumed.

"If you're attempting to make insinuations or accusations, Scout, you are mistaken." Vegas stepped up close to Jensen, invading her personal space. "The only dangers we face are the ones we're already familiar with."

Jensen wasn't convinced. "So, The Prime and General weren't aware the personnel of this facility were murdered?"

Vegas noted the silence. The team watched them closely. Curiosity, concern, and suspicion surrounded him. He looked back at Jensen with his own accusatory glare. The last thing he wanted was speculation and lack of confidence in his leadership. Unfortunately, he faced one issue that Scout Jensen had freely pointed out. Something he couldn't answer. He had no true idea what knowledge his superiors held. He was to conduct their orders. That was his job. It was what he had always done. It was the reason he now stood toe to toe with Jensen, feeling nothing but compassion for the younger woman.

Vegas took a step away. "I assure you, Scout, I was fully briefed on this mission. Any possible known dangers would have been brought to light, to secure our success."

Jensen wanted to believe him. She really did. She knew she had to step down. The whole team was watching. Maybe she would pursue her point later. When they were home. When they were alone, and she could express her concerns openly. If nothing else, Jensen knew her behaviour in front of the team was disrespectful.

"Apologies, Sir. I'm just concerned for all our safety. As General Tehera said, we must succeed."

Vegas wanted to place a reassuring hand upon Jensen's shoulder. He didn't. "And we will." He stepped away.

Feeling the tension ease, Kiernan placed her scanner away and tucked a lock of hair behind her ear. "I think we've wasted enough time here."

"We should continue," Jorca said, her eyes alive with excitement. The confrontation had amused her.

Seeing sadness in Jensen's expression, Kiernan pulled her to one side. "Are you alright?" Doing what Vegas couldn't do she placed a reassuring hand upon Jensen's arm and pulled her a little closer. Kiernan ignored the team who may have looked upon her behaviour with curiosity.

"Sometimes I feel like I've reached my limit. So much death surrounds us. We live in the shadow of such atrocities. We hide away from the barren truth above us. I've fought scavengers savagely bent on taking my life, to eat me. Their actions don't faze me. It's their nature. I have no qualms in defending myself against them. But this," she looked around at the bodies. "This is different. This was the act of taking life by the hands of another no better than the continent that destroyed our world. These people had loved ones and families. Why would anybody put such dire measures in place? Kill everybody? Why?"

Understanding more than she cared to admit, but not wanting to continue the direction of their conversation, Kiernan rubbed Jensen's arm gently. "People like us will never understand such acts. I don't believe it's in our nature to do so."

"How can one life be valued above another? Where's the sanctity?" Jensen felt her thoughts spiral.

Kiernan smiled softly, knowing that was a question not easily answered. "This is hardly the time to discuss such things, Scout, but I tell you what," she paused in thought. "If you ever feel like an in-depth conversation over a bowl of banal slop," she tapped the inter-communicator strapped to her wrist, "Just give me a shout."

"I might take you up on that, Minister."

Kiernan stepped away. "Any time." She noticed most of the team had travelled further down the corridor. Xoren was examining another body close by. She pulled her pack back onto her body. "And Jensen, we're allies. When away from duty and stuffy regulations, please call me Kier."

The younger woman's smile grew. "Then call me Jen.

CHAPTER 17

The engineering sector was a vast facility found on a second lower level of the station. It was an immense space half dominated by a crosshatch of partitions dividing individual workstations. Each workstation held the tools and materials needed for a specific task. The area was lit up to maximum illumination, but even with all the lighting, a shadow seemed to loom across the vast expanse. And the silence? The silence was chilling.

Major Vegas, Jensen, Jilya, Ruben and Raziko, otherwise known as Team Two, entered the facility via a stone stairway. At the base of the stairs was a double set of doors. These were locked by a similar mechanism that Jensen bypassed with the aid of her E.M.P disruptor.

Jensen paused mid stride and looked ahead of them. They stood atop a raised metal grid platform affording them a view over the engineering facility. It seemed endless. The workstations stretched out beyond the platform. She struggled to see that far into the distance. Jensen looked up at the ceiling, curious to see a hoist above the stations. It was attached to an integrated network of runways that spanned the entire facility, running to the far end, and disappeared beyond the operation sector. Jensen rose onto her tiptoes to look further across the room. She saw peculiarly shaped objects covered by material sheeting. What are they, she wondered.

"Major, what were they doing here? What were they evaluating?" She was instantly curious to know what inhabited the separate room at the far end. It was clear the hoists carried the engineered parts into that area.

Realising Vegas hadn't replied Jensen looked to her mission leader. Vegas stood by the platform rail arms folded as he stared out ahead. "Major?"

A moment passed before Vegas turned, his expression grave. He pulled the carrier from his back and placed it gently by his feet. Standing before his team, the Major took a breath and silently. Finally, he spoke.

"What I'm about to say stays within the confines of this station." Vegas pulled the breathing apparatus from around his neck and dropped it to the floor beside his pack. It was another moment before he spoke, drawing out the silence with palpable tension.

"You are all familiar with the events that caused the downfall of our planet. This is something we are taught from an early age." He looked into the eyes of each person one by one. "However, the information you were provided… that we were taught… isn't wholly accurate."

"Isn't accurate how?" Ruben asked suspiciously.

Vegas ignored the question and continued. "We were a smaller continent, separate to the three main superpowers. Victims of a war that occurred around us. The East used our lands to build a test site and store weapons of destruction, as well as using our subterranean landmass, due to its denser formation, to build the original prison for the criminally insane. This is the reason we, as an independent nation, survived the devastations. We had a ready-made shelter."

The team nodded all familiar with their history.

Vegas studied his team. His eyes drifted from Jilya, to Ruben, Raziko and finally Jensen. "This is a lie."

Felling an invisible vicelike grip claw at her stomach, Jensen swallowed. "A lie?"

Vegas nodded cautiously. "We were, we are the East." He took a breath. "It was our nation, our leader, who caused the devastations that destroyed our world."

There was silence.

A long and drawn-out stillness followed Vegas' words, as the weight of his revelation settled into their minds.

"You're lying," Jensen said, though she knew he wasn't.

Vegas didn't reply. He didn't have to.

"But…" Ruben looked to his fellow team. "But we…"

"Survived," Jensen finished. "We… was it … I don't…" She looked away. A thousand thoughts swarming her mind and no way to grasp one, pull it from the coil of confusion, and formulate a question; let alone a response.

Vegas pushed forward. "I know this is a lot to comprehend, but it's important you understand this if you are to proceed with the retrieval mission."

"Understand what?" Jensen stepped forward, "Understand that our survival was a lie? That so much of the world perished while our ancestors scurried to safety?" Jensen's ire rose. "We know the story. Capita knew there was no hope for this planet, so she planned to move her nation to a new world. The rest of the population…"

"Be damned," Ruben interjected angrily. "The rest of the world be damned."

"Why are you so incensed by this?" Jilya turned to face his colleagues. "We're not responsible for the actions of our ancestors. What matters is right now. What we can do to create a new world from that tragedy."

"A tragedy we created," Jensen pushed.

"No!" Jilya argued, "Not us. We did nothing. We can only work to create a new world from the ashes of that past."

"Empty sentiments," Ruben said, with a look as cold as the land above them.

"People," Vegas drew his team's attention. "Now isn't the time to draw contention from this revelation. We're here because we have a mission that will help secure our future. The past isn't ours to shoulder."

"Then why lie?" Jensen asked, a feeling of emptiness seeping into her.

Vegas forced a heavy sigh. "Because the truth is no less devastating. Nevertheless, this is our reality. We live with the consequences caused by our ancestors."

Jensen turned away.

Raziko, who up to that point had been silent, said, "So why are we here?"

"To…"

"Selfishly carry out the plans forged cycles ago by our dictating leader?"

"**No**," Vegas shouted, "Don't you get it? No matter what happed before, all we can do now is secure our future." He held out his arms and turned to face the engineering facility. "We're standing in the heart of Capita's plans. This is where they worked and created the technology needed for faster than light, universal travel. This was our future."

Turning, Jensen approached Vegas and stood beside him. "A future we don't deserve."

"From a past in which we had no hand," Vegas pressed.

"And the millions who died?"

"And what of those who survived? Were they not still innocent victims?" Vegas turned to look at Jensen. "We didn't devastate this world, Jensen, but we do have the ability and duty to deliver a future." He put his hand on her arms, drawing her attention. "For those who work together in the colony for a life deserving of them. All of them."

"I'm in," Ruben said. "For our people. For our future. For those who died and their family who survived. I'm in."

Jensen wasn't ready to back down. The revelation was still too raw. All her life she had believed a lie. The foundations upon which she built her belief structure were crumbling beneath her. She looked back at Vegas.

"Why tell us here? Why now?"

Vegas turned back to the facility and looked ahead. "Because the technology we've come to retrieve will reveal this truth. What you will undoubtedly see down there will confirm all I have told you." He looked back at his team. "As I said, this information is strictly confidential and comes direct from the Select Prime himself. Failure to keep this information classified will result in penance of the highest degree."

Spoken like a true Easterner, Jensen thought.

"What is that punishment," Jilya asked curiously. None had ever been exposed to the Select Prime's highest degree of penance.

"Only Commander Tehera knows. All those trusted with this truth have carried it to their last breath." Vegas looked directly at Jensen. "In time you will understand the reasoning."

Looking away, Jensen shook her head. "It's easy to keep a secret when it harbours so much shame."

"And if that's your reason for keeping this information close then so be it."

"It would be mine," Jilya responded, as he stood beside Jensen. A show of support.

Mine too, Vegas thought. "So," he looked to his team, "Are we ready to proceed?"

Realising Vegas' eyes were upon him, Raziko nodded faintly. "Sir."

Ruben, "Yes, Sir,"

"Sir." Jilya replied.

Studying the floor for long moments Jensen finally looked back at Vegas. "Yes, Major," her answer honest, but laced with the burden of guilt.

Something changed for her at that moment, and as Jensen looked over the facility workstations, she felt a palpable tension rise; the weight of a truth nobody wanted to accept. Acid churned within her stomach.

Vegas continued, "I know this is a lot to come to terms with so quickly, but we still have a job to do. Each of your consoles has been pre-programmed with data on the materials you need to collect. We are looking for design schematics, processors, and components. Possible locations and occupational titles of the individuals who worked in those areas are included, as well as a few scientists still known to us who worked on the design and construction of their craft."

"Their craft, Major?" Raziko looked back over the facility.

"Their craft, yes. Capita's scientists had begun construction of the first faster than light intergalactic space craft. Although we too have continued and advanced in this development, we are missing key components to complete our own construction. We are almost there."

The team looked out over the facility. It was, without a doubt in Jensen's mind, the single largest area of inside space she had ever seen.

Vegas lifted his carrier and secured it on his back. "You're all equipped with additional carriers. Find what you need and take as much as you can carry. We may not be able to use the storage vehicle for maximum haulage, but we can still retrieve as much of the critical components as we can." Vegas knew that would be a blow to the colony. They needed more recyclable alloys.

He opened a gateway to a set of ten descending steps. "Let's move, people."

As the team began making their way through the gate, Vegas pulled Jensen to one side.

"Jen, you know what you are looking for?"

"Yes, Major."

"And you are," Vegas paused, trying to find the right words to connect with Jensen. "And you are comfortable with our situation?"

Jensen took a step forwards, narrowing the distance between them. "I will never be comfortable with this revelation. You have just fractured the foundations that upheld the sanctity of the work we do, for the future of our people. I also know that nothing can change this, and our only step is forward. That is the only fact that keeps me from walking away."

"Walking away?"

She ignored his question. "I shall complete my orders as requested, Sir." Jensen turned away. She passed through the gate without another word and took the ten steps to the ground below. Raziko, Ruben and Jilya were waiting. Each scout looked at her with an expression Jensen found unreadable. Thinking they wished to discuss the revelation with her, Jensen shook her head, "Not now, guys."

Raziko stepped forward. "Jen, it's not that." He turned to the side and Jensen followed his line of sight. It was then that she saw it. Bodies, countless bodies of scientists and engineers who had worked in Capita's facility.

Jensen stepped closer and entered the maze of partitioned workstations. She looked inside the first cubicle. There she saw the body of a man lying collapsed over a workbench. Evidence of dried blood pooled around his head where he had fallen and punctured his forehead on the circuit board he was working on. Broken spectacles lay upon the puddle of aged blood. Jensen looked around the cubicle. She took note of the personal artefacts of the individual who had work there. Glossy images were still attached to the wall. She pulled one from a clip, looking at a picture of a happy family. It was a man, woman and two children. The picture was taken by the sea and an oceanic view stretched out behind them. The children were happy and smiling, proud parents holding them close. Carefully, Jensen replaced the image. She turned away and left the cubicle respectfully. Taking a left, Jensen stepped over two bodies before she entered another cubicle. There a younger woman was slumped within a rotating chair. Legs sprawled, arms hanging down, the woman looked like she had just fallen asleep at her desk. She wore the laboratory coat of a scientist; her personal identification card was still attached to the lapel. Jensen took the card. There was an image of the woman next to a symbol she'd never seen before. Not even a label named the woman.

"There's more," Jilya said, as he stood at the cubicle entrance. "Thirty or forty bodies. The further we look the more we find."

"But this is not why we're here." It was Vegas who appeared behind Jilya. "We need to concentrate on the mission. We have a narrow period." Seeing Jensen was about to argue, Vegas added. "We can't change the past."

Jensen's expression was cold. "But surely, we can take a moment to pay our respects, Major. To those whose lives were stolen from them so we could live now!"

"Don't make this an issue, Scout."

"How can I not when you heartlessly…"

"Heartlessly?" Vegas stormed forward standing toe to toe with Jensen. He towered over her, his ire infused. "Don't you think I felt exactly as you did? Do you not think I felt lied to and cheated when I learned this truth? It changes nothing. NOTHING. It's the past. A truth heavy with shame. But there is a reason they chose to obfuscate the fact and I don't question that. What matters is what we do now. For the hundreds of colonists who place their future in our hands."

She didn't want to back down. Jensen had so much more anger waiting to release, but she could see the sincerity in Vegas' eyes. She could hear it in his voice.

"But how do you deal with this?"

"This what?"

"Guilt," Jilya offered,

"Shame," Jensen continued.

Vegas took a step backwards. "By doing what's right. That's all I can do." Jensen closed her yes. A frown dipped above them. As much as she wanted to continue to vent her ire, she knew it was fruitless. Not now. Not right now, she thought.

"Fine. I can do that." She looked back at Vegas. "For right now." It was the best she could offer.

***

Staying upon the upper level of the Testing Station, Kiernan, Xoren, Jax, Jorca and Ziran had travelled a different direction from Team Two. They entered a cafeteria. Kiernan looked around at the scene before them in dismay. Bodies lay slumped over tables, faces in plates of dried food hanging over tabletops or prostrate upon the ground. Plates and cups still lay scattered over surfaces, stale crusts of what was once food congealed and dried to porcelain. At the far end of the room, Kiernan saw a service area light still shining above pots of putrefied foods. Military personal and kitchen staff lay near the servery, trays, spoons, and ladles scattered around them.

A stale aroma filled the room. Kiernan took a deep breath, as she tried to name the scent. She strode further into the room and stood by a table. Something on the floor caught a beam of illumination from the lights above them. She bent down to retrieve it. It was an old timekeeper. The face was cracked, and its hands bent. She presumed it must have been damaged during the mass extermination. Her eyes read the positioning of the timekeeper's hands. Mid-morn. Must have been when they died, Kiernan thought. Innocently partaking in a late breakfast or an early lunch. Kiernan rubbed her thumb over the cracked face, feeling a shard dig into her skin.

Noticing the rest of her team leaving through a side door, Kiernan placed the timekeeper into her pocket and followed. They found themselves in a long corridor. A single body dressed in full uniform lay across their path. Xoren took the lead and stepped over the body as he led the team down the corridor and through a maze of passageways.

"I believe we are almost there," Xoren stated, as he studied his console.

They came to a stop before a scarlet doorway. It would seem relatively inconspicuous if not for the double set locking mechanisms situated at the top, middle and bottom of the door.

"I hope we can still open this like the others," Ziran said, with concern. The locking mechanism was like none they had seen thus far. Xoren waved his E.M.P disruptor over the lock. Nothing happened.

"That's interesting," he commented.

"It really isn't as complicated as it looks," Kiernan said thoughtfully. She studied the lock. "If we just do this," she took a slim metallic tool from her pack and prized the casing away from the lock. "It's quite a simple lock. It just looks more intimidating for a reason."

"Being?"

Kiernan didn't miss Xoren's defensive tone. She pointed up to the corner above the door. The team looked, seeing a security camera. An operational light flashed, signalling the equipment was recording. It appeared all power had been temporarily restored to the Testing Station.

"Access was clearly limited to this area of the station. Entry gained solely by viewers on the other side of this door granting permission to security cleared personnel." Kiernan pointed to the steel bolts visible now the mechanism casing had been removed. "Nobody would try to do this while they were being watched. However," Kiernan used her tool to slide between the top two steel rods. She activated an unseen switch that released the rods, which then slid backwards out of the door frame and into the safety of the mechanism. "Almost too simple." The trigger caused the other two sets of steel rods to slide back with a mechanical jolt.

"And there we have it. Not particularly advanced considering the purpose of this Testing Station, but possible the budgets dictated where financing was spent." Kiernan stepped back as Jax pulled the door open. The team crossed the threshold.

They entered a bright passageway with a blank wall to their left and a row of mirrors to their right. Kiernan placed her hand upon the mirror and looked at her reflection. It was a two-way mirror, another safety measure. This meant they were heading in the right direction. The team walked past the mirror and under a moulded arch. They jumped as an alarm hollered at their presence.

"What the…" Jorca held her chest.

"Need clean pants?" Jax asked with a laugh.

"Calm down people," Xoren turned to face the team. "It's a form of elemental compound detector. Our equipment must have set off the alarm.

Kiernan thought of the specific items on her person that could trigger an alarm.

They found themselves before another door. This one not only had no evidence of a handle, but no visible signs of a lock.

"Now what?"

"Manual manipulation." Ziran dropped his pack.

"Manual what?"

"This." Moving fast, Ziran hurled his weight at the solid barrier. It didn't move.

"Want to try a twosome?" he asked to which Jax shrugged.

"Why not!"

The pair threw their weight at the door again. There was still little movement.

Kiernan turned to look in the mirrors beside her. They covered the upper half of the wall. She studied her reflection barely recognising herself. Where was the smartly dressed scientist in pressed suits and starched lab coat? Instead, was a woman covered in grime and dark clothing. She tucked her hair behind her ear and then jumped helplessly as her image shattered and the mirrored glass fell to the floor. Startled, Kiernan turned to see Jorca standing with baton in hand.

"If at first you don't succeed?"

"Smash the life out of it!" Jax finished. The pair laughed. Obviously, a private joke between the two.

"Sorry to disturb your personal inspection, Minister. Must keep moving, right?"

"I get the point," Kiernan said harshly. She watched Jax manoeuvre himself carefully over the lower half of the wall and through the shattered mirror frame. He entered the hidden room. Ziran followed. It was a security zone. A row of six monitors sat along a wide desk. Two uniformed bodies lay upon the floor. Ziran looked at the screens. The first showed the door they had entered. The next showed the room beyond. It was the last four screens that Ziran found most interesting. He clearly recognized holding cells with the remains of bodies lying within. Naked bodies. He leaned closer to silently count the bodies, but then jumped as a hand clasped his shoulder. He turned to see Jax. "Do you ever get the feeling you weren't told as much as you thought?"

"Frequently," Jax replied. The officer stared at the bodies. "I wasn't informed this was a prison."

"It wasn't."

Both men looked over at Xoren, who was peering over the dividing wall. He looked intently at the monitors.

"Then why the cells? Why the bodies?"

Xoren turned to the men. "It was a Testing Station for mechanical, as well as chemical, advances."

Kiernan watched Xoren's exchange with Ziran and Jax. She knew this information. She'd had briefing on what the station was testing and for what reasons. It was the sole reason she was there. She wondered how the men would react knowing the truth. How Jensen would react.

"They experimented on people?" Jorca investigated the security room trying to see the monitor screens over Xoren. "What were they assessing? Can I see?"

"I think we need to continue our directives," Kiernan said to steer her team's attention. The last thing she needed was a diversion into morbid fascination.

Taking the hint, Jax activated a switch and the second door opened. With a nod of thanks, Kiernan, Xoren and Jorca passed thorough the doorway. Jax took a door in the security room that brought him out into the same area as the team. Ziran moved to follow but paused next to a seventh monitor situated upon the wall. This one appeared to be connected to the elemental compound detector. Upon the screen was the skeletal image of one of his colleagues with a clearly visible firearm tucked into their clothing. He frowned, tapping the screen with his finger. He was unable to tell who the image was.

"Scout, are you coming?"

Ziran looked up, seeing Jax by the doorway. He nodded, unconsciously switching off the detector screen and filing the information away for future reference.

They had entered an outer office from the security room. A row of protective suits hung upon a far wall. They were made of a dull, colourless material with a sheen that glowed in the soft light of the room. In the centre was a table holding nothing but a single cup. The team looked around. Various restraints hung on another wall, including shackles, gags, and batons like their own. Next to the wall, beside the door, Ziran spotted more wares for personal safety. He picked up a weapon, like that which Kiernan concealed, and turned it in his hand, inspecting its construction.

"Designed for firing darts," Xoren offered. "Tranquilising darts."

Ziran placed the weapon back upon the wall rack.

Advisor Xoren turned to the team. "Ziran, Jax and Jorca can remain here cataloguing inventory. If you find anything of use from your supplied list, then bag it. Minister Kiernan and I will search further for the data files."

All eyes turned to Kiernan, aware she was the sub-head, and it was she who was to issue orders. Kiernan appreciated the sign of respect and smiled inwardly.

"That is acceptable, but I am capable of retrieving the data myself, Advisor Xoren."

Jax watched their interaction. "I can go with you, Minister. I am here to protect you after all."

Kiernan tucked her hair behind her ear. "It won't be necessary, Jax, but I appreciate the offer."

"You cannot be alone, Minister," Xoren pressed. "The data you are tracking down is of a sensitive nature. I insist I go with you."

She didn't wish for Xoren's company, but Kiernan couldn't swiftly conjure a reason for him to allow her the space she craved. Kiernan sighed and waved her hand dismissively. "Fine. I shall be busy, so allow me the space I need to complete my task."

"Of course, Minister."

Kiernan removed her pack as she approached another door. Her E.M.P disruptor made short work of the lock, and she was soon passing through the barrier and into the heart of the testing facility. Xoren watched from behind. He was impressed; Minister Kiernan was an intelligent woman. It was a shame, he thought, that she wouldn't be making the journey home.

CHAPTER 18

The chemical testing laboratory was broken into several areas. First were the holding cells; a line of ten translucent boxed cells, six of which still held the bodies of their test subject inhabitants. The last four at the far end were empty. Those doors were open, the occupants gone many cycles before.

Kiernan approached the first cell. Laying within was the body of one reasonably well-preserved corpse. The body lay face down. It was naked apart from restraints around its ankles. A chain was still attached to the wall. Kiernan stepped closer and placed her hand upon the translucent dividing wall.

"What were they doing to you?"

Standing behind her, Advisor Xoren spoke quietly. "This was a testing laboratory Minister. Considering the data that you have been sent to find, I'm surprised you had to ask that question."

"It was rhetorical," Kiernan said humourlessly. She knew what she was sent to retrieve, but these individuals could have been subject to many kinds of torturous experiments. "Who were these people?" She looked up the row of cells seeing bodies in an array of prostrate positions, and one she believed held a position of prayer.

"I believe they were prisoners."

Kiernan turned to Xoren. "And that makes it acceptable? To torture them because they were prisoners?"

"Right or wrong isn't the issue, Minister. I'm sure they were the most logical choice at the time." Xoren stepped away from Kiernan and looked around the room. He saw a partition wall to the left with a large window. Xoren stepped towards the window and looked inside. There was nothing but a single gurney equipped with leg, wrist, and head restraints. A urine-stained blanket covered its surface. Xoren turned back to Kiernan. "You act so disgusted by what you see, Minister and yet you work…"

Kiernan held up her hand angrily. She shook her head. "Do not even attempt to compare my work to whatever heinous crimes were committed here, Xoren."

"If there is no comparison, then why are we here?" Xoren had to stop antagonizing Kiernan, after all, she didn't know the truth of her directives.

Turning, Kiernan bit her lip. She wouldn't dignify him with a response. He wanted to argue. Why? She had no idea. The metallic taste of blood on her tongue told Kiernan she had bitten too hard, and she released her tender flesh. Was there a comparison? There never used to be, but that was before. Everything had changed. And her presence on this mission? It wasn't linked with her current project, but the request had come straight from Select Prime Abrahams and was linked to a proposed new project she was to head.

"Nothing is as it seems, Advisor," she said hollowly. What was the point of this conversation, she thought.

The older man smiled. "Of course." His sarcasm was not lost on Kiernan.

Having enough of Xoren, Kiernan walked away. She headed for a door in the far corner of the laboratory and opened it easily. Ahead lay a small walkway with two doors. Kiernan read the door plaques. One labelled as a materials store, the other filing. She chose filing.

Entering the room, Kiernan looked around. Cabinets lined the right and left sides of the wall. Each cabinet was five drawers high, and the drawers were labelled in alpha-numeric sequence. Thinking of the data she was to retrieve; she scanned the cabinet labels.

"Can you help? There are so many files here and it will take time." This was sure to keep Xoren busy and quiet.

Hearing Xoren enter the room, Kiernan turned just in time to see him strike out, hitting her across the head with his baton. Kiernan tried to duck, but only managed to dodge the full force of his strike. She was knocked backwards and fell with force into the metal cabinets. Kiernan reeled from the pain, feeling instantly nauseated and dizzy. Stars exploded behind her eyes. She slid down the filing cabinets and hit the ground heavily. Kiernan cried out harshly. She wrapped her arms around her head, as she felt a kick to her stomach.

"Stop!"

Another kick connected with her side.

Desperate to escape the onslaught, Kiernan tried to rise, but a third strike sent her sliding across the room. She felt her body hit a corner and she pushed herself into the wall. Kiernan held the side of her head. It thundered with pain.

"What are you DOING?"

Xoren remained silent, as he pulled an object from his pack and secured it to the wall. His index fingers flew over a small keypad, delicately hitting each button with practiced synchronicity. Once done, Xoren turned to look at Kiernan. Beside him a low rhythmic tone beeped out from the mechanism.

"I assure you; I will make this as painless as possible."

"Too late," Kiernan spat out. She looked down at blood covering her fingers. She coughed and then winced. Her ribs screamed in pain. Kiernan looked back at the object Xoren had fixed to the wall. "What is that?"

Xoren remained quiet as he approached Kiernan. He knelt to face her, and Kiernan pushed herself harder into the wall. Fear trickled through her veins. She could feel his breath on her skin, and her nerves pricked in revulsion.

Xoren's head tipped to the side. "The General and Select Prime are aware of your faltering commitment, Minister. Such a crime will not be tolerated. I've assured them a mere accident will eradicate the problem."

"Problem?" Kiernan wanted to laugh. "You're going to kill me because I-"

"Ask too many questions and won't do what is necessary for our survival." With a look of disgust Xoren rose to his feet.

"It's not that I won't," Kiernan argued, as if it was that easy to agree.

"Why I always have to be the one to rectify other people's mistakes is a constant mystery to me."

"Mistakes?" Kiernan moved to her knees.

Xoren twirled the baton in his hand. "How much time to leave the room before detonation?" he asked. He approached the explosive again, ready to enter in a countdown.

Wiping the blood from her fingers Kiernan took her chance. As Xoren keyed a countdown into the detonator's timepiece she acted quickly.

"Minister Kiernan to Scout Jensen and Major Vegas."

Xoren looked around swiftly. "NO… you…" He advanced, eyes burning with rage.

"Do you hear me? I need-" Kiernan cried out as Xoren kicked her wrist away. Her arm hit the wall and her communication device fell to the ground. Xoren stamped down, smashing it into pieces.

"Bad move, Minister."

As Xoren raised the baton once again, Kiernan reached into her side pocket and pulled out her automatic firearm. Xoren froze in alarm.

***

"This is Scout Jensen." Jensen paused and waited, but there was no reply. "Minister Kiernan? Please respond."

She was greeted with silence. "Kiernan-" Jensen paused, and her wrist fell to her side. A nervous flutter agitated her stomach. Jensen looked around the cubical she inhabited and the pile of electrical components she had placed to one side for carriage. She had already found half the material on her list. Jensen paused for a moment, then, decision made, she turned and left the cubicle.

Navigating her way through the maze of concentrated office spaces, Jensen passed the rest of her team who were too busy conducting their own directives to notice her.

All but Major Vegas. "Scout, where are you going?" He called, still feeling the burn of their confrontation.

Jensen never stopped moving. Instead, she broke into a run. "Minister Kiernan has requested our assistance and seeing as you don't appear to be answering, I will." She ascended the platform steps two at a time and disappeared from Vegas' view. He shook his head. They had work to do and Kiernan had her own team for help.

***

Advisor Xoren starred at the weapon aimed upon him.

"Where did you get that?" He took a step backwards away from Kiernan. He'd never seen the feral glare in her eyes before. He'd never seen that look on anybody before. "Put that down, Kiernan. You don't know if it works, and you might hurt yourself."

A painful laugh escaped Kiernan's lips. She held onto her side with her injured arm to ease the stab of pain shooting through her. "Are you really going to patronise me in your position, Xoren?" Kiernan pushed her body up against the wall until she was standing. Her ribs hurt painfully, and her head throbbed like a hammer was swinging around inside her skull. She was afraid, but she would never let Xoren see that. Kiernan didn't know what to do, but she would stall for as much time as she could. Either somebody would find them, or she would figure out a plan. Worst comes to worst, she thought, I'll shoot the deceitful wretch.

She watched him. His eyes moved back and forth from her to the weapon in her grasp. "I wouldn't try anything," she said, with as much confidence as she could muster.

Xoren held up his hands. "Just give that to me. Believe me, what I had planned was so much quicker than they intended. There is no way out for you."

Alarm sent violent tremors through Kiernan. "What does that mean? Are you trying to tell me I should allow you to kill me so I have an easy death?" Kiernan laughed. "Do you honestly know why they want me dead, or are you just following orders?"

"No, I-"

"Do you know what they have planned? What I'm investigating?"

"I know as much as I need to know. I know we are all working for the same goal; liberation for our people and a new world." Xoren was steadfast in his beliefs. Blind, Kiernan thought. She took a breath. She didn't think she would be able to stall for much longer. She felt nauseated, and exhausted.

"You know nothing," Kiernan challenged. "Do you even care?" She looked carefully into Xoren's eyes, gripping the firearm tighter. Studying his reactions. Something in his eyes told her he really didn't understand and was only doing as ordered.

"What if it were your life they wanted? If you believe so much in the agenda, would you give it freely?"

"Willingly, for the future of our people. We all make sacrifices." He replied without falter. "Kiernan, please put the weapon down."

Falling back against the wall, Kiernan tried to regain her focus. Her mind wanted to rest. Her thoughts wanted release. She needed sleep. She knew then she was concussed. She was losing the battle to hold her ground. Kiernan blinked and shook her head. If Xoren wasn't unpleasant enough to look upon already, she was suddenly seeing two of him. She felt a fresh trickle of blood run down her forehead and around her left eye.

"You know, Advisor Xoren. I'm aware of every sacrifice I've made, willingly or unwillingly, for the agenda. This isn't why we're here now."

Xoren took a step closer. He could see she was struggling to keep focus. "Why are we here, Kiernan?"

"Because the agenda is a lie." Seeing Xoren take another step closer, Kiernan aimed the weapon lower. "I've read a shot to the stomach is excruciating."

"Then enlighten me, Kiernan." Xoren remained still. "What is this knowledge you claim to have, that nobody else is privy? What do you know which enables you to boast superiority over the rest of us? Tell us why we are wrong in our lifelong commitment to an agenda designed to bring liberation for us all?"

Kiernan wanted to answer his question, but without presentable proof, she would have nothing to back her claims. And there was proof. She just needed to obtain it. Until then she had to keep her suspicions close and hope it wouldn't get her killed in the meantime.

***

It hadn't been hard to track the route the data retrieval team had taken. Following the pathway of strategically wedged open doorways, Jensen moved at speed. She ran through a cafeteria, paying little attention to the bodies around her. Running through a second door Jensen followed the corridors, only having to backtrack once before she passed through a doorway lined to one side with mirrors. She slowed and skidded to a halt over broken glass as she hit a closed door.

"Jen?"

Looking to her right, Jensen saw Ziran in a room beyond the mirrored walkway. She vaulted through the broken frame, seeing a row of monitors. "Where's Kiernan?" Jensen glanced down at the monitors but couldn't see her upon any of the screens. She looked back at Ziran, frustrated by the confused expression upon his face. "Where is she, Ziran?"

"She's with Advisor Xoren in the chemical testing laboratory. They were searching for the data stores."

Without so much as an acknowledgement of thanks, Jensen ran out of the monitoring room and into security. There Jorca was studying a rack of antiquated weaponry.

"Minister Kiernan?"

Without looking up, Jorca jabbed her thumb over her shoulder. Jensen followed and ran into the chemical testing laboratory. She found Jax crouched down, inspecting a body inside a holding cell. "Minister Kiernan?"

"Excuse me?" Jax rose and approached Jensen.

"Where is Minister Kiernan," Jensen demanded.

"She's with Advisor Xoren."

Jensen looked around the laboratory. There were several doors they could have gone through. "Which way did they go?"

"Why the rush? What's going on?"

Reaching out, Jensen took the burly man, who was a head taller than her, by the scuff of his coat and pulled him towards her. "Which way did they go?"

In a swift movement, Jax took Jensen's wrist and twisted it, spinning her around and pulling her into him. Her back against his body. He wrapped his arms under her chin and squeezed. "They're busy. Why don't you go back to nit picking through the dead and leave us here." He squeezed a little harder.

"What have you done?" Jensen gasped out. She could feel pressure mount, as her airways narrowed forcibly.

Jax wrapped his free arm around the wrist of the arm holding Jensen and pulled a little tighter. "Stay out of it, Jensen. They aren't interested in you."

Jensen could feel her head throb, as pressure mounted. She choked as she swung her body around in a futile attempt to free herself. She tried to pull his arm away, but to no avail. It only made Jax squeeze tighter.

"Pl… n…" She couldn't speak. She couldn't breathe. She couldn't-

A loud crack resonated from behind her, and Jensen felt her body fall as Jax released her. She hit the floor, as a second smack followed. Jensen couched and gasped for air. She saw Jax's body crumple beside her. She pushed herself away from him and looked up. Ziran stood beside the fallen body. Blood ran down his baton. His knuckles white from the strength of his grip.

"I knew there was a reason I didn't trust him."

Jensen tried to stand, but she fell. Her head swam. She moved to her knees, taking a deep breath, and tried to rise again. Her legs shook, but she was upright. "Thank you" she whispered, swallowing with difficulty. "Which way… did… Kiernan… and… Xoren go?" She took shallow breaths.

Ziran pointed his baton to a specific door. She turned as she heard Jorca gasp behind them. Knowing she could leave her to Ziran, Jensen continued, struggling to catch her breath as she passed through the doorway. She stopped as she heard Kiernan's distinctive voice.

***

Managing to keep Xoren talking, Kiernan sensed more than heard the arrival of help. Holding her injured arm against her body, she focussed on the man before her. Kiernan felt betrayed, hurt, and angered, but not only did she have to worry about Xoren, but the explosive fixed to the wall beside him. She could hear a low repetitive tone coming from the mechanism. Was it counting down? How much time did she have? Of one fact Kiernan was sure… if the bomb was to detonate, she was taking Xoren with her.

"What do you intend on doing if you stop me, Kiernan? I'm not the only one aware of your perfidy?"

"You have me all wrong, Xoren. There is no deception." Kiernan took a brave step towards Xoren. He took a step backwards. His hands held in supplication. This caused Kiernan to smile inwardly. "You don't have to do this, Xoren. Deactivate the explosive."

Xoren released a bark of hysterical laughter. "If I don't terminate you then my existence will be as worthless as yours!"

"And that tells you nothing of our Select Prime and Commander?" From the corner of her eye, Kiernan saw the door move ever so slightly. It was just enough to confirm somebody was just behind the barrier. "Xoren, what is the alternative to killing me? Why will your life be as worthless as mine?" Kiernan saw Jensen slip into the room. She stayed calm, fighting off the fog that invaded her dwindling clarity. Her head pounded painfully. Her eyes glistened with unshed tears. "Why do they want me dead?"

"Because your compassion will destroy us," Xoren answered. His response was seething, making Kiernan wonder what Xoren had been informed, in the order to kill her.

Kiernan felt the fight seep away from her. Would it be that easy to follow such an order? If Xoren would so blindly yield to this command, who else would? With a soft voice, Kiernan said, "Without compassion-"

"We have a chance of survival."

"Why did they order you to kill me, Xoren?"

The older man remained silent.

"There is another way." Kiernan wasn't sure what that was yet, but there had to be.

Xoren's eyes flickered around the room. He was thinking. For a moment he pondered Kiernan's words. Was there another way? He shook his head. "No, Minister. Not for you." Eyes narrowing to slits, Xoren charged at Kiernan.

Fear overwhelming her, Kiernan took a step backwards and pulled the trigger. Terror eclipsed her being when it didn't fire. She stumbled backwards and hit the wall behind her. Xoren advanced. The firearm fell uselessly from her hand. Jensen sprinted, reaching Xoren just as his hand reached out to grab Kiernan. She pulled the man backwards and threw him to the side. He collided with a metallic filing cabinet and dropped; the unit bounced back hitting the wall and its drawers sprung open. The weight of them pulled the cabinet frame to the floor. Xoren rolled away, missing the cabinet hitting him full force. He rose quickly, but Jensen was ready. Xoren reached for his baton. His expression dropped. The weapon was no longer attached to his side. It had fallen in the melee and lay out of reach in the corner. Xoren clenched his right hand, shaping it into a fist, but before he could throw a punch, Jensen moved. She pushed him hard into the wall with a solid kick to his abdomen. Then she punched repeatedly and again. Anger and fear took possession of Jensen, as she hit the man over and over. Fury at their situation, at the Majors revelation, at Jax's attack and at Xoren's actions. Her rage filled eyes burned into Xoren like scorched iron. Blinded by anger. She hit again and then wrapped her hand tight around Xoren's throat. She squeezed. Her grip tightened. A growl emanated from deep within her chest.

"Jensen," Kiernan called. "Stop."

Blood rushed to Xoren's face as his jaw dropped and he struggled for breath.

"He was going to kill you!"

Kiernan stepped closer, her body almost touching Jensen. She spoke softly. "Please don't lower yourself. He isn't worth it."

"How… How can you be so… so…?" Anger fermented within Jensen, but she did as bid and released Xoren. She placed her hand upon his chest keeping the bloodied man from moving. He gasped painfully. Blood ran from his nose.

"Not a nice feeling, is it?"

"Jensen…

"I should have killed you," she growled.

"Jen!"

Taking a sideways glance, Jensen looked at Kiernan. For the first time she was able to take a closer inspection. She saw the wound upon her head, and the way she was holding her arm. Blood trailed the side of her face. Jensen's anger surged. Reached for her tonfa, Jensen hit out quickly. The connection was sound. Jensen struck Xoren with enough force that he fell to the ground in an undignified heap.

Kiernan gasped and staggered backwards. She looked back at Jensen who regarded her with a cool expression.

"He's unconscious," she offered, with unapologetic appeasement. She turned from Xoren. Her eyes scanned Kiernan's injuries. "We need to get you out of here. I need to get Jilya to look at your injuries. He has the most medical training."

"What about him." Although happy to comply, Kiernan feared Xoren's reaction when conscious.

Jensen was less concerned. "He can crawl out of here on his hands and knees." She placed her palm on Kiernan's cheek and inspected the wound to her hairline. "That's some crack on the head, Minister. Your wrist. Do you think it's broken? What happened?"

Kiernan lowered her head and stepped away. The first of her unshed tears escaped her eye. "There was no reason for me to be here, Jen." Kiernan's words were soft. "This was their plan all along."

Jensen already figured that. She nodded. But why? She needed to question Kiernan further. She needed to question Vegas. Was he involved? She hoped not. It became startlingly obvious to her that deception ran deeper than anyone of them might have believed possible. She had questions and she needed answers. But first, to deal with Advisor Xoren.

Jensen watched Kiernan pick up the discarded firearm, and then wrapped an arm around her waist, as she began to lead her out of the filing room.

"I never found the data assigned in my directives."

Jensen stopped. "Do you need to-?"

"Let's just get out of here."

Nodding, Jensen reached out as they passed the explosive. The number 20 flashed on its digital readout in a bright scarlet. She pressed the button.

The countdown began.

"What are you doing?"

Jensen moved quicker, ushering her into a swifter exit. She didn't respond as they entered the chemical testing laboratory, and then broke out into a run. Kiernan held her arm close, as she limped beside Jensen. She saw the bodies of Jax and Jorca lying inches apart. "What!"

"Keep moving," Jensen urged, forcing Kiernan into a faster pace. She chanted the countdown in her mind. "Just keep moving."

Once entering the security room, Jensen found Ziran leaning over a computer. "Get to safety," she yelled.

The man looked up at her in alarm. "What?"

Jensen ran past him, pulling him with her as she entered the monitoring station. "Get down!" Pushing Ziran under a desk, she dropped to her knees, pulling Kiernan with her. Kiernan fell between the scouts, and Jensen reached out, pulling Ziran close and sandwiching Kiernan between them. She closed her eyes and voiced the remaining countdown. "Three… two… one…"

CHAPTER 19

Vegas was crouched upon his knees under a workstation. The desk was small, and his bulky frame struggled to fit under the counter enough to be able to gain access to the rear of an antiquated data processor. He had found the cubical of a known scientist renowned for his work on the galactic exploration project, and hyper-drive and soundwave technology. The Major's directive was to find the raw data for faster than light travel.

The construction of their craft was complete, as was the hyper-drive system. What was missing was the eradication of bugs in the main system drivers' ability to support the hyper-drive system for extended periods of travel. As well as the last piece of technology vital to their Ultimate Agenda. This information was contained within the data, Vegas was tasked to find. For cycles, they had toiled in effort to build and re-build their ship equipped to transport their future to a new world. A world free from poisonous radiation and endless dusk. The power source was ready, thanks to Kiernan's tireless efforts, the ship was assembled, and its hyper-drive system was almost complete. They were so close.

Locating the terminal needed, Vegas set to work downloading the station's information. Kneeling under the workstation, he pulled out his data console and connected it to the aged terminal. Once connected he could transfer the entire system's backup data store to his console.

Footsteps caught Vegas' attention and he looked up above the desk to see Jilya standing before him.

"Major,"

"Scout."

"Sir, we all heard Minister Kiernan's request for help. Raziko, Ruben and I feel we should send one of us to back up Jensen."

Vegas placed his data console upon the floor and rose fully from behind the desk. "Are you suggesting Scout Jensen can't take care of herself or a potential situation? Furthermore, are you insinuating Minister Kiernan's protective detail can't perform their assigned duties?" Vegas was still smarting after his confrontation with Jensen. He knew it and so did the rest of the team.

"Sir, I believe we should leave nothing to chance. If Kiernan did need help, then where was her protective detail and why didn't she summon them?"

Placing his hands upon the desk Vegas looked down with a sigh. Jilya was right. "Have you completed your directives?"

"Almost."

"Then you go and…"

Both men froze as the deafening sound of an explosion reached their ears. The station shook, lose objects on the desk between them rattled and rolled off its surface. Vegas looked up at the network of relays above them, seeing them shake with the force. The men's eyes reconnected. The sound of running footsteps reached them. Vegas stepped back from the desk in bewilderment.

"Looks like we're all going," he said, as he vaulted over the barrier.

Jilya followed him out of the cubicle, and they ran to the platform steps, "Major, do you think-"

"No point in presumptions, Scout, let's investigate."

The men turned to see Ruben and Raziko run towards them. They ascended the stairs at speed.

***

Her breathing sounded harsh, even to her own ears. Dust particles floated around them, settling upon the trio like freshly fallen snow. Jensen had never seen snow, but she had read about it. The lighting around them had shattered, but emergency beacons emitted a soft emerald glow. Jensen took a breath and coughed as dust hit the back of her throat. The sound of unknown objects falling around them forced Jensen to bury her head, still holding Kiernan until all sounds dissipated.

It was Ziran who spoke first. "Everybody alright?"

"I think so," Kiernan replied.

"Then does somebody mind telling me what… that… was?"

Jensen rose and shook her head to release the dust which had settled into her hair. "Later, Ziran. We must get out of here."

Pulling her head up from the ground, Kiernan coughed harshly. She blinked and shook, instantly feeling the wound on her head explode in pain as she moved. "Oh my." she groaned and held her head with her uninjured arm. Kiernan coughed again. Her ribs throbbed in pain.

"Can you stand?" Jensen asked, her concern clear.

"Without throwing up, I'm not sure. Give me a moment." Kiernan sat gingerly upon the floor.

Ziran stood and looked around the security station. All monitors had disconnected from the power grid. Their screens black. Fortunately, there was little damage to the room in which they had taken shelter, but Ziran could see evidence of the blast beyond. All the two-way mirrors had shattered from the blast's vibration and glass littered the walkway.

"Can I ask again? WHAT HAPPENED?"

Jensen looked cautiously at Ziran. Could she trust him? Maybe she needed to evaluate Ziran fist. "What happened to Jorca?"

"The woman went crazy. Accused me of double crossing the mission. Threatened to expose me for killing Jax…"

"What?" Kiernan said with a jump.

Ziran continued, his expression incredulous. "Didn't give me a chance to respond or explain before she came at me with her baton like a possessed scavenger. After what I'd saw from Jax I simply reacted." Ziran saw how closely Jensen was watching him, a wary glint in her eyes. He looked down at Kiernan, who was still seated on the floor. For the first time he saw her head wound, split lip, and the way she held herself in obvious pain. Ziran knelt and placed a tender hand under Kiernan's chin and angled it up for a closer inspection. "This didn't happen in the explosion." He looked around. "Where's Xoren?"

"Dead," Kiernan answered without regret.

"How?"

Rising slowly to her feet, Kiernan took a step towards Jensen. "What happened to Jax?"

"He tried to stop me from finding you." Jensen smoothed her hand slowly down her clothing brushing away the dust. "He would have killed me."

"I stopped him."

Kiernan looked between Ziran and Jensen. "Jax as well?"

Jensen nodded silently. Her mind whirled with paranoia. "There's something we…"

Approaching footsteps halted Jennens's words. Cautiously she angled her body to peer through the broken two-way mirror frame. She saw Jilya first followed by Ruben, Vegas and then Raziko. The four men stopped, skidding to a clattering halt over the scattering of broken mirrored glass.

Vegas looked around. There wasn't much evidence of the explosion in the monitoring room, but Jensen feared what they would find when they ventured back towards the laboratory. The Major turned his attention to Kiernan. Her visible wounds sent instant alarm through him. Impulsively, Vegas vaulted his bulky frame over the wall.

"WHAT HAPPENED?" he roared.

Ziran, bewildered and still unsure of what had occurred himself, looked to Jensen. Catching his movement, Vegas did the same.

"Care to enlighten me, Scout?"

Feeling she no longer knew who she could trust, Jensen faltered. She licked her dry lips as she looked at Kiernan. The dried blood and terrifying vision of what Xoren had tried reminded her of his and Jax's betrayal, of the foundations behind their actions and their implications. Who else was involved? Who issued the order? Most importantly, did Vegas know. Could they trust him?

"Scout," Vegas' patience was wearing thin. "What HAPPENED?"

"A chemical reaction," Kiernan said. "I can only surmise whatever they had stored and had been using here had degraded and become unstable over time." She looked at Jensen with a guarded expression. "I warned Xoren to keep out of the stores. He believed there might be useable materials."

"Jilya, Ruben, Raziko," Vegas turned to the Scouts, "Investigate, but tread carefully."

"Yes, Major." The scouts complied.

Once they were gone, Vegas folded his arms. "Do you want to try again? Please explain to me how a simple chemical spillage shook the entire foundations of this station?" He turned to Kiernan feeling he would receive honesty from one of his closest allies. "What happened that urged you to call for help? Help you felt you were unable to receive from your protective detail. Why call us?" He took a step towards Kiernan. "Most importantly, why are you the only one sporting injuries?" Still focussed upon Kiernan, his eyes flicked up to Ziran. "Maybe you can answer, Scout?"

Jensen watched silently, struggling to rid herself of her intense feelings of paranoia. Who could they trust? "Ziran wasn't present at the explosion, Sir."

Vegas remained focussed upon Kiernan. "Why did you call for assistance?"

Kiernan stepped away from Vegas. She took a slow breath and gauged her body's reactions. She feared she had broken ribs, but her breathing seemed a little easier. She was hopeful. Kiernan had no doubts in her trust for Vegas. She had known him for long enough to feel her faith in him was just. However, that didn't mean she was ready to impart the truth just yet. Xoren had tried to kill her. The Select Prime wanted her dead? Kiernan believed she had to discoverer the truth behind the ultimate agenda. She had already uncovered enough to label her a threat, but who else could she trust to share that burden?

Watching Kiernan's inner turmoil, Jensen knew there was more information she needed from her. The governing powers of the colony wanted Kiernan dead and the Minister knew why.

"Sir, you need to see this."

Vegas turned to Jilya, who was standing in the doorway. He looked back at Ziran, Kiernan and then turned to Jensen. "On my way," he said giving Jensen one final look before following Jilya into the security room and beyond into the testing laboratory. Everybody followed. There seemed minimal damage, until they entered the laboratory.

Jensen looked around, astonished that the small explosive device had managed to create so much devastation. The reinforced glass on each of the holding cells had shattered. The walls were cracked and broken, jagged fingers stretching out like forked lightning through the concrete. The ceiling was interspersed with fissures forking out above them. Portions of the ceiling had broken away and fallen. A piece lay upon Jax's body.

"Looks like they didn't make it." Ruben knelt and took Jorca's hand. It was cold and smeared with blood.

Vegas closed his eyes and pinched the bridge of his nose. "Where's Xoren?"

"Through there." Kiernan pointed to what was left of the doorway leading to the stores and filing room. The door was gone, the frame destroyed. Instead lay tons of concrete almost blocking their entry entirely. Seeing an opening above the rubble, Ruben approached what was left of the doorway.

"Scout, no!" Vegas yelled.

"Sir, there is enough room for me to slide through at the top! We need to see if we can find Xoren."

"Don't be foolish," Ziran yelled.

Ruben stopped and turned. "What if he's alive?"

Jensen looked up at the ceiling, hearing a loud crack above them. New fingers of expanding cavity streaked through the cement and stone, further fracturing its integrity.

"Surely we must try."

"Ruben!"

As the scout looked at her, Jensen angled her finger up to the ceiling. Ruben followed and looked up above him. The cracks opened, extending above him. Kiernan gasped.

"Move now!" Vegas yelled. He watched in horror as another part of the ceiling broke away and fell hard, trapping Ruben between it and the floor. Jensen closed her eyes, as she saw a splattering of blood shoot out from the impact.

"No!" Jilya yelled and turned away.

"Everybody out, now!" Vegas backed away, retreating to the safety of the security room. The integrity of the laboratory too compromised to remain safe. "Move quickly."

The remaining six members of Operation Hypogean ran for safety, escaping any more falling debris. The sound of crashing rubble drowned out their retreating footsteps as they ran out into the corridors. Kiernan moved as fast as she was able, trailing behind the team. The gap widening as she struggled to keep up. Her side screamed in pain, her head throbbed, and her stomach churned. She saw herself falling further and further behind. It was Jensen who noticed, and as they entered the cafeteria, she stopped.

"Jilya, Kiernan needs medical assistance."

Deciding the eatery was a good place to stop, Vegas slowed to a halt. "Re-group people. Jilya attend Minister Kiernan, and Jensen a word please."

Refraining from lashing out in frustration, Jensen knew she needed to think fast. Vegas wanted answers and she couldn't give any without compromising Kiernan's safety. If she could have a moment alone with Kiernan, she would be able to solidify a story between them. Two members of the team had been ordered to take Kiernan's life. She needed to know why, and if anybody else from the team was awaiting their opportunity.

Kiernan perched on a table, relieved to take a moment's rest. She closed her eyes and took shallow breaths. Images of Xoren's attack flashed through her mind. His expression, as he struck her with his baton. The look of aggression, as he kicked her across the floor. He enjoyed it she realised. A lump rose in her throat.

"Minister?"

Opening her eyes, Kiernan saw Jilya standing before her; concern was clear in his expression. He held a medical pack held before him.

"Do you mind if I take a look at your injuries?"

Kiernan nodded, afraid to use her voice for fear it may break and betray her attempt to remain calm. The team were all feeling the effects of seeing Ruben's death. Something she was sure wouldn't truly sink in until they were out of danger.

Placing his kit down to the right side of Kiernan, Jilya opened it and rummaged inside. He looked up at her head.

"Brunt force trauma," he said softly. "Do you feel sick, dizzy, tired?"

"Yes, yes and yes." Kiernan smiled. "Very tired. I know I must have a concussion."

Jilya pursed his lips and nodded. He began to clean her head wound, wiping gently around the area of impact. "Minister, if I may, your wounds are very particular to evidence of a physical…"

Kiernan shook her head, silently saying that he was not at liberty to finish his statement. Jilya held his silence for long moments, as he continued to clean her wound. However, eventually he spoke again.

"Minister. I am a medic and am sworn to a similar oath as Physician Angeles. Anything you say to me will be…" seeing Kiernan was about to protest, it was Jilya who shook his head. "Anything you say to me will be held in confidence, but I see now there is something more" he chose his words carefully, "sinister… going on here." He lowered his voice. "If you are unable to tell me that is fine but know you can trust me." Jilya then looked away, indicting his speech was over. He took a dressing from the kit and placed it over Kiernan's head wound. "That's one; where else?" He began to gently clean around her cut lip, respectfully ignoring the tear that ran down Kiernan's cheek.

Jensen's attention turned to Raziko and Ziran. The men stood in silent dismay. One of their own had died before them. Jensen felt it too, but she couldn't allow herself to concentrate on those thoughts. Not yet.

"Jensen?"

She turned to see Vegas standing before her.

"A moment?"

With a nod, Jensen looked back at her fellow scouts. Ziran had his hand upon Raziko's back. A show of comfort.

Vegas folded his arms. "We lost Ruben. One of our own. Another Scout. That's four of our team gone," he watched Jensen's expression and lifted his hand slowly, pointing at her chest. "The truth, Scout. Tell me the truth. Kiernan looks terrified and you look as tense as I've ever seen you."

Jensen relaxed her features and looked back at Vegas with indifference.

"Don't try that with me, Scout. Whether you believe me or not, I'm on your side and if Jax or Xoren or Jorca attacked Kiernan, then I need to know, or I cannot do my job."

"And what is your job, Sir?"

"To oversee this mission and bring the team home safely."

Jensen looked away. "It seems you have already failed."

"Damn it, Scout. I AM NOT JOKING."

Keeping herself calm, Jensen held Vegas' stare. "Neither am I, Major." She looked around seeing all eyes were upon them. "If you have questions, then I'm not the person you should be talking to. I have questions too, but I won't compromise Kiernan's safety until she is ready to talk." Jensen saw Vegas' expression fall. He didn't understand what she meant, but he understood Kiernan was the person he needed to speak to. He looked over at the Minister. She was sitting gingerly upon a dining table, as Jilya gently pressed around her side. Her eyes, however, were fixed upon his. Patting Jensen's shoulder Vegas walked towards Kiernan.

"How are you feeling, Minister? It seems Advisor Xoren took the brunt of the explosion?" Vegas now watched Kiernan's reaction. She was quicker, calmer, and more ready for his questioning. She knew him. She also knew she could trust him, but she wasn't ready to divulge the truth. Not yet.

"Cuts and bruises," she said. "Not sure if my arm is broken." Kiernan held said arm close to her body. She took some tablets handed to her, along with a canteen of water.

Jensen was instantly beside Vegas. "What are those?"

Holding up the container, Jilya exposed the lid portraying the medication he had handed Kiernan. "Painkillers. Do you need some? I have plenty," he said with a smile. Jensen cast a gaze between Jilya and Kiernan. Vegas between Jensen and Kiernan. Kiernan offered Jensen an almost imperceptible nod of assurance. She took the painkillers.

"Right," Knowing he wasn't getting the answers he sought just yet, Vegas glanced around at his team. "We need to collect our haul from the testing facility. We were ordered to find the possibility of a munitions factory somewhere within this station, but under the circumstances, I feel this is not in our best interests. We will collect the material from our directives and quit."

"Agreed," Kiernan said, as she slid off the table. She looked around. "I lost my pack in the explosion."

"The data?"

She lowered her head with a shake.

"Damn it," Vegas whispered.

"Actually," Ziran stepped between them. "I downloaded all the hard data files from a main terminal in the laboratory." He held up his console. "There's a good chance what you need is in here. I picked up as much as I could when we left, including Jax's pack." He dropped the console in the pack. "There's a lot of separate project files."

"Good work, Scout," Vegas slapped his back.

Kiernan remained impassive but took Jax's pack all the same.

"Gather your things and let's go."

CHAPTER 20

They walked in bewildered silence. Vegas took the lead; his thoughts fixated upon Kiernan. Jilya was next, pondering the origin of Kiernan's injuries. Then there was Ziran, who ran the events before the explosion over and over in his mind. Kiernan was next, silently running through the possibilities to questions she had yet to ask. Behind her was Jensen. She looked back and forth between the remaining team members, wondering if any of them carried an alternative agenda. Raziko brought up the rear. The last expression upon Ruben's face etched into his mind's eye.

Jensen remained close to Kiernan, a list of questions formulating within her mind. They needed answers. From their first meeting, Jensen had held the distinct impression Minister Kiernan was harbouring secrets. Her occasional, but noticeable, evasive reasoning further enhanced those suspicions. Jensen was never one to pry. Living within the colony, she fully understood the need for privacy. Especially when your only means of an escape was to enter a terrifying, toxic wasteland. Due to this, she respected a person's privacy, but with Kiernan it was different. She needed answers and she was sure Kiernan had them.

Jensen stepped up her gait as she stole a sideways glace at Kiernan. The Minister's features were tight. Worry lines etched trenches around her eyes and, at that moment, Jensen knew a battle was heading their way.

Almost reaching the stairway down to the testing facility, Jensen froze as a distant sound met her keen ears. She looked ahead seeing Vegas halt and turn. Their eyes met. They heard it again. A piercing scream echoed through the station. Followed by another. Then another and another. Different tones showing growing numbers.

Jensen watched Vegas' eyes grow impossibly wide. Realisation dawned. There was another scream. Followed by another. Each one different, varying in proximity.

"The explosion must have alerted them to our presence!"

Panicked, the team began to run. They sprinted down a short corridor and took a left. Retrieval of any more components forgotten, they headed for the exit. Ahead, the elevator shaft came into view, but what Jensen saw made her heart freeze in her chest.

She stopped as she felt somebody collide into the back of her as she stared ahead in horror. Scrambling down the elevator shaft were a hoard of scavengers.

"No!"

Unsure who had spoken, Jensen changed direction. "Run!"

The team turned direction and ran. Vegas led the way back towards the testing facility. A hopeful location of safety. Jensen looked to her side seeing Kiernan slow, and instinctively she reached out to take the wrist of her uninjured arm. In her other, Jensen pulled free her tonfa. They passed through a side doorway and reached the concrete stairway.

"Ahhhhgh!"

Jensen turned to see Jilya fighting with a scavenger. She thought they were at least fifteen fractions ahead of them. She wondered where this one had come from. Gripping the tonfa, Jensen released Kiernan's hand.

"Keep going," she shouted, as she ran to Jilya's aid.

Jensen ignored the call of her name, knowing she needed to help Jilya first. The man was taken off guard and pulled to the ground. Another scavenger was fast approaching. It came from the opposite direction, its eyes wild with hunger. Jensen swung out hitting it hard across the face. It bought her enough time to reach Jilya. The younger scout was gaining the advantage and had the scavenger pinned to the ground face down. In a swift move of logical thought Jensen pulled out a knife from her trouser leg pocket and pushed the blade down hard into the scavenger's neck. She severed the spine. The scavenger screamed but stopped moving.

"Where did you-"

"Move, Jil," Jensen ordered, as she pulled him from the ground and continued to run. Passing the first scavenger Jensen had knocked to the floor, Jilya saw it was rising.

"Jenson!" he yelled in warning.

Jensen turned seeing the scavenger moving as she skidded to a stop. She threw her knife to Jilya, and he caught it easily, swung the blade around and pushed it into the back of its neck. A new move used by Jensen, it was swift and effective. The scavenger fell back to the ground unmoving. They continued to run, terrifying screams drawing closer and closer. The gap between them, and the horde of advancing scavengers shrinking.

Kiernan hadn't stopped to pay much attention to her surroundings as they entered the testing facility. They ran through the mass of cubicles, Vegas ordering them to follow Raziko as he took a detour and disappeared into a workstation. Kiernan followed, unable to do anything more, as she pushed herself to move faster. As fast as her abused body was able. They reached the end of the cubicles and ran out into a wide-open space. Their footsteps echoed, their breathing sharp. Continuing to the far end Raziko, Kiernan and Ziran passed a peculiar shaped, shrouded object. It hung high above the ground. They paid it little attention as they ran, hearing the distant scream of scavengers loom ever closer.

Reaching the far end of the vast space, Ziran cursed, confronted by another locking mechanism. He fumbled frantically in his pockets desperate to find his E.M.P disruptor.

"Make haste, Scout," Vegas shouted. The Major had cleared the cubicles and was running towards them. He held his data console tight within his grasp. Behind him the team saw Jensen and Jilya sprinting towards them. Jilya was fast and he was easily catching up with Vegas.

"They're coming," Jensen shouted. "Open the door!"

It was less than ten fractions before the first scavenger broke through the cubicles. It screamed in triumph, eyes wide, broken teeth smeared with blood.

Ziran fumbled desperately, unable to find his E.M.P disrupter. Vegas pushed him out of the way. Finding his instrument in his breast pocket he used it quickly and deactivated the lock.

"Inside now," he yelled.

They were too close. Almost upon them. Two, three, four scavengers appearing from the workstations. Getting closer. Too close. They wouldn't make it.

"Weapons!" The Major bellowed, as he pulled his baton from his waist.

Jensen pulled the other two knives from her leg pocket. The automatic firearms would take too long to retrieve from her pack. She threw her pack through the doorway and turned back to the scene before them.

"Catch," she threw one knife at Raziko and the other to Vegas. Jensen readied her tonfa. Ziran had pulled Kiernan into the far room and stood guard by the door, ready to defend their sanctuary. A horde of scavengers swarmed the far end of the room, massing upon the inspection balcony at the entrance. Four scavengers were upon them.

From the doorway Kiernan saw the fight begin. The scavengers howled into the fray, clawing, and scraping, screaming, and gnashing. It was the first time she had seen a scavenger up close. Their lifeless eyes seemed hollow. Their putrid skin, pale and fissured, oozing with thick pus. They wore little in the way of clothing. The few scraps of material did little to cover even the most intimate of areas. It did seem, Kiernan noted, that those strips of material almost appeared to signify a symbol of status. Was there a hierarchy within the scavenger pack?

On the floor, the fight was fast and frantic. Attacks and counterattacks traded repeatedly. Jensen swung out her tonfa hitting a scavenger, and then again, as the team fought to gain advantage. Vegas quickly took down a scavenger, severing its spine at the base of its neck, the knife his new favourite weapon. Kiernan saw the glint of appreciation in his eyes, as the scavenger fell at his feet. To their left, Jilya had been knocked to the ground. His opponent gaining the upper hand, as it swooped down upon him, taking him off guard, as blunt and broken teeth tore savagely into the flesh of his exposed neck. Jilya's scream echoed through the facility. Panicked by the sound, Jensen stole a glance, seeing Jilya's predicament and fought harder to overcome her attacker. It was Vegas who reached him first. Once again taking advantage of the scavenger's position, he sunk his knife into the base of its neck and twisted hard. He felt the satisfying snap as its spine severed.

Raziko was on the ground, flipping repeatedly as he fought with a smaller scavenger. His opponent was fast and easily twisted out of the larger man's grasp. Time was running out and soon the hoard of scavengers would be upon them. Knowing this, Raziko fought smarter. Using his strength, he pushed the scavenger away, giving him enough room to jump to his feet, ready his baton and swing out hard, repeatedly. Breaking bone after bone and leaving his attacker motionless.

Jensen had taken to a similar method. Unable to overcome her opponent, who was upon her with clawing nails, gnashing teeth and a stench which threatened to drag her insides up her oesophagus, with gut-wrenching wretches, she had used her tonfa to hit out harder and harder. They were running out of time to escape.

Seeing the mass approaching, swarming through the cubicles, Vegas felt panic rise.

"Retreat," he yelled. "Retreat!"

Jensen looked up, seeing the first of the horde make their way through the cubicle exit. She hit out one last time, seeing her opponent fall to the ground as she turned to run. To her side, she saw Vegas taking Jilya by the ankles as Ziran took his shoulders, and together they hauled the wounded man to safety. Raziko was just behind them, as they ran towards the separate room.

Piercing screams echoed in mass. Running through the door Raziko turned, slamming it closed behind him, and activating the lock.

Zira's laboured breath was drowned out by the screaming and pounding of scavengers, desperate to reach them on the other side of the door. He gasped for breath. "I've never seen so many. That was so close." The door shook as the scavengers threw their bodies against the barrier.

"People," Kiernan looked around at the team who were in varying degrees of recovery. "Everybody, please." She looked back down at Jilya, his skin pale, his eyes searching hers silently, as she forcibly applied pressure to his gaping neck wound. "You're alright," she whispered. Kiernan pulled off her jacket, balling it into her fist as she pushed it hard against his bloodied flesh. "We need a med kit!"

"It's in his pack," Jensen said, at once rushing to help lift Jilya, so she could pull the pack from his back.

The hammering on the door continued.

Jensen threw the pack to Vegas, as she helped lower Jilya back to the ground. "We need to find a more comfortable place for Jil to dress his wounds."

Raziko looked around. The room appeared to be an assembly factory. It was large and whatever it held for construction must have been as wide as the double sliding doors at its opposite end. A crane hung high above, still holding a piece of moulded metal in its claws. It swung silently and ever so softly; the air disrupted by their presence. Around the side of the room, and situated halfway up the wall, was a wrap-around viewing balcony. A set of metal plate steps led up to its steel grid walkway. There were three doors on the left side of the room, the furthest was clearly a lavatory. Raziko looked back at the far side of the assembly bay and the double set of sliding doors. Could this be their way out? From his vantage point he could see no sign of mechanical operation.

Vegas stepped closer. "Jilya's losing a significant amount of blood. We need to move him to that bench."

"Will he make it?" Jensen whispered to Kiernan.

The older woman looked back with a solemn expression that spoke volumes.

"He will make it," Vegas said, as he brushed past Jensen and positioned himself by Jilya's head. "Ziran help me get Jil up to that bench. Kiernan keep pressure on the wound. Jensen bring the medical pack and Raziko clear the mess covering that work top!"

The team jumped into action and obeyed the Major's orders with swift precision. Raziko swept his arm over the workbench, knocking off several flimsy containers, small tools, and papers. Vegas and Ziran lay Jilya on the surface and backed away quickly as Kiernan inspected the wound. She pulled her coat away, blood still pooling. Jensen opened the medical kit and pulled out a large, medicated swab. She passed it to Kiernan, who placed it over the gaping wound.

Vegas took the kit from Jensen and peered inside. "Is this all we have? Some wraps, anti-infection solvent and painkillers? I need... he needs... more than this." Vegas looked at Kiernan. "Advice please?"

Kiernan pushed harder, as she leaned over Jilya and spoke softly to the young man. Helplessness engulfed her, and a lump rose to her throat. Copious amounts of blood had seeped through the swab and soaked the side of her jacket. Jilya's eyes tried desperately to connect and communicate with Kiernan, but they drifted away.

Looking back at Vegas, Kiernan felt helpless, "There's nothing we can do. He's -."

Gasping one last time, Jilya pulled a final breath through his slackened jaw. Blood gurgled in the back of his throat. Kiernan placed two fingers upon his arm. There was no pulse. "I can't...there's no..." Her hand fell away. A single tear slipped from her eye. "He's gone."

With a growl, Vegas turned. He stormed towards the door and kicked it repeatedly, "Damn you," he yelled.

The thumping and screaming of persistent scavengers stopped for a fraction, and then increased in ferocity. Vegas raked his blunt fingernails over his head frantically and then yelled out again, pounding the sides of his fists against the door.

Taking Kiernan by the arm, Jensen pulled her to one side. She could see the colour had drained from her features. Her blood-soaked hands trembled, and she clasped them together to hide her emotions.

"You're alright," Jensen said calmly, desperate not to acknowledge Jilya's passing and only concentrate on their situation. She needed to stay calm. She needed to focus. Kiernan seemed to look right through her, and Jensen pulled her closer. "Look at me."

Doing as asked, Kiernan focused her gaze upon Jensen. "Jen," she looked at Jilya's body, then to Raziko and Ziran, who had walked away consumed by their own grief. She looked to Vegas, who was leaning against the door. "Jen, how are we going to get out of here?"

Jensen pulled Kiernan into a reassuring hug. She peered over her shoulder looking around the room. With limited options, she wondered that very same question.

CHAPTER 21

The screaming beyond the door was relentless. Almost half a mark had passed, and the scavengers' savage cries continued. Their threatening presence loomed upon the remaining members of the team. A terrifying reminder of the horror that lay beyond the assembly bay.

Sitting on the floor, her back against the wall, Kiernan cradled her injured arm close to her chest. She stared over at Jilya's body. He lay upon the workbench across the room. A dust sheet had been placed over him, but one arm hung low from the tabletop. A trail of dried blood streaked down his arm and formed a congealed puddle upon the floor.

Looking to the left of the table, Kiernan spied Raziko slumped on the floor. He had one hand placed upon Jilya's uninjured shoulder as he stared down at the ground. Vegas remained by the door. He stared at the solid barrier watching as it shook with the scavengers' continuous pounding. The Major's expression stayed the same, frozen in a fit of concentrated anger, simmering thoughtfully.

In a separate room, Ziran and Jensen searched storage boxes. Unclasping the lids on the large containers, one by one, the pair searched for anything they thought might be of use. At one corner of the room, Ziran found a large machine that appeared to dispense packaged foods with the input of monetary units. He jabbed at the machine's buttons hopefully.

"Do you think anything you get out of there will be edible?"

Ignoring her question Ziran said, "What are we looking for in here, Jen?"

Jensen pushed a cardboard box to one side and grasped another. She flipped open its lid and stared down into the container's contents. More components.

"What are we looking for? Anything that might help us. Ideas? I don't know." She looked up at Ziran. "We're at ground zero in a cluster screw-up."

"We had no idea what would happen here," Ziran defended. "This was a mission into the unknown and we were as prepared as we could be."

"Were we though?" Jensen placed her hands upon her hips. "Seems information wasn't distributed evenly, and agendas differed. If you ask me, Ziran, this mission was doomed from the start."

Regarding Jensen silently for several moments, Ziran took a step closer. "Are you referring to Xoren and Jax?" Another step. "Your lack of clarification into the events back in the laboratory reveals more than you realise. The mistrust in your eyes speaks volumes. I know you fear for Minister Kiernan's life. After what I saw with Officer Jax I understand why. I won't demand you tell me what's going on, but if a time comes when you need back up, I promise you I am on your side."

Jensen looked away. She believed Ziran and his pledge of alliance spoke volumes. Her eyes clouded with unshed tears, but she was desperate not to let them fall. She needed to hear that voice of support. Looking back at Ziran, Jensen smiled. "Thank you," she said simply, and then turned quickly to face a metal locker. She pulled it open and peered inside. There upon the top shelf sat a first aid box. She grabbed it quickly, aware they needed more than the meagre medical supplies that remained in Jilya's med kit. Jensen tucked the box under her arm and continued her search.

Behind her, Ziran continued to watch Jensen silently. He looked out of the door briefly, just able to see Kiernan sitting on the floor on the other side of the assembly bay. Their eyes connected and he turned away, almost embarrassed to be caught looking. Staring back at Jensen, Ziran thought back to the laboratory. Jax had attacked Jensen and he had killed him. Scouts stick together. It was an unspoken rule. Xoren had obviously attacked Kiernan. Jensen had stopped him. What was happening? Ziran would stand by his words, and he wouldn't push Jensen for answers. He would uphold his vow to stand by her, but he wanted answers.

Finishing her inspection of the locker, Jensen closed the door and turned. She was surprised to see Ziran had been standing in the same spot for the past several fractions, staring into space.

"Are you alright?"

He nodded. "Just thinking." Without another word he turned to the stack of narrow files.

Jensen took the medical kit from under her arm and looked at the doorway. The scavengers' screams continued. Their banging and thrashing upon the door continued. In frustration she kicked a box across the room; it hit the wall with a crash that echoed into the assembly bay.

"Want to alert more of those things to our presence?"

Jensen looked over at Ziran, her eyes void of emotion. "Can anything else be heard over that relentless wailing?" she shouted, as if to prove her point.

Kiernan looked up hearing, Jensen's voice from the opposite room. The screams were getting to them all. Kiernan wanted to cover her ears and bury her head. Anything to drown out the scavengers' wails. Her head fell backwards, hitting the wall behind her. She wanted to be home, back in the safety and seclusion of the colony. Their haven. Kiernan imagined herself sitting in her laboratory, safe and happily embroiled in her work. Comfort and familiarity. Not enveloped in this feeling of terror and the all-encompassing shrieks of–

"Hey."

Opening her eyes, Kiernan saw Jensen standing above her. She knelt and twisted her body around, so she was sitting beside Kiernan with her back to the wall. An instant feeling of calm encompassed Kiernan as she felt her settle beside her. Jensen was silent as she studied her profile for a moment before speaking.

"Does it hurt?"

Kiernan looked at Jensen and the younger woman inclined her head towards Kiernan's arm.

"Oh. Yes, it does, but I don't think it's broken," she paused and moved her fingers. "The pain is receding, and I have a little more movement."

Jensen took hold of Kiernan's wrist gently and pulled it towards her. Cradling the limb softly, Jensen pushed the sleeve up Kiernan's arm. A delicate hue of multi-coloured shades marred the pale flesh. Jensen brushed her fingers over the contusion, feeling the swelling around the base of her wrist. "How did it happen?"

Kiernan jumped, as another round of hammering resonated from the door. She saw Vegas turn and disappear into the room Jensen had just vacated. His expression infused with frustrated ire. The Major hadn't spoken since she had declared Jilya dead. There was no way he could deal with the loss of half his team. It was the most people they had ever lost, and they were under Vegas' command.

Jensen looked at the door as it rattled with intent. She felt herself push back harder against the wall. She knew there was no way the scavengers would be able to breech the barrier. The door was re-enforced with osmium. It would take an explosive force to penetrate the portal, and even then it was more likely to fracture the barrier's surroundings than the door itself. Still, in all her cycles as a scout, Jensen had never found herself in a position where she felt so utterly helpless and trapped. She looked over at Raziko. He had moved away from Jilya's body and was walking around the double sliding doors on the opposite side of the room. It was their possible means of escape and if anybody could figure out the mechanical functioning of those doors it would be Raziko. Jensen pondered their choices. They could wait for the scavengers to eventually tire and move on. She knew the energy cell had a limited supply of power. It would eventually deplete and then the whole station would be plunged into darkness. Surely, they needed to find a way out before that happened.

Turning back to Kiernan, Jensen picked up the medical kit and placed it on the floor between them. Noting Kiernan's lack of communication, Jensen looked into her eyes. It was obvious the older woman was in shock. Weren't they all? Jensen wondered how best to reach out to her. Opening the medical kit she rummaged around inside, pulling out a bandage. She began a slow and delicate wrapping of Kiernan's arm, her attention moving back and forth from Kiernan's wrist to her eyes.

"Talk to me," she said softly, her eyes focussed on the bandage.

Blinking, Kiernan appeared to regain a measure of sense. She looked at her wrist seeing the impressive job Jensen had done of binding her injury.

"You've done this before."

Jensen smiled softly. "Once or twice." Next, she took a jar of salve from the box and dipped a cotton swab into the medicated mixture. She dabbed Kiernan's split lip gently. "Talk to me, Kier."

Looking away to order her thoughts, Kiernan noticed Vegas was now standing by Jilya's body. "I apologise for my reticence."

"It's fine. This isn't a familiar circumstance. Even I've never seen so many scavengers before and I've spent countless marks on the Barrens."

"You're scared?"

"Terrified!" Jensen smiled. "I know we need a plan, but right now I think everybody is trying to reconcile what's happened."

Kiernan winced as Jensen applied a dollop of salve to her lip. "We don't have time to reconcile."

Screwing the lid back on the healing gel, Jensen looked up at Kiernan. "How long will the power cell last?"

With a shrug, Kiernan looked up at the lighting. "The facility is draining a lot of power. I'd never have imagined the generator would be linked to so many of the main circuit functions. Without any form of kinetic or solar recharge, the cell will drain fast."

"So, they are rechargeable?"

Kiernan nodded her head. "When connected to the right inlet of course." She paused, "Will the darkness deter the scavengers?"

"The light should have deterred them. They're used to the darkness obviously and have adapted well over time." Jensen looked back at the door noting a slight decrease in hammering and screeching. "Time. We could wait them out, but with no idea how long it would take for them to tire and move on, we would only find ourselves at a disadvantage" Jensen dropped Kiernan's swab to the ground.

Watching Jensen, Kiernan picked up the jar of salve. "What is this?"

Unscrewing the lid, Jensen held it for Kiernan's inspection. "A healing solvent. It was created by Physician Scarlet. It supplies a protective covering and advances the healing process."

Kiernan noted the aroma. "It smells potent, but not offensive." Kiernan took the tin from Jensen. She noticed the younger woman's frown. "You have two lacerations on your neck and one on the side of your face." Seeing Jensen's surprise, she asked, "You don't feel them?"

Jensen prodded gingerly around her neck and winced when she hit an open wound. "I had no idea."

"I'm not surprised." Taking the kit, Kiernan began cleaning Jensen's wounds. She noticed Jensen flinch; an uncomfortable expression shadowed her features. Kiernan paused. "What's wrong?"

Looking away self-consciously, Jensen took the swab from Kiernan's fingers. She studied the smeared blood. "I'm not used to that."

Kiernan frowned. "To what?"

Jensen dabbed the swab over her neck. She smiled awkwardly, not wanting to continue the conversation.

"You've never been taken care of?"

Dropping the swabs to the floor, Jensen decided a change of topic was in order. She stared back at Kiernan. "Kier, why did Xoren want to kill you?"

Momentarily taken aback by the question, Kiernan looked away, seeking out the positions of the remaining team members.

"Kiernan?" Jensen moved to capture Kiernan's attention. She brought her focus back, seeing the tension rise in Kiernan's demeanour. "Please trust me."

"Trust isn't an issue, Jen." Kiernan looked down. She picked up a clean swab and placed a drop of salve upon it. Giving Jensen a look which told her not to resist, she continued to clean her wounds. "I discovered something. I think." She kept her voice low. "This discovery was noted by the authorities. That wasn't necessarily a problem, however my stance on certain issues changed due to my questioning regarding my discovery."

Once again Kiernan's evasive reasoning caused confusion.

"If the truth behind my discovery is anywhere close to what I believe it to be, it will change everything we've ever believed and worked towards. Unfortunately, I can't provide any clarification until I find physical proof, but if it is true…" Kiernan looked up at Jensen. She paused, finding the words to express the enormity of her statement. "Everything we've ever hoped for, everything we've worked for, it's meaningless. Our future… there isn't one."

Jensen's mouth worked, as she tried to formulate a response. She stopped Kiernan's hand. "What do you mean there is no future? What did you discover? Who wants you dead?" She held Kiernan's hand tighter. "Tell me."

"Commander Tehera and Select Prime Abrahams."

Jensen took a slow breath. "Why?" she whispered.

"If we get out of here, help me find the proof, and I'll tell you all." Kiernan's eyes were pleading.

The pounding on the door stopped suddenly and Jensen turned to look at the sealed barrier.

Vegas was back beside the door, one hand on its surface. He turned and looked back at Jensen, concern clear. Frustration clear. Anger simmering just below his surface.

Jensen looked back at Kiernan. "If we get out of this, I'll help you."

From the doorway, Vegas watched Jensen and Kiernan. Knowing both women like he did, he knew their conversation was deep; secretive. He folded his arms and watched in thought. Kiernan had sent out a call for aid. Jensen had answered. He wished now he had. Suddenly there was an explosion and three of his team were dead. Whatever had happened in that laboratory, Vegas needed to know before he delivered the mission report to Commander Tehera and the Select Prime. Whether the truth of those events was relayed to his superiors depended on **what** that truth was. At this point, all Vegas could be sure of was that Kiernan's injuries were the result of a physical attack and not the explosion.

A shriek resonated from beyond the assembly bay. Ignoring, once again, the barrage on the door, Vegas approached the women and knelt before them. "We need to discuss our options. We need to formulate a plan to get out of here." He turned to Raziko and Ziran. "Team, bring all the packs and drop them on that table over there." He pointed at a table to the far end of the room. "We're going to pool our resources."

"Escaping to the surface is one thing," Jensen said, looking up at Vegas, "But we still have the journey back to the vehicles, and then the ride back to the colony. I don't know about you, Sir, but I've never seen so many scavengers before in my life."

"How are we going to get out of here?" Kiernan asked, as she pulled Jax's backpack towards her, ready to share its contents.

"One step at a time." Vegas rose to his feet and followed Ziran to the table were Raziko was already emptying out the contents of his pack. Ziran was next, taking his packs and spilling out the contents. Vegas followed suit.

"So much for salvaging materials," Vegas said. "So many high hopes for this mission and mostly raw data collected."

"The primary requirement, was it not?" Ziran asked.

"True," Vegas conceded, "but this hasn't been the mission they'd hoped for."

True, Kiernan thought herself, but for vastly different reasons.

As the women reached the desk, Kiernan was first to empty Jax's pack out onto its surface. Jensen followed, accepting full disclosure as she allowed all her pack's contents to spill out onto the tabletop. Once everything was lay out for all to see, all eyes fell instantly upon the two automatic firearms, with Ziran and Raziko who reached for the unsanctioned weaponry.

"Where did you-"

"Were we not told to gather anything we thought might aid our mission and the colony?" Jensen asked evasively.

That statement was true.

"But where did you-" Raziko reached for a clip of bullets. "Does it work?"

"I can only believe so," Jensen replied, looking at Kiernan and then Vegas. "Where do you think those blades came from? You never got to search the stores in the generator room like we did." she smirked, "I guess you needed to know where to look."

"You always were the savvy Scout," Ziran commented.

Eager to change the subject from Jensen's ill-gotten gains, Vegas spoke quickly. "Right, so far we appear to have a better selection of weaponry."

Raziko pushed a clip of ammunition into the automatic firearm.

"Whoa! Jensen held up her hand. Careful with that. Untested and untrained!"

"I studied ancient weapons," Raziko defended, eager to try it out.

"We all did," Jensen said, as she reached out, taking it gently from Raziko's grasp. "But let's not draw any more attention to ourselves just yet." She placed the weapon back onto the table next to its twin.

Vegas searched the table of contents, pushing items out of the way to speedily assess what equipment they had at their disposal. His eyes fell upon something which Kiernan had emptied out of Jax's pack. "What's this?" It was a rhetorical question. He knew what it was but had little idea why Jax would have one in his pack.

All eyes turned to the device lying upon the table, and Ziran reached to pick it up.

"Don't touch it," Vegas warned, "I need to make sure it's not activated."

Jensen and Kiernan recognised it instantly as another explosive device. They exchanged briefed glances before looking back at Vegas. Vegas caught their exchange, his expression unreadable. Turning back to the mechanism upon the table, he peered over it and turned it gently around. It was inactive.

"What is it?" Ziran asked.

"Explosive," Kiernan said. "I've seen them before."

"Where was this?" Jensen asked, her suspicion rising.

"Looks like it came from Officer Jax's pack," Raziko offered. "Never seen anything like this before. Can't be standard issue."

Vegas took the device and studied it closely. "I'm aware of these, but we don't have much call to use them." Choosing to ignore the reason Jax had one in his possession, Vegas concentrated on their task. "This will come in good use." Mentally he scrolled through Jax's mission inventory. There was no mention of any explosives. He placed it back down upon the table carefully and eyed their equipment. "Certainly, a few more surprises up our sleeves than I initially considered. Suggestions?"

"How much energy do we have before the station powers down?"

Kiernan took a slow breath, "I'm unable to provide an exact time due to the unknown system drains on the generator. It's more than predicted, and without re-charge capabilities we're on borrowed time."

"That may stand in our favour," Raziko said.

"Scout?"

"The scavengers may see reasonably well in the dark, but I'd still favour my chances in the darkness."

Kiernan looked to the door where sporadic hammering continued. "But how many scavengers are out there and how will we overcome them?"

"That is the pertinent question," Jensen added, as a plan started to form in her mind. "What about those sliding doors over there," she pointed to the wide double doors on the other side of the assembly bay. "Can we get out that way?" She looked to Raziko.

The broad man shook his head solemnly. He'd checked and double checked the area looking for a function which would allow them to operate the mechanical doors. He'd found nothing. "They appear to be operated remotely. My guess is what they were building in here was Top Secret and movement was closely watched. Without the proper tools, I can't even begin to access or bypass operations to allow manual execution." Raziko folded his arms and looked back at the doors. "They're not moving, Sir."

"They were building the craft," Vegas said. "I can understand why movements were under surveillance. That really doesn't help us now. We must get out of here as soon as possible."

"How do you propose we do that?"

Kiernan inclined her head to the explosive on the table. "We have one advantage."

"They do pack a punch," Jensen agreed.

"How would you know," Vegas interjected. He fixed his gazed upon Jensen.

Their glaring standoff was broken by a resuming pounding upon the assembly bay entrance. The team members looked at the door and then back at each other. The silence that had risen between them rescinded as Jensen took one of the automatic firearms.

"Right," she took the clip out from within its grip and checked the rounds of ammunition before re-sliding it back into position. Making sure the safety switch was in place, Jensen walked off to the steps leading to the observation balcony. "We wait until the power dies." She ascended the steps two at a time. "Use the cover of darkness to our advantage." Jensen approached a window situated above the door and pulled a container across the metal grate flooring until it was situated under the window. Once in position, she climbed upon it, and looked out through the window and into the testing facility below.

Out on the factory floor she saw swarms of scavengers squabbling over the fallen bodies of their pack. Limbs had been torn from torsos, as they fought over the putrid flesh. Amber eyes shone in the soft light. The mix of blood with foul streaks of infected matter lay splattered across the floor.

Jensen looked further ahead as movement from the cubicles caught her attention. She closed her eyes and turned away. Noticing the reaction, the rest of the team raced to her. Only Vegas climbed the step to where Jensen stood. He looked out the window to the scene ahead. Cautiously Jensen did the same. What they saw unleashed icy claws of terror down their spine.

A single scavenger had appeared, dragging something in each hand. In its left was the body of Jorca, its hand well placed in her mouth to keep a firm grasp. To its right was the upper torso of Jax. His body had been half trapped in the fall of celling debris in the laboratory. The scavenger had pulled what was left of his body free and brought both officers bodies along to the feast. Jax's body was held at the back of his neck. The Scavenger's claw-like hand wrapped tight around the back of the neck and throat. Pulling its prize towards the horde and screaming out in victory, the scavenger dragged the bodies further past the cubicles, leaving a bloody trail from the torn remains of Jax's torso. Jensen felt her breathing quicken. She couldn't turn away.

The scavenger screamed again drawing more of the swarm's attention. It dropped Jax's body to the floor before taking Jorca with both hands and with swift and savage intent it tore her head from the body. It held the up to the horde and howled in victory. More screams ensued, as Jorca's headless body was thrown before the mass. They swarmed around the offering and tore into the untainted, fresh flesh with vigour. The primary scavenger, as Jensen had internally named it, held Jorca's head before it as it began feasting on her flesh, tearing into her face in rapture.

Feeling her stomach convulse, Jensen turned away, retching, and heaving in repulsion. She bent over, holding her stomach as she tried not to allow the meagre contents of her last meal spill onto the grated balcony flooring.

"What is it?" Kiernan asked, clearly disturbed.

Vegas turned from the window. "Feeding time," he said coldly. He placed one hand upon Jensen's back, as he walked past her limp body and descended the steps. "How long until power outage, Kiernan?"

"A mark or two at the very most," she said. Maybe less, she thought. There was no way to tell for sure. She would have to inspect the cell and that wasn't going to happen.

Vegas nodded in thought. "So, we have a route of delivery. He pointed back at the window where a pale Jensen was seated upon the box, they had used to stand upon. "We have a means of destruction." He then pointed to the explosive upon the table. "Now all we need is the cover of darkness." Vegas stood beside Kiernan. "For now, let's take the remaining time to prepare and regroup?" He looked at Kiernan. "And maybe you can explain what really-"

"Not now," Kiernan shook her head. "Away from here. Escape first. Talk later."

"And you will?"

"Will what?"

"Talk."

Kiernan's smile was forced. "I trust you, Vegas." She mentally crossed her fingers. "But not here. We're too exposed. I will explain all to you and Jensen when we are away from danger."

"And my report of the mission?"

"Hoping we make it back in one piece?" Kiernan smiled only half joking. "We already told you what happened. That you can report to the Commander and Select Prime."

With a sigh of frustration, Vegas pushed. "And when will I hear the unabridged version? Five of my team are dead, Kiernan. Don't you think I deserve to know why?"

Feeling her frustration rise, Kiernan turned to face Vegas fully and lowered her voice. She spoke firmly, knowing Vegas deserved answers, but needing him to understand she had to be ready to impart her knowledge. She couldn't afford to make another mistake. "Let's get home first."

Frustrated, Vegas turned and walked away.

Feeling weariness seep into her limbs, Kiernan moved to the side and slid down the wall. She sat back where Jensen had treated her arm. She wasn't surprised to see the younger woman approach her and sit quietly by her side. Her complexion was pale. Her eyes glazed and bloodshot from her stomach convulsions.

Kiernan tried to gain a closer inspection of Jensen, seeing the distant expression in her eyes. She placed a hand upon her back and moved it slowly in a reassuring manner.

"What happened out there?"

Jensen blinked. A single tear rolled down her cheek. "Some primary-like scavenger brought Jax's and Jorca's bodies in with it."

The older woman frowned.

"Dragging them, or what was left of them, to the horde for consumption." Jensen closed her eyes, as another tear escaped. She shook her head softly and tapped her finger upon the middle of her forehead. "I can still see it here. What they did. What that scavenger did to Jorca. I can still see it."

"Jen, look at me."

Jensen turned to look at Kiernan. "I can hear the sound of flesh ripping from her skull… and the blood." she squeezed her eyes tightly closed. "It won't go away."

Taking Jensen's face in her hands, Kiernan held her. "Jen, look at me. Look at me." She waited until Jensen re-opened her eyes. "I can't begin to imagine what you saw out there, but right now you must let it go. We need you. If we're to get out of here we need you." Kiernan held Jensen's gaze. "Nobody else is dying. Do you understand me?"

Pulling from Kiernan's grasp, Jensen looked away. For the first time in her life, she no longer felt the same sense of reassurance at the thought of returning home. Their haven. What was it really? Looking back at the woman beside her, she felt that more than ever. However, Kiernan still had faith. Kiernan wanted to escape and return home. Despite it all her new ally still wanted to fight. If Kiernan could do this, then so could she. "What do I have to do?"

Smiling, Kiernan said, "What you do best. One thing I've noticed about you is that you live up to your reputation."

Jensen frowned.

"You can get yourself out of any tricky situation. Jensen, you're quick thinking and wily. If anybody can get us out of here, you can. Consider our current situation 'tricky'."

Sagging, Jensen took a moment to consider Kiernan's words. They had discussed their possibilities with the equipment they had, but they had failed to discover the munitions store. That would have been a great advantage. Still, they had some unexpected additions in their arsenal. Jensen looked around the room. She studied her environment. Her mind whirled as the first puzzle pieces of her plan began slotting into place. She tapped her fingers upon her leg as her thoughts formulated an idea.

Kiernan watched her, seeing the change in demeanour, as Jensen's mind weighed the possibilities of their escape. Her dark eyes shifted around the room as those convoluted puzzle pieces nestled comfortably together.

Rising to her feet Jensen folded her arms and looked at the door. It shook with sporadic pounding. Although engaged in the primary scavenger's impromptu meal offering, they continued to affirm their presence. Jensen looked at Vegas, back at the door and then up at the mezzanine balcony and the window offering them a view into the testing facility beyond. There were so many scavengers out there. The plan needed to be executed with exact precision. They would have to be eradicated on mass.

Jensen looked back at Kiernan. "I know what to do. I have a-"
The sentence died upon her lips as the entire station was plunged into darkness.

CHAPTER 22

As the station powered down, the distant hum of its generated energy supply dissipated into a moment of absolute silence. Darkness draped its ominous presence over the facility. For several long moments silence governed, and Jensen heard nothing but the sound of her own anxious breath. Beside her, she heard Kiernan shift and rise to her feet. From beyond the safety of the assembly room, the team heard the tell-tale signs of scavengers re-acclimating themselves to the change in environment. Darkness had returned. Their scurrying and screaming continued.

Moving slowly, Kiernan held out her uninjured arm, trying to feel her way through the darkness. Her pace was cautious as she sought a path to the table where they had deposited their equipment. Her torch was upon that table. Kiernan moved slowly, one cautious step at a time. She sensed more than heard Jensen move behind her.

Slowing, the women became aware of another presence. It was Vegas. He moved towards them, stepping closer as one hand reached out to gain purchase of Kiernan's shoulder.

"A little sooner than expected," he muttered.

"Indeed," she agreed.

The darkness was absolute. Jensen felt her senses heighten. She could hear everything from Vegas' breathing to the footsteps of scavengers beyond the assembly room. She stopped, and instead of moving to the table of equipment she moved to the door.

Not realising she was closer than expected, Jensen hit the wall with a soft bump. She moved slowly, feeling for the door. Once found, Jensen placed her head against the barrier and listened. Light growls and snarls drifted to her ears. The scavengers were still close, not yet ready to give up on the prospect of a meal. This would work in their favour. Jensen smiled slightly, unseen in the darkness. Upon her last look out into the facility she had counted just over thirty scavengers. Luckily, they were still nearby.

A click behind her drew Jensen's attention. She turned to see Vegas, Kiernan, Raziko and Ziran bathed in a soft glow of light. They rallied around the table.

Jensen approached the table. "I suggest we don't take our time. The sooner we get out of here the better."

"What's your idea?" asked Vegas.

Jensen looked at the four team members cautiously. They weren't going to like it, but she knew her plan would work. She just had to convince them of that. Quickly.

Jensen took a slow breath and stopped in place beside the table. The torch light was soft and set to a wide beam, which produced a shaft of light that spread out horizontally as well as vertically.

"We have one explosive device courtesy of Jax's pack. Our best bet to eliminate as many scavengers as possible is to draw them all to one location and set off the explosive."

"Workable," Vegas agreed, "and what about bait to draw them to a single location?"

Looking down at the tabletop, Jensen traced her finger along its timber grain surface. She tapped her finger and took another breath, "A food source."

The team looked at each other and then back at Jensen, waiting for her to elaborate.

"What food source?"

Acknowledging his question, Jensen turned to look at Jilya's body.

Realisation dawned.

"Are you out of your MIND?" Raziko slammed his fist down upon the table.

"We can't do that," Ziran protested. "It's Jilya!"

"Jensen, really?" Kiernan touched Jensen's arm softly.

"I know it's Jilya, he was my ally too, but if we're to get out of here we need to use whatever means possible."

"Means? Jilya is possible means?" Ziran shook his head and walked away from the table, disappearing into the darkness.

Scraping her fingernails through her scalp, Jensen sighed in frustration. "What other choice do we have? Do you think I like this idea? Or that it was an easy decision to make? It wasn't, but nothing is going to draw the scavengers to a single location like the promise of food. If anybody has another suggestion, then let's hear it."

Seeing movement to her side, Jensen turned to see Vegas walk away. He approached Jilya's body and stood by his corpse. Vegas looked down, pulling the makeshift cover away from Jilya's face. "No! This will work. It's a good plan."

"Good plan?" Ziran appeared from the darkness. "You can't consider this a good plan?"

"It's a plan that has a high percentage change of working," Vegas said, taking a step towards Ziran. "I understand your feelings, Ziran, but disconnect yourself from your sentiments towards Jilya and the ally he was to us all. Step back and look at our situation. What choice do we have?"

Ziran was silent and so Jensen spoke.

"One thought turned it around for me," she said. "If I were the one lying on that bench and the best plan was to use my body as a means of escape, then I'd want you to make that choice so nobody else had to die."

Ziran turned, clenching his fists. He thought about Jensen's words, and the truth was so would he. He sighed. It still felt so hard to accept. It was Jilya. One of his closest allies. It wasn't the fact that he knew Jilya would willingly make that sacrifice. It was the nature of that sacrifice. Scavengers. Shaking his head, Ziran turned and then nodded. Approaching Jilya's body he laid a hand upon Jilya's chest. A show of respect. Leaning forwards, he whispered something unheard into the dead man's ear.

Jensen looked to Kiernan, suddenly feeling she needed support from the older woman. In the limited light it was hard to see her expression, but Kiernan, seeing Jensen's need for encouragement, took a step forward and placed her hand upon Jensen's upper arm. It was the support Jensen needed. She felt ready to put her plan into action. She looked around seeing all eyes upon her. Raziko still hadn't spoken.

"Are you ready?" she asked him, cautiously.

"Let's get on with this," Raziko said bluntly, displeased. but accepting of the plan.

Right, Jensen thought. Stepping away she took her torch from the table, adjusted it to a narrow beam and approached the stairs. She climbed them two at a time, ascending swiftly to the viewing balcony and then made her way to the window. It was dark, but Jensen could still see the amber-eyed glow of scavengers milling around the facility. They hadn't yet given up on the prospect of food. This was positive and her plan would have to be executed perfectly if they were to eliminate as many scavengers as possible.

Hearing steps behind her, Jensen turned to see Vegas, Raziko, Kiernan and Ziran. Silently they crowded around the window and looked down at the scene beyond.

"What's the structure of your plan?"

Jensen pursed her lips in a moment of thought before she spoke. "Our escape is quite simple. We need to get Jilya's body through this window, but in such a way that it will attract their attention."

"We could fasten a wide-yield torch to his clothing, so it casts light over the body," Raziko offered.

"Great idea" Jensen said with a nod, as her plan formulated and expanded in her mind. "If we put the explosive in a pocket of clothing and set it to a thirty-fraction countdown, that should be enough time for the scavengers to gather around."

"Hmm," Vegas peered below. "Ground Zero will be right by the dividing wall between us and them. We won't have much time to run to safety, and the blast will be right by our exit."

"True," Jensen pondered Vegas' point. "Then we'd better get it right."

Not wasting time, Jensen moved past the team and approached the stairs in the semi darkness. Outside she could still hear the scavengers scurrying around, searching for food. They needed to move quickly before any decided to venture further away from their current location. She wanted to eradicate as many as possible.

Descending the stairs, Jensen could hear the others follow. She made her way to Jilya's body. They formed a half circle around him. Unsure of what to say, the team stood for a moment of silence. Each put a hand upon Jilya's torso, head bent in respect. After a moment, Ziran spoke. He reached out and untied a decorative band that Jilya wore around his wrist and removed it. The bracelet was stained with blood.

"I will pass this on to Millie."

Jensen's heart sank. She had forgotten about Jilya's spouse. They were soon to be parents as Millie was almost full-term carrying their child. It was their second and last attempt at Genetic Reproduction.

"Commendable idea, Scout." Vegas patted Ziran's shoulder and then turned and walked away. The burden of the lives lost under his command becoming all too real.

Jensen watched him go, knowing he needed time to think. She also knew they needed to set their plan into action. Walking to the equipment table, she picked up the explosive device. She studied its digital readout. It looked the same as the explosive Xoren had used in the laboratory's file room. She wondered again who had given the men these devices. Their unknown threat.

"Do you know how to program a countdown?"

Jensen looked up at Raziko, pondering his question. “How hard could it be?”

“I don’t know. How sensitive is that device you’re holding? Once false move and maybe we all go boom!”

“I’m sure it’s a little more sophisticated than that,” Jensen replied. She watched Kiernan move around the table.

“I can set the countdown.”

Jensen wasn’t surprised Kiernan knew how to use the mechanism.

“This works on a similar framework as many of the timekeepers used in my laboratory. Its functionality has a replicated matrix for all our digital timing devices.” Kiernan accessed the control system and its timing functions. “Exactly how much time do we need?”

Jensen judged the distance between the far end of the assembly room and the window. “Thirty fractions. We will need to be armed and ready.”

Kiernan nodded more to herself. “This explosive may be small, but it packs a punch.”

“We must consider that not all the scavengers may be killed in the explosion. Worst case scenario, we need to be ready for them. We may still have a fight on our hands.”

Ziran picked up the automatic weapon. “And this?”

“Anything acquired for this mission, we use for this mission.” Jensen took the spare ammunition from the table. “Give the automatic weapons to Kiernan. Assure yourselves that not only do they work, but Kiernan,” she turned to look at the other woman. “You can use them.” She saw Kiernan’s wary expression, even in the limited light. “Remember the safety catch must be disengaged before pulling the trigger.”

Ziran handed the firearm to Kiernan, along with the ammunition. “I’ve studied ancient weaponry. I’m confident I can guide you in its proper usage.”

Staring down at the weapon in her hand, Kiernan hoped she had more luck than the first time. Safety catch? She forgot about that the last time.

***

After another tenth of a mark to finalise the plan, the team was ready. They stood again by Jilya’s body, each one with a hand upon his chest. The team was silent, consumed in personal thoughts. The plan was daring, with varying degrees of danger. At only half strength, timing was of critical importance. Little leeway could be given for margin of error if they were to successfully conduct Jensen's strategy for escape. It was daring. It was dangerous, and it was desperate.

Vegas looked at his team. He wanted to offer words of encouragement and support. His tongue felt numb. Words failed him as he searched his mind for something to inspire courage in his people. It was Kiernan who noted his struggle.

"If I may say something?"

Vegas looked up at Kiernan. He gave a single nod. Tapping her hand lightly upon Jilya's body Kiernan spoke boldly. "I may not have known Jilya for long, but what I absolutely saw in him in that short space of time was a man of integrity, compassion, and bravery. He, along with you all, cultivated my deep respect for the work you do for our colony." Kiernan looked at each team member. She felt a flutter within her chest. "He didn't choose this sacrifice, none of us would, but I have faith, along with you all, that he would do whatever was necessary to ensure the survival of our family. We all would." Suddenly those words sounded hollow to Kiernan, and she faltered. Wasn't that what the Commander and Select Prime were doing? Whatever was necessary to ensure the survival of their race?

Seeing Kiernan falter, Vegas continued. "As Minister Kiernan said, we will remember Jilya's compassion and bravery. We will remember the man he was, and we will pass that memory on to his offspring."

Raziko, who had remained quiet, spoke suddenly. "I pledge guardianship for his spouse and child."

Jensen looked up in surprise. What Raziko vowed was a significant offering. With this oath in front of four witnesses, he had pledged to shoulder all responsibility as Jilya was no longer able to carry this for his spouse and child.

"Right," Vegas removed his hand. "We all know what we're doing. Kiernan has set the timer. Ziran and I will carry the delivery method to the window. Jensen will activate the explosive. Raziko and Kiernan will construct our cover. Weapons at the ready. Are we set?"

Firm nods answered his question.

"Then let's do this."

At once, Kiernan turned and followed Raziko to the table that had once held their equipment. Everything had been packed away ready for their escape. Together they flipped the table onto its side, the top facing the door. Raziko dragged another table over and flipped it, further building their den of safety. A timber notice board was next, wedged between the tables, giving more height to their shelter. Kiernan knelt behind the barricade, as Raziko stood beside it. They watched Vegas, Ziran and Jensen as they readied Jilya's body. To his side, Raziko saw Kiernan study her automatic firearm and remove the safety. He had showed her how it worked and she was ready this time. He only hoped she had a steady aim.

By the table, Vegas took Jilya's legs. Ziran cupped him under the arms. Together they lifted his body and began to carry it to the stairs. Jensen followed, holding the explosive carefully. Once up the steps, they carried Jilya's body to the window. It was wide enough to push him through but offered no extra room to propel it away from their place of safety. Their plan had to be exact. They lay him upon the ground.

Stopping by the window Jensen looked out into the darkness. She couldn't see anything but eyes. Thankfully, many pairs of amber eyes. She could hear them too. Their attack upon the door had almost ceased with the station's power down, but their snarling and scurrying continued. Jensen knelt. She placed the explosive upon the floor and then took out a torch.

"A spare, right?" Vegas asked. "We need as many of these as we can for our escape and journey home."

"One of Jilya's," Jensen said, and then as an afterthought she strapped her own torch to his body and attached his to her jacket. She activated its beam and switched it to broad dispersal, illuminating Jilya's body.

"Ready?" Vegas repositioned himself by Jilya's feet and took them firmly. Ziran re-grasped the shoulders and together they lifted the body.

"Count of thirty," Jensen said as she readied her tonfa.

At Vegas' command, Jensen smashed the window glass, sliding her tonfa swiftly around the frame to clear every shard from the opening. Several screams reached their ears as the scavengers heard them.

In a swift movement, Jensen clipped the explosive to Jilya's clothing as Vegas and Ziran lifted his body ready to dispatch.

Nervous glances were exchanged.

Jensen held her breath.

The men lifted Jilya higher.

"On my mark."

They levelled the body to the window opening.

Vegas turned to Jensen. "On three, arm the explosive." He looked at Ziran. "On five we dispatch."

“Sir,” both scouts agreed over the escalating screams of scavengers. Their light was now visible, and the hoard was gathering.

“One… two… three…”

Jensen activated the device. A countdown of thirty illuminated on its readout. She stepped away.

“Four… five.” Together the men pushed Jilya’s body through the window and then they ran.

CHAPTER 23

A step ahead, Jensen sprinted down the stairs in the semi-darkness. At ground level, the group continued to run, making a hasty retreat to the safety of their makeshift cover. They slowed to a halt and ducked behind the tables, beside Kiernan and Raziko. They didn't have long to wait.

The explosion resonated throughout the facility with a physical impact that shook it to its very foundations. The ground trembled. The walls fractured. Debris shot out in all directions, as a sapphire ball of fire rose in turbulent flames. It illuminated the assembly bay with its bright hue. The team huddled for safety.

Jensen looked up, seeing sapphire flames lapping at the ceiling. They flooded out across its surface area, like an ocean of undulating waves, engulfing everything in their wake. She ducked her head and squeezed her eyes tight shut. Fear enveloped her. A searing heat bathed the team, radiating down from the flames above them. All around, the sound of falling wreckage echoed through the room and a loud groaning sound captured Kiernan's attention. She looked up, squinting as the heat of the inferno seared her eyes. She saw the relays above them buckling as portions of the walls gave way and the relays' weight pulled from the bracketing. It swung sideways, passing their shelter by mere inches as it crashed into the wall to their right. In the flames, Kiernan saw a part of the wall opposite them fall and the sight of scavengers engulfed in flames.

Seeing Kiernan peering above the barricade, her eyes wide in horror, Vegas pulled her back down into their shelter. Moments passed before the screaming slowly dissipated. The effects of the explosion subsided. The team waited several more fractions, welcoming the ensuing calm. The scavengers' screams turned to gurgling groans. Cracking and snapping flames lit up the assembly bay, supplying a glowing source of illumination. They looked up cautiously.

"That was slightly more powerful than expected." Jensen blinked, as she took in the scene, partly shielding her face. Even from their location, she was able to feel the heat of the dying flames.

Vegas looked around. "What was that?"

"The explosion might have triggered the release of built-up gasses in pipes within the building structure." Kiernan looked at the team who were now all peering over the barrier. Their faces illuminated by the glow of dying sapphire flames. "I can only speculate what unknown gasses might have backed up in those pipes."

Once nothing but the sound of crackling flames filled the air, the team moved slowly beyond the barrier. The flames still supplied a good source of light, and they were able to survey the scene. The left side of the wall, which had once protected them from the scavengers, had been blown apart.

"Everybody alright?" Vegas asked.

Raziko rose to his feet, bushing down his clothing. "That was immense."

Jensen shook her head, feeling fragments fall from her hair. "Indeed."

"I think it's safe to say the scavengers were eradicated in that blast."

"Ground Zero," Ziran replied.

Stepping away from their shelter, Vegas turned to address the team. His features glowed in the light of dying flames. "We can't waste time. There is still no knowing if the blast alerted more scavengers to this location, and I don't want to wait and find out. We take all we have salvaged and can carry and get out of here now. I will take point, Ziran will bring up the rear." He unsheathed his baton and new knife. "Weapons ready. When we get to the surface, we head straight to the transportation."

Nods of agreement followed Vegas' words.

Tentatively, the team began making their way through the assembly room. Alert, weapons ready, they moved in single file. Vegas led them to the gaping hole in the wall and they passed through easily into the testing facility. With the flames still flickering, they were able to see fragments of body parts strew upon the ground. From their vantage point, it was easy to spot scavengers who hadn't been killed in the blast. Most were now encompassed in lapping flames. Weak cries rose from burning lips, the stench was almost unbearable. With one signal, the team positioned their breathing apparatus to quickly cover the stomaching wrenching aromas.

They walked cautiously, alert, and vigilant, stepping over fallen debris and scattered body parts. Jensen, continually scanning their surrounds, was alert to any form of movement. They passed through the cubicles and made their way to the mezzanine balcony. They ascended swiftly and activated their torches as the flames shed no further light.

Vegas stopped and turned to the team. "Once we get to the elevator shaft, Ziran, you're up first."

The burly man nodded, but felt their escape seemed too easy so far. As they continued towards the elevator shaft, his concerns became justified. They heard the definite sound of scrambling, heavy footsteps and piercing breathing. They rounded a corner and were suddenly face to face with two younger-looking scavengers. They were bent over one of their own, sampling the repugnant meat. Kiernan didn't pause to think and in a moment of pure reaction, she raised her firearm and fired four shots. Each shot succeeded in hitting its mark. The scavengers were hit in the head, and both dropped to the floor.

"What the-" Jensen's jaw fell, and she looked over at Kiernan. "Really?"

Kiernan was frozen in position, her weapon still aimed upon the fallen scavengers. She blinked and then turned to look around at the team. "I just reacted."

"I think somebody else needs to be taking point," Vegas joked.

Soft chuckles were muted swiftly, as a scream met their ears. One tone. One voice. Hopefully, one scavenger.

Standing flush against the wall, Raziko slid along until he reached the corner of the corridor. He peered around it cautiously, baton in hand. He held his fist up to the team ordering them to remain quiet and then raised one finger. One scavenger. Another signal, they were to remain in position. Raziko disappeared. He slid along the wall, moving closer and closer to a scavenger that had begun throwing its body against a closed door. Suddenly, Raziko yelled out, swinging his baton around fiercely, and as his foe turned in his direction, the weapon connected soundly with its head. A satisfying crack followed the impact. The scavenger dropped and fell forward. Raziko hit out once more. He connected with the side of its head and the impact secured its fate.

"Anymore?" Vegas asked. He appeared beside Raziko.

"I think we're clear."

The team turned one last corner. The elevator shaft was in sight. Cautiously they approached. Ziran took point, knowing he was to ascend the ladder first. Keeping close to the passageway wall, they reached the shaft and stepped inside.

"You ready?"

"Let's do this." Assertively, Ziran climbed onto and up the ladder. He ascended in silence, and as he reached the top he peered out into the roofless building. All was clear. He listened. Nothing. Below him, Ziran felt movement and looked down, seeing Jensen.

"Good to go?" she asked.

"Let's go home," Ziran replied.

The team ascended the shaft and together made their way onto the Barren lands.

It was an eerie experience, re-entering the wastelands for that second time. Kiernan looked around as she stepped out onto the shell of a planet that had once been their home. It was calm. Disturbingly so. Uncharacteristically placid. On their journey to the Testing Station, Kiernan had gotten used to the crackles of lighting, howling winds and deafening thunder. Now there was nothing. The team looked around; none having ever seen such an event. Sometimes the tempest would ease for a few scant fractions. Sometimes the thunderheads would soften, but they had never lined up in such a way to create the moment of serenity they were now seeing.

Jensen looked up at the sky. Even the cloudbanks were still. The sky would sporadically light up with a silent flash of sheet lightening, but other than that nothing.

Adjusting his mask, Vegas positioned his earpiece and tapped his communicator. The team followed suit. "Have you ever seen this before, Scouts?"

"Never," replied Ziran and Raziko in unison.

Jensen had only once before seen anything remotely similar, but it was gone in less than ten fractions. "Nothing like this," she responded. She kept her eyes upon the sky. Searching. Hopeful. If she saw it again the others would see it too.

"We have to move." Vegas looked ahead. The land was calm with no howling winds or thunder. As such his senses felt more attuned to any potential foe.

The team set off, Vegas leading the journey back to their transportation. Jensen and Kiernan walked side by side. Ziran joined them. Raziko remained to the rear.

"It's unreal," Ziran commended. "To experience such calm. Maybe it's an omen."

"Hmm," Jensen agreed, distracted. She continued to look up at the sky. "Or maybe it's 'the calm before the storm', as the saying goes."

Ziran looked over to Kiernan and then back at Jensen. The calm before the storm? After what they had seen, maybe it was. A chill passed through his body, and unbeknown to him, through the women beside him. The trio shared a look and, although lost in thought, one thing was clear, if this was the calm before the storm, then what a storm it would be.

CHAPTER 24

Jenson awoke the next morn. Her head throbbing; her body stiff and aching. She opened her eyes thankful for the darkness of her room. She was home. Distant sounds echoed from beyond the corridors; a new rotation was underway. She blinked in a moment of disorientation and rolled onto her side, curling into a tight foetal position. Why did she feel so physically exhausted? The question lasted only a fraction of a moment, as the events of the earlier rotation flashed into her mind. Jenson sat up quickly. A harsh breath passed her lips. She recalled the mission, the scavengers, Xoren, Ruben and Jilya; even Jorca and Jax. Jensen looked around the darkened room. More memories flooded back to her. Kiernan and the attempt on her life. Secrets and unanswered questions. Jensen grasped the sheets by her side, pulling the material into her tight fists. They had escaped the testing station in a wake of sapphire flames and chilling screams. They had made it back to the surface and safely back to their land vehicles. She even had the surprise of driving the multi-person vehicle back to the colony. A task she would have enjoyed if not for the lack of instruction beforehand. It had taken several attempts before she was able to get the vehicle into gear and moving. She was a quick study, but learning to drive under that pressure was tough. Still, if she had a chance to drive again, she would in a heartbeat. Kiernan and Ziran had travelled with her in the multi-person carrier, Vegas took the empty storage vehicle with Raziko.

Swinging her legs off the bed, Jensen looked down at the floor. Her eyes travelled over her flesh, seeing an array of bruises covering her pale legs. Her mind drifted, still lost in the memory of the earlier rotation. They had been driving for no more than a quarter mark when a vision had caught her attention. Jensen had instantly hit the brakes, her passengers thrust forward in their seats with a jolt. Behind them, Vegas had screeched to a stop with an exclamation of surprise in her ear, and a flash of headlights in annoyance.

"Scout?" Vegas questioned.

"Jen, is everything alright?" Kiernan asked.

Jensen was silent. She looked up at the clement sky, as she extinguished the engine. The ensuing silence greeted them with its eerie calm. Although the storm was beginning to rise, the land was still serene. If not for that, Jensen may not have spotted it.

"Scout," Vegas pushed. "Jensen, respond."

Without reply, Jensen stepped out of the vehicle, closing the door behind her. She looked up into the sky. It flashed with blankets of sheet lightening. They were gathering in frequency. The storm was returning. But right before them…

Turning, Jensen looked over at the storage vehicle, hearing Vegas exit the driver's side with an annoyed slam of his door. He held his hands up in question. Jensen turned away from him and looked up at the sky.

"Scout?"

In response, Jensen pointed upwards. "Sir, remember? Remember what I told you?"

Vegas looked up at the sky. It only took a moment for him to see what Jensen was referring to. Straight ahead he saw it. A break in the cloudbank. In the parting of the dense clouds Vegas saw stars. A small quilt of darkness scattered with twinkling astral bodies. He could barely hold back his gasp of surprise. Reaching out, Vegas grasped Jensen's upper arm and stared in wonder. It was beautiful. It was hope.

The pair heard several more closing vehicle doors, as Raziko, Kiernan and Ziran joined them. Without question they followed Jensen's light of sight and stared up into the sky. The five gazed in wonder.

"What does this mean?" Raziko asked.

Not diverting his attention Vegas said, "It means we are closer than ever to our Ultimate Agenda."

That was true, Kiernan acknowledged, but instead of hoping she was filled with unmitigated dread. Devilish claws of foreboding scraped their icy talons down her spine. When they got home, she knew she needed to put her plan into action. Fast.

Jensen thought back to that moment. She had turned to look at Kiernan. The Minister's expression further underlined her need for answers. Sitting upon the edge of her bed, body aching, head throbbing and stomach growling, Jensen decided her first point of call was breakfast. Then she would visit Kiernan. Her list of questions was increasing.

Rising from her bed, Jensen moved to grasp her clothing when the scent of her unwashed body assaulted her senses. Sweat, smoke and the unmistakable stench of scavengers hit her full force. Before anything else she needed a shower. Jensen dropped her clothing. There was a knock at her door. Dressed only in briefs and a vest she opened the barrier. There on the other side stood a fresh faced, and professionally attired, Minister Kiernan. Her expression was anxious, but her smile genuine.

"Hello!"

"Jen, I apologise for arriving like this without prior notice, but I need to talk. Are you free?" It seemed at that moment Kiernan became aware of Jensen's state of dress. She blushed apologetically and took a step backwards. "I can come back."

Rolling her eyes, Jensen stepped aside allowing Kiernan entrance. "No please, no time like right now. We do need to talk. Excuse the unwashed appearance." Jensen allowed Kiernan to enter, hoping she didn't smell too offensive.

Stepping into Jensen room, Kiernan looked around. It was different from her personal chambers. So much smaller. She took a moment to survey the meagre array of personal possessions curiously, boots, a box, a congealed yet colourful polyvinyl mass and a small selection of tomes. She smiled slightly.

"Sit down," Jensen said, motioning to her unmade bad.

"Thank you." Kiernan sat at the bottom of the bed. She averted her eyes as Jensen swiftly pulled on her discarded clothing from the eve before.

"Sorry," Jensen fastened her trousers. "I still reek of the mission! I was just about to take a shower. It's amazing that the de-contamination procedure doesn't erase the stench of charred scavenger. And an odour so strong it seeps into fresh clothing!" Jensen knew she was babbling. She was nervous. Having a good idea why Kiernan was there, anticipation thrummed through her. She sat down upon the floor opposite Kiernan, surprising the older woman. Crossing her legs, Jensen clasped one hand around her bare foot. "Talk to me."

Folding her hands upon her lap, Kiernan thought for a moment. She had rehearsed her speech twice over and intended to visit Jensen after her visit with the Commander and rare audience with the Select Prime, but in a moment of clarity she changed her strategy. Seeing Jensen and setting her plan into action was paramount.

Tucking her hair behind her ear, Kiernan spoke. "I know you need answers. Before I can supply them, I need some concrete evidence. You said you would help me?"

Jensen nodded. She wanted answers, but knew patience was key.

"Good. Right." Kiernan faltered as her fingers clasped tighter around her hands. "Jen, I'm a scientist. It's my nature to investigate. I'm always seeking unasked questions so I can endeavour to unravel their truth."

"Right?" Jensen found herself holding her breath.

"When I knew I was going to be collaborating with you, I looked into your colonist file." Seeing Jensen's frown, Kiernan was quick to elaborate, "Colonist files are held on all our people. It holds medical records, ranks, progress reports and relevant history. Don't get me wrong, I already knew about you." Kiernan blushed, as Jensen quirked her brow in curiosity. "I read all your mission reports. They are a fascinating read, and I found your skill in the written word most enjoyable. You have a talent!"

Jensen quirked a bemused smile. This was something she had never heard before. She had a talent. Maybe it was her love of literature and reading?

"I digress." Kiernan took a breath. "I read your colonist file There I found an obscure passage relating to your parents, who didn't make much sense to me at the time. I was in bed… falling asleep." She re-tucked her hair behind her ear. "But thinking back now I re-read over that passage this morn, and I see a possible connection to a greater issue." Jensen still appeared confused, and Kiernan wasn't surprised. She needed to elaborate.

"Jen, the passage said, 'Subjects castigated. Deflection of esoteric documents confirmed. Links to colonist Lomax verified. Containment implemented.'

Jensen tossed the phrases around in her mind, as she tried to understand the passage. She understood the phrases, but they made little sense. "Right… so… 'Subjects castigated'. Who was punished here? My parents? If so, why? What are these 'Esoteric documents' they mention and who is colonist Lomax?" Jensen thoughts whirled. "I don't understand what this means, Kiernan. I've never heard of a colonist called Lomax. In which colony does he live? How did my parents know him?"

Kiernan looked seriously at Jensen. "This is what I need you to find out Jen. You see I investigated Lomax this morn and there is only one entry for a colonist named Lomax. This individual was born pre-devastations and was granted shelter in the colony as his father worked at the Testing Station."

"He died there?"

"No." Kiernan said seriously, as a small fragment of understanding filtered through her mind. "His father wasn't present when our world was destroyed, and the station inhabitants were exterminated. I can't find clarification into who his father was, but he and his family had a pre-allocated placement in Governance. This was until his father's death, when he and his mother were re-located to Labour. Evidence of his history past this point is sporadic at best. The last entry mentions an affiliation with your parents. After that, his trail goes cold."

"He died?"

Kiernan looked deep into Jensen's eyes. The last entry states only one word 'Tergiversate'."

"What does that mean?" Jensen asked, her confusion mounting.

"It means defect, but I'm not sure at this point what this refers to." Kiernan rubbed her chin. "The reference on his file and affiliation with your parents highlight many questions."

Jensen was silent. None of this made sense. Her parents died on a mission on the Barrens. Major Vegas informed her of that himself. He had even pledged guardianship, should she need it, in her journey through scout training.

"This all seems so-"

"I know, I know." With a frustrated sigh Kiernan rose, forcing Jensen to do the same as the Minister started pacing up and down the small space. "I would agree with you, but I noted the same authorisation code on the notes pertaining to your parents as I found on the evidence I'm collecting now." Kiernan stopped and faced Jensen. "I don't know who it is, and I don't know what it means, but it fills me with the same gut churning anxiety, and I can't ignore that, Jen. It's connected. I know it is. I just don't know how."

"This is what you want me to investigate?" Jensen was dubious.

Kiernan stepped closer. "Investigate. If I do, it will be noted. Discover what you can and share these findings with me and I in turn will share my burden with you. Maybe together we can blow this apart and find the truth hidden in this web of lies."

Turning away from Kiernan, Jensen stared at the wall in thought. She wanted answers, but instead she was left with more questions. "Find Lomax? Do you have any idea how old this person will be now?"

"About one hundred and ten cycles," Kiernan confirmed.

"And what if he died cycles ago?"

Kiernan had considered this. "Then speak to his family and allies. Speak to anybody who might know anything about him. Just don't give up. Trust me, Jen. We have something."

It seemed unbelievable, and yet Kiernan was absolutely convinced. Jensen wanted to disregard her words as nothing more than paranoia, but she had already seen too much at the testing station. Somebody wanted

Kiernan dead. Kiernan appeared to know why. That meant Jensen wanted to know why. And now her parents might have been involved? If this was so, how long had this labyrinth of deception been simmering beneath the colony's surface? Was this the true cause of her parents' death? It wasn't possible, was it?

CHAPTER 25

Vegas strode purposefully down the corridors of Governance workers' personal units. After hearing their meeting with the Select Prime and Commander Tehera had been delayed by four marks, he had decided on a visit with Scout Jensen to discuss matters about their mission. Unfortunately, Jensen was not in her room, and an attempt to contact her via their inter-communicator had been fruitless. While standing outside Jensen's door, Vegas had heard the wrist communicator sounding from inside her room. He doubted she was ignoring his call. Jensen wasn't there. That fact itself frustrated the Major. Once issued, Jensen was not to abandon the device until it was returned to command. With an internal growl, Vegas turned and instead headed in search of Kiernan. He had informed her of the meeting's delay and had a particularly good idea where Kiernan would have re-distributed her time.

Making his way towards the laboratories, Vegas headed away from the general Governance sector and towards the upper colonist sections. He strode through the corridors, arms ridged by his side. Anybody he passed could read his mood. They kept their distance; apart from one individual. Seeing the Major approach, Nicoletti was eager to corner him.

"Major Vegas, may I have a word?"

Vegas paused mid-stride, his attempt to mask his ire at Nicoletti's interruption failing. "What is it, Officer?"

The younger man paused for a moment as he registered the Major's brittle address. However, what he had to ask was more important than Vegas' reputed ire. "Sir, as of yet I have heard nothing of when Taura's body shall be released to me for carbonisation." Nicoletti's countenance hardened. "My spouse lost her life on the Barrens, and not only have I heard nothing about her Honourship for service, but until her body is released, I am unable to mourn. Taura was a well-liked and respected member of the colony. Repeated questions of when her Honourship will take place are frustrating when I have no answer for our allies."

Vegas' mood dissipated in the face of Nicoletti's heartfelt request. He released the reins on his coiled posture and placed a reassuring hand upon Nicoletti's upper arm. "That is unacceptable, Officer. Rest assured I shall speak to Physician Angelus to find out why this hasn't happened." He patted the younger man's arm. "Start making your arrangements for her Honourship, Officer. I shall see to the rest."

Their mission, as eventful as it had been, had left Vegas with the illusion that they had been away for longer than they had. Even so, the cause of Taura's death wasn't under question. Her body should have been released by now.

Nicoletti appeared to feel relieved. "Thank you, Major."

"Of course, Officer." Vegas took a step backwards. "Now, if you will excuse me?"

"Sir." With a nod, Nicoletti turned, allowing Vegas to continue his journey.

Eager to demand answers from Minister Kiernan, Vegas mentally ordered his list of questions. They had yet to unify their story for the meeting with the Select Prime and Commander. Kiernan had suggested he fall in line with her story. Vegas would do that for her, but he needed to know why. The possibility that Jensen knew more than he did bothered him. The younger scout was increasingly more confrontational and suspicious. Vegas struggled, not knowing the best way to convince Jensen that he had her best interests at heart. He always had.

***

Minister Kiernan and Physician Angelus stood side by side staring at the gurney before them. Upon its surface lay the double-bagged body of the scavenger responsible for taking Taura's life. The body had been kept chilled since its arrival. Unfortunately, that did little to keep the corpse adequately composed. The scavengers lived in a chilled environment. As such the decomposition process had begun. Already Kiernan could detect the aroma, which had become the single biggest trigger for her terror-filled memories from her experience in the Barren lands. The putrid stench began to filter into the Examination room. Physician Angelus covered his nose with his fingers. Kiernan had asked him to join her in the investigation of the corpse. It was a pure case of morbid fascination that urged him to agree.

Re-securing the reusable, poly-fibre apron around his waist, Physician Angelus hummed quietly to himself. It was loud enough for Kiernan to hear him, and she turned, looking at the taller man in question.

"Oh me? Nothing."

With a bemused quirk, Kiernan narrowed her eyes.

Angelus relented as he turned to face her. "Well, naturally, I'm wondering when you were going to elaborate." He waved his index finger around Kiernan's face. "Although I'm expecting the team later for post-exposure check-up, I'm obviously curious why your face looks like you've attempted to enter a room without opening the door first." He gave her a swift visual appraisal. "Body held favouring one side. Arm bandaged. An almost unperceivable limp, observable only by the trained eye of course. You did have assigned protection, right? Rest assured I shall be speaking to Officer Jax when we next meet!"

Knowing it was not her place to divulge the mission, Kiernan remained silent. Deciding a change of topic was needed, she instead turned back to the gurney and the body lying upon its surface. "I had the displeasure of encountering more of these then I ever thought possible."

"You did? How many? Records have never documented any more than three in a single encounter!"

"At least thirty."

"THIRTY. Did you find a horde's den? This is extraordinary. How did you survive such an encounter?" Angelus paused, giving Kiernan a closer inspection. "Now I understand the colourful swelling. Over thirty. How did you escape?"

Kiernan folded her arms in an unconscious manner. She stared ahead at the body. "I'm sure you will read all about it in the mission report."

Registering Kiernan's evasiveness and quickly noticing her reticence to discuss the mission details, Physician Angelus approached the gurney. "What say we pull out this flesh chomping fiend and open it up?"

Picking up the body bag together, the pair lifted it off the gurney and over to an examination table. As they placed it down, both were instantly aware of the consistency of the contents within.

"That doesn't seem promising," Angelus remarked, as he prodded the bag with his fingers.

"We really need to-"

Unexpectedly the door opened, and Major Vegas strode into the room.

Angelus regarded the Major with an arched brow, "Sterile environment!"

Ignoring him, Vegas looked at Kiernan. "I've been searching for you." He looked down at her naked wrist. No communicator! "Scout Jensen has also removed her inter-communicator; do you know why?"

His accusatory tone irritated Kiernan, but she refused to let it show. She knew Jensen had removed her communicator. She had suggested the move herself. “I’m preparing for dissection. This really isn’t the time.”

“Hmm,” Vegas seemed to relent. “We need to talk.”

“And we will.”

“Now,” Vegas pushed.

Without breaking her professional visage, Kiernan nodded once. She pulled off her poly-fibre gloves and dropped them onto the examination table. “Prep room,” she said and led Vegas into the side room. The prep room was small, housing a simple modesty partition and a sink for washing. A storage locker to the right held anti-bacterial solvents and spare smocks. There was a strong smell of disinfectant.

Once inside, Vegas closed the door and turned to face Kiernan. “The briefing being delayed for several marks works well in our favour. I need to know what happened, Kiernan. I can’t go into the briefing with the Select Prime and Commander if I have no idea what truly occurred during the period our teams were parted.”

Kiernan had wanted to delay this moment for as long as possible. She had hoped it would have been longer. Kiernan wasn’t ready to talk. She needed to hear back from Jensen. She needed several more marks at least.

“May I ask you a question?” Vegas nodded, so Kiernan continued. “Do you trust me?”

“I always have before,” was the Major’s response.

“And if I told you I couldn’t give you the answers you seek right now, would you accept that?”

Vegas folded his arms. “When we are due for a briefing. How could I?”

“Could you delay the briefing yourself?”

“Not without a solid reason.”

“So, you could.”

Vegas narrowed his eyes. “In theory.”

Kiernan turned and began a thoughtful pacing. “If I were to tell you that I’m currently working on the proof I need for the answers you seek, would you be willing to hold back for several marks until I’m ready to talk?”

“Jensen?” Vegas asked.

Kiernan nodded.

Forcing out a harsh breath, Vegas looked up at the ceiling. He still felt out of the information loop, and he didn't appreciate it. He was the Major. He was in a leading command role. Who were they to leave him waiting for answers? Vegas wanted to order Kiernan into divulging her secrets, but he couldn't. He liked Kiernan and he respected her. He worried for her safety. After recent events how could he not? However, Vegas wasn't the most patient of individuals.

Stopping Kiernan mid-pace, Vegas stood before her holding eye contact. "I'll delay the briefing for as long as I absolutely can without raising suspicion. You need to come to me before this rotation ends and tell me everything."

The Major's voice was absolute. He was reaching the end of his patience. Kiernan knew him well enough to see that. With a barely perceivable nod, Kiernan turned and closed her eyes. Please hurry Jensen.

CHAPTER 26

Entering Labour colony was easy with the upper-level authority token given to her by Kiernan. Jensen wasn't questioned once as she flashed her crossing token to the officers guarding the border between Governance and Labour. She recognised one officer, who had previously apprehended her for being in Labour without authority on a separate occasion. This time he allowed her entrance with a sweep of his hand. The officer, Llanos, in turn had recognised her. No words were spoken as Jensen crossed the border.

The passageways were quiet, showing most of Labour's colonists were engaged in their rotational occupations. Jensen walked down empty corridors, peering into rooms with curiosity. In small rooms she saw classrooms populated by mid-teen colonists selectively chosen for their future rolls. Taught by elders, retired from their positions, the teens were educated in more than one area to cover a broad variety of positions within the colony. If a post was of lower ranking and not needing more than half a cycle's instruction, young citizens were put to work early, quickly earning their keep within the community. Further education taught within the Labour colony would generally lean towards lower-level postings in Governance. Upper-Level postings were taught within Governance itself.

Jensen continued, passing assembly rooms where people constructed necessities vital for rotational life within the colony. Recycling, upcycling, everything was repaired or repurposed. Much of what Jensen, as well as other scouts had been able to scavenge off the Barren lands, would end up in these plants. Nothing was ever wasted.

As she continued further into the colony, Jensen had one destination in mind. She was looking for a particular person. At eighty cycles old, Mira was one of the oldest colonists still living within Labour. Jensen found her a most interesting individual who, like herself, had an interest in the history of their planet. In her spare time, she loved to educate herself and had a particular affinity for extinct planetary languages derived from colony records and scouted tomes, as well as alternative physicians' arts, such as muscle manipulation and understanding the physical form. Jensen had first met Mira after hearing about the woman's collection of tomes. She hadn't visited Mira in some time, but knew the older woman would have some answers to the many questions she held.

Rounding a corner, Jensen took a left, brushing her fingers over the cool rock walls as she made her way towards the Labour colony's personal units. She was looking for room 172. Her trek took her further away from the main hive of the colony, to the far outskirts of the colonists' units. After another fraction of a mark, Jensen reached room 172. She knocked lightly. There was no response. Jensen knocked again, harder, louder. A moment later she heard a soft reply. Jensen waited and soon the door opened.

Mira hadn't appeared to have aged at all from the last time Jensen saw her. Her hair was still long and ashen, pulled back from her face. If anything, Jensen thought she looked smaller, but her smile was just as welcoming as always. The woman pulled her into a strong hug.

"Jen, it has been a while. I'm so happy to see you. Please come in." Her welcoming embrace wasn't as strong, but Mira still oozed vitality.

Jensen stepped into Mira's unit. It was small, like hers, but filled with a lifetime of memories. And the tomes. Jensen always took a moment to read over the tiles and see if she'd discovered anything new. They were piled high against the wall in envious rows of reading pleasure.

"Still coveting my tomes," Mira laughed. "Feel free to borrow." She smiled with a wink, "I'll give you a five-rotation reading period before I expect it back!"

"I will take you up on that offer." Jensen stopped in the centre of the room and turned to regard Mira. "How are you?"

"Still keeping myself useful," Mira said with a smile. "It's the secret to longevity. Don't slow down too much or they catch up with you. "

"They?"

Mira smiled. "I have a feeling you're not here for a social visit?"

Jensen leaned against the wall and looked at Mira with a small smile. "Not this time. I've come for some information, that I hope you will be able to help me with."

Sitting down upon her bed, Mira patted the space beside her. "How can I help?"

Jensen sat down and twisted slightly so she could look at Mira. "I want to ask you about a colonist. His name was, or is, Lomax."

A glimmer of recognition flashed upon Mira's features. "Lomax?"

"You know him?"

"I knew him," Mira confirmed. She looked down at the floor. A wisp of a memory passed through her, and a smile touched her lips. "I knew colonist Lomax well. He was one of the last living citizens from pre-devastation."

Jensen nodded.

"Colonist Lomax encouraged my interested in the planet's extinct languages. He taught me my first 'second' language. You see, his family spoke two. His father worked for the government and defected from his homeland to work for ours. Lomax himself was a general labourer, domestic cleaning mostly, but he says that's what kept him fit and strong." Mira smiled fondly. "That was one of his secrets. He would say, 'for longevity, keep active in mind and in body'. I followed a lot of his advice."

Mira pointed to a corner of the room where a healthy plant stood. It was rare to see vegetation outside of the terrarium.

"That plant I grew from a single cutting given to me by Lomax. Every time it sprouts a new leaf, I remove the oldest… dry it… infuse it and drink it." She tapped the side of her nose. "Another secret."

Jensen looked upon the plant in surprise. "These secrets to longevity do appear to work."

"Indeed." Mira laughed lightly, but her smile quickly faded. "Now tell me why you ask about Lomax?"

"I need to find him."

Mira appeared bemused. "Lomax vanished about fifteen cycles ago. I can only presume he is dead by now, Jensen. He was a good and wise man. I do miss him."

"He knew my parents."

Mira pursed her lips with a nod. "I'm afraid I never knew them." She rose and turned to face Jensen. "Why do you ask about Lomax now?"

"When was the last time you saw him, Mira?"

"Jensen, it was such a long time ago."

"Please try."

"I'm afraid I can't remember," Mira said defensively, her demeanour changing in an instant.

It surprised Jensen to realise Mira's mood had shifted suddenly to a lack of trust. That had to mean she knew something. Surely. If she did, then was her safety in jeopardy too? Had she held the burden of clandestine information for all those cycles?

Rising, Jensen took one step forward, careful not to cause Mira alarm. She needed to choose her words carefully for Mira to believe she could be trusted.

"Jensen, I apologise. I'm tired. I think I need rest." Mira moved to the door. "Maybe you should come back in a rotation or two."

"Mira, please wait." Knowing she needed to gain the woman's trust, Jensen thought fast. Honesty. Always. "Mira," how do I word this? Jensen closed her eyes in thought and took a breath. Looking back at Mira, she said, "Somebody I am working closely with was targeted. An attempt made upon her life. She believes it's because she is aware of certain information about a conspiracy within the colony. She won't, at this point, divulge any more information. What I do know is that the authorisation codes behind this information match those sealed upon the archives detailing the truth behind my parents' death, and the disappearance of Lomax."

"You said your parents died scouting the Barren lands," Mira countered.

"That is what I was told. However, what if they didn't, and what if all this isn't circumstantial?"

Mira remained silent as she looked at Jensen dubiously.

"I don't want to say too much, Mira, but I've just returned from a mission to a testing station where an upper-level Governance advisor attempted to terminate this person's life." Jensen paused as she studied Mira's reaction. "I'll be honest. I don't know how this links, but I trust her when she says it does."

Turning, Mira picked up her warm infusion. She took a sip and then turned back to study Jensen closely. "I don't trust this unknown individual, Jensen, but I do trust you." Tapping her index finger on the side of her mug, Mira said, "Speak to Tovey."

"Tovey?"

"Go south," Mira said with emphasis, "Locate Tovey."

"But who's," Jensen paused, as Mira held up her hand.

"You may wish to return and talk again, but for now I can't help you."

Jensen turned with a frustrated sigh. Go south? That meant returning to the Primary colony. And who was Tovey? That was an unfamiliar name to her. Jensen wanted to push for more but knew Mira wouldn't be forthcoming. If Mira was to trust her, Jensen had to do as asked.

"I may see you again," Mira said mysteriously.

Pausing in the doorway, Jensen said. “You can count on that. I believe I need your help, Mira.” Turning, Jensen pulled the door closed behind her.

Watching her leave, Mira took another sip of her infusion. “I hope you’re wrong, Jensen.”

CHAPTER 27

The room was saturated by an odiferous aroma rising from the semi-decomposed body. Even while held within the confines of the refrigerator unit, the scavenger body's decomposition rate had progressed to such a level, it was currently the consistency of a partially formed gel-like structure.

Physician Angelus stood over the corpse; his face contorted in revulsion. A potent salve under his nose and a mask positioned carefully over the lower half of his face, did little to detract from the aroma. He pushed a spatula into the remains and scooped up a small amount of purified internal organ. Dish in hand, he dropped the sample upon its surface and sealed its lid.

Angelus handed it to Kiernan. "Now for the brain."

Kiernan looked down into the dish. Every sample they had taken appeared to have an amber hue that reacted to the examination room lights. A soft glow emanated from within the core of each specimen. Was this the toxic substance that had transformed the survivors of the devastations into the flesh-hungry scavengers they had become? Biting the corner of her lip, Kiernan labelled the container lid and placed it with the collection they had harvested.

"This is fascinating," Angelus said.

Kiernan looked over to see him slicing into the scavenger's skull with a scalpel. Its rate of decomposition continued to escalate to such an extent the skeleton had softened. Angelus was engrossed in his task, and she couldn't help but smile at his eager expression. It was a unique experience, and he was taking full advantage.

Turning back to her samples, Kiernan stared down into the first dish. She frowned as she studied the luminous glint shining from within the centre of the sample. It was like a sign of life emanating from within. Her mind whirled with possibilities.

"I have to try something."

"Hmm… excuse me?" Angelus didn't look up from his task. "No thank you, I couldn't eat at a time like this."

With a quirk of her brow Kiernan shook her head and took the first sample dish. Maybe she would just run a test or two while Angelus was preoccupied.

***

Within half a mark, Jensen was entering the main bazaar of the Primary Colony. The journey had taken longer due to a curious increase in border patrols leaving Labour. Even with a pass, colonists were being asked what their business was or had been. She decided against the discourse and instead took the back route.

Stepping into the smoky, stale environment, Jensen looked around. There were fewer people than normal. She frowned. Usually, no matter what time of rotation, there was always a steady flow of colonists milling around the bazaar. Several of the regular traders were missing, even Dicken was absent from his cart of unidentifiable fare. The chimney, which always churned a billowing plume of smoke up its flue, was inactive and cold.

Jensen walked through the bazaar. It was then that she realised the major difference. There were no playing children. That was unheard of. Needing to know more, she headed to the one person she knew would be able to provide her with answers. Approaching Flick's den, Jensen stopped short of entering when a voice called out to her.

"He's gone."

Jensen turned, seeing a slim woman with a shaved head. Her pale cheeks and sunken eyes emphasised the emptiness in her voice.

"Excuse me?"

"You're not from here," she said.

Jensen shook her head. "Where's Flick?"

"Gone."

"Where?"

The slight woman stepped closer. She looked around, seemingly checking her surrounds before she spoke again. "Taken."

Jensen stepped closer. Her curt responses were frustrating. "Taken where?"

"Don't know. Devlin came himself. He took Flick, and more besides. People are scared now. Hiding."

"And the children?"

"Not allowed here. To keep them safe you see."

The woman closed the distance further until she was standing before Jensen. She looked her up and down, giving obvious appraisal before asking. "You trading?"

"No." Jensen looked back to Flick's domain. "Flick was taken. With how many others? Do you know why? Do you know where they went or what's going on?"

"Many questions," the unknown woman took a step backwards. "No pressure. How do I know you're not with Devlin? Why are you here? You don't belong here."

Jensen withheld her frustrated sigh; she wasn't getting any help from this woman. She decided upon a different approach. "Do you know Tovey?"

"I know Tovey."

"Take me?"

"Does Tovey know you?"

Honesty. "No."

The woman took another step backwards, smoothing her fingertips over her bald head. "Why do you want Tovey?"

The questions were tedious. Jensen remained calm. "Please, it's important."

"Why do you want Tovey?"

"Mira sent me."

A flicker of recognition twinkled within the woman's features. Her eyes narrowed, and she circled Jensen, seemingly appraising her again. Trying not to appear bemused by the odd woman's behaviour, Jensen waited.

She had come looking for answers. Now Flick had disappeared? Never had she known for people to be so scared in the Primary Colony that they would hide the children away. Jensen peered around again. They were being watched, mistrust in the eyes of several observers.

"I don't have time for this," Jensen pressed forward. "What's your name?"

"More questions."

"I can help."

"Nobody can help us."

That statement was true. The Primary colony housed the forgotten people. Those who would be left behind. Nobody could help them, but they lived away from the tight control of Governance. Nothing could take that freedom away from them, or so they thought.

"I'm an ally of the southern people. An ally of Flick. If he were here, he would vouch for me."

"He's not here."

"But I can help find him." Patience reaching its limit, Jensen tried one more time. "Where can I find Tovey?"

"You can find Flick?"

"I would try."

"Follow me."

In an unexpected move, the unknown woman turned. She peered back at Jensen long enough to imply she was to follow her, and then she walked off, heading towards a narrow, rotten timber doorway.

***

Her brow furrowed in concentration. Kiernan peered down into the microscope. Angelus had completed his investigation of the body and Kiernan was examining the samples he had taken. Standing before the sterile work surface, she adjusted the magnification parameters of the eyepieces. Behind her, Kiernan could hear Angelus humming to himself as he cleaned away his equipment and loaded it into a sterile bowl.

In the centre of the room, upon the examination table, lay what remained of the scavenger. The temperature of the room, even though adjusted to a cooler setting, was still enough to further escalate decomposition. In Angelus' opinion, it now resembled an amber pile of mush. He was lucky to obtain samples from specific locations before they degraded to a sticky conglomeration of unrecognisable matter.

At the microscope, Kiernan added a droplet of translucent liquid to the sample she was examining. Its russet colour changed swiftly.

"My, my, my," she muttered to herself.

"A rather curious exclamation from the minister and scientist. Care to elaborate?" Angelus ceased his task and peered over Kiernan's shoulder.

"Look." She moved to the side and Angelus peered into the scope. He was silent for a moment, then moved away, blinked repeatedly, and then looked back into the scope.

"Hmm, did you add florogenoxide?"

"I did."

"Hmm… but… this means…"

Kiernan placed a hand upon Angelus' back. "This means the sample has a synthetic marker."

"Are you inferring that-?"

"The scavengers are not quite the product of evolution we originally surmised."

Angelus looked sideways at Kiernan. "Fascinating!"

Kiernan gazed back at the body. "Ziran downloaded all the information he could from the laboratory at the testing station. I need to see that data now."

"What are you thinking, Minister Savvy Pants?"

Stepping towards the body, Kiernan stared down at the liquefying puddle. "That I really hope I'm wrong."

CHAPTER 28

She'd never travelled this far into the Primary Colony before. Jensen was transfixed by her surroundings, as she found herself going deeper and deeper into what she identified as the original body of the mental hospital it once was.

Walking down a corridor lined with rooms on either side, Jensen noticed many of the doors were missing. She peered into those with barriers and saw families huddled around their children, a suspicious glare cast towards anybody who looked through the tiny windows. Jensen wanted to question the nameless woman, and ask her where she was taking her, but remained silent. A show of trust on her part.

Takin another set of stairs, the pair changed direction and descended to a lower level. Here the air was cooler, damper. There was a familiar aroma in the atmosphere. Ahead, the woman stopped by a door. She turned to look at Jensen.

"Tovey?"

Silently the woman opened the door. She stepped inside, holding the tattered barrier for Jensen to follow. She entered the small room, and the door was closed behind her. Taking a moment, Jensen looked around. The room was large. Almost twice the size of her personal unit. There was a bed to one side, covered with tattered blankets and a stuffed toy resting upon an overused, stained pillow. In a small pile to the side was a pile of tomes, curious artefacts Jensen found unrecognisable and basic furniture cobbled together with rusted screws. Jensen stepped towards the timber table. She ran her fingers over its surface.

"What can I do for you, Jensen?"

Turning swiftly, Jensen looked the mysterious woman before her. She was different. She stood taller and held herself straighter. An air of confidence changed her features entirely. Jensen would have believed she was looking at a different person.

"I want to speak with Tovey."

"I am Tovey."

"Excuse me?" Jensen arched a brow. "If you're Tovey, then why didn't you say-?"

"I couldn't be sure who was listening." Tovey's head dipped to one side. "Mira informed me of your approach. I was waiting for you. I needed to assure myself of your sincerity."

"How did Mira-"

"We can't give away all our secrets." Tovey smiled and circled Jensen. "You wish to discuss my grandfather."

"Grandfather?"

"Lomax."

Jensen was stunned. Not only had the woman before her transformed, oozing with eloquence and confidence, but she was the granddaughter? "What can you tell me about him?"

Tovey sat upon a chair against the smooth timber table. She folded her hands upon her lap. "My grandfather was born pre-devastation, but he lived most of his life in the colony. He outlived his spouse, and his son, my father. He fled here, taking me with him over ten cycles ago."

"And the reason he fled?"

Tovey remained still. "He was entrusted with information given to him by a scout."

Sitting down on the bed, facing Tovey, Jensen leaned forwards. "What scout. Who?"

"I don't know. I was too young at the time, and he never revealed the identity."

Jensen's mind raced. "What was the information?"

"Of that I am also unaware. As was my grandfather. He never asked, nor did he want to know. The information got the scout killed. All he knew was the information had to be protected from falling into the wrong hands. However, when knowledge of the missing information was uncovered and the scout disappeared, my grandfather fled Labour, taking me with him."

Looking down at the floor, Jensen pondered Tovey's revelation. "Where is the information?"

"Within a lockbox, its location is unknown to me."

Holding back a frustrated growl, Jensen asked, "Tovey, what can you tell me?"

A smile curved the edges of Tovey's mouth. "Now you are asking the right questions."

"I am?"

Tovey rose. She walked across her room to a shelf on the wall. There she took a small, framed picture and handed it to Jensen. "This was my grandfather, as a young child. It was taken with his parents."

Jensen studied the image. She saw Lomax standing between his mother and father. The child had a bright infectious smile, which mirrored his mother's. His father was different. He appeared pensive. The older man, with ashen hair and circular spectacles, carried a sadness in his eyes, which even the presence of his son could not eradicate.

"When was this taken?"

"Two rotations before his birthday. One rotation before the devastation."

Jensen looked into the fathers' eyes. "He knew."

"Little did my grandfather know that his birth celebration was to be a location to a new world." Tovey sat back down. "Moving with my grandfather here to the Primary Colony was tough. Losing him was worse."

"He died?"

Shaking her head, Tovey broke eye contact. "It was Devlin. He came looking for my grandfather, questioned him endlessly about the information given to him. Whatever was contained within those documents, he wanted it desperately. He beat him for it. In front of me, but grandfather never said a word. Pleaded his ignorance right until the end."

"End?"

"When they took him." Tovey's gaze faltered. "I've not seen him since. He was a strong man for his age. Healthy and full of vitality, but it's been so long now. He can't be alive. I want to know what happened, but I fear the truth."

Jensen took Tovey's hand. "What about the information? Where did he hide it?"

Shaking her head, Tovey pulled back. "He didn't bring anything with us. I wonder, even now, what he did with it. Not to mention what was sensitive enough that people died." Tovey rose to her feet and crossed the room. "Leaving me alone. Fending for myself. This isn't a great place for a child with no protection."

Feeling the sting of Tovey's words, Jensen wished for things to have been different for the young woman who had been left alone so many cycles ago. "I'm sorry this happened to you and your grandfather, Tovey."

The woman nodded. "Are you going to find out what happened to him?"

Jensen nodded.

"And will you tell me?"

"If you wish for me to do so." Jensen paused… "Tovey, is there anything else you can think of? Anything that might help in my search for the truth?"

Tovey was quick to nod in the affirmative. "My grandfather told me his father worked for the government, securing a future for our people, but somewhere along the way their work became distorted, and their focus changed. He said the weight of that work changed who his father was. It became a 'stain' that he could never remove. He secured a place for himself and his family within the colony. He tried to adapt to the new way of life, but eventually the guilt took him."

"He killed himself."

"And when he died, my grandfather, and his mother were moved to Labour."

Jensen looked down again at the image of a young Lomax with his mother and father. A young child so full of happiness and life. Ignorant of the events that were to unfold. She turned her attention to his father and the older man's haunted expression behind small bespectacled eyes. "What was his father's name?"

"Phoenix." Tovey was quiet for a moment before she asked, "Jensen, do you know what plagued Phoenix's conscience?"

"No," Jensen replied honestly. "I don't know yet, but whatever it was… it is…" her thoughts turned to Kiernan. "It's enough to kill for."

CHAPTER 29

Seated at the familiar setting of her desk, Kiernan stared at the screen of her terminal. Her fingers moved lightly over the keyboard. The sound of co-workers around her faded away as her mind ruminated over the results of the tests she and Angelus had undertaken. What they discovered should not have been. Now only one person could hopefully supply the answers she needed.

Lost in her thoughts, Kiernan jumped as a hand landed upon her shoulder. She turned to her left and looked up seeing Vegas standing beside her.

"Delivered as requested." Vegas handed Kiernan a data console.

"Is this all the data Ziran loaded from the laboratory?" she asked.

"That's what he says." Vegas took a seat beside Kiernan. "I have to hand that over, so whatever you need, may I suggest you make it quick."

Kiernan wasted no time in plugging the console into her terminal and accessing the information contained within.

Vegas watched her. "What are you looking for?"

Knowing she could not keep Vegas in the dark, Kiernan began to explain. "Angelus and I took samples from the scavenger's body." She scrolled through the mass of data that loaded upon her screen. So much information, Ziran had surpassed himself. However, she was looking for something specific. Kiernan began to key in search phrases.

"What did you discover?"

Pausing, Kiernan said, "Synthetic markers in the scavenger's genetic composition."

Vegas watched Kiernan's screen, not quite understanding, at that point, where she was leading him. One block of information flashed to another as she followed a trail of data that would lead her in the desired direction.

"Synthetic markers?"

"As in artificially created."

The Major rubbed his stubbed chin, as Kiernan's revelation began to herald understanding. He continued to watch as she accessed a file loaded with video clips. Kiernan browsed through the dates.

"Look at this," she pointed to the very last clip. "This was three rotations before the devastation." Deciding not to start at the beginning, Kiernan accessed the last clip.

Before the screen stood a smartly dressed man in a laboratory coat like Kiernan's. He couldn't have been more than forty cycles old, yet his hair was ashen, and his haunted eyes could be seen clearly through circular spectacles. His expression was detached, his voice emotionless. Kiernan activated the clip. The man started to speak.

"Test Vial 15 has proved successful in withstanding the effects of Amphibulartoxin. All twenty subjects injected with the vial have displayed immunity to the toxin with no current side effects."
The camera spanned out, giving a view of the laboratory at the testing station. Each of the ten cells was filled with three test subjects.

Kiernan gasped lightly, as she saw the individuals locked in the cells. They were naked. Their bodies showing signs of abuse and fading bruises. Each cell held a man, woman and child, sadness, and defeat in their eyes.

Stepping back into view the scientist continued to speak. "With these results comes increased confidence in total protection to a worldwide release of the toxin and the survival of our people."
The clip ended.

Vegas stared at the frozen screen; arms folded with one hand covering his chin. His brow furrowed in deep thought. Kiernan scrolled through to a random clip and activated the playback function.

The same scientist stood before the camera. His expression disturbed and clouded with emotion he was unable to disguise. In the background, out of view, the sound of cries for help filled the air. The scientist spoke, having to shout over pain-filled hollers of terror.
"Vial 3 is unsuccessful against the toxin. Subjects show no level of resistance."
The camera panned out to the holding cells. In the top corner of the first three cells a visible, amber-tinted mist seeped into the cell chambers. Within those cells, every man, woman and child inhabitant cried

out for mercy. Pain etched into their expressions, blood seeping from their facial orifices. Tears of terror, followed by horrendous reactions to Amphibulartoxin as it took over their bodies. The scientist moved into view.

"Physical reactions to the toxin consistent. Vial 3 is a failure."

He was visibly disappointed. "Commence tests with vial 4."

The clip ended.

Kiernan turned to Vegas with watery eyes. She took a composing breath and swallowed. "Why?"

Rising, Vegas walked around Kiernan placed his hand upon her shoulder. He knelt closer. "Explain."

Knowing what Vegas was asking, Kiernan elaborated. "My directive for the mission was to retrieve the data pertaining to a vial 15." She looked back at the screen. "Up until this moment I had no idea what vial 15 was."

"Why do our people want the inoculation to a toxin that has been presumably extinct in our world for over one hundred cycles?" Vegas leaned closer, aware that there were still people working in the laboratory, even if they hadn't seen what he had. "I want you to keep digging. Find out everything you can. Load the entire contents of Ziran's console onto remote storage and hand this back to me. I am going to push right now for a meeting with Commander Tehera. I will update him on the events, as I know them, and hand over this data."

"Is that wise?" Kiernan argued. "What if-"

"I can't be seen as withholding information, and the sooner I report the mission successes the better."

"Successes?" Kiernan was incredulous.

"You asked me serval time to trust you, Kiernan. Now I'm asking the same of you." Vegas rose. "Keep digging. When I return, I expect answers."

"As do I," Kiernan replied cryptically.

Vegas held eye contact for a moment more before looking away. He did not have the answers he wanted, but he had discovered more than he expected. With so many unanswered questions, how could he weave a believable lie for his superiors? And where was Jensen? What part did she play in Kiernan's plan? Vegas' mind ran amok with suspicions and presumptions. He realised meeting with Tehera may be a little more convoluted than he'd first thought.

***

Re-entering the main bazaar, Jensen was again struck by the lack of activity within the social hub. She stopped by the vacant spot left by Dicken's food cart and looked around. Still no children. Barely any traders. Jensen looked back at Flick's and frowned. Tovey appeared beside her.

"What's going on, Tovey?"

"It's him; Devlin. He comes every rotation. Sometimes he intimidates. Sometimes somebody disappears."

"Flick?"

"Flick, Dicken, Andreas, Willa. We never see it happen, but we know he took them."

Lacing her fingers behind her head, Jensen stared ahead. For what reason did Devlin take them? Was it to instil fear? That had certainly worked, but why the sudden increase in abductions? Jensen knew Devlin worked with others, his 'mob' as they were called. A militia of sorts that policed the Primary Colony without permission or election. She had only seen Devlin once in the flesh. It had been at a distance, and she had barely time to register his appearance before she was escaping back to Governance. Devlin was tall with thick hair. From her vantage point it had been all she was able to learn. Whoever Devlin was, he did not live within Primary Colony. His physical appearance was proof of that. He looked too healthy.

Tovey placed a hand upon Jensen's upper arm to gain her attention. "What are you going to do?"

"How long has Devlin cast his shadow upon the colony?"

"Since before my grandfather and I arrived."

Jensen nodded, thinking just that. A little piece of the puzzle hovered over its place, but a larger question manifested within Jensen's mind. For whom did Devlin work? Could this corruption really go as high as Kiernan believed? In the past, Jensen was sure Devlin was an opportunist who tried to rule by fear. For the most part it had worked. Nobody had revolted against him, due to the lack of an established governing body within the Primary Colony. Like all oppressors, Devlin had taken what he wanted, and the colonists allowed him in hopes of a peaceful life. His thug-like mentality had endured well in an ungoverned society.

Wordlessly, Jensen entered Flick's domain. Evidence of a struggle lay scatted over the floor. Nobody had dared to enter the room since. She bent down and removed a tattered tome from the ground. Her name was scrawled on the reverse. Something Flick had planned to trade with her?

"When did this happen?"

"Yester-rotation."

So soon! Taking the tome, Jensen placed it upon Flick's countertop. "How does Devlin enter the colony?"

"I can show you where he is last observed, but then after that is a dead end."

Jensen ran a hand down her leg, feeling the outline of the automatic firearm Kiernan had handed to her along with the crossing token. "Take me there."

***

The door opened more quickly than Vegas expected. Holding a box housing the data they had retrieved from the testing station, he watched Tehera's line of sight move swiftly to the hardware he was carrying. Without so much as a greeting, the commander stood aside and allowed Vegas entrance into his office. Vegas had spent many a fraction sitting in Tehera's office, receiving information or instructions. He knew the area well.

Entering confidently, he placed the box down upon Tehera's desk and turned to face the bearded man. He noticed Tehera appeared tired with deeply furrowed lines around his eyes furrowed and shadowed dark circles.

Vegas took the seat Tehera offered and watched as the commander walked around his desk to sit facing him. His frame remained rigid. His posture straight and unmoving. He clasped his hands upon the desk before him.

"Reports show only five of you returned. I've tried to contact Advisor Xoren with no success. I have two vehicles in the bay with no scouted supplies. I've delayed the briefing while I review your return and meet with Xoren, except my trusted advisor is uncontactable. Explain."

"We lost Advisor Xoren, Sir."

Tehera did not respond instantly, but the slight flicker in his right eye signified his mounting rage.

Vegas continued. "We were not prepared for the mission. Nothing could have prepared us for what we faced out there. We lost five members of our team and-"

Tehera slammed his fist down upon his desk. "WHAT HAPPENED?" Tehera yelled, his face turning an intense shade of crimson.

Vegas kept eye contact with Tehera. "An explosion caused by unstable materials killed Advisor Xoren in the station laboratory. The resulting structural instability of the surrounding area further took the lives of Officer Jax, Jorca and Scout Ruben. It inadvertently alerted a hoard of scavengers to our location, and, in our battle, we lost Scout Jilya, Sir." Vegas leaned forward in his chair. "We walked right into a scavengers' den; maybe twenty or thirty of them. Probably more. It was all we could do to escape with our lives."

"So, you failed." Tehera rubbed his bearded chin. "The whole mission was a failure, and I lost my trusted advisor while under your command."

Not reacting to Tehera's words, Vegas said, "And two officers and two scouts."

"It took a cycle for us to pinpoint the location of the testing station and identify the data needed for our Ultimate Agenda. Rotations and rotations of planning the search for materials vital to our goal… and… you… failed." Tehera pushed himself away from his desk and rose, circling Vegas. "How did unstable chemicals trigger an explosion that killed my advisor, one scout and two officers? How did you manage to alert a horde of scavengers to your position, and lose a seasoned scout in the battle? I want a detailed report on my desk within two marks." Tehera held onto the back of Vegas chair. The Major stared forward respectfully. "You are lucky I did delay the meeting with the Select Prime. We need to rethink our whole approach. You have put us back cycles, Major."

Vegas was silent, allowing Tehera to continue his rant. He could feel the commander's rage undulating from him in waves of ire. Surely, they hadn't set them back cycles?

"I will take your rank for this, Vegas-"

"With resect, Sir-"

"Your position-"

"Commander," Vegas rose from his char and turned to face Tehera. He took the box from the side of his desk. "These data consoles hold all the downloaded data from the station laboratory and the testing facility. Every project they undertook, every build, every creation, every schematic, every test conducted, they are all here." He handed the box to Tehera. "We may not have returned with as much as we anticipated, but we returned with what I believe is the most vital collection of data we could harvest."

Tehera was silent. Stunned. He looked down into the box and then back up at Vegas. "Have you studied the data?"

Instinctively quick to respond, Vegas said, "Negative, but both collections were obtained from the main terminals. Minister Kiernan and I are supremely confident everything we need is held within these consoles."

Passing Vegas, Tehera placed the box back upon his desk. He turned to address the Major. "Good work. The lives we lost out there will be honoured to our cause." He was silent for a beat, his gazed fixed upon Vegas. "Dismissed."

Stunned by the commander's behaviour, Vegas nodded. He had hoped for more discussion on the issues. He had expected a different outcome. Confused, but doing as ordered, Vegas turned and left Tehera's office, closing the door softly behind him.

Tehera watched him leave, his gaze never straying from the closed door. His eyes narrowed. He gripped the edge of his chair so hard the whites of his knuckles strained against his flesh. His chest rose and fell with rage. Pulling the chair from under his desk, Tehera threw it across the room, feeling undeniable satisfaction as it shattered against the wall. He balled his fists by his side and took a deep breath. Their plan was still on course. However, there were still loose ends to tie up.

***

Stopping against the wall, Vegas remained within earshot, hearing the clash of something being hurtled across Tehera's office. He took a step back, closer, to listen. There were no more sounds. Still suspicious, Vegas took another step until he was beside the barrier. There was silence for a moment and then a voice.

"*We need to talk… I just had a meeting with Vegas… I understand, but I had to agree due to the nature of the mission outcome… there have been unexpected eventualities we need to examine… No, Sir… Right away… Thank you.*"

Not wanting to remain should Tehera open his door, Vegas turned swiftly and moved away from the commander's office. Thoughts and suspicions escalating within his mind, he never saw Scout Ryan until they collided in the corridor.

"Major, I apologise."

Attempting to rein in his frustration, Vegas smiled stiffly. "Not a problem, Scout. You're in a hurry."

The Scout beamed with excitement. "Nothing is wrong, Sir. In fact, I was just about to meet with Commander Tehera. I wasn't aware you had returned, otherwise I would have reported the news directly to you, of course."

"News?"

"I have just returned from a routing vent inspection topside. All seemed standard, no issues. Then something happened."

"Happened?" Usually, an unexpected event on the Barrens would instantly trigger alarm however, Ryan didn't appear distressed.

"I was inspecting the last vent. It was clear with no obstruction. I was about to head back when," Ryan paused for effect. "A calm settled over the land. I have heard of it, but I've never experienced something so rare. Clement. It really happened, but that was not the remarkable part! I stood looking around. The storm dropped. Dust settled. I looked up at the sky and I saw it. A haze of violet. The sky, Sir, I saw the sky!" Ryan became more animated as he spoke. "The cloudbanks parted, and the sky opened before me. The most beautiful sight I have ever seen. As though it revealed itself just for me. It was just a small break, but Sir, it really happened."

In sunlit marks, Vegas thought, jealous Ryan had seen what the rest of them had only dreamed. Deciding not to relay what his team had seen on their journey back, Vegas grasped the younger man's upper arm and squeezed lightly. "What you saw might well be the break for which we've been waiting. A parting of the toxic cloudbanks might afford us the ability to try communication with our satellite. If it is still orbiting the planet that is."

"With hope on our side, Sir."

Vegas nodded. He wanted Ryan to keep the information close until he could be sure of Tehera's intentions, but he knew that would only raise questions he was unable to answer. He needed his team to continue like everything was running to its rotational routine. "This is exciting news. Another step closer to our Ultimate Agenda. Well spotted, Scout."

"Thank you."

Vegas watched Ryan head towards the Commander's office. He pondered this latest revelation. It was true that a parting of the cloudbanks could offer them the possibility to communicate with their satellite. That communication could offer the opportunity to retrieve the information stored within its databanks. Information they had lost many cycles ago. Information colonists had died for.

Watching Ryan disappear into Tehera's office, Vegas turned and walked away with increasing urgency.

CHAPTER 30

Four marks had passed, and Kiernan heard no word from Jenson. Still sat at her terminal, she worked diligently through the data retrieved from Ziran's console. It was a vast undertaking, so she had taken to researching key phrases to narrow down the parameters. Possible useful evidence was saved onto a separate file.

Copying another part of data, Kiernan paused as she read the file name. She was searching for specific evidence. Evidence which she had stumbled upon many rotations before. That which had been the original clue into signs of a conspiracy within the highest-ranking members of the colony. She had been searching for information, following a trail of data, which had begun with reviewing the requests presented by the Gene Cleansing team. Kiernan thought back to that moment. She pondered her decision to look further into a curious entry in the genetic data entries. That original and presumed innocent act had started her journey into a quest for truth.

This rotation, both Jensen and Vegas would be expecting answers and she still needed to find her solid proof. She needed to search harder.

With renewed determination, Kiernan turned back to her task.

"Minister Kiernan?"

Kiernan turned to see Officer Nicoletti standing beside her. "Oh, Nicoletti, apologies, I was engrossed in my work." She smiled at the younger man, remembering his spouse, Scout Taura. "How are you?" she asked sincerely.

Nicoletti didn't answer her question. Instead, his gaze drifted to the floor for a moment as he took a breath. "Taura's body will be released to me. I am beginning preparations for her Honourship."

"Well consider me there."

Although he did not know Minister Kiernan, talk of her allegiance with Jensen had spread around Governance. If Jensen liked her, then that put Kiernan in good stead with her colleagues and allies. It was rare an affiliation would occur between opposed ranked colonists of Governance.

"That's very kind of you, thank you, Minister." Nicoletti smiled and then blinked as he recalled why he had been asked to visit Kiernan. "Oh!" He dug his hand into his leg pocket and pulled out a small data disk.

"Major Vegas asked I pass this on to you." He handed the disk to Kiernan. "He said he made a copy for your perusal." Nicoletti frowned. "He also asked me to state that he is 'sure you understand the sensitivity of the document'."

Kiernan studied Nicoletti. "Indeed." She looked down at the disk knowing instantly that it was a copy of the files Vegas had taken from the Testing Station. The sensitivity was the fact Vegas must have copied the information before handing it to Tehera. It was a show of trust on Vegas' part. He was willing to stand by Kiernan's beliefs and help her in almost blind faith. Kiernan smiled to herself.

"Thank you for bringing this, Officer Nicoletti. And don't forget to keep me updated on Taura's Honourship. I will admit after only one journey up onto the Barrens, I have a renewed respect for the Scouts and the job they do for us all. Your spouse was a brave woman."

"She was." Nicoletti's eyes glazed. "I better leave you to your work, Minister." He took a step backwards and then turned quickly, eager to hide the tears gathering in his eyes.

Nodding once as the Officer walked away, Kiernan then looked down at the data disk. She tapped is lightly upon her fingertips before turning in her seat and inserting it into her terminal.

***

She'd never imagined she'd see this part of Primary Colony. The walls were dirt, nothing more than a carved-out tunnel in dank soil. The scent was strong and moisture heavy in the air. Jensen reached out and ran her fingers over the moist dirt wall. She squinted in the darkness and used her torch to look more closely. Life. A tiny creature appeared through the soil, knocking little grains of dirt to the ground, as it burrowed a path through the grit, out into view, and then back again, disappearing into the wall.

Tovey stood smiling at her behaviour, as Jensen placed her hand upon the wall and shone her torchlight into the hole the tiny creature had created. She tried to peer into the aperture. It was clear to her that Jensen had never seen such an insect before. Tovey was aware of the reputed sterile environment of Governance. It was unlikely any form of creature would exist in the aseptic community.

Unable to see into the crevice, Jensen pulled away and looked around. They had reached a dead end. This didn't make sense.

"So, this is where Devlin-"

"He comes from this direction. That's where we first make sight of him," Tovey confirmed.

Jensen looked around again. She stamped the ground beneath them. Nothing echoed back at her. "You're sure."

"Positive."

Reaching up, Jensen was able to touch the ceiling. Again, it was dense with no evidence of a partition. "There has to be another route of entry."

"Jensen, I have followed him. I was just close enough that I saw him turn the corner into this passageway, and yet when I got here, he was gone. There was nothing. It was like I followed an apparition."

"That isn't possible."

"I know that."

Jensen sighed. "Alright." She stamped the ground again. Nothing. She kicked the wall to her left. She kicked the wall to her right. Nothing. In frustration Jensen walked back along the passageway to its entrance, stamping her feet the entire distance. Nothing. She walked back hitting the ceiling with the side of her fist. Still nothing. Reaching the far end, beside Tovey, Jensen hit the wall before her. There was no evidence of a hollow background.

"See?"

Still not wanting to concede, Jensen said, "We're missing something." On impulse, she extinguished her torch light. The bright, wide beam vanished, and darkness enveloped them. As her eyes adjusted, Jensen looked around. There! Bending down, she looked closer into the corner of the passageways dead end. It was practically invisible… unless one was looking for it. A tiny, almost imperceptible shaft of light. She reached out and felt the far wall and that's when it hit Jensen. The side walls were slightly soft and could crumble under touch. However, the far wall, which was essentially the passages dead end, was solid. Jensen rose.

"I think maybe we have to push."

Following Jensen's advice, Tovey placed both hands upon the wall. Jensen followed suit, and together they pushed.

For a moment there was no response, but then the wall started to move. Fraction by fraction it started to slide backwards. As it did, the minor shaft of light increased, first to a narrow beam and then a wider stream of bright light that illuminated the passage.

The women stopped. They had moved the wall back far enough for them to slide through the gap. Jensen peered through its opening. Inside the walls were a russet brick construction with metallic lights fixed along its surface, that Jensen estimated at about every four strides. The brick passageway continued as far as they could see, and the walls shone the further it went.

"Where do you think it leads?"

Jensen squinted, as she followed the line of wall fixed lighting into the distance. "My guess," she blinked as realisation dawned upon her. "To the truth."

With only a moment of cautious anticipation, Jensen slid through the gap. "Come on."

"Jensen, I can't."

Stopping, Jensen turned around. "What do you mean?"

"I must stay here. With my people."

"What people?" Jensen stepped towards Tovey. A light shone straight above her. "The dwindling masses. Tovey come with me and make this right. Help us figure out what's going on, and what happened to Flick, Dicken, Lomax, and everybody else who has suffered at the hands of these people. My parents too."

Blinking in surprise, Tovey took a step and then froze. "I'm afraid."

"So am I."

Bolstered by Jensen's words, Tovey passed through the gap and into the artificially lit brick walkway. Together they pushed the barrier closed and then looked ahead.

"Ready?"

Tovey nodded.

"Let's go."

***

Kiernan discovered the data files on Vegas' disk were less than half the size of those Ziran had retrieved from the laboratory. However, the content was specific. Each file had dedicated information about specific areas of construction. It was the craft, their craft. The original designs and schematics for the ship that was to take them to their new world. Kiernan knew their ship's construction had originally begun at the testing station. The craft had been deconstructed and most parts transported long ago, when the colony was still in its infancy, and Primary was its original foundation. In a location separate from Primary, the craft was stored ready for reconstruction. Kiernan knew not all its parts had been salvaged for safe harbour before the devastation. As such, they had to use whatever they could scout and scavenge, to finish its build once again.

On the information Kiernan was searching, she was finding nothing new. They already had the ship's blueprints and build designs. Almost a hundred cycles of scavenging and using every possible material had assured them the craft was fully reconstructed. All, but for one remaining item, the power source. That was Kiernan's role in the construction. She had spent many cycles designing, building, and evaluating the perfect renewable power source. A containment of renewable energy so immense that it could not only power an entire craft but effect its ability to sustain faster-than-light speed. That creation of sub-particle energy had been Kiernan's life's work. The energy cells used on their mission to the testing station had been but a mere infinitesimal fraction of the primary source's power. A source that, at that moment, was situated in the centre of her Laboratory. It stood a little higher than Kiernan and its casing was a slim pyramid. Even in a power down state, a glow emanated round it. It was complete and ready for adaptation into the craft. They were so close to completion.

Closing a file, Kiernan continued to the next. She wasn't sure what she was looking for, but she would know when she found it. One file led to another and then another. Kiernan stopped as a word jumped out at her. Cannon. She opened the file. A Dispersal Cannon? Kiernan studied the data. It was the schematics of a cannon designed specifically for their craft. Kiernan tapped her fingers upon the tabletop. What was this? She sat back in her chair, staring at the diagram before her. Her mind raced. So far everything on the disc was knowledge she was familiar with; until this. Why would their craft, built to transport them to a new home, need a 'Dispersal Cannon'? Furthermore, what was it?

***

There was a point, while walking through the passage, that the walls changed from a russet brick to metallic sheeting. Jensen stopped to study the wall, seeing fastenings upon the bricks where the sheeting had once been affixed. She brushed her fingers over the bracket holes.

"What is that?" Tovey asked.

"Looks like they are taking down the original wall covering to utilise the material," Jensen presumed. "There are still tools here." She pointed to the implements used to remove the metal covering. "I think they are in the middle of the task." Jensen looked around. "We need to keep moving. Others might be back at any moment."

They continued at a faster pace. Jensen wondered when they had started to cannibalise the colony's construction itself for useable materials. She knew Tehera had hoped they would salvage such materials from the testing station. Were they really in such dire need that they were reduced to stripping materials from the Haven? Was this safe?

Official word was their ship was in Phase Quattuor. That meant the craft was complete and the final parts of internal assembly were underway. Jensen believed they would fulfil the Ultimate Agenda in her lifetime. She was sure many colonists before her had hoped for that, but Jensen genuinely believed it was so.

"Look… there."

Jensen peered ahead to where Tovey was pointing. There was a door. The first of several. As they approached, they noted it held a window. Both women peered inside. A storeroom. Nothing of importance. They continued to the next door. Again, it appeared to be storage. Jensen sped up her gait to the third door. This was wider, but the glass was mottled and obscured their view. Noise drew their attention, and they stepped closer, recognising voices and the sounds of construction and mechanical tools. The noise echoed from within. The room beyond was vast. Jensen tried the door, but it was locked. She looked closer, trying to decipher a blurred image of an immense shape in the warehouse-like space. Could it be?

"Do you think that's-?"

"I do,"

Both women looked closely. Nobody, but those involved in the building of their ship, had seen it. Even those working on the ship were not allowed to discuss it. Everybody had a job, a role, within the colony. Some were not allowed to discuss that role. It wasn't considered a curious covenant, but Jensen wondered whether it should have been.

Looking up, and following the blurred lines of the craft, Jensen had to acknowledge it was an impressive size. Its shape was long, and she could just decipher its lines meeting to a point at one end. The front she would presume. It was sleek and its shape gave it an aerodynamic quality. She knew this was for efficient travel at faster-than-light speed. Jensen wished she could see it properly. Her whole life she had waited for this moment, yet it was still just beyond reach.

Knowing they needed to continue, both women backed away from the door. They walked the length of the vast space beyond the separating wall, and reached an end with two doors, one to the left and there other to the right.

"Which way?"

"Good question."

Neither door had a window, or a sign of its destination beyond.

"Maybe we should split up?"

Jensen shook her head. "No, we must stick together. If we-"

The sound of voices coming from the left door aided Jensen in her decision. Fearing being caught, Jensen tried to push the door to their right. It didn't move.

"It's locked?" Tovey announced incredulously and looked around in panic.

The voices drew closer.

Jensen studied the doors lock, and although slightly different in shape, she noticed a familiarity in the mechanism. In a moment of faith, she thrust her hand into her leg pocket and removed her E.M.P disruptor. She waved it over the lock. It opened.

"No way!"

Hearing voices closing in on them, Jensen pushed open the door and crossed the threshold, pulling Tovey with her. They closed the door together.

Tovey fell against the wall. "That was close."

With her ear against the barrier, Jensen listened as the voices opened and closed a door behind them, and then drifted away.

"How did you manage to…?" Tovey looked down at the device in Jensen's hand. "How did you know? What is that?"

Jensen held up the E.M.P disruptor. "A leap of faith. The lock looked familiar. I took a chance. This area was built during the colony's original construction. This had to be the case, as the ship is here, and it was transported from the testing station where it was originally designed and fabricated. The testing station had similar locks." Jensen shrugged in relief. "A leap of faith!" She pushed the device back into her pocket. "One of the colony's mottos is never throw anything away." Jensen grinned. "Mine is never give anything back." She winked.

"Good motto," Tovey agreed. Turning she looked ahead. Another passageway. This one was older, appearing more like something she would see at home in the Primary Colony. "Where are we?"

They could hear dripping, distant yet repetitive. It was dark, but small lights fixed to the celling illuminated a shadowy path. They followed. Jensen noticed a heavy presence in the air. Her breathing was tight. The air was thick due to a mix of stagnant water and dense natural gasses.

The women walked with caution. They reached a small room sealed shut by a door made of metal bars. The room was empty. They passed four more empty rooms.

"Containment cells?" Tovey looked to Jensen who only frowned in discomfort.

They turned a corner. More cells on both sides. Jensen shook a cell door. It was secured using an antiquated locking mechanism. Jensen tried another door. This was open and it creaked on aged hinges as it swung wide. The cell was empty.

"Who's there?"

Jensen looked to Tovey. It was a male voice.

"Hello?" A hand appeared further down the passage and reached out through cell bars.

Cautiously they approached. It was Flick.

"Flick!" Tovey knelt and took her ally's hand, holding it against her chest. "What happened? Where's-" she paused as she noticed the spread of contusions covering Flick's face and body. He was naked. "Are you… are you well? Do you hurt?"

"They took my one good tooth." Flick pointed to the gap where the crooked and stained tooth once stood.

Tovey laughed, as tears filled her eyes.

"Flick," Jensen pulled his attention. "What happened?"

"Devlin."

"We figured that. Why?" she asked softly.

"They need to do tests. We make good… 'subjects'. Who in colony is going to miss us? Outcasts. They use us much as possible. Keep us living longer. Like magic. Keeping testing. Unless they use the big one."

"What's the big one, Flick?"

"Don't know," Flick winced, as he coughed. He pushed his body harder against the bars, despite his bruising, and pushed his face between two metal bars.

"Then how do you know all of this?" Jensen asked.

"Owen?"

Tovey frowned, as she thought. Recognition soon sparked a face in her memory. "Owen? He disappeared almost a cycle ago, Flick."

Flick nodded. "Owen." He pointed to the cell opposite him. "In there."

The women turned to see a body lying on the floor, facing away from them. It was by the far wall, naked and visibly malnourished. Scars, bruises, and cuts marred pale, emaciated flesh.

"Hope he's sleeping. Hope he's never waking. He's done."

"Did he tell you this, Flick?"

Flick nodded again. He closed his eyes and swallowed in pain. "He doesn't want me. He said so."

"Who?"

"Devlin. I'm too much trouble." Flick looked to Jensen who was knelt by the bars beside Tovey. Concern was clear in her eyes. "He found our last trade."

Jensen searched her mind. The data consoles!

"How?"

"Don't know. Didn't say. Promise."

"She believes you, Flick."

Although Tovey tried to assure Flick, Jensen wasn't so sure he hadn't told him. She didn't blame him. Devlin and his men terrified the Primary Colony. Only now was Jensen beginning to understand just how much influence he had.

Flick held Tovey's hand tight. "Owen told me they have people here. Prisoners. He said he's taken to places. For tests. He was sure he saw him."

Jensen rose and looked around, searching for a way to release Flick from the cell, while keeping an eye out for approaching danger.

"You have to find him."

"Find who?" Tovey asked in confusion.

"He's somewhere."

Kneeling, Jensen said, "Flick you're not making sense. Do you know how they keep you in here? Is there a key?"

Flick pulled Tovey's hand. "He's alive. He's somewhere."

"Who?"

"Lomax!"

CHAPTER 31

Enforcement Commander Tehera stood outside a wide set of double timber doors. A plaque adorned the right door, indicating the room beyond was the personal office of Select Prime Abrahams. He hadn't knocked. The Commander needed a moment to rehearse details one more time before he had to offer a full explanation to the leader of their colony. Tehera already knew Abrahams was furious that the team hadn't been able to retrieve the materials set out in their mission directives. As such, the Select Prime had already issued an order for all non-essential, wall-mounted ores to be removed and re-used for their base compounds. There was one part left to be built for their craft.

Hand poised ready to knock, Tehera was taken aback when the door swung open, and he stood face to face with his Select Prime. Although not in the least bit intimidated by Abrahams' position, height or girth, Tehera respected his Prime enough to take a step backwards and lower his head in esteem.

Regarding Tehera, his right hand and trusted Commander, the Prime remained in his doorway, "I want Vegas and Kiernan in this meeting. Send word and return with them in no less than half a mark."

Not letting his surprise show, Tehera nodded and backed away from Abrahams, not turning his back until he was five paces away.

The Prime watched Tehera leave before disappearing back into his office and closing the door behind him.

***

She had found it. Kiernan didn't know exactly what it was she was looking for but knew she would know when that moment occurred. Chair pushed to the edge of her desk and wedged tight between the two, Kiernan moved closer to her terminal, reading the information on its screen. She blinked, resting her chin in her hand, as she read over the schematic once again. Why would a craft, built for the sheer purpose of transporting inhabitants to a new world, need a cold store facility capable of housing two thousand Cryo-Preservation Chambers? Chambers no larger than… she ruminated on the size calculations… her head maybe? Nothing in all her cycles working on the energy requirements of the craft had the power consumption of two thousand Cryo-Preservation Chambers been a sub-component.

Needing to know more, Kiernan extended her search to include 'Cryo-Preservation Chamber'. As an afterthought she set up the same search parameters on the data Raziko downloaded from the laboratory.

Now she had to wait.

"Our presence has been requested."

Kiernan jumped. She turned to see Vegas. A serious expression shaped his features.

"Now?"

"Now." Vegas looked around. Many of Kiernan's team had already left. Their work rotation had ended, and a new team would soon arrive. Moving closer, Vegas spoke freely. "Whatever you need to tell me, you do so now. We can't wait for Jensen to return. I'm not walking blind into an encounter with our Select Prime if I don't know the facts."

Studying Vegas, Kiernan agreed with a single nod. She couldn't hold back the truth any longer. Turning, she switched off her terminal screens. Kiernan wanted the search to continue while she was absent.

"Alright." She rose. "Let's talk."

Pushing the chair under her desk Kiernan shrugged off her laboratory jacket.

Vegas sighed internally. Finally.

***

Jensen stood staring into the cell opposite Flick's. Owens body hadn't moved, yet instead of concern, her mind remained fixed upon Flick's last words. It couldn't be true, could it? There was no way Lomax could still be alive. The man would be over one hundred cycles old. It was impossible. How many hits to the head had the delusional younger man received? Was that even Owen in the cell opposite? Arms folded; Jensen shook her head as she looked down at the ground. Her light hair shrouded her face as she frowned with disquiet.

Behind Jensen, Tovey knelt beside Flick, holding his hand. "My grandfather can't be alive, Flick. It's impossible." Releasing Flick's hand, Tovey tried the cell bars, pulling and pushing with force. "We need to get you out of here."

Stopping Tovey, Flick placed his own hand around hers, wrapped around the bar. Flick spoke firmly. "Owen played dumb. Like no sense, but he saw, he listened, he heard. Searching for a lost cure they were. Do tests on us. Try to recreate cure for toxin. To stop it. But Lomax, he wouldn't say. So, to punish he must watch. Suffering. Again, and again."

Fragments of Flick's words began making a twisted sense to Jensen. She turned and knelt in front of Flick. "What won't Lomax say, Flick?"

Flick shrugged.

"Are you saying Tovey's grandfather, Lomax, is being kept alive until he shares his knowledge?"

Flick stared back and forth between Jensen and Tovey.

"Flick, Lomax is alive?"

"Alive, yes." Releasing Tovey's hand, Flick reached through the bars and took Jensen's shirt. "Devlin is bad. His people are bad. You stop them."

"How!" Tovey exclaimed. "How do we stop a man who obviously works for the governing force of the colony? And where is my grandfather, Flick?"

Acknowledging Lomax was alive didn't feel as unbelievable as Jensen thought it should have. Nothing was surprising her anymore. She held onto Flick's hand, easing it off her clothing, but keeping hold of his cold appendage. Tovey had asked two particularly important questions. Firstly, how do you stop a dangerous force who seemed to have the backing of their Select Prime? And secondly, if Lomax was alive, where was he? Jensen's mind whirled.

"I need to speak to Kiernan. We need a plan."

"Jensen, if my grandfather is alive, help me find him."

Jensen studied Tovey. She wanted to. "Tovey, we need to stop what's going on. To uncover the truth. I owe it to every colonist who has lived and died for a cause that was a lie, and a woman who is risking her life right now to bring the truth to light."

Rising, Tovey looked down at Jensen. "And what about my grandfather?"

"We will find him," Jensen rose, resolute in her course of action.

Tovey wasn't convinced. "I want to find my grandfather, Jensen, I admit that, but why do they have him? Because he has vital knowledge they want. Help me find him. He might hold the key to the answers you are looking for."

Rubbing the back of her neck, Jensen considered Tovey's words. She was right, but so much time had passed, and she had agreed to check back in with Kiernan. She worried for her safety. There was Vegas, but Jensen still didn't know if the Major was trustworthy. They were stronger together and they needed to fight this battle as a team. But Tovey did have a valid point and knowledge was a powerful tool.

"Flick, can you survive here another mark or so?"

"Going nowhere."

"Which way did Owen say they took him for tests?"

Flick pointed to their right. Further into the unknown. "You return for me?"

Jensen felt Tovey grasp her arm. Hope. "You know we will."

"I be here."

The pair watched as Flick moved away from the bars and into a darkened corner. He hid in the shadow of darkness.

Silently, Jensen and Tovey headed further into that unknown.

***

They stood outside two doors. Before them was the entrance to the meeting room. The place where they had received their orders for the mission. Where Jensen and Kiernan had first met, and the Minister had put Jensen in her place in spectacular fashion. Vegas smiled at the memory. To their right was a windowed door. He recalled seeing Jensen peer through this door, seeing the stairs beyond. It would have been the first time she found evidence of a lower level to the colony. He remembered her curiosity. Had only five rotations passed since then? It seemed so much longer.

Passing through the doorway to the stairs, Kiernan closed it behind them and began her descent down the staircase. So far, they had walked in silence, but she knew Vegas would stop her and demand answers.

Their footsteps echoed as they took each step. Kiernan knew they would have to converse quietly. Sound could easily travel in the narrow stairwell. Vegas paused between the levels. They stood on a wide platform plated with a cross-hatched metallic tread.

"Talk."

Kiernan took a breath. She kept her voice low. "Some time ago I was performing a simple task." She recalled the moment with absolute clarity. "Reviewing department equipment requests. It was something I'd started to do to pay closer attention to stock control. I noticed an anomaly between equipment and material usage versus the department orders. It was more an idle curiosity at first."

"And?"

"And I noted the usage of materials for genetic harvesting and storage had over tripled that of colonists donating and requesting cleansing and reproduction procedures."

Appearing confused Vegas asked, "Meaning?"

"Meaning why would they need that much equipment and material? It opened a host of questions about ova harvesting, containment, and management. Simple mathematics."

Vegas nodded, only partly understanding what Kiernan was referring to. "And?"

"And so, I started to look further." Kiernan stepped closer to the wall. Her voice softened. "I began to look back into historical records, and the first point I noted a familiar thread in requests versus demand was back over the past twenty cycles. Twenty cycles, Vegas."

The Major thought. Twenty cycles? The length that Abrahams had served as their Select Prime. A position he had taken after his father, Select Prime Crane, had died. As per colony laws, offspring assumed their parent's position and were educated to the standards needed to undertake that role. Abrahams was heir to his father's ranking, just like the monarchy of old. He was much more solitary than his late father, but had proved to govern the colony as efficiently as the Prime before him.

"That could be a coincidence, Kiernan. Making such an accusation is punishable by incarceration. I hope you realise this."

"Of course. Why do you think I've been so closed on offering an explanation until I could uncover solid facts?" Kiernan was visibly affronted by Vegas' lack of faith. "Anyway, I started asking questions. Innocent queries really. I asked the genetic harvesting and cleansing teams about these figures."

"And?"

"Nothing. Nobody had an answer for me. Their figures were legitimate, which was even more confusing. I wondered if maybe the figures were being intercepted and fabricated. So, I dug deeper."

Vegas folded his arms, unimpressed by Kiernan's revelation.

"I started to uncover separate authorisation codes on embedded requests. Then I investigated all the female colonists who had entered the reproduction and genetic cleansing program. Know what I found? That in each case at least ten ova were removed and treated. Why ten? Only one is supposed to be removed, processed, fertilised and re-planted for gestation."

"And the men?"

"Only enough to fertilise one ovum. So again, I started to ask more questions," Kiernan paused…

"And?"

"And suddenly I'm assigned on a mission to the Testing Station."

Vegas frowned, tried to speak, but quickly changed his mind and remained quiet.

"I've started seeing that authorisation code increasingly frequently. It was on Jensen's parents file about *esoteric documents,* and a colonist named 'Lomax'. Then it was the password into a file I found on the disk you sent to me. Know what was in the file?"

Vegas was silent. His expression grim.

"Schematics for Cryo-Preservation Chambers to be stored onboard our craft. Two thousand of them… Vegas if-"

"Wait," Vegas rubbed his face with his rough hands. "Give me a moment; this is a lot to digest." He turned and walked the short length of the platform between the stairs. Vegas looked around fearing unwanted attention. "What does this have to do with Jensen's parents?"

Kiernan could only offer a mild shrug. "At the moment I don't know, but I've sent her to follow a lead and hopefully find out."

If it were possible Vegas paled further. "Some things are best left alone."

"Not if-" Kiernan paused. "Vegas… do you know something about Jensen's parent's deaths?"

"Only that it almost broke her, so I pledged my guardianship through her scout training."

Kiernan was surprised. "I never knew that."

"I just wanted to help, but I recall her being so devastated by her parent's death that she was unable to get out of bed. I don't want old wounds opening on a fools' errand."

Feeling a flash of rage, Kiernan stepped towards Vegas fiercely, and pushed him against the wall, surprising herself as well as the larger man. "This is no fool's errand. Whatever I discovered was just enough for higher powers to believe it necessary to end my existence. I think I'm scraping the surface of the truth, but I know something much more sinister is afoot. Do you understand? I haven't been alone since we returned. I've remained either in my laboratory or any place where there are multiple colleagues or colonists. I don't know who I can trust. I've hardly slept or eaten. Vegas, I'm terrified; all I can do is search for answers."

Vegas took a deep, steady breath. "And you're about to walk into the belly of the beast."

Allowing her arms to drop to her sides, Kiernan acknowledged Vegas' words for the truth they were. However, she held her head high, resolute and determined. "Are you with me?"

They were on the precipice of dangerous territory. Vegas could admit the prospect worried even him. He wanted to tell Kiernan to back away. He hoped it wasn't too late to change the minds of higher powers and convince them her interest had dissipated, but if any of what Kiernan said was grounded in truth, he was duty bound to uphold justice.

Holding out his hand, Vegas watched Kiernan take it in a firm shake. "I'm with you."

It was then that the lower door opened, and Commander Tehera stepped into view. "Prime is waiting."

Exchanging looks, Vegas placed his hand upon Kiernan's lower back. "On our way."

The pair descended the second set of stairs and passed through the doorway towards Abrahams' office.

CHAPTER 32

They seemed to go on forever; dark, dank corridor after dark, dank corridor. Narrow passageway after narrow passageway. It was the reality of a subterranean life. Jensen could tell when the passages were built and usually by whom. Those built pre-devastations were carved out with the luxury of time and with no expense spared to materials used. Some were re-enforced with brick, timber beams or alloy sheeting. Others carved out of the soil and clay of the natural elements. It all depended on what area of the colony you happened to be. Jensen decided she'd had enough of claustrophobic spaces with limited vision. Even with her torch set to widespread illumination, the darkness still encroached upon them, looming around the edges of their vision. There was lighting in the passage, but they knew not to activate it, instead relying on limited torchlight. How she longed for a time she would escape underground living.

Taking a sideways glance at Tovey, Jensen took a fraction of a moment to study Lomax's granddaughter. If everything she told her was the truth, then it was indeed possible he might hold the answers to longstanding questions. However, the man would be over one hundred cycles old. What did that mean for Lomax? What physical state would he be in?

"You're looking at me." Tovey turned to Jensen.

"Sorry... just thinking." Jensen looked away. They were approaching a door.

"Do you think our ancestors ever once considered their future included an insect-like existence in a maze of oppressive winds? My grandfather would speak about his life before the devastations. Such fantastical tales he told." They stopped by the door, "Do you really think we'll ever feel the sun on our faces or wind blowing through our hair?"

Jensen offered a pointed look to Tovey's hairless scalp.

"Figuratively speaking, of course," she added with a self-conscious smile.

Placing one hand upon the barrier, Jensen put her ear on the aged timber. "I think anything is possible. Remember... I go up onto the Barrens. I've seen our world. Even for those who don't make it to the new world, this world is changing. It's healing."

"It is?" Tovey was instantly fixed upon Jensen. Hope glistened in her eyes. It hit Jensen again how it must feel for those colonists who would be left behind in the Primary Colony. The faith they held that eventually their world would become habitable again.

"The thunderheads are breaking, and the cloudbanks are parting. It may happen sooner than we think." Closing her eyes, Jensen listened. She heard voices echo from within the room beyond. She pointed to the door and then placed her finger upon her lips. Tovey nodded; her thoughts still captured by Jensen's words.

The echo of voices showed the room was spacious. She tried the handle. It dipped and the door moved. Pushing just a fraction, Jensen moved so she could peer through its gap. Through the small opening she could see two individuals dressed from head to toe in teal coveralls. They had their back to the door, and as such Jensen was able to look further into the room. Only one side was visible, but she saw a scene remarkably like the laboratory at the testing station with a row of translucent cells. Three were occupied. In the third cell she saw Dicken. The food vendor was seated upon a raised sleeping pallet, huddled into its corner. In the second cell was a woman Jensen was unfamiliar with. She was huddled into the cell corner, next to Dicken. A need for comfort? Jensen thought. In the first cell lay a body strapped to a sleeping pallet. Jensen was unable to name this colonist. Looking back across the row of cells, she noticed the floors of the last three were covered in what she believed to be blood. There were no bodies, but the spillage still looked fresh and shone in the overhead lighting.

Gripping the doorknob, and with her face still wedged in its opening, Jensen looked back at the individuals dressed in coveralls. Protective clothing? She watched them working, still with their backs to her. From what Jensen could see, they appeared to be working with chemical solutions. Taking advantage of their preoccupation, Jensen continued to scan the area. She pushed the door open a little further. The far workstation was larger than expected and a third worker appeared. Behind them, she saw a row of four metallic examination beds with straps to hold their subjects. Further back and closer still, she saw a large, square, padded area with chains attached to the ground. Closer still, and nearest to the door, was a waist high platform, like the examination beds, but re-enforced with chains rather than straps.

"What's in there? What are you looking at? Tovey asked in a whisper.

Jensen looked back at Tovey. "I can see Dicken and another colonist. They are locked in cells. There's blood… not theirs-"

"What?"

"Beds with restraints and chains, workstations, and terminals. I don't know what they have been doing here, Tovey, but-" Jensen looked back into what she had internally titled 'a torture chamber'. Her complexion paled, "Many colonists have lost their lives here."

"Let me see." Tovey ducked lower, positioning her head under Jensen so she could observe the cells, seeing Dicken and another primary colonist familiar to her, Fatima. She saw the empty cells, splattered with blood and the single body strapped to a sleeping pallet.

"Jensen these people are fiends. We need to get Dicken and Fatima out of there." Her line of sight returned to the body restrained upon the first cell's sleeping pallet. She could see an assortment of translucent tubes feeding unknown chemicals into the occupant's body. Each tube was attached to an unrecognisable beeping device.

"Jensen, do you think…"

It had crossed Jensen's mind. A head of tangled, ashen hair, long and dishevelled; a withered body, so fragile upon the pallet's surface. Nobody could survive over ten cycles of that, she thought. Jensen hoped the body was not Lomax.

Taking another look around, Jensen made a bold move. The reinforced, waist-high block was within reach, at no more than six paces from the door.

"Run," she whispered quickly, as she pointed to the block and then pushed the door open enough to make her way swiftly towards their impromptu hiding spot. Tovey followed, making sure the door closed silently behind her. Both women dropped to the ground behind the raised platform, taking a moment to catch their breath. Their new position offered a full view of the workroom.

Jensen felt the blood freeze, as she spied more cells to their right. What was contained within forced an icy blast of horror to slice through her. Scavengers. Two of them, shackled to the ground with thick metal chains. They shared a single cell and moved agitatedly within the narrow confines. A flash of memory hit Jensen, as she recalled seeing Jorca's head within the grasp of a scavenger's hand, as it sunk broken teeth into her dead flesh. Jensen trembled as she shook the thoughts from her mind and looked back at the scavengers. They appeared subdued, awake, but not fully coherent. Both moved slowly, side to side, vacant eyes staring into nothing. Their flesh cracked and oozing. Jensen could smell the putrid pus from memory alone.

Shocked at the vision, Tovey couldn't feel herself rising from behind the safety of the platform until she was unexpectedly in full view. She had never seen a scavenger in the flesh. Only ever hearing about them. Word of mouth spread rapidly in close confines. Scavengers were the fiends who ate naughty children for disrespecting parents; or so children were told. They were the shrieks in the shadows; the foul smells travelling though colony vents.

Fixed upon the sight, Tovey wasn't aware she had exposed herself to the scavengers until her movement attracted their attention. What followed, Tovey could only describe as the most horrendous sound she had ever heard. They began to scream, throwing their bodies in her direction. Chains restricted their movements, they fought with a savage ferocity.

Seeing that Tovey had unveiled herself; Jensen was quick to pull her down before she was spotted by the scientists. Thankfully for them they didn't seem overly concerned by the scavengers' behaviour and continued with their work.

Jensen kept her hand on Tovey's shoulder. "What were you thinking?" She whispered harshly.

"Sorry. I've never seen a scavenger. I lost myself."

The scavengers continued to scream, but their volume lessened. Jensen thought they must have been affected by some form of tranquilizing agent for them to calm so quickly. However, Tovey's actions worried her. "They saw you. They are aware of you now. They will want you." She looked back at the cells; thankful the scavengers were bound by chains. She forced her body lower, terrified by thoughts of being caught. What would they do to them if they were discovered? Would they suffer the same fate as Owen and Flick, or would they be locked up in testing cells like Dicken and Fatima? Anxiously, Jensen scanned the area again. There were doors to the right. Should they try to reach them? Jenson feared what lay beyond. What if it wasn't a way out?

The scavengers' screams continued sporadically. Jensen was brought out of her thoughts by the sound of voices. She looked up above the platform to see the scientists packing away their equipment. Had the scavengers' restlessness upset their working environment?

"I think they're leaving," she whispered.

Tovey nodded hopefully and tried to make herself as small as possible behind the platform. The sound of rattling chains was disconcerting.

Peering around the side of the platform, Jensen watched the scientists. They took their time packing their equipment away. Acknowledging their motions, Jensen wondered what they were working on that caused so much destruction to the lives of the Primary Colonists. What was their goal? The possibilities sent a chill through her.

Beside her, Tovey looked back at the cells. From her position she could see only the first two cells. She looked at the body lying upon the sleeping pallet. The individual was old, that was clear, but nothing from her current distance proved if the individual was Lomax. Judging by what that person was going through, she hoped not.

The lights above the scavengers were extinguished. They were shutting the workroom down. It was late enough into the rotation to end their shift. Perfect timing, Jensen thought. She watched them, not able to understand what they were saying, but when they removed their head covers, two scientists were familiar to her. Fawkes and Lorenzo. She had met them both in her first briefing for their mission. Jensen felt a weight of apprehension drop into her stomach. Who else knew the secret depths of deception within the colony? Fawkes and Lorenzo chatted with a third scientist, and they laughed. Jensen watched, her ire rising. As the trio completed their tasks, they stopped and looked over at the scavengers with mirroring expressions of twisted amusement. For a fleeting fraction of a moment, Jensen pitied the scavengers. Continuing to talk quietly amongst themselves, the trio headed towards the side door. It was another exit! Two scientists departed, leaving Fawkes by the opening. The tall, thin man looked over at the cells. An expression crossed his features, one she could not recognize, but she felt unease.

"Just leave," Jensen muttered to herself. She closed her eyes, and held her breath, as the remaining lights were extinguished, and the workroom was shrouded in darkness.

***

It was the first time Kiernan had entered the Select Prime's office. Taking advantage of the opportunity, she took a moment to look around his personal space. It wasn't as large as she expected, but it was decorated with the most unique of items. Spanning the expanse of the far wall was a row of fitted floor-to-ceiling shelves. Upon each level sat items of antiquity passed down from one Prime to the next. Situated on the very top shelf, and filling its entire width, was a collection of hidebound tomes. On the second shelf down sat a row of what Kiernan easily identified as weapons varying in age and region. Some were primitive in design, others more advanced. On the third row down was a collection of different items, from frames holding tiny metallic discs, rich in design, to sculptures, pottery and plaques in languages Kiernan had never seen.

"Sit down," Select Prime Abrahams ordered, and the trio obeyed. Vegas sat in the middle with Tehera to his left and Kiernan to his right.

Kiernan took another moment to finish her swift scan of the shelves. On the fourth shelf sat what she could only presume was antiquated scientific equipment. The shelf below held more tomes, older and more fragile in appearance. On the shelf below that sat a row of boxes in assorted sizes and materials. On the last shelf, Kiernan felt her attention piqued the most. Spread out along the entirety of the bottom shelf sat a row of reading materials, all soft covered, dull, and creased with age. She was intensely curious as to the nature of these slim, colourful bindings.

"Well," Abrahams began, as he scrapped his fingernails over his scalp, "Who wants to begin explaining this cluster catastrophe that was your mission?" His eyes narrowed in upon Vegas.

Staying calm, Vegas spoke directly. "What eventuated on our mission, Sir, could not have been avoided."

Abrahams didn't speak, allowing Vegas to continue. "First of all, we faced a rubble field of unknown distance. Our sensors were unable to pinpoint its origin or end point. With limited resources, we had to make the decision to travel up and over. This had to be done on foot. Luckily, we were sixteen furlongs from the station's location. We travelled with packs only, but it destroyed our hopes of bringing back workable materials."

Abrahams' eyes slid to Kiernan's and then back to Vegas. "You lost two officers, two scouts and Tehera's advisor. How?"

As Vegas began his description of what happened, Kiernan again looked around Abrahams' office. There were pictures upon the wall. Reputedly, Abrahams' office walls were adored with works of fine art from their world, pre-devastation. One such painting she recognised from a tome she had read. She continued looking, seeing two boxes in a corner. She recognised them from the medial suite. On top of one of the boxes was a small, translucent vial. Kiernan frowned; was the Select Prime hoarding medical supplies?

"And how exactly did it happen, Minister Kiernan?"

Kiernan jumped, hearing her name. "Excuse me?"

"What caused the explosion?"

Realising she had drifted off in thought, Kiernan was quick to pull her thoughts into order. "Advisor Xoren offered to help me find Vial 15. My search led me to data and equipment stores." Kiernan took a breath. "In the equipment stores, Xoren discovered a stash of chemical supplies. I warned him to keep away, but he was convinced he could find something of worth." Kiernan watched Abrahams and Tehera exchange glances. "Whatever he found had become unstable over time. It triggered an explosion with Xoren at ground zero. I tried to request help, but Scout Jensen got there with only enough time for us to seek cover. The blast caused the station's integrity to be compromised and Jax, Jorca and Ruben were caught in the fallout."

Abrahams' expression twisted into fury. "And what of Scout Jilya?"

"Scavengers," Vegas offered. "The explosion alerted more scavengers than we've ever encountered. Ever. We were outnumbered. We manage to escape, but not without casualties. Luckily, the remaining team members did escape, but the mission was not without cost. We lost five good colonists in the process."

"And what of the data," the Prime asked.

"Major Vegas has handed over all retrieved data from the station. I have analysts searching the information."

Abrahams directed his attention towards Tehera in a silent question.

The Commander folded his hands together, "So far, the results are… extremely… rewarding." His eyes gleamed, but his expression soon changed. "I currently have Raziko and Ziran on lockdown. We have yet to notify Jilya's spouse." Another look passed between Commander and Prime. Abrahams nodded slowly. "And what of Scout Jensen?"

"Currently unlocatable."

"Find her," Abrahams ordered. "We cannot have colonists knowing the team has returned if their loved one hasn't." Abrahams turned back to Vegas. "And what of viable materials at the station?"

Vegas had watched the exchange feeling the same sense of dread as Kiernan. "Sir?"

"Were there salvageable materials for utilisation?"

"An abundance, unfortunately."

"And the possibility of a second mission? To return and reclaim our much-needed alloys? If reports of antiquity remain correct, there was one part of the craft that didn't make it here in time. That section we had to rebuild using valuable materials. Resources are low. This rotation alone I gave the order to cannibalise materials from the lower section of the colony. The denser alloys used in the craft build are vital."

"Sir," Kiernan spoke. "Are you proposing we send another team to retrieve the original section of the craft to recycle the materials?"

Abrahams rose. "As well as other materials, yes."

"With respect-"

"We have first-hand intelligence. We will be better prepared." Abrahams turned to Tehera, "Begin proceedings, Commander."

Vegas rose swiftly. "This would be a suicide mission. To send another team out there? Only half my team returned. I believe you gained the most relevant of data. Sir, Prime, sending another team out there would be-"

"Not another team, Major. You will be returning, as well as Minister Kiernan, Scout Jensen, Raziko, Ziran and another five selected individuals of our choosing. You will complete the mission."

Feeling fear travel down her spine, Kiernan's stomach twisted into knots of apprehension. "Sir-"

"Commander, begin choosing another five credible members for the team."

Vegas turned to Kiernan before looking back at Abrahams. "We should really-"

"This meeting is finished. I am extremely busy and must continue with my agenda for this rotation." Abrahams looked from Kiernan to Vegas and then Tehera.

The Commander rose and took a step towards the door. "I will have a mission draft for you by the end of the rotation."

"Excellent." Abrahams opened his door and said nothing as he waited for the occupants to leave his office.

Realising now wouldn't be the best time to fight the Prime's decision, Vegas exited swiftly, closely followed by Kiernan. They heard the door close before they realised Tehera hadn't joined them.

Memories of the mission bombarded Kiernan's mind and she felt her heart rate accelerate. Not again. She couldn't go out there again. "Vegas…"

"Shhhh..." Placing his hand upon Kiernan's back, Vegas directed her back into the stairwell. They took the first flight of steps.

"I can't go back there again, Vegas. None of us can. It would be suicide."

Folding his arms, Vegas stared down at the floor, his thoughts in overdrive.

"Do you hear me?" Kiernan asked and took Vegas' arm.

"I hear you," he replied. "Kiernan will you tell me the truth of the events which led to Xoren's death?" He had spotted a hole in Kiernan's story and hoped the prime and commander hadn't.

"Of course," she agreed. There was no point holding back any longer. "But will you answer me one question first?"

"Apart from how I am going to stop this second mission?" Vegas ran a hand through his short, dark hair. "Yes, you can." He felt weary. So much had happened and Abrahams wanted a second mission?"

"What is the Dispersal Cannon?"

He was ready to feign ignorance, but acknowledging Kiernan's honesty, Vegas knew he had to return her trust. There was a greater battle to face. However, in supplying Kiernan with this information he would have to admit his part in the Ultimate Agenda... and that he had lied to her. Was it too late to turn back? Vegas released a sigh, "It's a weapon." Looking around, Vegas guided Kiernan back up the stairs. "I will explain, but not here. Come with me."

With an impending sense of dread, Kiernan followed.

CHAPTER 33

As darkness surrounded them, Jensen felt her body sag in relief. The scientists had left. Finally. In the cells, the scavengers became silent. Was it cultivated behaviour, Jensen thought? How long have they been locked in those cells?

Pulling the torch from her pocket, Jensen altered its beam to a low-range setting. She didn't activate it until she was sure they were truly alone. She listened for several more moments, fearing the scientists' return. All remained silent apart from Tovey's shallow breathing.

"I think we're safe," Jensen said, as she activated the torch beam.

Tovey nodded. She took a calming breath. "What are they doing here, Jensen?"

"I don't know." Jensen kept her torchlight away from the scavengers' line of sight, hoping not to aggravate them anymore. "Come on." They made their way towards the holding cells. Jensen shone her torchlight into Dickens cell, illuminating the vendor and Fatima huddled together in their corners. A thick, transparent divide separated them.

Tovey placed one hand upon the cell, as she moved closer, her head rested upon the cell door. "Jensen?"

Looking closer, Jensen sighed. "They're dead!"

"No… no… no, no, no… oh, no…" Tovey hit the side of the cell with her fist. "Why? Why do this? These were good colonists. My allies. How can they be so heinous and uncaring with our lives?" Tovey couldn't hold back her tears. Silently, she wept.

Frustrated, Jensen placed a hand upon her shoulder. "We will make them pay for what they are doing to us."

"How? They've done what they want for cycles. How many others before you have tried to revolt against them, Jensen? How many have failed? How many others have become nothing but expendable test subjects?" Tovey wiped the tears from her cheeks.

Tovey's words highlighted a valid point to Jensen. Had others tried to bring their leaders' clandestine network of deception to light? Had her parents?

Taking a step away, Jensen looked around in the darkness. There was only one way to find out. She approached the first cell and shone her torchlight onto the form on the sleeping pallet. The face was turned away, but she could clearly see the waist rise and fall with a steady breath. Jensen search for the cell doors' opening mechanism. There was none. She frowned.

"What are you doing?"

"Trying to get inside. How do you think this opens?"

"I don't know." Tovey looked around, trying to distract her sorrowful thoughts. "Let's find out."

***

Vegas had retreated to the seclusion of his personal unit, taking Kiernan with him. If there was a safe space to talk without interruption, it would be there. Entering the room, Kiernan sat down on a single chair. She looked around briefly, familiar with the surroundings. It was a double room like hers, having the benefit of a separate sleeping chamber. The outer room was sparse, two chairs, a table, and a data terminal. The walls were as plain as the cold stone floor. Vegas had done little to make his personal space feel more like a comfortable retreat.

Sitting on the chair at his table, Vegas turned to face Kiernan. "You have a question."

Kiernan nodded. "Explain to me the purpose of a dispersal cannon."

Leaning forward, Vegas clasped his hands together, his arms resting upon his thighs. "It's a weapon, as you know. A powerful cannon built with a sole purpose. It has the capability of releasing a biological weapon into the atmosphere with a widespread dispersal rate."

"Our atmosphere?" Kiernan asked in alarm and confusion.

Shaking his head, Vegas knew he would have to provide Kiernan with a candid explanation. Trust went both ways, but in doing so, he would have to admit he lied about his knowledge of Vial 15 and the tests conducted many cycles before at the station. "As you know, the ship will soon be ready to transport us to the new world."

Kiernan nodded.

"As you are also aware, this planet was found before the devastations… in a neighbouring galaxy. A planet capable of sustaining life, with its own sun, a breathable atmosphere, and an abundance of vibrant vegetation."

Again, Kiernan nodded. This was common knowledge to all colonists. It was the reason they worked so tirelessly. For that chance to escape their lifeless world for a new, flourishing planet full of light and colour.

The Major shifted in his seat. "However, what you are not aware of is that this planet, our future world, already supports life."

"It's inhabited?"

Vegas nodded. "They are a primitive race. However, co-habitation is unlikely. The plan is to eradicate the current population."

She mustn't have heard Vegas correctly. Kiernan blinked, narrowed her eyes, and leaned forward. "Excuse me?"

So far, her reaction was tame. Vegas hoped that was a good sign. "The cannon will disperse Amphibulartoxin into the atmosphere. Complete population eradication should occur in a total of seven rotations based upon the planet's size. We shall be protected with the inoculation of Vial 15." Vegas elaborated. "For cycles, our people have worked to re-create Vial 15 after the original data was stolen, but countless tests proved unsuccessful. Thankfully, retrieval of the data from the testing station means our work is complete. We have the toxin and the inoculation from its deadly effects." Vegas paused, as he noticed Kiernan's complexation change from pale to a russet ire glow. "Kiernan?"

The Minister flew from her seat. "Tell me, Vegas, right now that you are joking?" She knew he wasn't. "Are you out of your mind? You are not serious? The Prime is accepting this? To exterminate a global population for our benefit? This is unacceptable. This is out of the question. It's abhorrent. It's criminal. It's… it's…" Kiernan paced Vegas' room. "It's diabolical." She turned to glare at Vegas. "You cannot be alright with this!"

Vegas raised his hands in a placating manner. "I will admit it took a long time for me to accept, Kiernan. The wheels are in motion. There is no going back."

"It cannot be."

"Kiernan, this is happening."

"I won't allow it."

"You can't stop it. Many cycles ago we lost the data. All we have left to pinpoint the planet's location was lost to us… stolen."

"Stolen?"

"But the data is still on our satellite, and with the cloudbanks clearing, and the gasses disappearing from the upper atmosphere, we will soon be able to communicate with the satellite and plan our transport trajectory. We're so close."

"To murder?"

"To a new life."

"Vegas do you hear yourself? This is-"

"I understand, Kiernan. I struggled with it too. It took me a long time to accept the plans, but you've been up onto the Barrens. Even if the cloudbanks disperse completely, do you really think there is a life to be lived up there? It's a desolate wasteland filled with the ashes of the dead."

"Our planet. Our deeds. Our price to pay."

"Not our deeds. We are victims too." Vegas argued, his need to justify the decisions bolstering his conviction, "but we have a chance."

Kiernan held her hands out beseechingly towards Vegas. "To make the same mistakes as our ancestors did and destroy a world?"

"To live again."

"It's wrong, and don't think I didn't realise you lied to me. You knew the whole time about the tests with Vial 15. How could you?"

Vegas refused to lower his head in shame, even though for a moment that was exactly how he felt. He was fighting for their future. "It's in motion. The cannon build is underway. Vial 15 will soon be synthesized on mass for the full protection of our people. All we need is the planet's location and we are ready." Vegas rose before Kiernan. "You've been up there, Kiernan. I thought you of all people would understand our need to escape this world?"

"I do, but at what cost? Another planet's population? Really? Are we that far down the evolutional chain of enlightenment?"

Vegas turned away from Kiernan. He pushed his hands into his pockets and stared down at the ground. "The burden becomes easier to bear when your actions are for your people's future. The lure of a new life becomes harder to resist."

"Not for me." Kiernan turned and approached the door, but as her hand reached the handle she was stopped. Vegas placed his hand over hers.

"Where are you going?"

"To find another way."

"I can't let you do that." Vegas pulled Kiernan's hand away and steered her from the door. "If you think they wanted you dead before, how do you think they will react if they discover you intend to thwart their plans?"

The weight of Vegas' words sent a heavy stab of fear plunging into Kiernan's chest. How indeed.

CHAPTER 34

The search hadn't taken long to find the cell's remote activation switch. Adjusting the isolation dial, Jensen opened Cell One. The door slid left as it opened.

Tovey stood on the threshold, afraid to enter. She jumped as a scavenger shrieked behind her. Jensen watched her, understanding her reticence to enter.

"Let me."

With a nod of acceptance, Tovey stepped to one side, allowing Jensen access into the cell. Eyes focussed upon the presumed sleeping body. Tovey held her breath.

As Jensen entered the cell, her absolute first sensation was a change in temperature. It was cooler. She felt the tiny hairs upon her skin prickle in reaction. She took a glimpse around the small containment room, alert for any form of monitor designed to detect movement. Nothing was visible. The sleeping pallet wasn't pushed against the wall, like the other cells, so she walked around to afford a better view of its occupant. Face half covered by long, ashen hair, she could tell the individual was old. The skin was pale and wrinkled with a growth of wiry facial hair.

Reaching out, Jensen pushed a tangle of locks from the face. Weary eyes fluttered open, causing Jensen to step back in surprise.

Tovey walked into the cell and then froze. She studied Jensen's expression with a queried look.

"He's awake."

Feeling her heart rate increase, Tovey circled the pallet. She gazed down upon the figure lying upon its surface. Vacant eyes moved into her direction. They connected.

"Grandfather?"

Lomax blinked, and a single tear slipped from the corner of his eye. Just one tear, as if it were all the moisture his body could afford to lose.

Covering her mouth, Tovey dropped to her knees before Lomax. She couldn't hold back her own tears. "Grandfather. I'm so sorry. All these years I thought you were…" she closed her eyes, willing her tears to cease for the sake of her grandfather. Looking back Tovey pushed the hair from his face. "It's really you!"

An imperceptible smile curved the corners of his lips.

Tovey's eyes hardened. "What have they done to you?"

Standing to one side, Jensen felt emotionally vacant. In any other situation she may have been moved by the scene, but the threat of being discovered forced her feelings in check. She scanned the area beyond the cell, paying close attention to the scavengers. Their eyes glowed in the darkness. They had ceased their harrowing screams, but Jensen knew they were watching. She could feel their eyes upon her. Tovey's voice brought back her attention.

"We need to get him out of here."

Jensen looked at the device Lomax was attached to, and the array of translucent tubes pumping a cocktail of assorted coloured chemicals into his body. They were attached to his neck, arm, waist, and foot. Jensen knelt beside Tovey.

"How?" She felt a hand grasp her arm. It was Lomax. He closed his eyes and moved his head in a negative motion.

"Why?" Tovey asked in desperation. "We need to get you out of here, Grandfather."

Lomax's face twitched in an expression of frustration. He moved his lips slowly, licking them in preparation to speak. The skin was torn and peeling. His lips moved, but no sound came forth.

"Slowly, Grandfather." Tovey stroked his forehead.

"Arm," Lomax said in a croaked whisper.

"Remove the line in your arm?"

Lomax nodded.

"What is this?" Tovey asked, as she lifted the tube carrying an emerald liquid into his arm.

"Alive," he replied.

Tovey dropped the tube. "No! What! Grandfather, I cannot. No. You can live!"

Jensen followed the emerald liquid to the machine which regulated its transfer into Lomax's body. So that was the chemical that kept him alive?

"Must," Lomax croaked. "No… more… pain."

"Pain?"

"No… more… killing."

"What do you…?" Tovey rose. "I've just found you!"

Understanding both sides, Jensen had to stand by Lomax. She couldn't imagine what the man had been through.

"He needs release, Tovey."

Lomax's eyes travelled to Jensen and remained fixed upon hers. A sense of familiarity passed through her, as she looked into the old man's eyes. She moved closer to him.

"I know you," she muttered.

Lomax stared at Jensen for a fraction longer. A tiny smile upturned the corners of his cracked lips. "Jensen."

She had seen him before when she was younger. Much younger. When her parents were still alive. She never knew his name, but she recognised his face.

"All grown," Lomax said.

"I met you… before… with my parents."

Lomax gave a small nod.

"You were a good ally to them." She recalled the memory. Even then, Lomax was an old man. She remembered he walked with a cane. Jensen continued to search her memory. Her mother and father. A meeting. She was there. So was Lomax. They met in a back-passage entrance to Labour. Her father handed something to Lomax. It was a little too large and Lomax was unable to carry it with two hands due to his need for a cane. He held it awkwardly under one arm.

"My father gave you something."

Lomax nodded.

"To hide?" She searched her mind. "To protect. In a box-like container"

A nod.

"Lomax… what was in the box?"

Reaching out, Tovey took her grandfather's hand. She brushed her thumb over this pale flesh. She could feel every tendon and bone."

"Truth," Lomax replied.

"You know what happened to my parents?"

"Yes."

"Please. We need to know what's going on to stop it."

"Cannot stop… inevitable… can only chose… path."

Both women frowned, confused by his answer.

"What do you mean, Grandfather?"

"I used to… tell you… stories… remember?"

Tovey smiled at the memory.

"Remember story… of treasure thief?"

"I do. The thief stole the king's jewels and gave them to his lover then they escaped, but the king tracked the thief down and killed him and his lover."

Jensen looked from Tovey to her grandfather and back again. She watched as a silent understanding passed between them. "Tell me?" she asked. "Not the story. Tell me of the truth."

***

Seated back in Vegas' spare chair, Kiernan stared at the door handle opposite. She had almost escaped the Major's unit. His words had stopped her. Were they a threat? She looked at the man she no longer knew. He stood in the centre of his room, arms folded, and his expression pensive.

The total annihilation of a race? That was not what she had worked all these cycles for. Had their own history taught them nothing? She felt sick. Surely, they had learned from the misguided, single-minded actions of Capita. They had moved forward, building hope for a future growing out of the remnants of their past. It had felt like a noble cause. But now…

Taking the second chair, Vegas positioned himself in front of Kiernan. He moved his head into her line of sight.

"I appreciate this is a lot for you to digest. I can only ask that you contemplate on our discussion and try to see from a unique perspective."

"You absolutely cannot-"

"**Kiernan**," Vegas shouted, making her jump. He held up his hands apologetically. "Understand that right now we have a more important issue at stake."

Feeling helpless, Kiernan dropped her head into her hands. "I don't know what to do about anything anymore." She looked back up. "Do you realise you have just shifted the axis of my entire belief system? I don't know how to come back from this."

"Then let's begin to change that." Vegas reached out and took Kiernan's hand. "Will you tell me what happened at the testing station?"

"I've already told you."

"No, what really happened. How Xoren, Jax and Jorca died?"

"How will all this help us now?"

That was a good question. Kiernan's reaction to the truth had allowed Vegas to view their situation from an unfamiliar perspective. Something he hadn't done for a long time. If he could get Kiernan to do the same, then maybe they could carve out a new future based on a mutually beneficial set of beliefs. Would Kiernan believe that?

"I want to know the lengths Tehera, and Abrahams will go."

"I think that is already apparent."

"You were going to explain everything to me, Kiernan. Can you do that?"

Kiernan relented with a sigh. "Alright." She tucked her hair behind her ear, wondering if Jensen had been able to uncover any information. Where was she? Tehera and the Prime were looking for her. Her fears for Jensen's welfare rose.

***

"So, we are agreed on the new directives."

"Of course," Tehera replied. He sat facing Abrahams, a data console between them. Its screen displayed the new guidelines for Abrahams proposed second mission to the station. They had spent the last mark planning the details. Information that would be handed to a select group of individuals with only one purpose in mind.

"Our Ultimate Agenda isn't far away from completion, Commander. Nothing must interrupt our plans. I will do whatever I have to, to succeed."

"Yes, Sir."

"And you have individuals in mind to deal with Kiernan and Jensen?"

"I do."

"More capable than the last?"

"Scout Ryan, Sir."

A smile curved Abrahams' lip. It never reached his eyes. "An excellent way to prove his commitment."

"My thoughts exactly."

Abrahams balled his hands into fists. "If you don't see to our problem, Commander, then it will be more than just Kiernan and Jensen marked for termination."

Tehera had little doubt of that. "Understood."

CHAPTER 35

Resting on her knees, Jensen placed herself before Lomax. The old man looked incredibly fragile. She feared, should she touch him, he may bruise. Tovey wanted to move Lomax, but to where could he be moved? It wasn't right he should spend what was left of his life, however long that may be, strapped to an unconformable looking sleeping pallet in a locked cell. How long had Lomax been hidden away in this room of torture? Jensen looked around, seeing amber eyes still upon them. She was certain if they moved the eyes would follow. Scavengers had excellent vision in the darkness. Jensen had little time to ruminate on the reasons the scavengers would be locked in that cell, but she did wonder on the purpose of the area in the centre of the room, with strong metal restraints secured to the ground. What level of torture had the colonists, scavengers and Lomax been subjected to?

Focusing back upon the old man, Jensen saw his familiar eyes upon her. She watched as Tovey dabbed a water-soaked rag upon his lips. His cracked tongue reached out to capture the droplets of moisture.

"Do you think you can talk, Grandfather?"

Reaching over, Jensen released a strap that was holing Lomax's torso to the pallet. His tattered clothing scrunched in the movement, exposing a large pressure sore on his side.

"Can we move you to a more comfortable position?" Jensen asked with concern.

Lomax shook his head "Don't move. Not… anymore."

His words set concern bells ringing in Jensen's mind, but outwardly she only nodded in response.

Receiving another dab of water, Lomax tried to clear his throat. His chest rattled; congestion loosened. How long had it been since he had last spoken? When he did speak, it started as a broken whisper.

"Your parents."

"Yes." Lomax had her full attention now.

"Known them… since… they were children."

Jensen smiled at the thought, having never heard stories about her parents as children. Growing up in a subterranean colony, enriching stories were hard to come by. She often wondered what they had been like as children, how they met and fallen in love.

"I taught your mother… the combat arts."

"You did?" Jensen had no idea her mother could fight with impressive discipline. It was a dying art. She moved a fraction closer. Jensen was eager to hear more, but she acknowledged more vital information was needed.

The small upturn upon Lomax's lips faded, as he stared at Jensen. An understanding passed between them. He knew what she needed to hear. Lomax blinked slowly and took a breath, "Jaxon, your father came… to me… many cycles ago. I was… still living… in Labour." Lomax paused and Tovey took the opportunity to offer him another dab of water. He accepted, his voice becoming clearer, stronger. "He was… concerned."

"Why?"

"He was scouting a new… area of the Northeast Barrens… when he found a hatch… like the one used to… enter and exit the colony. Never seen or used before. He was curious about its function." As Lomax spoke his voice continued to strengthen. "Jaxon opened the hatch, which was situated between the skeletal remains of two full … standing trees and entered."

"What did he find?"

"He called it a central store for a collection of our planet's art, history tomes, precious materials, and data. The store was expansive and as he scouted the data and precious artefacts, he came upon something… unexpected. In one area he found a stash of data intended for viewing by a Select Prime only. Naturally… he looked. What he found was information about the craft build, satellite downloads detailing locations of the new world, craft schematics, audio-visual data, recordings… … so much data… revealing and… potentially damaging."

"Did he tell you what was so revealing? Damaging?"

"No," Lomax paused, "Only a little, but nothing I felt was important… at the time. However, what he did tell me was that he had taken some of that data, files, and audio-visual recordings. He stole them."

A feeling of disquiet began to rise within Jensen's stomach. She and Tovey exchanged expressions of caution.

"There is a process for material transfer when returning from a scouting mission," Lomax began.

Jensen nodded. "Yes, I am a Scout."

"Of course, you are." Lomax recalled colony politics. It had been many cycles since he had lived within the ordinance of a governed society.

"What is the material process?" Tovey asked.

Jensen explained, "You deposit your pack contents into a separate channel which cleanses them on a conveyer. Once you are through your De-Con you can retrieve your findings and report them in for cataloguing and allotment."

"Right," Tovey looked back at Lomax to continue.

"Jaxon left the De-Con taking his pack with its entire contents. His actions sparked the curiosity of Officer Xoren."

"Advisor Xoren?" Jensen confirmed.

"Yes, Officer at the time, who in turn reported his actions to Major Tehera."

"Now Commander," Jensen informed, unaware Lomax was already aware.

Lomax continued. "Jaxon confirmed he hid his pack before returning to your unit, but he did share his findings with Tomei." The old man swallowed, and Tovey offered him another dab of water which he accepted before continuing. "Worried by Jaxon's reckless actions, and needing advice, Tomei came to me. This was the same rotation as your father came to see me, only marks apart."

"They both looked to you for sage advice," Jensen noted.

"I told her what I told Jaxon… to return the items before anything was noted as missing. Jaxon agreed he would, but he wanted to investigate the data before returning it. He did so with Tomei."

"What did they discover?" Jensen moved unconsciously closer.

"Tomei told me of only one file. However, what they did discover threw colony life off its axis for them both. At once the information Jaxon stole became proof-"

"Of what?"

Lomax paused and took a slow breath. "They knew they had to return the files before the theft was discovered. It was agreed Tomei would find the hatch on her next scout and return the files to avoid suspicion. However, something went wrong. Tomei was followed by the newly promoted Scout Xoren. He followed her to the hatch, but she became aware of his presence before she returned the files, and so returned with them."

"Her location would have pinpointed her intended destination."

"But Xoren still reported back to Tehera. With the files in their possession, Jaxon and Tomei needed to hide them. I agreed to conceal them for safekeeping. The last time I saw you was the meeting with your parents to receive the files. I took the box and Jaxon kept its key."

"Key?" a flash of recognition sparked a memory in Jensen's mind.

Feeling weary, Lomax paused to take a calming breath.

"Do you need to stop, Grandfather?"

Lomax shook his head. "Have to do this. Important. This has been with me too long. I asked to meet Jaxon and Tomei one last time. I decided to hide. I feared the repercussions. We were to meet in Labour's social complex. They never arrived, so I sent Mira to find them. Pass on my message that I was leaving."

"Mira?"

"She saw it happen."

"What happen?"

"Your parents… apprehended. Captured, I can only presume by order of the Select Prime. The last sighting of Jaxon and Tomei was them being taken by Captain Vegas."

Jensen felt the very breath leaver her body. Looking away, it took a moment for her to breath. Her heart stammered. Her body felt cold. "Vegas?"

"Along with Major Tehera and Xoren, they were the last colonists to be seen with Scouts Jaxon and Tomei."

His name resonated in her mind. Vegas. The man who had pledged his guardianship to look after her when her parents died. Jensen shook her head. It couldn't be true.

"You know, Captain Vegas?" Tovey asked, noticing Jensen's reaction to his name.

"I know him." Jensen gripped the sleeping pallet until slithers of timber penetrated her skin. She stared intently at Lomax. "Vegas?"

The old man nodded slowly, seeing the anger, hurt and betrayal shimmering in her eyes. Those emotions fought for dominion, and it was anger that reigned supreme.

"What did they do to my parents?"

"As far as I know, and for as long as I remained free, Jaxon and Tomei were never heard from again. Official reports said they were killed upon the Barrens."

Jensen rose. "Everything he did for me. He lied to me. How could he when all the time he knew the truth?"

"Jensen-"

"He betrayed me and my parents."

"You need to calm down and not lose focus," Tovey said cautiously. "Remember why we are here."

Looking back at Lomax and Tovey, Jensen forced herself to calm. A thought occurred to her. "Kiernan!"

"Who?"

"I need to find her. I need to let her know. She set me on this path. She is following her own leads. Vegas lied and she might be in danger."

"I think we are all in danger, Jensen." Tovey looked back at Lomax. "Grandfather, what do we need to do? Do you know how we can get you out of here?"

Lomax shook his head. "No get out for me. They keep me alive like this for punishment. Death is my salvation and so they refuse me."

"You cannot die, Grandfather." Tovey took Lomax's hand. "Please?"

"Death is all I desire." Lomax looked up at Jensen. "I have released my burden. Now please release me from my torture."

Feeling the depths of Lomax's request, Jensen knelt beside Tovey. The man had been kept alive by unnatural means. His body already appeared to be in the first stages of decomposition. His translucent skin, fragile and ready to fester. "I feel… if ever there was a gift you could give your grandfather, Tovey, it would be peace. His mind, though still alert, is trapped within its failing body."

"I don't want you to die!" Tovey cried, tears filling her eyes.

"I cannot come back from this. Please," Lomax begged.

Jensen watched as Tovey's mind fought the battle between her desires and that of her grandfather's. There was, however, only one honourable decision. Jensen rose, feeling the need to give them time together. She looked ahead into amber eyes. The reality of their situation felt suffocating. Was this how her parents felt? Jensen knew she needed to get back to Kiernan. She had discovered more than she expected. Vegas. The Major sprung to mind. A most unwelcome of thoughts. He had lied to her. Whatever had happened to Jaxon and Tomei, Vegas no doubt knew it all. She felt her anger bubble within. She needed to find Kiernan. She needed to find an escape. Another thought occurred to her. She needed to know the location of that box of stolen files.

CHAPTER 36

He hadn't left her side. Major Vegas went with Kiernan back to her laboratory and was perched on the opposite side of the room, conversing with a domestic. Before his revelation, Kiernan might have felt comforted by his presence. Now she was fighting persistent feelings of paranoia. She looked around, seeing the eve shift beginning their routines. This group was smaller than the team who worked the morn shift. Although their world hadn't seen light in one hundred cycles, they still clung to the rituals of a planetary solar orbit. Sometimes Kiernan preferred to work during the eve shifts. It was quieter and easier to concentrate.

Seated before her terminal, Kiernan's finger was poised over the activation button. She looked from the blank screen to Vegas and then back again. A swift decision had her changing her plans. Turning on the screen, Kiernan ignored the search results that had loaded while she was gone, and instead downloaded those results onto a data console. Keeping one eye upon Vegas, Kiernan cleared her recent activities from the data log. Once her task was complete, she shut down her terminal and discreetly slipped the console into the back of her clothing. Kiernan then rubbed her eyes and yawned widely for effect. Vegas looked up from his conversation and watched her approach. The domestic politely left.

"I can't continue, Vegas. I'm so tired."

"It has been challenging," he offered.

"In many ways," Kiernan agreed.

Vegas studied Kiernan for a moment. "Jensen hasn't returned yet."

"I know, but if I don't get some rest my cognitive ability will suffer. I'm sure Jensen is fine." She wasn't. "She might have already returned and retired for the eve." She doubted it. "Maybe you could check?" She hoped he wouldn't. Kiernan knew Jensen would come straight back to her with whatever she had discovered; if anything.

"Hmm," Vegas led Kiernan towards the exit. He placed his hand upon her back, a fraction above the concealed data console and felt her stiffen slightly. "Being the well-bred Major that I am, I shall escort you to your unit. I want to be sure you get there safely." He was sincere.

"Of course, thank you." Kiernan closed her eyes for a moment, hoping Vegas didn't move his hand any lower.

***

It was a hard decision to leave Tovey with her grandfather, but she had been insistent. She wanted time alone with Lomax. She had accepted his request to unhook the feed prolonging his life and wished to spend his last moments together. It was understandable but dangerous, and Jensen needed to return to Kiernan. An agreement had to be made. Jensen left her with the automatic firearm, after a brief instruction on how to use it. Her parting words were a simple plea, "Whatever happens next, find me. Do what you can to get to me."

Tovey agreed.

Taking a chance, Jensen took the route by which the scientists had left. It had quickly directed her back towards the Northern Colony. Her journey took her past a set of double doors with circular windows, Jensen paused for a closer look. They were frosted from the inside and looking closer Jensen realised it was ice. She tapped the glass. The crystalized water molecules were obvious. Intriguing. Being underground, finding cold storage was easy. However, she had never seen a room solely constructed for hyper freezing. She tried the handle. Locked. With no way to open the door, Jensen continued. She passed through another door and walked down a passage ending with two doors. To the right was a stairway, to the left the office of the Select Prime.

"Abrahams," Jensen whispered, surprised to be standing outside the bureau of the illusive Select Prime. With piqued curiosity, Jensen placed her ear against the door. She heard movement and a murmur. She continued to listen. Jensen could count the number of times she had seen the Select Prime on one hand. More movement. The sound of footsteps approaching. Swiftly, Jensen ran to the doorway leading to the stairway. She passed through the barrier and peered curiously through a small window. She saw Abrahams' door open and the Select Prime himself appear. He held a small container of liquid. She watched him walk away in the opposite direction. Ever curious, Jensen waited for him to pass through the door at the end of the passageway. She followed.

***

He was gone. Tovey had removed the chemical feed keeping her grandfather alive and watched as he slowly and finally passed away. She hadn't cried. She wondered why, thinking that maybe being able to see Lomax at peace was comforting more than upsetting.

Kneeling in the darkness, her grandfather's hand still within her grasp, Tovey placed her forehead upon his cool appendage. She closed her eyes. How was she to escape this room of torture? How would she find Jensen? Could she find her way back to the Primary Colony? So many questions bombarded her mind, that Tovey suddenly questioned the logic of being left alone. She had a weapon, but she had never used one before. She didn't want to attract attention to herself before Jensen and her accomplice had managed to figure out their plan. What was their plan? Persistent thoughts dominated her head so much so that it took a moment for Tovey to realise she was no longer alone.

A single light illuminated the workstation as two colonists entered the workroom. Tovey jumped in alarm, hearing voices, and she warily peered over her grandfather's body. Two individuals approached the cells. Still in relative darkness, Tovey remained close to the makeshift bed and watched cautiously. She saw two colonists enter the cells of Fatima and Dicken. Feeling her heartrate accelerate, Tovey watched as her ally's bodies were slung over capable shoulders and moved out of the containment rooms. The unknown workers chatted quietly, laughing together, as they carried the bodies across the room and over to the scavengers' cell. The door was open, and Tovey could only watch in horror as Dicken and Fatima were thrown inside. The scavengers attacked the recently deceased bodies, tearing into flesh with abandon. Screams of delight filled the room and Tovey clamped a hand over her mouth, restraining her tears.

The feeders watched. They laughed and cheered the scavengers on as they tore into the dead bodies with fervour. Stomach wrenching sounds of teeth sinking into flesh, tearing, ripping, assaulted Tovey's senses. She huddled herself into a ball, hands over ears, and closed her eyes. It would be over soon.

They watched the scavengers consume their fill a moment longer, and then the feeders sealed the cell doors and left. Lights were extinguished. Once surrounded by darkness, Tovey knew she needed to escape the 'torture room' as she had so aptly named it. She wanted to return home, but she needed to find Jensen. Lomax had left a parting message.

***

Jensen made it back to Governance. Traversing its hallways with a feeling of trepidation, she realised she had no idea where Kiernan's personal unit was. She found her laboratory first, but was informed she had left less than a mark before with Major Vegas. Jensen knew she needed to find them hastily. Now she needed to find the upper-level personnel units.

"Jensen!"

Hearing her name, Jensen turned to see Officer Nicoletti approach. They hugged.

"Where have you been? I've been asking around and nobody has seen you. If not for Major Vegas, I wouldn't have known you'd returned at all."

Jensen looked around cautiously. A move not un-noticed by Nicoletti. "I've been preoccupied with errands," she said evasively. "How are you?"

"Same," Nicoletti answered with a sad smile. "But I do have news. Taura's body had been released to me and I'm holding her Honourship and carbonisation next rotation eve." He searched her eyes. "Jen, I really need you there."

"You don't even have to ask." Jensen hugged Nicoletti again. "Anything I can do?"

Pausing slightly, Nicoletti took a breath. "Can you read her tribute?"

"Me?"

"Who else?"

Jensen felt a tremor of emotion pass through her. His request was a profound honour. "It would be my privilege."

The officer smiled in relief. "That's great. Taura often said you had a way with the written word. It may be considered a forgotten art, but I know you can and will do her memory justice."

"You can count on it."

With a pleased nod, Nicoletti said, "Even Minister Kiernan has confirmed she wishes to attend. I know she didn't know Taura at all, but it does mean a lot to know the sacrifices involved in scouting are being acknowledged… if only-"

"I know." Jensen rested her hand upon Nicoletti's shoulder. She offered him a reassuring smile, as her thoughts veered. "Speaking of the Minister, I need to find her. Do you know where the upper-level units are?"

Nicoletti looked at Jensen bemused. "Of course, I do. I used to be a Dispatch Officer. I know the colony with my eyes closed. Straight ahead, second left, right, left, left and third right. There is an access pass needed for the door, but bypass with code Three Zero Seven and you gain admittance."

"That easy?" Jensen asked dubiously.

"It's the Dispatch Officers' admittance key. If questions are asked, you are on your own. Minister Kiernan is unit forty-three."

Thanking her ally, Jensen left. His directions proved to be right, and she soon found herself standing before the door to unit forty-three. She knocked and waited.

"Who is it?" Came a disembodied voice.

"Kiernan, it's me."

The door opened at once, and Jensen found herself being pulled inside by one immensely relieved and happy to see her, Kiernan. Holding her ally, Jensen felt the fierceness of Kiernan's hug.

"Where have you been?"

"Following your lead, as instructed." Jensen pulled back and looked deep into Kiernan's eyes. Exhaustion and fear were clear. Her tension was palpable. She took a step backwards. "What's wrong?"

"Oh, Jen." Kiernan pulled Jensen to a small couch where they sat, and she told her everything she had discovered since they had parted that morn. Once she was finished, Jensen sat in silent disbelief. Kiernan started with her original discoveries, followed by the tests, Vial 15, the dispersal cannon, the dissection of the scavenger and a second mission to the Barrens. How long has she been gone? Jensen took a moment for Kiernan's update to process.

"Right," she said. "It's my turn." Jensen then began her update... Mira, Tovey, Devlin, the discovery of the holding cells and Flick... the torture room, Lomax, and the scavengers. The truth of Lomax's story and her parent's theft and discovery.

Kiernan listened, piecing Jenson's story together with her own and creating a much larger and more disturbing picture. She rose from her seat and walked to the centre of the room. "So, this is what we have so far... Your parents stole vital information, which not only threatened to expose the truth behind the work our past leaders were conducting on biological warfare, but the history of our planet's destruction and who was truly to blame. A fact that never became known because the Environmental Summit never aired in the Eastern Continent unless you worked for the government and had access to their direct feed."

"Like Lomax's father," Jensen offered.

"Exactly." Kiernan thought, "So their theft was discovered, and they hid the evidence with Lomax, but were themselves captured by Tehera, Xoren-"

"And Vegas."

"Yes." Kiernan tried to keep her mind focussed. She couldn't and didn't want to think about Vegas. "Lomax evaded capture and fled to the Primary Colony, but eventually he was located, and he too was captured."

"Where they have tortured him, ever since, for the location of the missing files. As he has never given it, they have simply kept him alive, prolonging his misery."

Kiernan nodded. "The missing files, which also hold the formula for Vial 15 and the location of the new world. Obviously due to the toxic atmosphere they have been unable to communicate with our satellite, which after so long we can only hope is still in orbit. And without the formula for Vial 15, they have been trying to re-create it using Primary Colonists as test subjects. Which means the colony and its inhabitants have been known all along."

Jensen ran a hand through her hair. "And they have been using it as their private holding ground for potential test subjects."

Her thoughts in motion, Kiernan continued. "The mission to the testing station was to harvest practical materials, find the dispersal cannon schematics and the original data on Vial 15, but they sent me, as I've been asking too many questions. The reason it took so long for the mission was 1., their attempts to obtain the information from Lomax, and 2., their efforts to pinpoint the station's location. Plus, the craft re-construction and further builds took time.

"I'm sure Capita never envisioned one hundred cycles of subterranean living before the craft would be worthy of testing. Her arrogance surmounted her. She acted before her plans were finalised. Too focussed on the televised performance."

Jensen rose to face Kiernan. "All along they planned to travel to the new world and exterminate its inhabitants. A new world, untainted by the plague of our peoples. She wanted to colonize it as her own. Probably wanted to be its new world leader."

"Yes," Kiernan jumped in. "So, her actions prevented the full build of the craft and delayed the cannon build. However, subterranean life became more demanding than expected when focussed upon little things like survival. Vegas recovered the cannon schematics, and the build is underway. I've checked the progress updates and we should be ready in twenty rotations. My power source is set for insertion within the next three."

"I have a question." Jensen took a step closer to Kiernan, "you said you discovered the scavengers bore synthesized genetic markers, meaning they were created. How?"

"My guess is that during the many tests at the station. They inadvertently altered the genetic makeup of the test subjects and created the original scavengers. Judging by their location, they stayed close to 'native soil'. Disregarded test subjects who didn't die, but instead thrived in the toxic atmosphere and increased in number."

"And our people are aware of this?"

"Possibly not until now," Kiernan confirmed.

"Right." Jensen tapped her thigh in thought. "So that leaves several unanswered questions. What are the Cryo Preservation Chambers?"

"I'm still looking into that." Kiernan picked up her data console and waved it before Jensen. "I have a mass of data to read. I've only suspicions right now."

"What we really need to ask is," Jensen started tapping her fingers with each question, "How do we expose the truth? How do we stop this? How do we confront Vegas? How do we confront Tehera and the Prime? How do we find Devlin? How do we stop the second mission?" Jensen sighed, "But most of all, what do we do next?"

Feeling an all-encompassing sensation of weariness, Kiernan dropped down onto the nearest chair. "I don't know, Jen, I just don't know."

***

Vegas stood before Commander Tehera. He had been summoned not long after leaving Kiernan and had made his way directly to his superior's office. Poised within the centre of the small room, Vegas faced the Commander. He'd been asked one question and Tehera waited for him to answer. There was no time to consider his response. Honesty could only be delivered with a direct and immediate reply. 'What had Kiernan discovered'?

CHAPTER 37

She was dreaming and somewhere in the recess of Jensen's mind she knew this. It was a re-occurring dream. Snippets of familiar events triggered her memory, unwelcome as they were. She was on the Barrens. It was during her first cycle as a scout. She was still acclimatising herself to the chaotic elements. It was eve. Acid rain was falling. Dressed in full protective clothing, and keeping her sight upon the ground, Jensen moved with swiftness, propelled by the raging wind. She was heading back to the colony. The hatch was no more than four furlongs away.

It was hard to hear anything over the storm, however something alerted Jensen to a possible presence. She stopped in her tracks and looked around for signs of movement. The rain was easing, making it easier to see her surroundings. Keeping still, Jensen deactivated her torchlight. Total darkness surrounded her. It wasn't like during the sun-lit marks when the distant sun's weakened light-waves broke through gaps in the toxic cloudbanks creating colourful hues across the ashen land. It was hard to hear over the raging wind, but fearing possible scavengers, Jensen continued to walk in the darkness. She kept her direction heading true to the hatch location. She moved slowly. Every time she felt uncertain of her surrounds, she would activate her torch light long enough to seek out a familiar landmark and then extinguish it again. Her progress was slow. A stark contrast to her heart rate, which hammered anxiously within. Counting her steps, Jensen walked to the tree stump. She activated her torch. She was there. Looking right, she searched out a right-angled wall formation. It was twenty-nine steps ahead. Extinguishing the torch, she continued, counting nervously as she went. 1, 2, 3. Her hand reached out in the darkness. 7, 8, 9. Grasping at the empty space ahead, Jensen groped blindly, hoping not to feel anything before her. 15, 16, 17. She was over halfway. 21, 22, 23. She readied her torch. 27, 28, 29. Jensen activated the torch, and its bright light illuminated the savage features of a scavenger standing directly before her. Its distorted features elongated as a piercing screech erupted from its foul-smelling mouth. Jensen screamed and pushed out as she saw bloody, broken teeth advance upon her face.

"No!"

"Jensen, WAKE UP!"

Jensen opened her eyes, her heart hammering, her breathing laboured and sweat tricking down her temples. Taking a gasped breath, she looked around in confusion. She was lying upon Kiernan's coach, a crumpled blanket around her waist. Slowly, her senses returned. Taking a calming breath, Jensen fell back onto the cushions and covered her face with trembling hands.

"Are you alright?"

Kiernan had been awake for over a mark already. She had positioned herself in a chair opposite Jensen, as she read her data console. When Jensen's somnolent distress began to escalate, she decided to wake her.

"Bad dream," Jensen replied.

"Ephialtes?"

Jensen looked up at Kiernan. "Absolutely." She moved to a seated position. Kiernan re-took her seat opposite. The younger woman's features were still flushed.

"How long have you been awake?"

"Not long," Kiernan said. "A mark or so. Thank you for staying last eve."

Jenson chuckled. "You didn't have to persuade me."

"Hmm," Kiernan's smile faded.

Jenson acknowledged the fact that both women felt safer together. She looked down at the console by Kiernan's side. "Any results?"

Following Jensen's line of sight, Kiernan looked at the console and then picked it up. "Indeed."

"Really?"

"So… the Cryo-Preservation Chambers were designed to carry fertilised embryos to the new world. The chambers, once activated, will develop a foetus to full term. Seems an efficient method for transporting a greater number of beings to colonise the new world." Kiernan activated the console and scrolled through the data. "There was some detailed information here. What I do not understand is why this wasn't de-classified, even to upper-level politicians. It was never a pre-requisite for energy requirements needed to power over two thousand Cryo- Preservation Chambers."

Jensen's mind began to ponder. "Is there anything in the craft's energy requirements that could calculate to a similar power specification?"

"Are you thinking subterfuge?"

"Quite possibly."

"I could check. Why?"

Jensen recalled her earlier discovery. "Suspicion."

"Based on?"

There was a knock at the door. Kiernan jumped.

"Expecting anybody?"

Kiernan shook her head. Cautiously she rose and stood by the barrier. Another knock.

"Kiernan, are you there?"

"Vegas," Kiernan mouthed.

Jensen felt her anger rise. She rose from the couch.

Another knock.

"Kiernan, I know you're there. Open the door."

"Damn it," Kiernan whispered. She looked over at Jenson, offering an apologetic gaze, but Jensen was ready.

In the corridor, Vegas watched as the door opened wide enough for Kiernan to peer through its gap.

"Now isn't a good time, Vegas."

"What's going on?" he asked, instantly suspicious.

"I'm not dressed, can you come back later?"

Her casual approach was anything but, and Vegas wasn't convinced. "No, Kiernan, I won't. I need to speak to you now." Vegas' eyes narrowed as he heard what he clearly recognised as Jensen's voice suggest Kiernan comply. It appeared to be the permission Kiernan needed. She opened the door wide enough for the Major to enter. Vegas stepped through, closing it behind him. As he turned back to Kiernan, he had no time to register Jensen advance upon him, rage burning in her eyes, as she pushed him savagely against the door. Her expression recognisable, her emotions true, and it took Vegas only a moment to understand the hatred in her eyes. She knew. How wasn't important. He could only stand against the door, as a betrayed and hurting Jensen pounded her fists against his chest repeatedly.

As tall as Vegas stood, as stiff as he was, Jensen's attack hurt more emotionally than physically. She continued with her assault. -

"Jensen STOP!" Kiernan yelled, shocked by Jensen's attack. She wasn't prepared for such an outburst and Jensen's aggression was palpable. It was only when her fist connected with Vegas lip, and he tasted blood that the Major grasped both of her wrists to make her stop.

"That's ENOUGH!" he shouted.

Shocked to feel restraint, it was all Jensen needed to regain a measure of sense. Anger thumbing through her veins she glared at Vegas unmoving. "You killed them."

Vegas sighed, but his expression was sad. "No, I didn't."

"You betrayed them," Jensen spat. "Their deaths are on your hands."

That he couldn't argue, however it was not as Jensen believed. "Allow me to explain."

Jensen glared at Vegas. How could she believe anything he would say to her?

"What reason do I have to lie to you?" he asked perceptively. "Everything I've done since that moment has been for you."

His words surprised Jensen, and although fighting her internal voice telling her not to believe him, Jensen held open her hands, showing she was backing off. Vegas released her wrists, and she took two steps backwards. She stood beside Kiernan.

"Explain."

Nodding, Vegas wiped the blood from his swollen lip. "I was still a scout when Tehera approached me saying two fellow scouts were conspiring to sabotage the Ultimate Agenda. I was surprised to learn it was Jaxon and Tomei, as I was familiar with them both and considered them trustworthy and capable scouts."

"Then why believe him?" Kiernan asked.

"He offered me evidence detailing their unusual behaviour, which I had noticed, so it seemed to match his story. They had stolen information and were conspiring with colonists from Labour. Tehera asked me to help in their capture. He said he needed to stop them before the damage was unrepairable. I thought I was doing the right thing."

A single tear fell from Jensen's eye. "What changed your mind?"

"When we apprehended Jaxon and Tomei they fought valiantly. Jaxon said they would never hand over the files, and that the colonists deserved to know the truth. Tehera told your father the future was not theirs to dictate, but that of the Select Prime. Your mother… Tomei… she refused to hand over the files. She said her daughter deserved to grow up in a safe, trusted environment." Vegas paused; his stoic expression wavered as he recalled the moment. "Tomei… she turned to me and broke down. She begged me to look after you, Jensen. She knew what would happen to you, but the right level of intervention could stop it."

"What would they do to me?" Jensen asked confused.

Kiernan sighed. “The Select Prime would declare your parents traitors and banish you from Governance, stripping away your right to follow in your parent’s footsteps. You would have lived your life in Domestic, shamed by your parent’s traitorous acts.”

“Yes,” Vegas wiped another drop of blood from his lip. “I pledged my guardianship to stop your exile. That way you could continue your life in Governance as a Scout.”

Jensen glared at Vegas. “Why would you do that?”

“Because at that moment, I believed your parents more than I did Tehera’s story. I doubted I could have stopped what had happened to your parents, but I regretted my part.”

Allowing Vegas’ words to sink in, Jensen stepped away and sat back down upon the couch. “Why did you never tell me the truth?”

“How could I?” Vegas sat in Kiernan’s chair “I knew if anybody was to follow in Jaxon and Tomei’s footsteps it would be their daughter. I risked too much pledging my guardianship. I had to keep my intentions transparent if I were to prove myself trustworthy to Abrahams and Tehera. The actions of a sympathetic fool, Xoren had said.” Vegas allowed his head to drop into his hands and was silent for a moment before looking back at Jensen. “I’ve led you whenever possible. I’ve given you every opportunity to gain experience. I made sure you were in the right place at the right time to discover the existence of the Primary Colony. I made sure you were placed on the mission to the testing station. I even made sure Nicoletti passed on the dispatch officer admission code to return to Kiernan last eve.”

“What?” Jensen was shocked.

“I thought you were working with Tehera,” Kiernan admitted. “You backed their plans for the dispersal cannon, the-”

“Don’t get me wrong,” Vegas interrupted Kiernan. “I want off this world. I want our promised land, as much as any other colonist. I just want what we deserve, not what the Select Prime desires. His plans are warped, obscure delusions of grandeur. We could have a full life in a world unspoilt by the ravages of our ancestors’ deeds.”

“Seems like you’ve kept your hands clean while others have done your dirty work,” Jensen said.

“You’re wrong.” Vegas leaned forward. “We are here right now because of me. We can change the future for us all, but we don’t have much time.”

“What do you mean?” Kiernan sat down beside Jensen.

"Commander Tehera summoned me last eve. He demanded to know what you have discovered."

Kiernan gasped softly, but confident after Vegas' explanation that he had misled the Commander. "So, you had to lie."

Vegas swallowed. "No. I told him the truth."

"What?" Jensen rose in alarm, followed by Kiernan.

"How could you?" Kiernan exclaimed. "How are we-?"

"Wait…" Vegas silenced Kiernan as he rose. "By the time this rotation ends, I guarantee Select Prime Abrahams and Commander Tehera will no longer hold any semblance of power in the colony. If we work together now, we can turn the tides and expose the truth." Vegas checked the time. "But we must move fast. Tehera is disbanding Abrahams' second mission, it was just a ploy to finish Xoren's failed task. In a quarter mark, Enforcement Officers will be here to apprehend you for perfidy. If the truth is to be revealed, you need to leave. Now!"

CHAPTER 38

She didn't mean to pull the trigger, but she hadn't meant to be seen. Tovey made the decision to follow the feeders the eve before, in the hopes of taking a similar path to Jensen. She wasn't prepared to encounter them, still in a side room, changing out of their blood-splattered coveralls. What was more, she wasn't prepared for the unexpected recognition. For in the illuminated space, she instantly recognised the feeders as two of Devlin's militia and right hands. That shocked moment of realisation resulted in Tovey reaching for the weapon Jensen had given her and firing in swift succession. She emptied the full round of ammunition into them both.

For cycles, Devlin's right hands had evoked terror in the Primary Colony. They had conducted his bidding, creating a fear that never ceased. They had beaten both her and her grandfather before taking Lomax away, she believed never to be seen again. His torture had been unimaginable. Tovey had killed them both, a reaction of circumstance for sure, but she felt no remorse and only a glimmer of satisfaction. However, the ricochet of the weapon fire had been louder than Tovey imagined, and fearing capture, she quickly dragged the bodies into a nearby cupboard. She changed into the feeder's fresh clothing, took an access card, and continued her search for Jensen.

***

It seemed that in the space of only four rotations, Kiernan found herself on the run with Jensen again. First had been the unexpected appearance of Devlin in the Primary Colony, a sighting she had not seen herself, and now they were running from Tehera's enforcement officers. When had her life changed so dramatically? She looked ahead at the woman leading her through a narrow channel. Jensen, it seemed, already had a plan. She had yet to share the details, all she knew was Jensen was heading back to the Barrens.

With every noise, every voice that echoed, Kiernan looked around in anxiety, fearing the enforcement officers were closing in on them. Increasing her pace, she drew closer to Jensen.

"Can you please tell me here we are going?"

"I have an idea." Jensen said without slowing. "I want to go back to where this all began."

Kiernan stopped for a moment, and then realising Jensen hadn't slowed, she sped up her pace once again. "What began?"

"My parents. Their discovery. The store of artefacts." Jensen didn't stop moving. "If we're to find answers, what better place to start?"

Jogging to catch up, Kiernan grasped Jensen's arm and pulled her to a stop. "Explain."

Looking around cautiously, Jensen was quick to elaborate. "Because there must be another entrance to that artefacts store. There cannot just be the one upon the surface. There is no way the Select Prime would risk going up onto the Barrens to recover data."

Kiernan thought back to her meeting with the Select Prime. "There is a collection of artefacts lining a row of shelving in Abrahams' office."

This information further solidified Jensen's theory. "I need you with me, Kiernan." Without waiting for a response, Jensen continued moving.

Comforted by her words, Kiernan followed. "Explain to me how we're going to get up onto the Barrens. Access is always supervised."

"Very true, however it's also half a mark into Nicoletti's shift. Something tells me he will be more than willing to accommodate anything we need."

"I hope so," Kiernan replied. Jensen's contacts had to be more dependable then the upper-level ministers and scientists, who would be presumably aligned with the Select Prime. Kiernan wondered who she could trust.

***

Vegas sent word for a select group of individuals to meet with him. He needed an area of neutral ground, but still secluded enough for a private discussion. Vegas had chosen the examination room in the medical suite. Physician Angelus was already present, standing in the corner, arms folded with his fingers drumming upon his upper arm in suspicious irritation. Vegas had entered his examination bay, taking over, as Angelus had so vehemently accused. He had called a meeting in the physicians' workspace. The audacity! If he wasn't himself invited to the gathering, he may well have threated to order him out!

It was eight marks into the new rotation. Vegas watched the door, knowing the recipients of his request to meet were soon to arrive. They were all colonists he knew were loyal to Jensen, Kiernan, or himself. The door opened and the first to walk in was Whylen, followed by Scout Ziran. Vegas pointed to an area of seating as the door opened again. In walked Scout Raziko, Minister Pavo and Captain Lucia. Raziko looked to Vegas and then the Physician, wondering why the meeting was in such a peculiar location.

"Don't look at me," Angelus said as he approached the team, "I've been hijacked just like the rest of you." He took a seat next to Raziko and then turned to the Major. "I'm assuming we will be informed as to why we've been dragged away from our busy schedules for a chit-chat?"

Vegas ignored him. He continued to watch the door, awaiting one more individual. It opened and Officer Nicoletti walked in.

"Sorry," he said. "I was in the middle of something."

Knowing exactly why Nicoletti was late, Vegas nodded and held his hand towards the empty seat, silently requesting he join the team.

"You're all here because I need your help. We need your help… Jensen, Kiernan, and me. A series of events has become known, which has cast doubt upon those who lead us. So, before I tell you why you are here, let me first present you with the facts.

***

She felt a shunt as the capsule reached the surface. Kiernan took a breath and nervously brushed a hand down her protective clothing. She caught Jensen's eye relaying an expression of support. Hanging the breathing apparatus around her neck, Jensen began to climb the rungs towards the hatch. It was silent in the lift. A contrast to the tempest Kiernan now knew raged beyond.

Reaching the seal, Jensen began the process of opening the portal. There had been no scheduled scouts for the past two rotations, so she was confident they wouldn't encounter any other scout upon the surface. Jensen felt secure in the knowledge their whereabouts were still unknown. She trusted Nicoletti, and although her plan was risky, she was confident in their course of action. She hadn't discussed their next move with Vegas, agreeing the less he knew the better. Vegas was gathering help and she offered Raziko, Ziran and Nicoletti as loyal allies. If strength was in numbers, then they had to make the most out of the troop Vegas would assemble.

Releasing the last seal, Jensen looked down at Kiernan. "Ready?"

With a nod, Kiernan pulled the breathing apparatus over her face. Jensen followed suit and, bracing herself for the tempest, Jensen pushed open the hatch. Instantly the howl of the wind invaded the lift. Jensen looked up, climbing further out and onto the surface. She felt the power of the storm as it thrust against her and turned around, holding her hand out for Kiernan join her on the Barrens.

"Fierce!" Jensen shouted, and pushed the hatch closed behind Kiernan. She turned, looking around at the lay of the land, recognizing landmarks. The second hatch was northeast. A burnt-out post marked their direction. Jensen knew of the location Lomax had described. She had seen the two trees, but had always passed the area, knowing it had been scouted long before. Unless the gales pushed new materials onto scouted lands, they were not to waste their time re-covering any area.

"How far do you think it is?" Kiernan asked, shouting over the storm.

"Not too far. I recall the area well. They are the only two fully intact trees I've ever seen. Who knew they unknowingly stood as a marker for a secret entrance back into the colony!"

They began their journey in silence, fighting through the savage winds. For mid-morn, the sky was lit with a wave of amber and emerald hues. It was more colour than Jensen had ever seen. Was the toxicity increasing? She made a mental note to discuss it with Kiernan when they returned to safety. It would be several furlongs before they reached the marker. Jensen stopped long enough for Kiernan to reach her, and together they silently pushed through the roaring gale towards their destination.

***

The door to Commander Tehera's office flew open with such force that it hit the wall. Three framed images fell to the floor, each frame shattering upon impact. Seated at his desk, Commander Tehera looked up with a start. Select Prime Abrahams stormed into the room. He strode towards Tehera's desk and leaned over the surface, bracing his hands upon the worn timber.

"Why do my officers report Minister Kiernan is unlocatable? Why do they say Scout Jensen is truant? And most importantly why is Major Vegas unreachable? I questioned his loyalty, but you assured me he was committed. His faced infused with ire, "Why am I asking these questions when I should trust you to deal with the menials?"

Opposed to Abrahams' terminology when referring to his lower-level colonists, more because he was sure outside of his presence, he too was labelled as such, Tehera fought a flash of rage. "With respect, it has been but a mark. The colony isn't large enough for us to lose subjects indefinitely. I've increased officers between the colony boundaries, as well as lesser-known back passages. I doubt it will be long before we find them."

Abrahams didn't move, his face inches from Tehera. "Minister Kiernan should never have returned from the mission."

"I understand," Tehera replied, "but maybe if you could enlighten me on what infraction she has breached, I can-"

"Am I to explain myself to you now?"

"Of course not, Sir. However, you ordered her termination without explanation. I think-"

"I don't require you to think, Commander Tehera. I require you to execute my orders. Has my promise in lieu of your service not been enough assurance to you? Will your stature in the new world not-"?

"No, Sir. You have been more than generous, and I am appreciative of the offer you have bestowed upon me. I guarantee I will not fail in my duties." Uncomfortable with the proximity Abrahams continued to enforce, Tehera pushed his chair away from the desk. "I only wonder whether I could amend my approach if I knew of the Minister's infraction."

"All you need to know is that Minister Kiernan has overstepped her bounds into areas that are no concern of hers."

Tehera averted his eyes, wondering what Kiernan had stumbled upon which had caused Abrahams to act so aggressively. Minister Kiernan was a valuable member of their team. She was head designer of their craft's energy system. She contributed greatly to genetic reproduction and cleansing. Plus, as Minister of Acquisitions, her support and methodical approach in the distribution of commodities had aided the colony in their balance of supplies. Kiernan was vital. Tehera's curiosity grew, but it wasn't for him to question. The commander rose from his seat.

"I shall increase officer presence on border patrol until the targets are detected."

Abrahams finally took a step backwards. "Use whatever force necessary to apprehend the threat to m – our agenda. Terminal enforcement is recommended."

Holding Abrahams' stare, the commander gave a sharp nod. Done.

***

The examination bay was silent. Vegas studied his team, staring back at him with varying degrees of disbelief and consternation. The major stood tall.

"Any questions?"

Ziran was the first to speak. "Raziko and I were there on the mission. I can say on behalf of us both, Jensen already knows she has our support. You both do."

"Thank you," Vegas replied, and then looked at the remaining occupants of the room.

Nicoletti was next. "You know I'm in."

With a small, almost imperceptible bow of respect, Vegas acknowledged Nicoletti. The officer had no time to mourn the death of Taura. Vegas felt tremendous guilt in pulling him into their cause, but Nicoletti had changed. Gone was the upstanding, rule abiding officer he knew. Nicoletti's allegiance had diverted from honouring the Ultimate Agenda and those who pushed for absolute resolve. A shift that would work in his favour.

Physician Angelus was next to speak. He rose, his index finger tapping his lip thoughtfully. "First of all, I can verify the rather colourful version of our Minister Kiernan who returned from the mission. Injuries that were, without a doubt, the result of a physical attack. Added to that, our good Minister was jumpy and withdrawn. Very unlike her, as I'm sure you will agree.

Vegas began a short pace back and forth. "As I said, you are here because we value you as allies and colleagues. So, I must ask you," he stopped and looked towards the back row of seats where Lucia, Whylen and Pavo sat. Three upper-level colonists who Vegas believed were loyal to him.

Whylen rose unexpectedly. "I have long had my suspicions. I've worked with Kiernan, and I know the areas she has researched. I'm with Kiernan."

Making a mental note to ask Whylen to elaborate, Vegas looked next to Pavo and Lucia. He saw the hesitation in them both, but feigned ignorance and waited.

Lucia was the first to speak. "I hope you accept that in order for me to fully understand your claims, more proof is needed."

"Right," Vegas looked to Minister Pavo. "Do you too require more evidence, Minister?"

Pavo hesitated before he spoke. It was a mere fraction of a strike, but enough to trigger alarm in Vegas.

"Maybe we could reconvene," he rose, "When Kiernan and Jensen can provide the relevant evidence?"

Disappointed, Vegas nodded to Ziran.

The scout rose, pulling an automatic firearm from under his shirt. He aimed it at Lucia and Pavo. Shock coloured their expressions.

"I'm afraid we can't do that," Vegas said with force.

***

The sun must have been high in the mid-rotation sky, for the amber and emerald hues blended in magnificent array. The tempest had calmed, making it easier to journey across the Barrens. Ahead of them, Jensen clearly saw the two fully intact skeletal trees Lomax had described. They stood out in dark contrast against the sky. The pair approached in silence. Kiernan looked up at the trees, never having seen such a sight. They may have been burnt out remnants of a magnificence long gone, but to Kiernan they stood as testament to the world that once was. These towering beacons were once alive with flourishing vitality. A lump of emotion wedged itself in her throat.

As they neared the location Jensen, started to scan the ground. So many cycles had passed since her father had entered the hatch. Cycles of ash and charred debris had littered the ground since then. There was no obvious sign of its exact location.

"Where do we look?" Kiernan shouted.

Jensen removed her tonfa. "Anywhere and everywhere," she replied as she began hitting the base of her weapon upon the ground, hoping to detect evidence of an alloy portal built into the surface.

Unsheathing her own baton, handed to her by Nicoletti, Kiernan mimicked Jensen. The space between the trees wasn't too large. As such it didn't take them long before Kiernan heard the distinct clunk of timer hitting lead.

"Jensen!"

Stopping her own search, Jensen saw Kiernan fall to her knees and begin scraping at the ground. Jensen was quick to follow. Together they worked to uncover the hatch.

"Was that too easy?" Kiernan asked.

Jensen looked down at an identical alloy access hatch to the one she had used countless times in the past. "I guess we will soon find out!"

CHAPTER 39

No lift! Of course not. Jensen stared down the hatch opening that disappeared into absolute darkness. She shone her torch into the vertical tunnel, seeing only ladder rungs.

"How far do you think it goes?"

"Only one way to find out," Jensen replied. She looked up at Kiernan. "I don't suppose polite courtesy will work in that instance?"

Arching an eyebrow, Kiernan took a step back and swept her hand in a chivalrous gesture towards the entrance.

Jensen smiled, as she secured her tonfa and torch to her belt. "Didn't think so." She slipped into the hatch, holding onto the rungs securely as she began her descent. When enough room was clear, Kiernan followed.

With each step, Jensen counted their descent. At one hundred and fifty rungs she started to worry. Were they halfway? What would they find at the bottom of the hatch? Feelings of uncertainty crept into her mind, and Jensen tried to rid herself of such thoughts.

"Jen?"

"Yes?" Jensen looked up, keeping an eye on Kiernan's boots, as they neared her fingers.

"What is it you hope to find down here? Really."

Pausing for a moment, Jensen spoke honestly. "This is where it all started. The discovery of this place changed the course of so many lives. I want answers. I want to know the truth. We've lived our lives being fed a utopian future, which I no longer believe was ever ours. Not for all of us. Not in the way we've been led to believe." Jensen shone her torch into the darkness. "I think it's time we knew the truth." Jensen frowned. "Hold on a moment."

Kiernan froze, as Jensen took another three steps and then paused. "I can see the bottom."

The women continued. Within another fifteen steps they reached the bottom. Jensen stepped off the ladder leaving room for Kiernan. Using her torchlight, Jensen looked around. The area was small. She doubted there was a de-contamination process beyond. Finding a door, she examined it closely.

"No lock?" Kiernan asked. "Strange."

"No lock, no handle, no visible form of access at all."

"This has to be the right place, but-" Kiernan couldn't help but wonder, "If this is what your father found, how did he enter?"

"Hmm," Jensen stepped closer, shining her torchlight around the frame. She peered closer, running her fingers over the surface. "Look here." She shone light over a specific area."

"Prizing marks!"

Reaching into her pack, Jensen pulled out her prizing tool. "Never leave the haven without it." Setting to work, Jensen wedged the tool into the door jamb and slowly prized the barrier open. As it started to move, Kiernan helped and together, they pushed the door open. Kiernan slipped out her baton and braced it between the door and its frame. Jensen investigated the room beyond. More darkness.

"There must be lighting here somewhere."

Kiernan felt along the wall until she found a wide metallic switch. She pulled hard, and with a whir of energy, the warehouse was bathed in bright light.

"Oh... my..." Jensen looked around in awe at the largest subterranean space she'd ever seen.

Overcome by the vision before them, Jensen and Kiernan walked into the expansive warehouse taking in the sights. It was a step back in time, into their world history. Paintings, sculptures, idols of antiquity. Display cases loaded with unrecognisable objects. Shelving stacked high with tomes and other colourful cases filed alphabetically. Furniture, electronic devices and a collection of land, air, and oceanic crafts. Seeing an area which appeared to be temperature controlled, Jensen approached the unit.

"Seeds," Kiernan said, reading a sign to the left. "Vegetation for the new world."

"Is the new world still in its infancy?"

"It's..." Kiernan looked away. How could she tell Jensen the truth Vegas had revealed? "The new world is established, but nowhere near as advanced as ourselves." Knowing it wasn't the time to engage in that discussion, Kiernan changed the subject. "Do you see anything that may indicate evidence of classified data?"

"Not yet." Jensen looked around again, still overwhelmed by their surroundings. "They can't possibly think all of this will fit in the craft.

A thought stuck Kiernan. "Maybe it depends upon the intended number of passengers?"

"Have you seen it? The ship I mean."

"Only once." Kiernan thought back to the one and only time she had been granted access to the craft. "During the design of the upgraded energy source I was given access to log calculation and design specifications. The original power source for the craft had proven insufficient so I had to rework schematics and reconfigure the origin source for a cleaner and more stable matrix and distribution of power. I only had one opportunity to see the craft and was never given a 'tour' so to speak."

"Hmm," Jensen continued to investigate the wealth of planetary history around them. "I saw it. I think. Yester-rotation through a frosted window. The space it is stored in must be larger than this, for it was gargantuan." Jensen looked down another isle of shelves to what appeared to be a glass-like cell at the end. Curious, she headed to the mysterious cell. Kiernan watched her disappear around a corner and followed. She stood before a polycarbonate container with a clouded surface area making it impossible to see within. It stood twice as high as Jensen and three time as wide.

Taking a step closer, Kiernan recognised the authorisation code upon its door. It was the same one used in the original files that had started her quest for answers. It was the same authorisation code relating to the documents concerning Jensen's parents.

"This is it."

"I think so too," Jensen agreed. She ran her hand over its entrance. There was unmistakable evidence of an upgraded locking mechanism sealing the door. Her father's theft, she presumed. Jensen waved her E.M.P disruptor over the lock. Nothing happened.

"That was a long shot."

"Not sure it's that kind of lock." Kiernan pointed to a circular area. "I believe this is a biometrics mechanism."

"Never heard of such a device," Jensen commended.

"They're installed in the craft."

"So how do we get in?" Jensen thrust her shoulder against the door.

"I don't think we can." Kiernan looked around and then walked back to the main warehouse.

"Where are you going?" Jensen asked in frustration. She wanted to search the cell.

"Maybe we will find something," Kiernan said, disappearing behind a tall row of racking.

***

Raziko stood outside the medical supply closet. Arms folded; the Scout stood firm. He took a step back to listen to the conversation within. Before him, Angelus, Nicolette and Whylen were seated in different areas of the medical bay. The men were silent, pensive, waiting. Vegas' move was unexpected by the other inhabitants of the room. The Major had escorted Lucia and Pavo into the closet. Ziran remained beside him.

Inside the storage closet, Vegas watched Ziran bind Lucia to Pavo, back-to-back. He then tied their hands together, right to left and vice versa. Then he bound their feet. They were secured and immobile.

"Vegas, you will be stripped of your rank and privileges. Do you understand? Please reconsider your actions."

"I think we're beyond that now, Lucia." Vegas stood tall. Arms hanging by his sides, he focussed his attention upon his prisoners.

"Then explain why you are doing this?" Pavo asked. "This is ridiculous. What do you hope to achieve? We are allied colleagues."

Vegas remained silent as Ziran finished securing Lucia's feet together. He never thought Lucia or Pavo would waver if he were to request earnest help.

"We are, but I expected more. Obviously, your loyalties lie elsewhere."

Neither responded.

Finishing his task, Ziran backed away. He grasped his weapon from a shelf and positioned himself besides Vegas. The firearm remained aimed upon the impromptu prisoners.

"Unfortunately, you will not be leaving here until you supply me with the information I need. I want to know what the Select Prime has promised you for your loyalty."

Again, the response to his question was silence.

The major folded his arms. "If you don't speak, you won't be leaving this room."

"And if we speak, but you don't like what you hear, will you still allow us to leave?"

Vegas remained calm, but Lucia's words rang true. His actions, as well as the situation, was unprecedented. Law and order had always been a simple task in a colony, with only several thousand inhabitants to support. Contention within the ranks was rare. Vegas realised, if he didn't stand by his convictions, their current actions would be futile. Everything Jensen and Kiernan were doing, would mean nothing if he didn't play his part.

The belief had always been that the colony, although running in a hierarchy, still worked together for a mutual goal. It appeared the lives of the many worked for the benefit of the few. Vegas wouldn't be one of those few. He was not a pawn, and it was time to act.

Looking at Ziran, Vegas saw concern in his eyes. Although Vegas had previously requested his support should there be any resistance, he had never thought it would be needed. He needed time to reconvene with his ensemble of colleagues; and Pavo and Lucia needed time to consider their co-operation.

"Ziran? A word outside. Let's give our guests a moment of deliberation."

Ziran nodded and followed Vegas out of the closet, much to the protests of their captives.

Closing and locking the door behind them, Vegas turned to the remaining occupants of the room. Nicolette, Angelus, Raziko and Whylen awaited instruction. None appeared comforted by the turn of events, and Vegas tried not to feel overwhelmed by the gravity of their situation. There was no turning back now.

"I need you to go back to your rotational roles. We need to be seen as behaving normally. However, I'd like you to consider if there are other colonists who would align with our cause. We must move quickly if our plan is to succeed."

"Where are Jensen and Kiernan?" Raziko asked.

Vegas looked to Nicoletti, and the team received an unspoken answer.

"Why topside?" Raziko continued to quiz.

The Major sighed. "There is still more we need to discuss for you to understand the background of this matter." He hoped imparting this knowledge would further install trust in the team.

"Hmm, so while you all go scamper away, I'm left babysitting the bondage duo. Why do I feel like I've drawn the short pipet here?" Angelus' eyebrow arched so high it threatened to disappear off his face.

"Excuse me?" Vegas asked, confused.

"Never mind that. I'm left guarding hostages! This was not how I planned my morn and I refuse to harbour illicit endeavours."

Vegas took a deep, calming breath; this was becoming an increasingly complex situation.

***

Their search through the warehouse had opened Jensen and Kiernan up to so much about their planet's history. Both women were overwhelmed but were unable to genuinely appreciate what they had discovered. Not when a greater quest was upon them. At that moment, it was finding a way to get into the polycarbonate cell.

Kiernan passed stacks of colourful containers. Each one was labelled in a manner she was unfamiliar with. Different languages? After all, their planet had hosted an array of multi-lingual nations. More than she expected it seemed.

"Kiernan... Quick!"

Jumping at the sound of her name being called so urgently, Kiernan turned to see Jensen skidding around the corner.

"This way. You must see this!"

Spurred on by Jensen's excited tone, Kiernan dashed to follow. Jensen led her to a far corner. She stopped beside a row of tall, metallic containers, shaped in a half circle.

"Jen?"

"Take a look!" Jensen said, as she pulled thick steel rods to the side and opened the first container's double doors.

Kiernan gasped. "Oh... My..."

CHAPTER 40

Staring at the contents within the container, Kiernan's hand covered her mouth. She knew exactly what she was looking at. Although she had never before seen the items Jensen had unveiled to her, Kiernan could not only tell what they were, but the chemical acronym etched into the side of each item confirmed her suspicion. She took a step closer as Jensen opened four more containers, each housing more of the same. Once the last door was open, Jensen stood back beside Kiernan. Every shelf within each container held a row of bullet-shaped capsules as long her forearm and as wide as her head. Two thirds of the casings were translucent. Contained within was a cerulean substance which appeared alive. The mist of particles undulated in hypnotic waves.

"Kiernan, what is this?"

Rubbing the bridge of her nose, Kiernan mentally calculated the number. Twenty per container, four containers. That's eighty. More than enough.

"Kiernan?"

Taking a step closer, Kiernan reached out and ran her hand over one of the casings.

"What are they?"

Looking back, Kiernan took an anxious breath. "They are missiles loaded with Amphibulartoxin."

"What?"

"Enough to wipe out life on a potential new world."

"Potential?"

"Our new world."

"The new world is already inhabited?"

Kiernan cleared her throat. "Currently, yes."

Frowning, Jensen searched her mind. "Amphibulartoxin. Why does that name sound familiar?"

Holding her hand near a missile, Kiernan watched the cerulean glow shone against her pale skin. "At the testing station, it was the airborne toxin that killed the workers. All those bodies we found."

Thinking back, Jensen recalled the way Kiernan described the workers' deaths. It was a horrifying experience. "Why were those people killed?"

"I can only presume they secured the people they wanted to save from the toxin, those who made it to the colony, and they eradicated the rest. To stop the knowledge of classified data from escaping."

Looking back at the missiles, Jensen noted how each one was strapped into place. Securing it in such a way that there was no possibility of it falling from the shelving. "How dangerous is this?"

"A covering of a surface no larger than your finger could wipe out the entire colony."

"And they plan to eliminate our new world's current inhabitants with this?"

"Yes."

Jensen re-sealed each container. "That can't happen. We must stop them."

"Isn't that what we're doing?"

From the corner of her eye, Jensen spotted something unexpected. She turned to study the object, recognizing a large prizing bar designed to open the larger, timber crates. Impulsively, Jensen grabbed the heavy bar and ran out of sight.

"Jensen?" It took Kiernan a moment to understand what Jensen had in mind. She ran after her, rounding the corner in time to see Jensen standing before the translucent cell by the far wall. Jensen swung hard at its surface. The tool bounded back, jarring Jensen's body, but a small dent had been made. She swung again, and again, and again. Over and over Jensen swung, the banging and clattering echoing around the vast warehouse, as she thrust the bar repeatedly into its surface until the small dent became a larger and larger. The surface started to crack and splinter. Jensen kept on swinging until the splintering spread out across the entire surface of the cell's door and the dense material started to buckle. She panted, her breath beginning to labour. With one final swing, and a grunt of effort, the cell door disintegrated into small, cube like pieces that scattered out across the ground.

Breathing hard, Jensen dropped the prizing bar to the ground. A bead of sweat trickled down her forehead. "Look at that," she said with a smile. "Simple after all!"

Kiernan closed her slackened jaw. "Indeed."

Without hesitation, Jensen stepped into the cell.

Contained within were rows of filing cabinets to their right and timber containers to their left. Straight ahead was the brick wall the cell was constructed into.

"Which side do you want?" Jensen asked.

"I'll take the cabinets."

"Right," Jensen pulled up her sleeves. "Let's get to work."

***

He had no idea where he was. Not surprising, as he had material covering his head. With arms bound behind his back, Nicoletti was unable to remove the hood that irritated his skin and restricted his vision. His breath was harsh, muffled under the fabric hood, limiting his ability to pull in fresh air.

Nicoletti was alert to every sound. He tried to recount his steps, wondering how he had found himself in this situation. He was returning to his post. That was the last memory he recalled before waking up in a seated position, in this unknown location. The distant sound of a faint crackling caught his attention, as did the aroma of heated metal. That was a known aroma and common in the colony. It was the small of metal being smelted down for repurposing. That meant he was far from his post. Near engineering, maybe? He struggled again against his bindings.

"That will do you no good."

Nicoletti paused. His heart beating faster. "Who's there? Is this a joke? It's not funny. Let me go!"

Suddenly, Nicoletti was blinded by a bright light, as his hood was removed, and he found himself under a blinding spotlight. He squinted against a piercing beam aimed directly into his face, and tried to look around, but his head was then grasped in a vice-like headlock. Now he was unable to move at all.

"What is this?" he yelled, followed by a yelp of pain as a fist hit him soundly in the face. His head swam groggily, as warm blood slipped from his nose and down his throat. Nicoletti gurgled and gagged on the tangy, metallic liquid.

"Do I have your attention?"

"Yes."

"Good-"

"What-"

"I'm asking the questions."

Nicoletti attempted to nod, but his head was held firm. He tried to look around, but the bright light in his eyes limited his vision. He could only just make out the dark shadow of a torso and head standing before him.

"You allowed Scout Jensen and Minister Kiernan access to the Barrens. Why?"

Nicoletti remained silent.

"Why did Jensen and Kiernan enter the Barrens?"

"Don't know."

"So, you did allow them access."

"Never said that."

Another slam of pain, as a long object hit Nicoletti in the torso. He gasped and cried out in agonising pain. He felt a crunch. Something had broken. A bone? A rib? His heart beat even faster as his panic rose further. He gasped for breath.

"You allowed them access." That wasn't a question.

"Yes."

"Why?"

Nicoletti pressed his lips together. Another strike to his torso had him crying out in agony. The pain erupted around his chest and then suddenly he gasped as his breathing laboured. With every attempt to pull air past his lips a sharp stabbing sensation racked his body. He cried out again, fighting for breath.

"You… hit… him…too… HARD," the voice said, laced with fury. "HOW CAN I QUESTION HIM?"

Fear burning through his nerves, Nicoletti tried to breathe, but every attempt brought agony. Every gasp becoming increasingly restricted and painful. The taste of blood overwhelmed his senses.

"What use is he to me now, you fool. DAMN IT."

Feeling his head released, Nicoletti felt his chin grasped firmly. A head of thick, messy hair loomed into his blurred view.

"He's dying," he heard the voice say. "Struggling to breath. Won't make it." He felt his head fall, as he struggled and gasped for air. Agony. Pure agony.

"Leave him."

A voice behind Nicoletti spoke. "But Scout Jensen and Minister Kiernan entered the Barrens. Where did they go?"

"Hmm," The controlling voice appeared thoughtful. A cursed whisper echoed around the room. "Come with me." The urgency in that command was clear, as an echo of footsteps faded into the distance.

He was beginning to feel lightheaded. A mist invaded his thoughts, but the pain was receding. Nicoletti continued to gasp. Blood gurgled in the back of his throat. He knew he was dying. How has this happened? He thought of Taura. The memories calmed him, as the fog in his mind expanded. Then suddenly a single set of footsteps moved closer. Nicoletti felt his hands released from their binds and he fell from the chair into the arms of an unknown saviour. Without the light in his eyes, Nicoletti was just able to see a woman pulling him into a comforting embrace.

"It's alright. I have you. I'm so sorry. I wanted to wait and help when they were gone. I'm too late." A soft hand brushed over his face. "You're not alone. I have you."

Feeling a calm ease over him, Nicoletti's distant gaze drifted. His desperate gasps for breath slowing. His vision darkened. He could feel his face caressed by a soft hand.

"I have you," the voice repeated.

Darkness overwhelmed him, but he wasn't afraid. He was safe and he was warm. He was going home.

Tovey watched as Nicoletti took his last breath and then felt his body sag in her arms. She reached up and closed his eyes. A solitary tear slipped down her cheek. She had no idea who this person was, but when she saw Devlin and two more men bring him into the room, Tovey could only hide in the shadows. It's what she had been doing, slowly moving from one location to another, to find Jensen and avoid detection. She'd never expected to run into Devlin, but as her firearm was out of ammunition, she could only wait helplessly lest being captured too.

Easing Nicoletti's body to the floor, Tovey rose and stepped away. She looked around the brick room. It was dark, apart from the single light that stood in the centre, shining upon the now empty chair. The room appeared to have a purpose, torture, and interrogation. She needed to find a way out of there. Quickly.

CHAPTER 41

Kneeling among five open, half empty boxes, Jensen held the current box-file upon her lap. She flicked through the pages, searching. She wasn't sure exactly what she was looking for. Something she could use as evidence. Everything she had found was information she either already knew or it didn't bring any ground-breaking revelations.

She picked up another box-file and opened it quickly. "Did you know a deep space probe discovered the new world? It's situated in solar system like ours and has-"

"I have it!"

"Hmm?" Looking up, Jensen saw Kiernan holding several sheets of paper. "What?"

Kiernan stared down at the top sheet, her eyes growing impossibly wide. Jensen's request for her to elaborate was cut short, as a strange sound capture their attention.

"What was…?" Jensen rose and the file upon her lap fell to the floor.

Kiernan folded the papers. "I don't know, but-"

The sound grew louder. A disembodied clanking.

"We need to get out of here before-"

Jensen was silenced, when part of the brick wall at the far end of the cell began to move forwards and slide open. That moment of shock, in seeing the hidden wall open, was enough time for their unexpected visitors to stumble upon Jensen and Kiernan inside the Select Prime's storage cell. Surprise mirrored the faces of Jensen and Kiernan, as well as the two high-ranking Enforcement Officers who stood at the secret chamber's entrance.

"Any point yelling *run*?" Jensen asked.

Both officers pulled out their batons. The shorter of the two shook his head with a nefarious grin. "On your knees. Hands behind your backs."

The women obeyed. Jensen looked over at Kiernan, as she sunk to her knees. "I'm sorry."

"Not over yet," Kiernan replied, so softly that only Jensen was able to hear.

Hands swiftly bound behind their backs, both women were hauled to their feet and escorted back through the hidden doorway.

They were led through a back passage. More passages. This one was well lit and sterile. The walls were stark, shining in artificial light. Jensen tried to memorise their journey, and as they passed through a narrow doorway, they found themselves in a longer corridor that Jenson recognised. She was there the yester-rotation, after leaving Tovey with Lomax.

The officers stopped them at a door to a presumed domestic supplies cupboard. When the barrier opened, Jensen realised this was anything but. The room was large and dark, with a single bright light shining upon a lone chair in its centre. Kiernan scanned the periphery of the lighting edge, spotting a body lying upon the ground. It lay on its back with arms by the sides. A tremor skittered through her body. Kiernan nudged Jensen. She saw the body. A cautious glance passed between them. Their tension mounted as the officer placed a second chair next to the first already in the light. Both women were led over and forced into the seating. Jensen tried to peer down at the body upon the floor, but it was half lying in the darkness and the light was too bright. She felt her arms pulled behind the chair and secured at the rear. Kiernan followed and then tatty hoods were placed over both of their heads.

Then there was silence. Nothing, but the harsh sound of nervous breath met their ears. Jensen struggled against her bound hands, but to no avail.

"Have they gone?"

"Doubtful," Kiernan whispered back. "No doubt guarding us from the shadows. Watching."

"Is…" Jensen found herself feeling fearful for the first time. "Is this Abrahams?"

"Not his mode of operation. This is somebody else."

"Who?"

"Who indeed," said a voice from directly behind them. It was low and gravelly, like a deep whisper. "You have given us quite the run around."

Jensen held her breath. Footsteps circled once. Then again. They stopped and a deep sigh met Jensen's ears.

"I have questions. You will answer them candidly and without hesitation. Failure to do so will be… painful. I recommend against failure to obey."

"What do you want?" Jensen asked.

"Question 1, Scout Jensen…"

Jensen's heart missed a beat.

"What exactly were you hoping to find in the data store?"

Jensen replied honestly. "Anything that might help."

"Help what?"

"Discover the truth."

A low laugh followed her reply. "Do you not yet understand that as a governing body, the Select Prime must make difficult choices? Carrying the weight of those choices is a burden that others are lucky not to bear. Sometimes truths must stay hidden for the good of the masses to avoid misunderstanding, fear, and a downward spiral into anarchy. There is contentment in ignorance."

"Should that be one man's choice?"

"It is the Select Prime's choice, and I work in his favour, under his orders. For the good of the many."

Jensen twisted her hands against her bounds. They were tight.

"And what is your intention for the many?" Kiernan asked.

"Liberation, as has been the Select Prime's intention all along."

Suddenly finding her head held in a solid grip from behind, Kiernan gasped.

"Minister Kiernan, as it appears you think you can ask questions… your turn. How did Advisor Xoren die?"

"Explosion at the testing station," Kiernan replied, as best she could with the arm wrapped around her head. A solid punch hit her direct in the stomach. Kiernan gasped in pain, struggling to catch her breath, as that pain radiated through her midsection.

"What are you doing?" Jensen struggled in her chair. "That is the truth. That explosion killed four of our people."

"What caused the explosion?" the voice asked.

Something in the inflection of that voices caught Kiernan's attention. "It was-"

"Let's get to the bigger question." Jensen said, interrupting Kiernan. "My parents stole information and for all these cycles you still haven't been able to find it. You may now have the formula for Vial 15, but you still don't have the location and co-ordinates of the new world that you are so desperate for. Unless the toxicity clears from the sky, you will never be able to communicate with the satellite. Right now, the only known location is in that stolen information. Only one person knows where that is." As soon as the words left her lips, Jensen knew she had made herself prime target for their interrogator.

"I'm aware you released Lomax from his prolonged… stay with us. Nothing escapes my radar."

Jensen felt that was too bold a statement to make and obviously not true at all. "And there is now only one person who knows the location of those files."

"Who?"

Jensen laughed, to which she received her own punch to the stomach.

"Tell me who has the files."

"I don't know!"

A punch to the side of her face had Jensen seeing stars.

"Stop!" Kiernan shouted.

"Who?"

Feeling her eyes sting with unshed tears, Jensen shook her head to clear her thoughts from the pain. She needed to think, but a muffled voice caught her attention.

Kiernan tried to listen, hearing only the words *two marks* and *cover*.

An irritated sigh was expelled from the disembodied voice.

"You have a brief period of respite, while I address an urgent matter for the Select Prime. Use this time to consider your options… or lack of them."

That's it? Jensen thought.

Footsteps moved away. "You come with me. You stay here and watch them."

Realising he was leaving one officer behind, Jensen reconsidered their odds. A door opening and closing signalled the departure of their interrogator. Kiernan remained quiet. She listened. One set of footsteps began to pace around the edge of the room.

"Jen?"

"Yes?"

"How are we going to…?"

"Careful," Jensen whispered.

Kiernan understood.

The women sat in silence, and Kiernan pondered over the conversation she barely overheard. Two marks. What happened in two marks? And that voice. She knew that voice. The inflection of certain words was clear. She began to understand the level of danger they were facing.

"Excuse me, Officer?" Jensen called, "Do you mind?"

Footsteps drew closer. "What?"

"I'm really struggling to breath. Please could you remove the cover for a short while?"

There was an abrupt laugh in response.

"Please?" Jensen feigned anxiety. It wasn't hard. "I can't breathe. Just for a moment. Please."

Silence.

"Please."

Another moment passed and the hood was pulled from Jensen's head. The officer strode away.

"Thank you," Jensen said and took a large pull of slightly fresher air. She noted Kiernan's hood remained. "Are you alright, Kir?"

"Not really."

Jensen nodded but didn't reply. She needed to think. To weigh their options. One moment she thought they were about to enter a lengthy interrogation; the next said interrogator was abandoning them, with little in the way of relevant information. He was due to return, but what had caused such a turn around. The bright light shining in her face made it difficult to see, but it did draw her attention to the body lying close by. Reaching out, Jensen used her booted foot to slip into the pocket of the body's clothing and pull it closer. Her second attempt worked, and she was able to move the body enough for a blood-splattered face to slide into view. Jensen gasped.

"Nicoletti!"

"Quiet," shouted the officer.

"What is it?" Kiernan asked. She heard a muffled sob stumble from Jensen's lips. "Jen?"

"It's Nicoletti. My ally. Taura's spouse."

"The Decontamination Officer?"

"He's here. Dead. They… they…"

Kiernan recalled Nicoletti. "How… when?"

Unable to hold back tears, they silently fell for her friend. "This is my fault."

Jensen's words stuck Kiernan with the pain she could feel behind them. "Don't. Don't think that. None of this is your fault, Jen. We are all victims here."

Unable to wipe the tears that rolled down her cheeks, Jensen took a ragged breath. "I must stop this, Kir. How many more will be hurt or die?" She struggled hard against her bindings in rage.

"Stop that," the officer yelled. Footsteps drew closer. "That's it." The hood was returned to Jensen's head, but it only made her struggle harder.

"If I have to tell you-"

A heavy thud silenced the officer. Then they heard the distinctive sound of his body hitting the ground.

Both women remained nervously silent.

"Well placed bricks as doorstops can have other uses."

Jensen jumped in instant recognition.

"Sorry I took so long. I've been trying to find a way out."

"Who's-?"

"Tovey?" The hood was pulled from Jensen's head. "What are you doing here?"

"Lost and hiding mostly, but more importantly saving your lives!" She looked down at Nicoletti. "Before I'm too late again."

"What's going on?"

Tovey pulled the hood from Kiernan's head, and then began untying her hands. "We need to get out of here before Devlin returns."

Jensen turned sharply. "That was Devlin?"

"That wasn't Devlin," Kiernan argued. "That was Abrahams. I recognise his voice. He tried to disguise it, but-"

"That was Devlin," Tovey insisted. "I saw him. I know him."

Jensen looked from Tovey to Kiernan, as another piece of the puzzle fell into place. "Oh no."

CHAPTER 42

Retracing their steps, Jensen and Kiernan led Tovey to the warehouse. Having taken the officer's baton, Tovey held the weapon in a ready position, as they made their escape. They soon found themselves back in the data cell. Offering no time for explanation, Jensen picked up her tonfa and the trio made for the exit. Tovey had little time to process the sights around her, but twice she had to stop herself from colliding into a corner as an unexpected object caught her eye.

Reaching the door, Jensen passed through, followed by Tovey and then Kiernan, who pulled her baton from the door frame. It closed behind them. Darkness.

"One moment." Jensen activated her torch and shone it up the ladder shaft.

Tovey gulped. "How far is-"

"You will be fine," Kiernan assured her. "Jensen will go first, then you and then me."

With a nod, Jensen began her ascent. Holding her torch carefully, she directed its beam towards the hatch. Hearing voices behind her, Jensen concentrated upon reaching the surface. It seemed quicker than their descent, and before long she reached the surface hatch. Releasing its seals, she pushed the access open.

Instantly she was greeted with an unexpected silence. Disconcerted, and forgetting to secure her facial apparatus, Jensen climbed the remaining rungs of the ladder and climbed out onto the Barrens. Pulling free her tonfa, a move more out of habit due to her apprehension, Jensen grasped the timber cautiously. She looked across the Barren lands, realising she could see further than ever before. They must have been entering the twilight marks, and yet the still atmosphere and visibility was like nothing she had seen before. Was it a clement? It seemed like it, only more so, as not a sound infiltrated the calm.

Turning slightly, Jensen looked up into the sky. She couldn't control her gasp. The cloudbanks had not only parted but separated to such an extent that there seemed more visible sky than toxic mass. Vast blankets of stars shone above her, twinkling in their splendour. Staring up in wonder,

Jensen cast her gaze over the stars as though trying to count every sparkle of light.

Behind her, Jensen heard Tovey and Kiernan ascending the hatch rungs, but she was unable to pull her attention away from the vision. In awe she turned, bracing her tonfa upon her shoulder as her gaze followed the sky. And then the breath left her body. There, straight ahead and hanging low in the sky, Jensen saw the moon. The once brilliant orb was displaced, split into two pieces and held in a fractured orbit. Rubble and dust formed a broken ring around its mass.

"Jensen?"

Hearing her name, Jensen turned.

"Is that… is that the moon?" Tovey asked.

Jensen looked back up at the sky in silent wonderment.

"It's happening." Kiernan appeared beside her. "It's really happening. The world is healing."

Letting the tonfa drop from her shoulder, Jensen allowed it to hang lightly within her grasp. She stared up at the moon. It was not the object of majesty she had read so much about. That once glorious orb was a mere shadow of its former brilliance.

"I never thought I'd live to see this moment," Tovey said. "Is it usual to feel overjoyed and yet heartbroken at the same time?"

"No," Kiernan placed her hand upon Tovey's back in a comforting gesture. "I know exactly how you feel."

An exchange passed between Kiernan and Tovey. "I've heard a lot about you," Tovey said with a smile.

"You too, it's a pleasure to meet you, Tovey."

"We shouldn't remain stationary. It's too dangerous." Turning, Jensen looked in the direction they were to travel. "Scavengers prefer the darker marks." She wanted to stay and stare up at the sky. To drink in the sight before them, but Jensen knew danger was always close.

It was enough to spur the trio into action. The women began their journey home.

Watching Jensen from behind, Kiernan wasn't surprised she showed little reaction to what should have been a magnificent and most-anticipated vision. Placing her hand upon her stomach, Kiernan could feel the rapidly swelling bruise from the punch she had received. And the man who delivered that painful blow… Devlin… Abrahams. It didn't matter if Tovey saw their interrogator and knew from first-hand experience who he was, Kiernan recognised his voice. The inflection within his tone was most definitely Select Prime Abrahams. That it was one and the same made perfect sense. The man controlling the hidden agenda would resort to adopting a second personality to outlet his nefarious nature. How many colonists had Abrahams killed in pursuit of his personal agenda? Unconsciously she placed her hand over the folded papers she had hidden under her shirt before they were discovered in the data cell. Evidence of a personal agenda she now knew to be true. She had the proof. Her original discovery, so many rotations ago, now becoming clear. They had to stop Abrahams.

Wondering how they would do that forced Kiernan to stop in her tracks. 'Devlin' had abandoned his interrogation upon notification of a prior engagement. Something which was to occur in two marks? She thought back to interrogation room and the body lying upon the floor.

"Oh no!" Kiernan sprinted to catch up with Jensen. "Taura!" she said in alarm. Receiving a look of confusion, Kiernan elaborated. "Devlin… Abrahams… he had to leave due to his presence being required in two marks! Less than that now. It's Taura's Honourship! What appointment will a Select Prime keep if there is no family member to preside over a colonist's Honourship?"

"Nicoletti!" Jensen said, understanding Kiernan's alarm.

Tovey looked between the two women. "What?"

Jensen explained, "If you can recall colony life, an Honourship takes place to commemorate the life of a family member and ally who died serving the colony. It is a time when all colonists assemble, either at the ceremony itself or a communal point, to pay respects to that colonist's work for the Haven. If in the extremely rare occurrence there is no family member to head the Honourship, then the Select Prime will preside over the ceremony, as a mark of respect.

Kiernan grasped Jensen's arm. "Jen, I have a real sense of foreboding."

An unspoken understanding passed between the two women, and then the trio set off with haste. They ran, moving faster and faster towards the colony, and their collective fate.

CHAPTER 43

Arms folded in a controlled state of annoyance, Physician Angelus stared at Vegas. The Major had yet to leave his medical suite. Why he couldn't linger in another physician's suite he had no idea. Well, he did, but his continued presence was starting to vex the fastidious physician. Head bent to one side; Angelus studied Major Vegas. His expression was perplexing. He sat outside the door to the supplies store, his thoughtful countenance changing only as an idea would come to mind that he would then quickly disregard. Angelus felt unable to work, not only due to the major's presence but the illegally held colonists bound in his supplies store.

"Exactly how long do you intend in keeping those two? You do realise you're interrupting my routine!"

As much as Vegas had tried to ignore the penetrating, accusatory stare of Physician Angelus, he couldn't ignore his comment. As scenario after scenario passed through his thoughts, each one abandoned as a futile possibility, Vegas began to realise only one outcome may possibly work with the desired success.

Taking a deep breath, Vegas rose and faced Angelus. "I'm trying to find a way out of this situation. Unfortunately, I cannot move them from your store right now."

"Well, isn't that terrific! How am I supposed to function amid this unlawful activity? I'm not a natural vessel of deception."

"I could gag them?"

"And within four words you made a tricky situation increasingly absurd. Besides, that store is soundproof."

Vegas checked the wall's chronometer. "It's Taura's Honourship in one mark. There are things I must do before then. I can't release them. Not yet. Not before-" Vegas studied Angelus. "What would you suggest?"

Angelus stepped around his desk. "If you're leaving me with them, I may feel a little safer if you were to leave that automatic firearm in my possession."

Vegas pulled the weapon from under the rear of his shirt. "This?"

"Security."

"Do you know how to use this?"

"As much as you, I'm sure."

Increasingly irritated by Angelus' sarcasm, Vegas placed the weapon on the counter. The illegal contraband seemed to be changing hands so often. This weapon he had secured for himself after the mission. Jensen had not asked for it back. He was the Major after all.

"I can only ask that you err on the side of caution… for obvious reasons."

Angelus retrieved the firearm. "Major, I assure you not only will I show caution, but may I remind you, I'm one of the very few who is actually capable of removing and treating the sort of injury this can cause."

"And yet that doesn't fill me with confidence," Vegas only partially joked. "Please just guard our detainees until my return."

"As you pointed out, it's Scout Taura's Honourship. I shall be in attendance."

"Then secure the medical suite when you leave. Understand?"

Glaring at Vegas, Angelus merely nodded. "Of course."

"Problems?"

"Not one."

"Good. Then await my word." Vegas turned towards the door. A moment of silence after his parting remarks to Angelus was broken only by the sound of a loud burst which ricocheted around the medical suite. Vegas stopped, feeling a shocking sensation which radiated through his side. He looked down as moisture soaked his clothing. Pain, sharp pain, intensified rapidly. He had been shot. He tried to turn, to look at Physician Angelus, but shock overtook him, and he fell to his knees and then towards to the ground.

Angelus looked down at the firearm. The shot was louder than he expected, but such an effortless way to dispatch a potential threat without getting his hands dirty. Dropping the firearm into his lab coat pocket, Angelus unlocked the supply closet door and entered.

"You couldn't just play dumb like me?"

Lucia and Pavo both looked to Angelus in surprise.

"You think you are the only two the Select Prime has promised a deal within the new world? A good physician is a highly sought commodity." He approached the pair with a scalpel. "Now let's get you untied before any more interruptions. An internal communication from Abrahams has requested our presence at once. My presumption is an upcoming event that means it's time to thin the herd."

***

Jensen released the hatch, not at all surprised to see the lift capsule still at the bottom of the shaft. With Nicoletti no longer at his post, it was probable the entrance had been suspended. This was a fact Jensen had been fully aware of, and why she had chosen to return to the main colony entrance instead of trying to navigate their way back home from the interrogation room. With the entrance on lockdown, there was no need for officer presence. Perfect.

Kiernan peered down the hatch. "Where's the lift?"

Jensen shone her torch light down into the shaft, highlighting the ladder rungs.

"Not again!"

"I'll go first." Jensen said, as she swung around and into the hatch. She knew how to access the escape portal in the lift capsule.

"More?" Tovey asked.

Kiernan could only nod. "So, it seems."

Dropping down into the lift, Jensen examined the twin access doors. She removed her prizing tool and set to work separating the mechanical barriers. Behind her, Tovey soon entered, followed by Kiernan.

"Jen, there can't be more than a mark before Taura's Honourship."

"Working on it," Jensen grunted, as she prized the lift doors open and stepped into the reception zone.

A small part of her recalled seeing Nicoletti's smiling face as he would greet her upon return. Instead, the room was dark, lit only by the emerald glow from a security beacon.

"My guess is everybody's congregating in the communal hall. We couldn't have picked a better time to return unnoticed."

Kiernan nodded, as she looked around the reception zone. "There will be nothing more than a skeleton shift of enforcement officers for the next two marks."

"How far away is the communal hall?" Worried about the prospect of being caught, Tovey considered potential threats, as Jensen open the mechanical door into the de-contamination chamber. They passed through without activation. A move Jensen no longer considered since she had seen the reduction in toxic cloudbanks. After all, she hadn't worn her facial apparatus on their journey home. An absolute first. Maybe it was seeing the moon for the first time, but Jensen's adherence to protocol was slipping and she didn't care at all.

Passing through the de-con chamber, the women stepped out into changing rooms. Jensen opened her locker and retrieved a clip of ammunition. She handed the clip to Tovey.

"Empty, right?" She said, recalling Tovey's rhetoric on how she eradicated the feeders while they travelled back.

Tovey replaced the clip and handed the weapon back to Jensen. "I can't have this."

With a nod of understanding, Jensen handed it to Kiernan. It was, after all, her firearm originally. "You know the drill."

Accepting the weapon, Kiernan placed it in her pocket.

"Are you ready for this?" Jensen asked. Her thoughts were on stopping Abrahams, not realising they were about to rewrite not only their futures but the future of every colonist in the Haven.

CHAPTER 44

There was silence as the Vestibule inhabitants absorbed Abrahams' orders. None dare look at one another, fearing any exchange of reservation would result in the swift termination of life. But it was a means to an end. Right? After this, nothing would stand in the way of the Ultimate Agenda. The new world was almost within grasp.

Abrahams' select group stood in a line, Angelus, Lucia, Pavo, Scout Ryan (who'd always kept one eye on Jensen, as per Abraham's request), Fawkes and Lorenzo. Commander Tehera stood beside Abrahams.

Abrahams addressed his line-up, "You all have your orders." He circled the group. "None of you are going to disappoint me." That was a statement.

"No, Sir," came the mechanical response.

"Exactly."

***

The first to leave the gathering were Captain Lucia and Minister Pavo. Lucia's directive was clear, to follow through with the completion of an instillation she had constructed half a cycle prior. Lucia's mind wandered back to seeing Vegas' bloody body as she and Pavo exited the store. She didn't blame Vegas for his actions. If the situation were reversed, she too could imagine acting in a similar fashion. However, it was not, and loyalty only stretched so far when personal gain was motivation.

Luckily, Captain Lucia had certain skills. She was a highly efficient electrician and had aided in the upgrade of the Re-cycled Air Purifying systems as well as the wind turbines, the vital machinery that converted the planet's raging tempest into a main power source for the colony.

It was Lucia who supervised every dip and rise in power created by the turbines' generation, and it was she who reported her closely watched findings to Select Prime Abrahams. When a total cessation of generation was recorded, it was Lucia who had instantly directed those findings to the Select Prime. Abrahams had then ordered Minster Pavo to supply real-time footage of the Barrens, where they discovered a clement and a fifty percent clearing of the cloudbanks. At that point, satellite communication would become of paramount importance.

Lucia followed Pavo to the Transmission Vault. A small but dedicated area designed for off-world communications. There, they split. Pavo retreated to his workstation, where he would try to communicate with their satellite. Lucia moved to a small, and recently installed, workstation built for one purpose. The Transmission Vault was perfectly situated above a junction between Domestic and Labour. It was the perfect base to join the multi-strand wire conduits from each colony to a specific location for generation of the most effective charge.

Sitting at her desk, Lucia fired up her terminal and the Conduit Electrical Detonator. To her right, Pavo attempted first communication with the satellite.

***

Angelus headed back to his medical suite. His fingers twitched with increased nerves. Shooting Major Vegas had been an impulse move, but one he was sure Abrahams would have approved. Unfortunately, that had not been the case. Nobody was to work without prior knowledge of the Select Prime. Because of this Abrahams had set Angelus two tasks. 1. to dispose of Vegas' body. 2. eradicate any evidence displaying wrongful conduct. Easy, Angelus thought. Still, the daunting task did set his nerves on edge, and as he passed through the doors to his medical suite, intent on first pouring himself a cup of his personally brewed spirit, he froze. Where was the body?

Pulling out Vegas' firearm, Angelus rushed over to the smeared blood. He followed the trail left on the ground. The smear turned to droplets that moved around the edge of the medical suite and towards the supply closet door. Gripping the automatic weapon, Angelus pulled the closet door open. Then everything went black.

***

The chamber was dark and eerily quiet. Lorenzo refrained from activating any lighting as he stood at the entrance, pulling on his protective coveralls. Once ready, he turned to Fawkes, who had finished adjusting the tight coveralls over his own gaunt frame.

Picking up two small projectiles, Lorenzo accepted the syringe Fawkes handed him. "How much?"

"Transportation time only. We want them back on form in no more than half a mark."

With a thoughtful nod, Lorenzo loaded the two darts with the required amount of tranquilizer. "This should be adequate."

"Good." Fawkes picked up the tranquilizer pistol and loaded the first dart. "Let's get this over with."

***

He was informed Scout Jensen and Minister Kiernan were being held in an interrogation room deep in the chambers of the Governance engineering sector, close to where the craft was situated. Following Abrahams' orders, Scout Ryan was sent to retrieve them, staging a daring rescue. His theatrics were short-lived as the interrogation room was empty. Only the body of Nicoletti remained. He was told they were being held for the murder of a colonist. Was it really Nicoletti? A close ally of Jensen? Ryan acted only as per Abrahams' promise for his future, but finding Nicoletti's body and the interrogation room otherwise empty, Ryan knew this would anger the Prime.

Heading back, Ryan chose a different route. Intending to intercept Jensen, he knew of one fact with absolute conviction, Jensen would not miss Taura's Honourship. With that in mind, he investigated lesser-used paths that would lead to the same destination, the Communal Hall. Scout Ryan was correct, but he was not expecting a third individual. Her pale complexion and overall state of appearance led Ryan to believe she was not a Governance colonist. As he approached, the unknown colonist averted her eyes quickly. A sign she felt out of her depths. A sign she was not meant to be there? Jensen's and Kiernan's expressions never faltered.

Ryan stopped before Jensen. "I was on my way to Taura's Honourship. It starts soon. I'll walk with you?"

Jensen was quick to ask, "Weren't you going in the wrong direction?"

The question didn't faze Ryan. "Thought I heard footsteps."

"Ah." Jensen moved passed Ryan to begin their journey together. "Better not be late. I need to be near the front. Nicoletti has requested I speak."

"Right." Ryan remained composed. "No doubt you will do her proud. Nicoletti hasn't arrived yet but may have by the time we arrive."

Kiernan gave Ryan a sideways glance; her lack of trust was rising.

Continuing to follow Jensen, Scout Ryan looked back to Tovey. "I don't believe we've met?"

As Tovey prepared to answer, Kiernan said, "Tovey's from Domestic. She knew Taura well and wanted to attend her Honourship personally."

It was a request that could be granted by ministers such as Kiernan. The experience was more personal, being present at the Honourship and not in the Communal Halls of Domestic or Labour, simply listening to the ceremony upon the amplifier system.

"Ah, permission has been cleared?" Ryan asked, appearing over curious.

Kiernan stiffened. "I gave permission."

"Of course."

'Thank you', Tovey mouthed, to which Kiernan gave a single nod.

At the head of the group, Jensen found herself questioning Ryan's behaviour. Was that nerves she detected in his voice? If so for what reason?

"So, you were previously at the gathering if you noticed Nicoletti's absence?"

"Hmm," Ryan appeared distracted. "Oh, yes."

"Why did you leave?"

A moment of thought. "Lavatorial needs."

"Inoperative?"

"Queue."

"Must have been long?"

"Taura's Honourship has most of the colony in attendance, as you can imagine."

"What about the lavatory outside the hall?"

Ryan stopped. "Most inquisitive, Jensen!" He watched Jensen, as she turned and saw the suspicious glint in her eyes. She knew. He thought about continuing his deception, but knew either way, they were all heading to the same destination. Suddenly, the prospect of what may occur caused a tremor of uncertainty to travel through him. At Taura's Honourship? Select Prime Abrahams was set upon achieving his plan at this time and destination. It was ahead of the known schedule. He didn't understand why, but it was not for him to question.

Seeing that tremor, Jensen took a step toward Ryan. Tension rose and Kiernan reached for the firearm hidden in her pocket.

"If your intention is to assure our arrival, then you have wasted your time. If you have more underhanded intentions, then I'm sure Kiernan will not think twice about using the weapon she now has aimed at you."

Without moving, Ryan used his peripheral sight to gain a sideways glance at Kiernan. Jensen wasn't bluffing. It was enough to convince him. "You killed Nicoletti."

"Never."

"What do you want?"

"Exactly what is coming, so lead the way, Scout?"

"I'm on your side."

"You're on your own side, Ryan. I'd wager you don't even know what is really going on, but let me assure you, you're about to find out."

Jensen stepped to the side. "Lead the way."

Without another word, Ryan obeyed.

CHAPTER 45

The small vestibule situated behind the governance communal hall was a sparse area. Used mainly as a waiting room, it held four chairs, one against each wall and a low table in its centre. The stark walls stood out, contrasting against the four uncomfortable chairs, two of which were currently occupied. Upon the chair facing the door sat Commander Tehera. Facing him was Select Prime Abrahams, who studied the commander closely. Feeling the weight of the prime's stare, Tehera fidgeted in frustration. Abrahams' glare seemed accusatory, but why? He had conducted every task Abrahams had asked of him.

"Our plans have taken an unexpected turn, Commander Tehera. My hand has been forced, and as such my plans must be brought forward expeditiously. Certain issues will need to be addressed as a matter of urgency. Once the Honourship has reached its conclusion I would like for you to 'tie up' any loose ends."

"Sir?"

"If either Minister Kiernan or Scout Jensen survive this next mark, I want you to terminate them."

Tehera studied Abrahams. He wasn't sure anybody would survive his plans, but if that was this order. "Yes, Sir."

"By now Scout Ryan has 'rescued' Jensen and Kiernan from the clutches of Devlin," Abrahams allowed a sly smirk to curve his lips, "I'm sure they believe they are following their own intended strategy." He leaned forwards in the chair. "What happens now shapes our future and we must do whatever possible to ensure the pendulum swings in our favour, Commander. My plans are in motion, and I will not end this rotation without success. Are the officers ready?"

"Yes, Sir."

"Good."

***

As they approached the communal hall, Jensen could see through the double doors and within. The room was teeming with colonists. For a moment, Jensen thought of her ally Taura, and the true testament to the person she was judging by the mass of colonist awaiting her commemoration. If Nicoletti was there, he would have been proud.

Nearing the entrance, Jensen spotted Raziko standing outside. She stood back, whispering for Kiernan and Tovey to lead Ryan inside, confirming she would join them after she spoke with Raziko.

He waited until they were alone before he spoke. "Vegas has reiterated the plan. Abrahams has his officers standing guard inside, but the scouts are ready. Whatever the prime has in store we're prepared. Just waiting upon Nicoletti to arrive."

Not wanting to dishearten Raziko by informing him of Nicoletti's death, Jensen nodded. She patted her ally's arm. "Let's wait inside. We will make Scout Taura proud."

The pair entered and the doors closed behind them.

***

A hush fell over the hall. It was a silence that stretched out as the Governance population awaited the arrival of Officer Nicoletti. Upon a large podium, at the front of the hall, stood a single pulpit beside an image of Scout Taura. Jensen found herself staring at the image, sadness clawing around the edges of her heart. But there was no time to feel sadness, or anger. There was only a need for retribution. For them all.

The silence continued until quiet whispers drifted through the hall. Where was Nicoletti? It was at that moment that the vestibule door opened and Commander Tehera followed Select Prime Abrahams to the podium. Applause rose at the rare site of their colony leader. Tehera took a seat at the edge of the podium, while Abrahams approached the pulpit. An overhead light shone upon his balding head.

"It has always saddened me that my busy schedule leaves little time to meet with the loyal colonists of Governance, but what saddens me more is this being one of the few occasions a Prime must attend. The death of any colonist is an unhappy event, but the death of a colonist who gave their life for our Haven must always be marked with the utmost commitment. No Prime must ever let that mark of dedication go without remembrance." Abrahams cast his gaze around the room. He noted the location of his enforcement officers close to the pulpit and along the sides. He spotted Scout Ryan, Jensen and Kiernan standing a third of the way up the hall. No doubt traumatized after their encounter with Devlin. Abrahams then looked up the sides of the hall where his ministers sat in segregated balconies. Everybody was present. "I had hoped, while making this introduction, that Officer Nicoletti would have arrived to begin Scout Taura's Honourship..."

Jensen felt hatred seep through her pores.

"But until he does, I shall cover as best I can, relaying the pride and thanks of our colony."

Once again, Kiernan heard the rise of whispers circulate around the crowd. Where was Nicoletti? Why wouldn't the Prime wait? What was the rush? Kiernan looked around, feeling the vulnerability of exposure, in a sea of faces. The ministers were seated in the balconies. In earlier gatherings, she herself would be situated there.

"Scout Taura was indeed a well-liked and hardworking Scout. She brought much wealth to the colony on her scouting missions, as well as analytical data." Abrahams paused and rubbed a hand over his bald head. The adhesive from the hairpiece he wore while in the guise of Devlin irritated his scalp. He studied the sea of faces once again. His eyes connected with Jensen. "I could continue on the worthy attributes of Scout Taura, a credit to our colony, but her close ally, Scout Jensen is here, to honour her memory."

Swallowing down the ball of anxiety which had lodged itself within her throat, Jensen made her way to the podium. Soft applause encouraged her journey, as she climbed the six steps and approached the pulpit. Standing before the man she loathed, Jensen could only bow her head in false respect and then take position. She looked out into the crowd and the faces before her. There were no children at an Honourship, and though attendance was considered mandatory for a colonist who died in service, she knew some faces were missing. Physician Angelus and Major Vegas for a start. Where was Vegas?

Jensen looked down at the microphone. It transmitted her words through an amplifier that relayed the Honourship to the gathering of colonists in Domestic and Labour. All would be congregating to honour the passing of Taura in their communal halls. She began to speak.

"It's a sad fact that not many will know Taura as well as I'd have liked you to. She could appear so reserved and quiet, not one to be the centre of attention unless she had something to say. To those who knew her, Taura had a sharp sense of humour, she was brave, caring, fun to be around, and most of all she was a caring spouse. There wasn't a rotation that passed that she didn't make me laugh. Even if I were only walking down a corridor and somebody fired a random projectile at me; I always knew it was her.

She had a presence. She had wisdom and bravery, and when something needed to be said, Taura would say it." Jensen looked around the congregated faces, seeing smiles, and tears of sadness. Looking to the left of the podium, Jensen noted Abrahams seated beside Commander Tehera.

"Taura believed in our cause. She believed in the Ultimate Agenda and dedicated her life to the pursuit of that… dream… hoping that reality would be something she would see in her lifetime. Like we all do. For Taura that never happened." Jensen looked across at her fellow colonists once again. "Maybe not for any of us." She saw the commander rise swiftly in her peripheral vision. "Taura's life was taken in one of the most horrific of ways. The greatest danger to us all, we believed, lay in wait upon the Barrens." Her eyes connected with Abrahams. "Maybe that was never true after all."

As Abrahams rose, Jensen said a soft 'thank you' and left the pulpit. There was no going back now. The gauntlet had been thrown before Abrahams. Jensen made her way back through the crowd, feeling pats of support. She looked to her right, seeing Ziran's eyes upon her. They had been throughout her speech. She hadn't had time to discuss her plans with him, or Raziko, and only hoped Vegas had relayed her own messages of instruction. Where was Vegas?

Taking the pulpit, Select Prime Abrahams features seemed hubristic. Jensen recognised that expression. The gauntlet had been accepted.

"Thank you, Scout Jensen, for so eloquently laying down the foundations for the remainder of my candid announcement."

Jensen felt her stomach drop. A hand lightly grasped her forearm, and she turned to see Kiernan relay an expression of concern.

"This is it," she whispered.

Jensen nodded slowly. "Are you ready?"

A gleam shone in Kiernan's eyes. "Bring it on."

Adjusting the microphone, Abrahams continued, "Scout Jensen touched on a point I want to elaborate upon. Scout Taura gave her life for a cause she believed in. A cause that I believe in… that all your ministers believe in, and that you yourselves believe in… the quest to claim a new world as our own. A cause that started before we were born but that has endured through time. Even now, we are dedicated to continuing that quest for our ancestors, and our future generations. Am I right?"

Applause.

"There is not one of us here who wouldn't give our lives for the Ultimate Agenda." Abrahams paused again, waiting for the continued ovation. When it came, Jensen turned to Kiernan.

"They don't see what he's doing!"

"I think it's time," Kiernan said, and as the applause died, Kiernan rose her hand. "Select Prime, a question if you please?"

"After I have finished."

"No," Kiernan pressed. "NOW… Sir."

A slow smile spread across Abrahams' lips. "Minister Kiernan?"

"The craft is an exceptional feat, and the product of cycles upon cycles of hard work and dedication from our colonists, but is it true that it is not equipped to fit all colonists on-board?"

"That is a challenge we must face," Abrahams confirmed.

"A challenge?" Kiernan pulled the sheets of folded paper from under her shirt. She gripped them tightly. "Wouldn't you agree it is a fact?"

"There is no doubt being a Select Prime comes with difficult choices to make for our colony. Some of those choices are made easily. Others are not."

"Could you elaborate?" Jensen asked.

Abraham smiled. "I have to make choices regarding the population and passenger manifest for our craft, but there are ways to earn your place."

Instantly, an eruption of protests broke out among the Governance congregation. Jensen was positive that sentiment echoed throughout the neighbouring colonies of Domestic and Labour.

***

Colonist Mira stood within the congregation of Labour's communal hall. She had easily recognised Jensen's voice requesting elaboration from the Prime. She knew this time would come. When Lomax confided in her about the contents of a mystery box he had been given, Mira knew their falsely promised future would eventually be exposed.

***

Raising her voice, Kiernan continued. "Earn a place? This was never instructed as part of the requirements for the Ultimate Agenda."

Abrahams remained calm, and in control. "This was always part of our agenda. How many colonists call Governance their home; and Domestic and Labour combined? It's been my dedication to assure as many colonists as possible have a place aboard our magnificent craft."

"Is that so?" Kiernan opened the papers in her hand. "Then maybe, Sir Prime, you can explain to us... in the Genetic Cleansing and Reproduction Project, why you sanctioned the removal and storage of-"

A loud crash sounded throughout the hall, as Abrahams slammed his fist down upon the pulpit. "As Select Prime I do not have to answer to-"

"Oh, but you do," Jensen pushed.

With a nod of Abrahams head, an officer stepped forwards, placing a hand upon Kiernan's shoulder, to escort her from the hall. Kiernan pulled away, but his grip was strong. Beside them a second officer approached Jensen, but Raziko and Ziran were fast to support them. Ziran aimed his automatic firearm against Jensen's apprehender's head, Raziko a sharp and deadly blade.

"Give me a reason not to pull the trigger," Ziran seethed.

Both women were released, but a surge of surrounding officers acted swiftly. As a small unit formed a barricade around the podium, several more advanced upon Ziran and Raziko. Once again, their attack was countered as a formation of scouts surrounded the officers and a standoff ensued. A heavy silence fell upon the communal hall. The officer beside Kiernan stood down, after a nod from Abrahams, and Tovey took both officers weapons. Kiernan straightened her shoulders with confidence. "This conversation is overdue, Sir. Shall we continue?"

He had never expected there to be so many scouts willing to stand against him. Where was their loyalty? Abrahams' hands trembled with rage, but he forced himself to remain calm. He looked to Tehera, who was awaiting his command. Abrahams then looked back at Kiernan. "Minister, if you are once again referring to my authorisation to harvest genetic material... yes. It was a clandestine approach, but one implemented to ensure the future of our people, by stockpiling reproductive cells."

"No, that isn't what I'm referring to." Kiernan looked down at the papers in her hand. "What I'm referring to is the lack of male reproductive cell harvesting. Why just female?"

"That's-"

"Why?" Kiernan continued. "Because you already had a donor in mind." She held up the papers, as Jensen watched absorbed. This was Kiernan's show. It was hers to deliver. This was the reason the Select Prime had ordered Xoren to kill her.

"I have a full breakdown of your genetic data... and its compatibility with every female colonist's harvested reproductive cells."

"That's ENOUGH." Abrahams slammed his fist upon the pulpit again, but the surrounding crowd only watched with riveted attention. "I order all-"

"No... you... DON'T"

Hearing a recognisable voice, every colonist turned to see Major Vegas standing at the side of the podium. He aimed his firearm at Abrahams.

Shocked gasps echoed around the hall as his overall appearance was acknowledged. Vegas was pale, his skin ashen, and blood soaked one side of his uniform. He could barely stand, but Vegas used all his might to keep his weapon aimed upon Select Prime Abrahams. There was one round of ammunition left in the firearm, and it was for Abrahams alone.

"Please continue, Minister Kiernan."

Receiving consent from Vegas, Kiernan reined in her shock and looked back at Abrahams. "Each and every one of those cells... taken without consent... has already been fertilized by yourself and stored in cryo-preservation chambers, ready for the maturation of your offspring upon reaching the new world. A race fathered by you."

Gasps, murmurs, and whispers of alarm circulated the crowd. Outbursts of anger rose with intensity. Jensen thought back to the freezer she had passed on her way from the torture room. She recalled passing Abraham's office and him leaving with a vile that he transported instantly into that room. "It's true," Jensen said loudly. "I know its location."

Taking a step forward, Kiernan drove her point home. "Your service to this colony has been warped by your delusion of supremacy. How many more colonists could travel to the new world if not for the space you've allotted for your immense hoard of cryo-preservation chambers? A new race of our people fathered by you."

Jensen looked up, seeing the shocked faces of the ministers of the colony. The Prime Select's deception ran deep.

Abrahams trembled, rage clouding his vision. Embarrassment colouring his cheeks. He was a force ready to erupt. Seeing his opportunity, Vegas readied his weapon, but as he closed his finger upon the trigger Commander Tehera dived at him from the side. He knocked Vegas to the ground. The weapon fired, accidentally hitting an officer guarding the Select Prime. She fell instantly. Vegas struggled with the commander, but his weakened stated allowed Tehera to gain the upper hand. He found himself upon his back, the commander delivering punch after punch to his face. Before anybody could run to his aid, the hall froze as Abrahams issued a command.

"STOP!" All eyes turned back to the Prime. The row of enforcement officers tightened their flank around the podium. "My work has only ever been for the good of our colony and its inhabitants. As I said I must make the tougher choices." His voice dropped to a softer tone. "Like now."

Watching Abrahams, Jensen wondered what he was about to say. He had no defence against his actions. She looked at his flank of officers seeing indecision in their faces.

Abrahams spoke into an inter-communicator strapped to his wrist. "Captain Lucia."

"Yes, sir, Prime," came her disembodied voice.

"Has Minister Pavo made contact with the satellite?"

The crowd held their breaths. This was news they all had been waiting on for cycles.

"I can confirm the satellite has been located."

"And the data?"

"Data currently appears scrambled, possibly degraded due to the passage of time, Sir, but Pavo is confident he can retrieve the information."

Abrahams grinned widely, as controlled elation filtered through the crowd. "That is excellent news."

"Sir."

"Oh and, Captain Lucia?"

"Yes, Sir."

"I authorise you to activate the charges."

Silence… and then a deep breath. "Acknowledged."

Raziko looked to Kiernan, who in turned looked to Tovey. Jensen looked to Ziran and then Kiernan. When Kiernan's eyes connected with Jensen's, understanding dawned upon them both.

CHAPTER 46

It was instantaneous. Not surprising for an expert in munitions. Captain Lucia was, after all, the creator of the incendiary device adapted into missiles loaded with Amphibulartoxin. Setting a relay charge of explosives into the structures of Labour and Domestic Communal halls had been the task for which she would be highly rewarded in the new world.

The blasts resonated throughout the colonies. The sound carried further, via the recycled air purification system. It intensified the body of the explosion, carrying the screams, cries and sounds of the falling roof structure throughout the subterranean expanse. Masses of concrete and metallic ore fell upon the colony inhabitants, expertly charged by Captain Lucia.

Reaching the people of Governance, desperate cries of the injured and dying were met with abject horror. Helpless, all they could do was listen, as the sounds of shocked terror met their ears. Within moments, alarm set in. Panicked, the ministers fled from their balconies, retreating to areas of presumed safety. Around Jensen and Kiernan, Governance colonists erupted in fear. Some fled the halls, others falling into each other's arms in a need to ease their shock. Others still, including enforcement officers ran, desperate to reach those in trouble with a desire to help.

Kiernan looked up at the pulpit where Abrahams remained. A calm expression formed his features. His burning ire had dissolved, replaced with a look she could only describe as satisfaction. She then looked to Jensen, who was rooted in shock. She watched, as over half the communal hall's occupants fled, but found she was unable to react. Jensen looked back up at Abrahams, disgust running through her veins. She felt tears fill her eyes and cloud her vision. Never had she expected Abrahams to commit such a vile, vengeful act. Their eyes met and held in a silent duel.

As the first rumbles of falling stone faded, and the background reverberation for cries of help filled the vents and travelled through the hall, Jensen felt her body pushed left and then right, as people rushed past her. She clutched her chest, a pain filling her soul. How many had died? How many hundreds of lives had Abrahams just exterminated? She looked back at the Select Prime, his hubris settled fully into his serene expression.

More colonists rushed past her, and Jensen turned to see Tovey standing before her.

"Now, Jensen, we have to act now."

Looking around, Jensen searched out the familiar faces she needed; Raziko, Ziran, Kiernan and Tovey. Ziran led the scouts, and she trusted him in that task. So far, they had performed admirably. There was no sign of Ryan, he must have disappeared in the hysteria. Vegas? Jensen searched for the major, seeing him prostrate upon the ground. He was alive, that she could see from his limited movements, but he'd received some punishing blows from Tehera. The commander? Where was he? Frantically searching for Tehera, Jensen suddenly saw him advancing towards her.

Two shots were fired in the hall, and everybody froze.

Effectively gaining attention, Kiernan lowered her firearm and aimed it at Tehera. The commander halted in his tracks.

Ziran aimed his firearm at the Select Prime.

"It's over, Abrahams." Jensen stepped forward. "It's time for you to step down. You're guilty of theft, murder, conspiracy-"

"Not including your time spent as 'Devlin'," Tovey added. "Kidnapping, assault, torture and horrendous crimes against our people."

Jensen continued, "You are guilty of so-"

"Do you think I wouldn't go down without a fight, Scout Jensen? I am the Prime, as is my birth right. Everything I do helps the people."

"Everything you do benefits yourself," Jensen countered, she glared at Abrahams, watching as the Prime's features twist into an expression she could only identify as mania.

Abrahams moved forward and leant into his microphone. "RELEASE THEM!"

Surprised by his outburst, the team turned as the vestibule doors swung open and two scavengers stormed into the hall. Tovey felt her heart freeze. It was the scavengers from the torture room, where Lomax had been held.

Terror erupted, as the first scream left a scavenger. The remaining occupants of the hall scrambled, fighting for escape. Trying to stop them from reaching the colonists, Jensen, Ziran and Raziko charged towards the flesh-hungry beings.

Piercing screams filled the hall as the ravenous scavengers attacked. Feeling he had the advantage, Ziran aimed his weapon upon an advancing scavenger, but it was shockingly swiped from his hand.

Disregarding the firearm, Ziran fought the scavenger as only a scout knew how.

Raziko dipped to the ground, taking the second scavenger with him. He threw the being over his head, as it flailed and swiped, desperate to grasp flesh. A colonist, who had been hiding at the side of the podium, tried to run past. The scavenger reached out, pulling at his leg, and sinking rotten broken teeth into his flesh. The younger man cried out in pain. Using its preoccupation, Jensen made her move. She slammed her boot into its back and the scavenger was thrust to the ground. It lost purchase of the young man's leg as its teeth were torn from the punctured flesh. In a rapid move, and as Raziko held its legs, Jensen straddled the scavenger's back. Grasping its head with both hands, she twisted firmly. Jensen heard its neck break as the spinal column was severed. The being screamed helplessly, immobile, and barely alive.

From his pulpit, Abrahams continued to watch with rapt attention. His flanking officers had abandoned him. Most had fled the hall. Abrahams felt no need to worry anymore. If this was his time, he would take as many lives as possible with him, including the engineers of his downfall. Besides, there was something most enthralling watching the scouts battle flesh-hungry scavengers. Where else could he possibly wish to be? It was the first time he'd ever seen his precious scavengers living their full potential.

Tehera had watched Ziran's firearm fly from his hand and slide towards Vegas' prostrate body. His gaze turned to Kiernan. She held her firearm upon him, but anxiously watched the scouts battle with the scavengers. Tehera would take his chance. He ran towards the firearm, but Kiernan caught him.

"Don't," she yelled. "I will shoot you, Commander."

Tehera smiled, and she knew he was going to call her bluff. Running for the weapon, he heard three short, sharp bursts. His prize was almost within reach. He took another step before realising his left leg refused to co-operate. Tehera looked down. Blood began to soak through his clothing. Then he saw more blood soaking into his front. He looked back at Kiernan. She'd hit him. Twice? He offered her a small smile, but Kiernan's blank expression didn't change as she pulled the trigger six more times, emptying her weapon's clip into the commander. The vitality faded from his eyes as Tehera fell to the ground. Dead.

The moment it took for the scouts to register Tehera's demise was all the time the first scavenger needed to lunge upon Raziko. It swiped sharp talons across his chest, cutting deep. The claw-like nails sliced between his ribcage, slicing into his heart. Raziko cried out, as pain surged through his body.

Jensen and Ziran ran to his aid, but it was too late, Raziko joined Tehera upon the ground. Ziran roared with anger, charging the larger scavenger, as he kicked and punched out in retribution. He thrust the being against the wall and Jensen was quick to follow, retrieving a discarded baton from the floor and swinging hard. A brief instant before her weapon struck the scavenger their eyes met, and she could have sworn she saw recognition in its eyes. It knew it was about to lose its life. She appreciated that acknowledgement, understanding that it would die for its actions. Jensen swung repeatedly. The polished timber buried deeper and deeper into the scavenger's head until brain matter seeped through the broken skull. Jensen continued hitting out, for Raziko, for Jilya, for Taura.

Unexpectedly, her name being called softly, filtered through Jensen's rage.

"Jensen?"

Jensen stopped and turned to see Tovey standing a safe distance away.

"Jensen, it's dead. You can stop. You killed it."

Looking back at the bloodied form, Jensen registered the amber pus seeping out from the scavenger's skull. Its body broken. Its life extinguished. She dropped the baton and stepped away, sweat tricking down her skin. Her hands trembled.

Looking around, Jensen saw Ziran kneeling helplessly over Raziko's body. Kiernan stood further back, a blank expression in her eyes. Shock. The bodies of trampled colonists lay scattered around the doorways, but all others had escaped the hall, fleeing for safety or in the aid of the Domestic and Labour colonists. Harsh breathing filled the hall.

Kiernan dropped her spent weapon.

Jensen heard a ringing in her ears, as reality settled upon her.

"Most impressive, Scout Jensen."

Why was Abrahams still standing there? "Your leadership is over, Abrahams."

"Devlin," Tovey added.

Abrahams diverted his gaze to Tovey. "The granddaughter. I recall the time we spent together." His expression grew sinister. "We did have fun!"

Tovey looked away, as unpleasant memories surfaced.

"Step down, Abrahams," Jensen pushed. "You are guilty of so much wrong against our people. For me, your downfall started the moment you killed my parents."

Abrahams appeared confused, "But Scout Jensen, I never killed your parents."

Jensen narrowed her eyes, as Abraham's gaze drifted to the scavengers and then back again. Unrestrained glee formed his features. "I believe you just did."

Stepping backwards, Jensen looked to the scavengers. "You lie."

Abrahams shook his head. "Death was too lenient of a punishment for perfidy."

A dim ringing began in Jensen's ears. Shook her head. "No!"

"I like to be creative with my punishments." Abrahams looked at Tovey. "As I'm sure Lomax would attest. I was particularly impressed by the way you repeatedly caved your fathers head into a-"

"STOP!" Jensen breathed heavily. Rubbing both hands over the back of her head, she roared with emotional pain. "I'll kill you!"

"Excuse me?" Abrahams stepped around the pulpit. "You ruined my plans. My birth right to lead the colony to a new world. How dare you!" Abrahams boomed.

"You're lying!"

"Why?"

"Because-"

"If you think I will allow you to escape without retribution, you are wholly mistaken. I will personally make sure I taint… spoil… shadow, every aspect of your life, Scout Jensen, from now until-"

A single shot echoed through the hall, shocking all inhabitants, as Abrahams' rant was prematurely interrupted. Jensen continued to stare at Abrahams, watching as the bullet hole in the centre of his forehead began to seep with blood.

Feeling a tremor run through her, Kiernan looked around. Who had taken the shot? She then spotted Vegas, in a semi-reclined position, firearm still in his hand. As his last grasp of energy left him, he fell back to the ground. She ran to his aid.

Jensen watched Abrahams body slump, and then fall from the podium to the floor. The scavenger, barely alive and with a broken neck, reached out. It pulled his body closer and sunk jagged teeth into the side of his face, whimpering in delight. Jensen watched, but she felt nothing.

"He's dead."

She didn't respond to the sound of Tovey's voice.

"It's over."

Turning, Jensen looked at her blankly. She was numb. She barely blinked, as thoughts failed her. What was Tovey saying? She turned to see Kiernan desperately checking Vegas' vital signs. Ziran still knelt beside Raziko's body. She turned to the scavengers, one was beaten to a foul pulp against the wall; the other, paralyzed, was gnawing at Abrahams' face. Jaxon and Tomei, her parents? That flash of recognition in the scavenger's eyes, just as she delivered her killing blow, appeared in her mind. Was it?

Emptiness seeping into her core, Jensen felt her spirit fracture as she walked slowly out of the hall.

CHAPTER 47

How long has it been? Major Vegas mused, as he shifted in his observation bed. He hadn't thought he would survive, but rotations later he awoke in Physician Scarlet's medical suite, very much alive, and very much feeling the pain of his personal ordeal.

He opened the one eye that wasn't still swollen shut to find Minister Kiernan sitting by his bedside. She appeared tired, worried, like the weight of the world was upon her. Vegas shifted slightly, turning his attention to Kiernan.

"How long have I been here, Kir?"

Kiernan took a relieved breath, happy to finally see Vegas responsive. They had feared the worst. Vegas had lost a tremendous amount of blood, but Physician Scarlet, although constantly in the shadow of Angelus, proved herself a skilled healer. Kiernan reached out and took the Major's hand. "You've been unconscious for three rotations. You terrified me." She tucked her hair behind her ear. "I'm so happy to see those, or at least one, broody dark eye!"

Vegas tried a smile, feeling his swollen features twinge in pain. "Ouch! I've a feeling this is going to sting for a while."

"Well apart from the fact your nose may have spread a little unevenly across your face, I'm sure you will regain full health." Kiernan tapped his hand lightly. "Was it Angelus who shot you?"

"Yes. I woke up in his medical suite sometime later. Never hit a major organ. You'd think a physician would know where to fire to inflict the most harm. Anyway, he returned to, I can presume, clear his mess. I was waiting."

"I thought as much when we found the body." Kiernan's mind drifted to the events since their final encounter with Abrahams. "I'm so glad you're awake."

Vegas' frown barely visible around his swollen features. "Where's Jensen? Is she all right?"

"She's fine," Kiernan assured. "Of a sort. As far as I know anyway. She hasn't left her unit since you shot Abrahams. She won't open the door, won't speak, but we know she is in there. Tovey has tried to draw her out with no luck, but she did manage to get her to eat a few mouthfuls of food yester-rotation."

Vegas recalled the last moments before he shot the Select Prime. He could understand why Jensen would have reacted so devastatingly to the realisation the scavengers she killed were her parents. "I had no idea Kiernan!"

"I do believe you. I understand how hard it must have been to navigate the path of enforcing colony law and politics, mixed with your own sense of right and wrong." Kiernan's mind drifted back over the last few rotations. "A lot has eventuated since, Vegas. A lot. Governance colonists and enforcement officers have united. All survivors from Domestic and Labour have been moved to Governance. Only a few are still receiving medical treatment. Lucia, Pavo, Fawkes and Ryan have been apprehended and detained. They are awaiting judgement."

"That will be difficult without a Prime or Commander. What of the council of ministers?"

"Currently disbanded… or I should say awaiting you."

"Me?" Vegas gave a half-hearted chuckle. "What can I do?"

Colonists are demanding a democratic vote to elect a new Select Prime."

"Reasonable," Vegas agreed, something he always thought should have been in practice for such a powerful role.

Kiernan smiled. "Well, the people have already decided that they want you as their new Prime."

"Me?" Vegas laughed again. The action caused pain to shoot through his body.

"It's practically a majority vote. Who else do they trust to finish the construction of the craft and lead the people to their promised new world? It's you, Vegas."

"I'm not the right choice."

"You are their choice. A democratic choice."

Turning from Kiernan's encouraging gaze, Vegas considered her words. Could he?

***

Another two rotations had passed, and Jensen still hadn't left her unit. Tovey sat on the floor outside, her legs outstretched, feet upon the opposite wall. Jensen was in there. That, she was positive. Tiny amounts of food had been accepted, but only when she had left. Tovey was thankful, at least, that she was eating.

Resting her head against the wall, she looked up at the celling. Her thoughts drifted to the marks after Abrahams had been shot. Events passed through her mind like a blur, but one moment stood out. Going to free Flick.

***

Tovey had travelled alone, only taking a couple of wrong turns before finally finding Devlin's holding cells. Most of the colony was open and colonists were free to cross from one section to another. As such, it was easier to navigate the subterranean passageways without fear of being caught.

Armed with clothing, Tovey first found the key before unlocking Flick's cell. The younger man was hiding in the shadows.

"Hello?"

"Flick, it's me, Tovey."

Flick appeared in partial light, his bony hands hiding his unclothed form. "Took longer than I thought."

"But I'm here now," Tovey threw the clothing over to Flick. "Put these on and we can get out of here."

Flick scrambled to cover his body. "Heard explosions."

"A lot has happened."

"Lots?"

"Devlin is dead."

"That is lots." Once clothed, Flick appeared fully into view. "Will you tell me?"

"Of course."

"On way home?"

Tovey smiled. "What if I say we're not going home? What if I tell you we're going to Governance?"

Flicks eyes widened. "Governance," He whispered, having never dreamed he would see the colony itself. "Really?"

"Yes."

"Lots has changed." Flick followed Tovey out of his cell. "What about our people?"

Tovey smiled as she looked back at Flick. "A lot has changed, Flick, but there are still many changes to come."

***

That had been five rotations ago. Since then, Flick had spent his time recovering in the personal unit of the late Select Prime. It seemed fitting.

Hearing a shuffle coming from Jensen's unit, Tovey spoke again.

"I'm glad you ate, Jensen. I have food for you here. I'd really like to see you and be sure you are alright."

There was no response.

"As I've said every rotation, Jensen, I have a message to deliver personally to you." It was Lomax's last message before he slipped away. "Please open the door so we can talk."

***

On the other side of the door Jensen sat with her back to the solid barrier. She stared straight ahead, seeing nothing but the manifestation of thoughts within her mind.

All this time her parents had been alive, but in the most unimaginable of ways possible. Jensen wondered if they kept any memory of their former selves, a thought that had repeatedly come to mind. Did they recognise her? She thought maybe, but hoped not. Tears filled her eyes again.

Wrapping her arms around her torso, Jensen slid sideways to the floor. The ground should have felt cold against her skin, but she felt nothing. Jensen wondered how many lives had been tainted by Abrahams actions? How many lives had he taken? How much pain had he caused? How many colonists lost their lives in the explosions? All they ever wanted was to work towards a better life. That promised new world. An ideal fed to them for the gain of one individual. Jensen wanted to rise above the shadow Abraham had left, but thoughts of her parents, and what they had endured, refused to vacate her mind. The memory of the scavengers last expressions, before she delivered her killing blow, haunted her.

Every rotation since, as Jensen woke from a restless sleep, she cursed the new morn, wanting her misery to end. She wondered what the point was. Working towards a lie. Even with Abrahams gone, his stain left a mark upon her conscience that she was unable to ignore. And she was tired of trying.

Re-focussing her attention back into her unit, Jensen rose to a seated position and looked around her four walls. They were closing in around her. She was sure. She'd lost count of how many rotations she had been there, but the room was getting smaller. They were trying to suffocate her out of this room of solitary abyss, but she was stuck in a subterranean hell with a barren wasteland above her. Why would she want to go back to that? Let them suffocate her.

***

Back outside Jensen's unit, Tovey looked up as she heard footsteps. It was Kiernan. Between them they had divided time trying to coax Jensen out of her room. When Kiernan wasn't visiting Jensen, she was taking care of colony business and trying to rebuild its command structure with a politically democratic foundation.

That morn, Vegas had been released from the medical suite. Tovey heard the colonists bid for him to stand as Prime and, from what she understood, Vegas had agreed. As such, he had called a meeting for all colonists later that eve. Nobody knew what Vegas was to announce, but word was he was to officially accept the position.

"Nothing?" Kiernan asked.

Tovey shook her head.

Stopping, Kiernan looked down at Tovey. "This cannot continue anymore." She hammered upon the door. "Jen, this is Kiernan. This must stop. There is a world out here and it needs you." She placed her hand upon the barrier. "Jen, I get it, I really do, but if you stay in there… even after death, Abrahams wins. Don't let him. Don't allow him to beat you." Kiernan looked down at Tovey. "Have you told her?"

"No." Tovey rose. "I want to tell her face to face."

"If we don't act soon, I have no idea if you will ever get the chance." Kiernan hammed upon Jensen's door again. "Jen, listen. Tovey has a message from Lomax. It was to be delivered to you alone. I'm waiting to hear this and I'm sure, deep down, so are you."

There was no reply.

"Just tell her. Just give her the message."

"But" Tovey said with pleading eyes.

"What do we have to lose?"

Forcing out a deep breath, Tovey agreed. She took a step closer to the door. "Jensen, before my grandfather died, he gave me the location of the stolen files that your father gave him." She paused and listened. "Jensen, I know where they are. I can tell you. We can all go together right now to retrieve them."

***

Rising, Jensen stood by her door. A glimmer of hope sparked anew within her. Placing her hand upon the door, she lay her forehead upon the cool barrier.

"Honestly?" It was the first word she had spoken in rotations. Her voice was hoarse from lack of use.

"Promise," came the earnest reply.

Turning, Jensen approached the shelf and pulled her mother's hand-carved box from its position. She lifted its lid and retrieved the key from within. The key she had spent cycles wondering about. Now, now she knew its function.

Cautiously, Jensen opened her door.

"Take me there."

CHAPTER 48

It was a surreal experience, crossing the boarders from Governance to Labour with no restrictions. What was at once clear was the fallout from the explosion. Governance colonists had worked hard to find survivors and clear the dead. The smell remained. It was the scent of death, which was slowly transforming from an aroma of blood to a strong rotting stench. A sign there were more bodies to be found. And the rubble! Much of the ceiling in and around the communal halls had come crashing down, crushing many below. Blood stained the remains; a devastating reminder of what Abrahams had inflicted upon his people.

"So, Mira had the box the whole time?"

"Grandfather said she kept it safe and close, as per his request. Hidden in plain sight."

Kiernan frowned. "In plain sight? I wonder how."

With one hand in her pocket, Jensen held the key in her grasp. "I'm thinking maybe her unit."

"Sounds quite possible." Kiernan looked to her side, taking a surreptitious glance at Jensen. She couldn't describe the comfort she felt in seeing Jensen again but wondered what was going through her mind.

Jensen led the way to Mira's unit, room 172. They were far enough away from the main blast that there had been insignificant damage in the social housing section. As such, it was easy to navigate the journey to Mira's room.

Passing unit after unit, their doors open, with a scarlet symbol on the front. The symbols differed, showing if the inhabitants had been found alive or dead. There were many more symbols for the dead than living. Jensen felt despair creeping into the edges of her mind. So much death. So much betrayal.

As they reached Mira's door, Jensen knocked, an action more of habit. There was no symbol upon Mira's door. She had not yet been found. There was no answer.

"I had to try," Jensen mumbled as she tried the handle. The door opened, and with an intense feeling of anticipation, the women stepped into Mira's unit.

The familiar scent greeted Jensen. A mix of steeped leaves and botanical scents created by Mira. Jensen smiled at the memories recalled.

Tovey turned to Kiernan. "Where do we look?"

"Everywhere, I think." Kiernan approached the bed and crouched down to look beneath its frame. "Look everywhere. If she kept it close, it shouldn't take long to find."

They began searching drawers, in and around the bed, and in the wardrobe. Not being a large room, it didn't take them long to realise it didn't appear to be in the unit.

"It has to be here," Jensen said, frustration clear in her voice. She wasn't leaving without it. Not now. Not after all this time. She looked around again, studying every item of furniture and possible location as she tried to recall the size of the box from her last memory of it being handed to Lomax by her parents. When her eyes moved to Mira's plant, she frowned. Mira's plant was her obsession, the leaves picked fastidiously to dry and consume. The large corner shrub sat upon a platform draped with a multi-coloured scarf.

"Kiernan, can you that lift plant in the corner. Put it on the table?"

Curious, Kiernan accommodated the request. Bending down, Jensen pulled the large piece of fabric away, revealing the aged lock box. She recognised it instantly.

"Hidden in plain sight," Tovey muttered.

Lifting the container, Jensen sat down upon Mira's bed and placed it upon her thighs reverently. She gazed down in wondrous anticipation.

"Are you going to open it?" Tovey was anxious to see what the box held.

"I think Jensen needs to do this alone." Kiernan placed her hand upon Tovey's shoulder. "Maybe you could come and help me with the preparations for the Major's address?"

Not looking up from the box, Jensen nodded. "I can meet with you both later?"

Tovey failed in hiding her disappointment as she followed Kiernan to the door. She stopped behind Kiernan at the exit.

"Know where I am if you need me?" Kiernan said softly.

Jensen nodded. She didn't look up. That was all right. Kiernan knew how momentous this moment was for Jensen and was happy that it had managed to lure her from her unit.

"See you later, Jen."

"Kir?" Jensen looked up unexpectedly. "Do you think they knew?"

Kiernan paused mid-stride. Her heart lurched. She knew instantly what Jensen was referring to. Her eyes clouded with tears. "No, Jen, they didn't know. They weren't your parents. Not anymore. Not for many, many cycles."

Desperate to seek comfort in Kiernan's words, Jensen nodded. She wanted to believe that.

Hearing Kiernan and Tovey leave the room, Jensen pushed her key into the lock. It turned stiffly. Her heart accelerated as she lifted the lid and peered inside the box.

***

Several marks later found the colonists of Governance and the survivors of Domestic and Labour congregating back in the communal hall. This time, it was Vegas who waited anxiously in the vestibule. Dressed in his uniform, he stood before Kiernan as she adjusted his lapels and straightened his necktie. Her eyes drifted up to his swollen face, noticing his nose had spread a little wider across his face. At least the swelling around his eye had reduced enough that he was able to open it again.

"Looking good," Kiernan said with a wry smile.

"Liar," Vegas laughed. "But I won't complain."

"Lucky for you."

Vegas continued to chuckle. "I'm simply happy to be out of medical. Too much thinking time."

Kiernan sat down upon the chair Abrahams had occupied six rotations before. "Able to write a good speech?"

With a secretive smile, Vegas sat before Kiernan. "I guess you will find out."

Crossing her legs, Kiernan leaned back in her chair. She'd worked long rotations filled with a heavy number of political matters to resolve. Lorenzo had not been found, and although his apprehension was high on the enforcement officers' agenda, she knew it was only a matter of time. Nobody could hide indefinitely.

"So, what's left to brief me on?"

Swinging her foot back and forth, Kiernan pondered Vegas' question. "Minister Pavo was telling the truth. The data from the satellite was degraded. I'm afraid we have been unable to retrieve the stored files."

"At all?"

"Nothing. All earlier data referring to the new world, stored on the satellite, has been irrevocably lost."

"Damn it." Vegas fought the desire to kick the table before him. Without that they were no closer to navigating their journey to the new world.

"Good news is that we still have access to its telescope, so we are able to study the neighbouring galaxies."

Vegas slumped further into this chair. "That's cold comfort, Kiernan, if we must begin our search again. I have no idea how long it took our ancestors the last time they found the new world, let alone how they co-ordinated the search. All that data has gone." Vegas dropped his head into his hands. "And I was hoping my first speech as Elect Prime would be filled with positive news."

Kiernan leaned forward. "Jensen has the box."

"Box?"

"The data files her parents stole. The whole time it was in the possession of a colonist, Mira, in Labour. We retrieved it earlier."

Rising swiftly, Vegas began to pace the vestibule. The location of the new world was reputedly contained within the files Jensen's parents had stolen. "And?"

"Tovey and I left Jensen to open the box alone. It was something she needed to-"

"I understand, but I want those files Kiernan!"

"I know… and you will." Kiernan rose, "As for right now," she checked the walls chronometer, "I believe you have a speech to make, Elect Prime Vegas."

"And Jensen?"

"She will be here."

Trusting Kiernan, with a nod of acceptance, Vegas took a deep breath and opened the door. Kiernan walked out and he followed. Together they stepped up the podium, but it was Kiernan who stood before the pulpit. Wrapping her fingers around the microphone, she looked out among the mass of faces who had been waiting patiently for them to arrive. So many more faces, including the survivors of the explosion.

"Colonists of Governance, Domestic and Labour. By now you are all fully aware of the eventualities which have led to this moment. I'm not here now to reiterate those events. I'm here on a positive note. The people of our colony have spoken, and on this first democratic undertaking, the vote for our new Elect Prime was practically unanimous. I introduce to you all your new Elect Prime, Vegas."

Colonists rose from their seats as applause and cheers filled the communal hall. Vegas took the pulpit, allowing a moment for the people to show their elation. In the balconies, even the ministers appeared pleased with the choice. This was due mainly to one announcement Vegas was soon to make. A decision that needed ministerial backing.

Looking to the back of the room, Vegas saw the door open, as Scout Jensen slipped inside. The highly sought-after box held under her arm. Vegas turned to Kiernan, who had also witnessed Jensen's arrival. They watched, as she purposely made her way to the front of the hall, taking a seat beside Ziran, Tovey and Flick. Jensen nodded once to Vegas. A silent acknowledgement of his unspoken question.

As applause subsided, Vegas began to speak. "It's an immense honour to be elected as your new Prime. Unexpected, but an honour none the less." Vegas had made a silent pledge with himself in his decision to accept the role. He would not let the people down. Looking around the sea of faces, he spotted Domestic and Labour colonists mingled in with Governance. Is this how it should have been all along? No segregation? No divisions imitating a class-like structure?

Looking to the front of the line, where Jensen sat beside Ziran, Vegas saw the two Primary Colonists he had yet to meet. Discussions of how to approach the Southern colony was on his agenda. One of many changes he intended to instigate.

"I do have a great deal to get through, one of the most important of which being the re-establishment of our efforts to finalise our journey to the new world." Vegas looked again to Jensen, seeing her nod in confirmation. She had the data. "The countdown will begin," Vegas announced, much to the joy and applause of his colonists.

As the clapping eased, Vegas said, "But first, as your Prime, it is my duty to select my direct officials. I can think of no others, who not only deserve, but are more than capable of the task I am about to bestow." With one last gaze across the mass of faces, Vegas announced, "For the position of First Advisor to the Elect Prime, the position, of course, goes to Minister Kiernan."

Hearing her name, Kiernan refrained from outwardly showing her shock, however surprised she was by Vegas' announcement. Giving him a pointed look, explicitly showing that she wished he'd have advised her first,

Kiernan took a step forward, to stand beside him, and offered a slight bow in acceptance of the honour.

"Really?" she asked, from the corner of her mouth.

"Who else," he replied.

When the applause quieted, Vegas spoke again. "And my Commander of Enforcement… I'm sure you can agree… could be none other than Scout Jensen."

Rapturous cheers filled the hall at Vegas' announcement, confirming it was a position well chosen. Jensen looked up at Vegas. She tapped her chest in query. Vegas nodded with a laugh, and so Jensen rose, box still within grasp. She mounted the steps up the podium and stood before the colonists of Governance, Domestic and Labour. The cheers continued and so Jensen leaned into Vegas.

"May I say something?"

Surprised, but not opposed to her request, Vegas took a step back, allowing her to take the pulpit. Jensen placed the box next to the microphone, as her accolade eased. She opened the lid. Vegas couldn't help but peer inside, desperate to discover the contents held within. He spotted a large folder and a small box-like contraption, that he was unable to name. He watched Jensen remove that device, close the box lid, and place the peculiar item upon its surface. The crowd hushed and so Jensen began to speak.

"I never expected to be up here again so soon. If ever. I stand before you now a reformed, and shrewder, person. Knowing you are aware of recent events makes this easier to convey. Some of you will also be aware of the reasons why these events occurred. A deception that started over fifteen cycles ago."

A feeling of unease settled into Vegas, but he stood back, allowing Jensen to speak.

"Murder, torture, abuse, kidnapping, theft, deception. Those are but a few of the crimes committed against many of us at the hands of Abrahams and his chain of command, who we believed were there to protect us. As a scout, I saw enough horror upon the Barren lands to believe this was indeed our Haven. How wrong I was." Jensen activated a switch upon the device. She moved slightly to the side and a bright light illuminated the wall behind her. "I lost hope. Almost completely. I didn't see a point to this life and was ready to give up. Then I found this." Jensen activated another button and a beautiful image of a thriving planet appeared before them all. She began to scroll through the images. "Data of our new world portrays a planet of unrivalled beauty." She let the images scroll from rolling hills, snow-capped mountain ranges, golden sandy beaches, vast forests, endless oceans, isolated islands, cerulean skies, and starry nights. "Mountains, lakes, streams, life on land, air and in the oceans. One sun, just like our world, and a fully formed beautiful moon. Everything we could ever wish for."

Jensen looked out to the people, seeing expressions of awe and joy. Expressions that matched how she felt the moment she saw the images on the device that she found in her father's box. As a slow applause turned into rapturous cheers, Jensen looked at Vegas, seeing his face transformed into absolute reverence, as he stared at the images. He felt it too, utter veneration.

"This is the new world," Jensen said, raising her voice to be heard over the ovation from her audience. "This is our world. Our promised land. This timeline, our lifetime… this world is within our grasp!"

The picture changed to an image taken by their satellite showing the world. An image taken from space. A planet of blue and green.

Standing at the pulpit, Jensen pointed at the image. "This is what we were promised, and now I say to you… let us go and claim our new world!"

Louder cheers erupted from her audience. Beside Vegas, Kiernan stared out at the scene, torn as she appreciated the peoples' exhilaration, but wondering if they understood the cost.

At the pulpit, Jensen continued, her voice rising louder and louder. The reaction of her audience boosting her spirit. "Let us go to our new world, take what was promised to us, and if anybody or anything should dare to deny us, then we will rise above them and STRIKE... THEM...DOWN. We will take our new world, armed with enough firepower to remove any threat, any who dare to say this is not our right." Jensen looked up at the image in devotion. "They call this planet 'Earth', and this is our promised land!"

The hall burst into cheers, joy, and cries of excitement. Jensen looked at Vegas, seeing him beam with exhilaration. His hunger for their new world, and desire to leave this hellish planet behind, plainly visible.

Beside them both, Kiernan watched in horror. This was not how it was supposed to be. This was **not** Jensen. Not her Jensen? Something had happened. Had the trauma caused her to lose her empathetic nature? Her kind heart? Her beauty? She needed to stop this.

"We are ready. We have paid our dues," Jensen shouted. "And planet Earth shall be ours!"

Just The Beginning… End of Part 1

ACKNOWLEDGEMENTS

I want to start by thanking my amazing partner, Jay, for helping me make this possible. For never wavering in her belief in me, and standing by me whilst I worked part time to write this novel.

To my mum, for reading, supplying encouraging feedback and for always being there.

To Eden, for creating the super impressive front cover.

To Amanda, for her amazing editing skills in helping me with vital fine tunings.

And to Justine, for crucial content reading and humorous feedback.

ABOUT THE AUTHOR

MJ lives in Derbyshire, England, in the heart of the National Forest. MJ's passion for writing was re-ignited whilst becoming a certified mindset and personal development coach. When not working, MJ loves being outdoors and enjoys traveling with partner Jay, walking, cycling, and spending time with family and friends. MJ continues to have a passion for ancient history, and in any spare time can be found upcycling furniture, restoring ancient coins, writing, and playing the guitar.

Printed in Great Britain
by Amazon